Someday Autumn Will End

The Soul Remembrance Trilogy: Book One

Someday Autumn Will End

The Soul Remembrance Trilogy: Book One

Jared A. Perrin Sr.

Copyright © 2020 Jared A. Perrin Sr.

Copyright © 2020 Jared A. Perrin Sr. All rights reserved

The characters and events portrayed in this book are fictitious. Any similarity to real persons, living or dead, is coincidental and not intended by the author.

No part of this book may be reproduced, or stored in a retrieval system, or transmitted in any form or by any means, electronic, mechanical, photocopying, recording, or otherwise, without express written permission of the publisher.

Cover design by: Jaiandre Perrin

Dear Reader,

If you are here, I am already truly grateful to you for opening my first novel. Writing this book took me on a journey that I couldn't have ever imagined. What started out as jotting a few things down just for the fun of it, quickly evolved into crafting what you have before you.

My inspiration to write comes from a lot of different things. Life, love, relationships, parenthood, nature, video games, dreams, and movies. But most importantly, from music. I've heard it said that music was the language of the soul, and I believe that. It has the power to touch people in so many ways. In this book, I used music to take my mind to all sorts of different places in order to create the story I wanted to tell.

We all know that no movie is complete without a soundtrack. I believe that no book should be without one either. It's those movie moments where a subtle song plays in the background, setting the scene just right, that elicits the perfect emotional response. Sadly, these are the songs that often go unmentioned in the credits, or are absent from the soundtrack.

As you follow along with the story, keep an eye out for the dreamscape sequences. These are where the music really played a pivotal role in my creative writing.

If you would like to listen to the exact song or combination of songs that shaped the chapter, you can find the complete playlist on my website.

Thank you for reading, and I hope you enjoy reading it as much as I enjoyed writing it.

Happy reading!
Jared A. Perrin Sr.

www.jaredaperrin.com

*To all the people who encouraged me along the way.
Even those who didn't realize they were doing it.*

Prologue

Nothing happens unless first a dream.
　　- Carl Sandburg

Am I too late? I jump into the large aquarium. The water is warm and hazy. Lights flash and loud music blares from somewhere. I have no idea what I am doing. I have no plan. I just know that she needs me. I feel strong currents in the water moving me towards the glass. I kick my feet and swing my arms as fast I can, determined to get to her. No matter how hard I try, the distance between us barely closes. In the distance I can make out a large shadowy figure quickly moving towards us. Out of nowhere, a huge shark closes in on her. I can see the panic on her face as she realizes what is swimming towards her.

I am grief-stricken. I yell out to her. "Swim to me!"

She looks at me. I can see panic has overtaken her, and she cannot move. I swim faster, determined not to lose her again, but the shark is swimming much faster than I am. I muster everything in me. I kick my feet and swing my arms with everything I have. With a whoosh, I am there just as the shark arrives.

I grab her and hold her close with one arm. With

my free hand I give the shark a punch. It recoils as if it doesn't understand what has just happened. She is holding me so tightly I can feel her heart beating against me. The shark, angry as ever, readies its second attack. It charges at us again, its mouth wide open. Not exactly sure what I am doing, I flip both of us backwards to avoid the attack while unleashing a massive kick to the underside of its mouth. It reels in pain, swimming every which way. Blood fills the water as it swims back into the abyss from which it came.

I gather myself. I look around to make sure the shark has not returned. I hold her close by my side and swim upwards. As we reach the surface, the crowd cheers in amazement at what they have just witnessed. I'm not sure what to make of what is going on. I don't care. I've saved her. She is safe. She is with me.

"Are you okay?" I ask.

"I am now. You saved me. You always save me. I love you," she replies softly.

I am completely moved by her words. I hug her close. "I love you too," I whisper.

We hug for what seems like hours. At some point, the music stopped and the crowd is now silent. I have no idea how long it has been. I look up towards the stands. Everyone is gone. The stadium lights slowly begin to dim.

She gently turns my face back to hers. "Look at me. I love you, but we can't stay here. If we ever get separated again—"

Her words are drowned out by the loud music that is suddenly playing again over the speakers in the stadium. I turn around and survey the stadium. It is still empty. I turn back to suggest that we leave, but she is gone.

"Kaleb. Kaleb, wake up. Wake up. I know you hear your alarm. Don't just lay there, sleepy-head. It's your first day of second grade, and you're going to be late."

Part One

Chapter 1 - Late Arrival
-Kaleb-

I walked into the office a lot later than I'd planned. I tried to quietly get to my cubicle without anyone noticing. Sometimes I felt like people were taking bets on how late I'd be each day.

I got to my cubicle without anyone seeing me. Even though we didn't have to be at work by any certain time, everyone got there before me, and like any office environment, there were gossipers, rumor-starters, know-it-alls, and social judges that had an opinion on everyone, and how they should do things.

I quietly sat down. My old, crappy office chair creaked a little bit. "Good morning, sunshine," a voice from over the wall said in what I took as a judging tone.

The voice came from Brenda. She sat across the wall from me. She was probably just sitting there waiting for me to get in so she could say that. Something about that phrase always annoyed me. It's one of those things that was always said to people who aren't early risers, like that's a bad thing.

"What's so good about it?" I mumbled under my breath.

"What's that?"

"Good Morning, Brenda." I enunciated each word and said them loud enough so she could hear me, but just low enough that the rest of the office couldn't.

Brenda was one of those social judges. She got in at 6:00 and thought everyone else should too. Little did she know, we all knew that she didn't do any work when she got in. She just read those cheesy romance novels till about 7:30, before everyone else got in. We never knew exactly what she worked on the rest of the day.

I turned on my computer and settled in. I really wanted some coffee, but I didn't feel like walking to the cafeteria. I was a bit grumpy in the morning, so it was probably best for everyone that I stay in my cubicle for a while. I couldn't deal with cheery people that early in the morning, but after my coffee, I would gladly be your best friend.

After about an hour of checking and responding to emails, I decided to go to the cafeteria to get some coffee. I was still sleepy and didn't feel like doing anything but going back to bed. Unfortunately, coffee didn't wake me up at all, although I tried to convince myself otherwise. It did, however, satisfy my morning hunger.

The cafeteria was empty, and of course, the coffee pot was empty as well. There went my plan of getting in and out. I opened the cabinet, got the coffee, and poured it into the filter. As I was waiting, Tammy came in. Tammy was like my work wife. We had our little morning routine. She was a lot older than me, but carried herself like she was younger than me. She was easily the coolest person in the office, and had a great sense of humor.

"What's up, grumpy?" she said.

"Living the dream," I replied cheerfully.

"Yeah, you wish you were. More like a nightmare, at this place."

She was also one of those people who called things as she saw them. Well, that is, if you agreed with her. If you didn't, she was just viewed as negative. I happened to agree with her more times than not.

"What's going on with you?" I asked.

"Same old stuff. You know."

I knew she was dealing with health issues and a lot of things outside of work. I could feel that that day was worse than others, despite the act she put on.

"You tell your parents about us yet?" I grinned.

She laughed. "Nope! I'm still waiting on you to tell yours."

"I'm working on it. You know how they feel about old, short, German women."

"Oh, they'll love this one!"

"I bet. I'll bring them around. I'm sure they'll grow to love you just as I have," I said as I made a choking gesture around my neck.

She laughed. "You're such an ass. How is it that you always know when I need a good laugh?"

I shrugged. "I don't know. I just get a feeling, I guess. We can't have you walking around here being sad. It ruins morale."

"Well, I will make sure I come find you when I am feeling down. Even though you're an ass, you always know how to make me laugh."

"It's what I do." I smiled. "Make the check out to me."

"Good luck with that, honey," she said. She flashed a flirtatious smile. "Catch you on the flip side."

As she walked out, Kaje walked in. He was my best friend. He was the closest thing to a brother that I had. You name it, we've been through it. He was there for my saddest moments, my happiest moments, and everything in between. We grew up together and had worked at pretty much the same places since we entered the workforce.

"What's up, sleepy? You couldn't wait for me?" he asked.

"I figured you had already been in here."

"How many times did you hit snooze today?"

"Only about four times. Maybe five. Maybe ten."

"Dude, that is so crazy. Can't you just put your phone across the room or something, so you have to get up and turn it off?"

"You know I've tried that."

"Oh, yeah. The alarm just becomes part of your dream."

"Exactly."

He laughed hysterically. "Remember that time you swore you were in New Edition because you fell asleep with them playing on repeat?"

I laughed right along with him. "Whatever, man. I was like ten years old. Besides, I was in the group, for one night, at least."

"Yeah, okay, Ralph," he said, still laughing at me.

We both laughed for a bit longer as we got our coffee. "Why do you need coffee? Do you even need sleep to function?" I asked.

Kaje could sleep one hour and have the energy of someone who slept twelve.

"I drink it for the taste, the aroma, and the richness," he said with some horrible accent.

I rolled my eyes. "If you say so. I'm headed back to my desk. We still on for lunch?"

"You know it. Don't forget about the BAM before lunch."

Kaje liked to come up with acronyms on the fly. Sometimes they were easy to figure out. Other times I was just stuck scratching my head in wonder.

"Let me guess. Boring ass meeting?"

"You got it!"

"Oh, great! Looking forward to it. Joy is me," I said sarcastically.

I grabbed my coffee and headed back to my desk. That meeting was the last thing I needed. I knew I'd be lucky if I didn't fall asleep in the first five minutes of it.

I got back to my desk and sat down. I grabbed my headphones out of my bag. I always listened to classical piano or new age music to help me relax and take my mind off the fact that I was at work. Before I could start playing my music, I heard a voice from over the wall.

"On break already, huh?"

Brenda was nosy and always kept track of everyone's movement, especially mine. I felt bad for her some days. Other days I just wanted to tell her to mind her own damn business.

"Finish your novel already?" I said, just low enough to not be fully heard.

"What's that?"

"Never mind." I pushed play and started my playlist.

I hoped that annoyed her as much as she annoyed everyone else. If she said something in response, it was lost in the ether. My music was on, and I was in my own little world. My work day had officially begun.

Chapter 2 - The Joys of Meeting
-Kaleb-

The meeting bored me to tears. The fact that the room was freezing was one of the only things that kept me awake. That, and I was sitting in the front row. I sat next to Kaje. We always talked about anything and everything during meetings. Being in the front row limited what we could say to each other, so we decided to save our conversation until lunch. He did manage to tell me that he'd rather be getting his wisdom teeth reinserted, then pulled again with no anesthesia than be in that meeting. I coughed and cleared my throat to cover up my laughter.

Just as I was able to contain my laughter, the company president handed the microphone to the vice president to say a few things. That was absolutely the last thing I needed at that moment. Whenever he talked, he ended every sentence with a long humming sound. It was especially troubling when the last word of the sentence ended with the letter "m."

"You may hear rumors about our profit margins shrinking due to the weather this quarter-mmm. As

I've told you with all the rumors you hear, don't concern yourself with them-mmmm. The weather probably won't have an adverse effect on our gain share this year-mmm. Although this weather is not typical for this time of year, these patterns are becoming more and more common-mmmmm."

Everything about the meeting reminded me of a time in high school chorus when everyone had to pick a song and sing a solo in front of the class. The choir teacher made it absolutely clear that if anyone was caught laughing at anyone during their performance, they would receive a failing grade on their performance. I didn't really consider that an issue for me. I wasn't one of those kids that made a habit of laughing at people trying to do their best, especially with singing.

Most people took the class to get an easy "A". When you think of a choir class, you think of singing as a group. We never even considered the fact that we would have to sing a solo.

It was Tracy Gordan's turn to sing her solo. While just about everyone in the class dreaded that moment, she happily headed to the front of the class. She walked with an air of confidence, almost as if she signed up for the class just for that moment. She handed her song selection to the teacher who sat at the piano. As the piano played, she rocked back and forth. A smile formed on her face as she waited to join in. We all waited in anticipation of what we were about to hear.

"*There are people in the world...*"

Her voice belted out a melody in a tone which could only be described as some sort of cross-bred farm animals being tortured. It was unlike anything I had ever heard in my life. I was in total disbelief at what I was hearing. I looked around the room to see how other people were reacting. John, who was one of the nicest guys in the class, was squeezing his hands together so tight, it was as if he was trying to cause himself pain. His face was completely red, and I swear I saw drops of sweat running down his forehead as he tried to hold his laughter in.

Meeko was sitting at the end of the seated risers, maybe about three rows up. The next thing I knew, I saw her fall over the side. I wasn't sure she even had time to brace her fall. I never did see her come back up.

I coughed a few times and even threw in a fake sneeze for good measure. I didn't want to laugh, but it was really hard not to. As I looked around the room, I saw everyone doing whatever they needed to do to not laugh. I remember feeling so bad for Tracy, but also wanting her to hurry up and finish before the whole class failed.

I looked down at her to see how she was handling everything that was going on. She was in her own world. She was in an absolute state of bliss. She swayed back and forth, smiling and singing like her voice was moving mountains.

Eventually, the vice president finished his speech, and the meeting was just about over. I could hear everyone gathering their things in anticipation of walking out.

"Before we adjourn, does anyone have any questions-mmmmm?" he asked. There was a ten second pause as everyone looked around. "No? Okay then-mmmm. Have a good—"

"I have a question about our gain share target," a voice from the back of the room yelled out.

"You have got to be kidding me," I mumble, probably a little bit louder than I meant to.

Mindy asked the question. She was notorious for asking stupid questions at the absolute worst times. Everyone turned and looked at her with bad intentions in their eyes.

"The ME strikes again," Kaje whispered.

"The who?"

"Meeting extender."

"Right!" I said with disdain. "Looks like we won't be going to lunch anytime soon."

Judging by the looks Mindy was getting from people around the room, I thought she was going to need a police escort to get back to her desk safely. It wasn't so much that she always had questions. It was the fact that they were always at the very end meetings, and they were always questions that had already been answered.

About fifteen minutes and four questions later, we were finally dismissed. Everyone hurried out of the room, fearing there would be another question. Seeing as though Kaje and I were in the front row, we were the last ones to head out.

"Hey, guys. Pretty informative meeting, huh?" Liza, our manager, asked us as we were walking out.

She looked at us with her big, blue, piercing eyes. She vigorously nodded her head up and down as she asked us the question. She did that whenever she asked a question that you are supposed to say yes to, as if she was using the power of her eyes and her nod to compel you to agree with her.

"I must answer yes to your question," I thought in my head, with the voice of someone under a spell.

"Yeah, it was a pretty good meeting. We were just discussing that," Kaje replied.

"Good. I'm glad you guys were engaged in the meeting."

We began walking out of the room. I gave Kaje a fist bump. "Good save."

"Dude, I had to say something. You were probably doing your 'The power of Liza compels us' bit in your head," he said, and he couldn't help but laugh.

I laughed. "Yep! You know me all too well. I hope you are ready for lunch because I was ready a half hour ago."

"I know that's right."

"Okay, I'll meet you by the doors in three minutes."

"Maybe even four?"

I laughed. It was one of those inside jokes that only we got.

Chapter 3 - Lunch Time Special
-Kaleb-

Since we were both more out of shape than we liked, we made a habit of walking the trail outside of the building at lunch. It was a scenic trail that actually led into a regional park. To the dismay of our managers, employees were able to take an extra thirty minutes of lunch, as long as they were doing something active like walking outside or working out in the on-site fitness center. That was a mandate passed down from corporate. It was supposed to promote more engaged and healthier employees, as well as lower healthcare premiums.

    Our managers were pretty old-school. Their mindset was, what worked for centuries must have worked for a reason. That type of thinking made for a very tense work environment sometimes. We once had a meeting with our managers to discuss how we felt about the stressfulness of the work environment. Their solution was to put a box of Legos on a table near the printer. We all felt like that was an insult to our intelligence, so no one touched the Legos, out of principle.

It was still warm enough outside that we didn't need jackets, but I brought mine anyway. Kaje looked at the jacket and shook his head. We headed out the side door. There was less traffic in and out of that door, so there was less risk of bumping into someone we didn't want to walk with us.

"What are you getting into tonight? You want to go shoot some hoops?" I asked.

"I'm supposed to be meeting that woman I met at the grocery store," he replied.

"Oh, that's right! The one with eight kids."

"Yeah, right! The one with zero kids. I'm not dealing with someone with kids. It's hard enough just dealing with them. Women are crazy nowadays."

"I know that's right. You know they say the same thing about us though."

"Exactly! It would be just my luck that I find one that's not crazy, and she actually does have eight kids."

We laughed. "I'd just start calling you 'Octodad,'" I said. We laughed even harder. Kaje's laugh was loud and infectious. People who passed us either looked at us like we were crazy or they wished they were walking with us.

"What about you? What letter in the friend-zone Rolodex are you on tonight?"

That was a common joke he made. He loved pointing out the fact that I always had female friends, but I never committed to anyone. Although he knew I was, at one point, he liked to point out that I hadn't been in a real relationship since.

"Whatever, man." I was still laughing from my previous comment. "I'm still going to the gym whether you are coming or not. I'm not really in the mood to deal with anyone tonight. You know how I get when I get around someone who is going through something."

"Dude, I still don't know how you deal with that. Absorbing what other people are feeling. What are you called again? An imp-hat?" He snickered a bit when he said it. He was always a bit skeptical of anything he couldn't explain. I really couldn't blame him because I was the same way. I really couldn't explain to anyone exactly what I felt. I just knew I felt what I felt.

"Empath. Mr. Comedian. You know what it's called."

He laughed. "Yeah, I know. I was just trying to get you to absorb some of my wittiness."

"Start displaying some, and maybe I will," I replied playfully.

"Ah, I see what you did there."

Kaje and I rarely argued. We learned a long time ago to just respect each other's opinions. Things could get pretty heated when discussing sports. Mainly, the occasional Jordan versus Lebron debate, but we never got too serious, just a little passionate about our stances. Outside of sports, we pretty much always had the same opinion on things anyway. Most of the time we even acted the same. And even though we don't look alike at all, it was crazy how much people mistook us for one another.

I looked at my phone and noticed the time. "We better start heading back if we are going to get back in time. You know Brenda probably has one of those kitchen timers in her cube."

"Right! Probably one for each of us."

I laughed. "Why are we still here again?"

"I was just asking myself that same thing. I've just been feeling like I'm bigger than this place. Not just this place, this whole corporate life thing. I just feel like there is something bigger out there for me. You know, I still haven't given up on my music. I still put out feelers from time to time."

Kaje kind of stumbled into corporate life. I always thought he would be in music or television. He was much more confident than he gave himself credit for, and he always had a presence about him that I admired. People were drawn to him, and it wasn't just people in his peer group. It was people from all different walks of life. He always had people vying for his time, whether he liked it or not.

He would say the same about me, but in my opinion, it was different. People were not drawn to me like they were to him. I always believed that my outward persona was different than my inward persona. What I thought I put out there for the world to see, was a bit different than what they actually saw. Growing up, I was very shy and it never truly went away. I just got better at faking it. I tended to attract people with my niceness, a warm smile, a funny line here and there, and my willingness to listen.

My willingness to listen was dangerous for me because there was always a chance of attracting the wrong type of person. My mom always warned me to watch out for what she called "energy vampires." She said I would know them when I met them because they would sap all my energy. She was right. I had come across more than a few.

I made a little joke to break the sudden seriousness of the conversation. "So, you're just going to leave me here in this dump, huh?"

"I'm not going anywhere, anytime soon, but it crosses my mind a lot lately. Besides, you don't have to stay here, you are only staying because you have a thing for Brenda."

"Man, that's not even remotely funny. I almost just threw up in my mouth."

We laughed really hard. Hard enough that we had to stop walking and gather ourselves before we headed back to the building.

"Did you pack your lunch or are you going to the cafeteria?" I asked.

"Nah, I'm going to check out the specials in the cafeteria."

"You better hit that salad bar. We didn't just walk for no reason."

He waved me off. "Whatever. Monday is my hungry day, and a salad is not going to cut it today."

"Alright. I'm going to head back to my desk."

"You aren't eating?"

"I'm not really that hungry. Plus, if I eat anything, I'll need a nap afterwards."

Kaje chuckled. "Dude, are you ever not sleepy?"

I laughed. "When I'm sleeping." It was funny because it was true.

"It's because you are always listening to that yogascape music, or whatever you call it. I would tell you that you should take a nap at lunch, but we know what happens when you do that."

I palmed my face. "Yes, we do."

The last time I took a nap in my car at lunch, I had a dream that I woke up from my nap, went back to work, attended a couple meetings, made significant progress on my project, then headed to my car to drive home. When I woke up, I thought it all happened and I just took a quick nap before driving home. I then proceeded to drive home. That was a fun story to explain to my manager.

"I'm heading back. Maybe I'll nap and dream you went to the salad bar," I said.

Kaje laughed. "That's about the only way you'll see me at the salad bar today. I'm HAF."

I laughed, shook my head, and headed to my desk. "I'm not even going to try to guess what that means. Catch you later."

Kaje laughed at me. "Later."

Chapter 4 - Clock Watching
-Kaleb-

The rest of the day felt like it went on for days. I had a headache from staring at spreadsheets the whole day. All I could think about was going home, but every time I looked at the clock, it was the same time as it was the last time I looked.

I thought about what Kaje said at lunch about being bigger than that place. It was times like that when I wondered if there was even something else out there for me. I looked at spreadsheets and code so much, sometimes they found their way into my dreams. Talk about a waste of a dream.

I often thought about what career path I would have chosen if I got the chance to do it all over again. The answer always eluded me. I was stuck in my little cubicle with my spreadsheet dreams.

I needed a break from staring at my computer, so I went over to Kaje's cubicle. Ron was in his cube. Ron and I always had a difference of opinion when it came to a lot of different things, and I always had a hard time hiding the fact that he annoyed me, so I turned to head back to my cube. Ron saw me and called me over.

"Oh, great. Joy is me," I mumbled. "What's up, fellas?"

"Ron was just showing me some pictures on his phone," Kaje said. He shot me a look and rolled his eyes with disdain.

Ron liked to go on social media and look at half dressed women all day, then he would save pictures and show us. He excitedly showed us a new picture, like the barely dressed woman in it looked that much different than the other hundred he tried to show us the day before.

"Don't you get tired of looking at the same type of pictures all the time?" I asked.

When Ron got flustered, he had a slight stutter. "I d-d-d-don't look at the same type of pictures all the time. I explore different b-b-beautiful women whenever I look."

"You're exploring their beauty, huh?" I asked in a somewhat facetious tone. Kaje couldn't help but laugh at that.

"You act like you don't g-go on any social m-m-media and look at women," Ron said.

"Oh, I do, quite often. I just don't look at what you look at. I mean, I look at beautiful women on there. I just think there is something refreshing about seeing a woman be tasteful and not feel like she has to show tons of cleavage or be half-naked to get likes."

Ron swiped through a few photos on his phone. "These women aren't half-naked."

Kaje laughed. "I'm not complaining, but they might as well be. Half of them had on clothes, but they were about three sizes too small."

"Look, you can look at whatever you want to

look at. I was just wondering why you always seem to search under the hashtag 'thicker than a snicker?' What's wrong with the hashtag 'classy women?'"

"Wh-wh-whatever. These women are classy. You don't think they are classy just because they s-show c-c-cleavage?"

"That's not what I'm saying. Classy women show cleavage, but they don't do it just so people will look and follow them, or for some sort of shallow validation from strangers. If a woman has to show cleavage or be half-naked to get attention, it says more about her than the guys she's attracting. Would you date a woman that went on social media and dressed like that?"

"I'm not trying to d-date them. I just want to l-look at them."

I sighed. "You didn't answer my question."

"Would I date a woman that looked like that? Yeah, I-I would."

That was also why I had a hard time dealing with Ron. It was hard to have a meaningful conversation with him because he always dodged the question.

I sighed again. "I didn't ask you if you would date a woman who looked like that. I asked if you would date a woman that went on social media and dressed like that."

"Yep, I would. Are you saying that you wouldn't date a woman who looked like that?"

"Well, first off, I wouldn't—"

"First off, she would just be your 'friend,'" Kaje interjected.

"Ha-ha! Funny guy. As I was saying, I wouldn't date a woman based on her pictures, alone. I would want to get to know her first, then maybe try to understand why she feels the need to put pictures like that out there. However, if I was dating someone who started putting pictures of herself out there like that, I think we would need to have a serious discussion about whether I was providing the validation that she is seeking, if she feels like she needs to get it from strangers on the internet."

"Okay D-D-Dr. Phil Kaleb. I don't have t-time to analyze women like that."

"Maybe you should make time. I'm just saying that you can gauge a lot about a woman by the hashtags she uses."

Kaje laughed. "He doesn't have to worry about making time. None of those women want him anyway."

"Ouch!" I said.

Ron couldn't help but laugh. "S-s-screw you, Kaje."

We all got a good laugh out of that one, and once Kaje started laughing hard, it was hard for anyone around him to not laugh just as hard. As we were cracking up, we got a little too loud. We heard Liza's door open.

"Uh oh," I said. We all exchanged worried looks.

"I can hear you guys. Full on!" Liza said angrily. Her big, blue eyes gazed intently at us.

"Sorry," we all said in unison.

The apology satisfied her. She turned and went back into her office.

"Full on!" I mouth to them as I made an exaggerated pointing gesture. Kaje put his hand over his mouth and started laughing again.

"Man, I'm out of here. I'm not letting you get me in trouble." I quickly headed back to my desk. I had a few things I needed to finish up anyway. It was almost time for me to go home, and I had already caused enough trouble for the day. I was pretty sure I was being closely watched after that outbreak of laughter. Management doesn't like for us to be out of our seats. We always joked that Liza had one of those plaques on her wall that said "The beatings will continue until morale improves." The truth was, she wasn't that tough on us, but her management style did take a bit of getting used to.

Tammy popped her head over my wall. "Stay out of trouble this evening."

"I always stay out of trouble. Unless I'm with you." I winked.

She blushed. "Oh, you are so full of it. Have a good evening, trouble."

"Thank you. You do the same. Go straight home. I'll see you tomorrow, bright and early.

She laughed. "Yeah, right. Bright and early, my ass."

I laughed. "Hey! The road to my cube is paved with good intentions."

"I'm sure it is. Goodnight, sweetie."

"Goodnight."

I looked at my clock. Thirty more minutes and I was on that paved road out the door.

Chapter 5 - Evening Flow -Kaleb-

Kaje walked by my desk as he was heading for the door. "You still planning on going to the gym tonight?" he asked.

"That's the plan. I have my bag with me, so I'll probably just kill some time first. Maybe I'll go to the mall."

"If you are going to the mall, I'll go with you."

"Cool. You know it'll have to be the crappy mall. I don't feel like dealing with that traffic on the way to the other mall."

Kaje paused. "Yeah, that's cool. I'm down."

"Don't you have to get ready for your date?"

"It's at seven. I don't need that much time. It's not supposed to be some big event, especially since it's on a weeknight."

"Where are you meeting?"

"Chuck's Diner. I figure it will be quiet on a weekday. We can talk and keep things light."

"Dude, are you joking?"

"No, why?"

"How many dates have you gone on with women you met there?"

Kaje thought about it for a minute. "Only like four or five."

"And you aren't worried about running into any of them while you're on this date?"

"Not really. What are the odds of that?"

"I would say they are pretty high."

"It'll be alright. It's not like it ended badly with any of them."

"That's technically true, if you don't count the fact that you just stopped talking to them when you realized they weren't a good match."

"What was I supposed to do? Keep going out and wasting both of our time?"

"No, but a phone call or text with an explanation is always a good option. Or better yet, have a little more patience. Sometimes people don't show their true colors on a first date because they are nervous."

"I hear you. I just don't know how that phone call would go. 'Hey, thanks for the date. You were boring and you bored me. Let's not do that again. Bye.'"

We started laughing.

"Yeah, go with that. Actually, send that in a card. That's a winner."

"You know what I mean though?"

"I do, but if you are looking for perfection on your first date as a barometer for a second date, you might not give anyone a second date."

"I guess."

"Okay, let's try this. Make a vow to give Octomom at least three dates, no matter what happens. Well, unless it's a complete disaster."

"Hmm, I guess I can do that. How about you vow to meet someone with no intentions of keeping her in the friend zone."

"How did this become about me?"

"I'm just saying. You have all this advice, but you don't apply it to yourself."

"Whatever. You know exactly why I'm not trying to be in a serious relationship."

"You still claiming that's the reason? How long ago was that, again?"

"How about we just focus the conversation on you. Three dates. Consider somewhere other than Chuck's Diner. You can let me know how it went when she leaves while you are in the bathroom."

Kaje laughed. "Yeah, okay."

I gathered my things and shut down my laptop. "Ready to head out?"

"I was ready hours ago."

"I know that's right. I'll meet you there. Let's go in the back entrance. I don't need to be anywhere near the food court. I'm starving."

Kaje snickered. "I knew you would be. You should have come to the cafeteria with me."

"Yeah, whatever."

When we got to the mall, it was pretty desolate. The number of stores that had closed since we were kids was astonishing. Considering the time of day it was, it probably would have been empty anyway. Most people had real adult things to do after work, and security kept nearly all the teenagers out, unless they had a parent with them.

Kaje pointed to a young lady walking out of the department store in front of us. "Whoa! Check her out. She is an FMS! How old do you think she is?"

"Old enough to fool the security guards, apparently."

"Get out of here! She is at least twenty-four."

"Bet?"

"How old do you think she is?"

"I'll give her seventeen at best."

"No way!"

"Hurry up and go ask her before she walks away."

Kaje laughed. "I don't want to know that bad."

I shook my head. "You just don't want to walk all that way."

"That too, especially in this old, creepy mall. They need to fix this place up. Look, some of the lights down there are flickering."

"You scared of the scary dark?"

"Nope. I'm just not going down there."

I laughed. "Mmhm. Sure, you're not. You have a date with your future wife in a couple of hours. You don't need to mess that up."

"Future wife? You are crazy. I'm just hoping she is cool enough for a second date."

"Oh, yeah. The perfection barometer."

"Whatever. Come into this store with me. I need to look at a pair of shoes."

"To go with your other hundred pair?"

"Just come on. You can get a pair too."

"Not from there. I'm not bougie like you."

We walked into the store. Kaje looked around at several pairs of shoes. I just walked around, browsing. The place wasn't my style. I tended to dress more on the casual side, while Kaje always looked like he was ready to go out for the evening.

Kaje waved me over. "Watch this," he said. He had a sneaky grin on his face.

"Oh, boy. You are about to get us kicked out of the store."

Kaje walked up to a completely unassuming customer and frantically asked him about the country of origin of the shoes he was holding, and if any animals were harmed while making them. He asked if he could see them in a size thirteen for his left foot and a size nine for his right foot. The poor guy was so caught off guard, he could barely respond.

"Excuse us," I said as I moved Kaje away from the confused man.

Kaje laughed uncontrollably. "Did you see the look on his face?"

I laughed. "You are a fool. We should go see if there is a store that sells handbaskets."

"I'll be right back. I'm going to see if they have these bad boys in my size."

"I'll just wait right here. I don't need to see you cause any more trouble. And make sure you leave that man alone!"

I walked around the front of the store for a few minutes, looking at things that I would never buy in a million years. Occasionally I would go check the back of the store to see if Kaje was finished. It had been close to fifteen minutes and he still wasn't finished. I headed towards the back to see what was taking so long.

As I headed towards the back, I heard a somewhat familiar voice in the front of the store. As I turned to look, I briefly saw a woman go by. She was moving very quickly. A strong feeling of déjà vu washed over me. It halted me in my tracks. I felt like I'd experienced that moment before. I couldn't shake the feeling that somehow, I knew the woman, and that she was in need of some kind of help.

After I got my bearings, I walked out into the mall. There was no one in the mall except an elderly woman and a few other random people. I quickly walked towards the exit. The woman I saw was nowhere to be found. I slowly walked back to the store to see if Kaje was finished. Before I got there, I saw him walking towards me.

"Dude, you okay? Why do you look like you don't know where you are?" Kaje asked.

"I just had a serious case of déjà vu."

"Uh oh. What happened this time?"

"I was waiting for you to checkout, and I heard a voice that sounded oddly familiar. I turned and saw this woman walking by."

"Well, did she look familiar?"

"That's the thing, and I know you are going to call me crazy, but she was walking so fast that I didn't get a good look at her. The weird thing is, she felt familiar, if that makes any sense. Almost like I've experienced being around her before."

"Yeah, you are crazy, but what else is new? Was it you-know-who?"

"No. It wasn't her."

"So, did you go after her?"

"So, the crazy thing is, I did, but she was nowhere in the mall. The stores between here and the exit aren't even open, so she couldn't have gone into any of them, and unless she is faster than Usain Bolt, she wasn't getting to that door before I could see her."

"Dude, I swear you experience the craziest stuff."

"Yeah, I guess I do. That one shook me a little bit

though."

"I'm sure you will probably run into her again, somewhere. Maybe at the track," Kaje said as he laughed.

Through my wonderment, I managed a small laugh. "Right."

We headed to the exit. We both kind of looked left and right to see if we saw her.

"Well, we know she's not hiding in one of these crevices," I said.

"Do we? Maybe she lives in the mall." We cracked up laughing.

"And on that note, I am out of here. Have fun with Octomom tonight. Let me know how it went."

"Alright. Talk to you later. Don't let me find out that you came back up here searching for her home."

I laughed. "You won't." I knew I would have never heard the end of it if I did.

Chapter 6 - Night Life
-Kaleb-

It was a long ride home from the gym. I stunk it up on the basketball court because I couldn't get my mind off of the woman at the mall. My focus was more on her than it should have been. I spent the majority of the games trying to remember where I heard her voice before. Basketball normally took my mind off of things, but even then, she was still on my mind.

I got home and planned to just chill on the couch. My knee was bothering me from basketball and my back felt tight. No sooner than I walked in the door, I heard a voice on the other side of the door.

"Open the door, you non-basketball playing scrub."

I opened the door and let Kaje in.

"Really? Scrub?"

"That's what Dave said you were playing like."

"Whatever. That's what he plays like every night. Anyway, what are you doing here? Shouldn't you be out on your date?"

"I had my date. It's over."

"That was quick. She walked out on you?"

Kaje rolled his eyes. "Please. I walked on her. She was practically begging me to stay."

"Ah, okay. Now you can tell me what really happened."

Kaje smiled. "It went okay. She's cool. A little reserved for my taste, but cool."

"Remember I told you—"

"Yeah, I know. I plan on going out with her again. If she'll actually go out with me again."

"Uh oh. What happened? Did she find out about your trail of destruction?"

Kaje laughed. "Not really, but guess who came in and kept shooting disapproving looks at us?"

"Oh, boy. Let me guess. Toya?"

"Exactly. It was almost like she knew I was going to be there. She probably hasn't been there in months."

"I never did like her. Have I mentioned that before?"

"Maybe nine or ten times."

Kaje and Toya became an item shortly after high school. We all knew her in school, but let's just say she didn't really hang with the cool kids. He always thought she was pretty, but when guys are young and dumb, we worry more about our reputation than our relationships, so he didn't even think about dating her then.

Shortly after high school he ran into her, and they started dating. He was big into his music and small acting gigs, so he always wore nice clothing and kept himself in shape. She was always more on the heavy side and dressed very plain. He didn't necessarily mind this, but she always thought he did, regardless of his assurances.

She began working out with him and slowly upgraded her wardrobe. He was excited to see the changes in her, so he went all in with helping her with whatever she needed. We would tease him because they would often wear matching outfits when they worked out, and sometimes they even matched when they went out.

Several months had passed and Toya was looking great. She lost a lot of weight, had a new hairstyle, and really nice clothes. Kaje would bring her everywhere. She was his support system. She was at all of his shows and auditions. He would always say they uplifted each other.

One thing that bothered him was how she craved attention. Whenever any guy paid attention to her, she ate it up. It was like she couldn't get enough.

A few months later she broke up with him. She told him she wanted to see other people. Kaje was furious. He never said anything to her about it, but he always told me how pissed he was about it. He felt like he built her up just so she could go be with other guys. Over the next few months, she would try to get back together with him when things didn't work out with whoever she was dating. They never had a serious relationship again, but they talked and occasionally did things together. One day she disappeared again to date some other guy. He got sick of the cycle and cut her off.

"How did Octomom react to her and her stalker looks?" I asked.

"Nandini was a little uncomfortable, but we dealt with it."

"Oh, have you confirmed she doesn't have eight kids? Do I have to call her Nandini now?"

Kaje laughed. "Whatever, man. I told you she didn't have eight kids. You were just hoping she did so you could keep calling her that."

I grinned. "I might call her that anyway. Nandini. I like that. Is that an Indian name?"

"Yeah, she is from India, but she has been here since she was a child."

"That's pretty cool. Maybe she will teach you some culture."

"Whatever!" Kaje said. He looked a bit bashful.

"So, did she ask about Toya?"

"Yeah, I gave her a brief synopsis of the situation. She seemed to be understanding, but the date ended shortly afterwards."

"You think it ended because of that?"

"I don't think so. She had made mention that she couldn't stay late. We'll see though. Maybe I'm the one that won't get the second date."

"I'm sure it's fine. Just be open and honest, and it'll work out."

"Yeah, I know. That damn Toya, still messing things up after all these years."

"I told you not to go to Chuck's. There's too much baggage in that place."

"Yeah, I probably should have taken that advice."

"The funny thing is, knowing Toya, she probably would have shown up anywhere you went."

Kaje laughed. "I know, right!"

"I'm glad it went somewhat well, besides that little drawback."

"Yeah, me too. It was a good date, but now I'm starving."

"You just came from a diner and you are starving?"

"Man, I was too nervous to eat. I didn't want to eat and then have the BGs.

"BGs?"

Kaje got up and walked to the refrigerator. "Bubble guts. I know you know what that is."

"Nope."

"It's the sound your stomach makes when you eat something bad and need to run to the bathroom."

I laughed hysterically. "It's probably a good thing you didn't eat."

Kaje grunted. "You don't have anything in this refrigerator."

"You mean I don't have anything unhealthy."

"Yeah, that too. I need some real food. I should have gotten something at the mall. Speaking of which, you know I fully expected you to go back up there."

I tried to act like he was way off base for thinking that. "Did you? Why would I have done that?"

"Dude, don't front. You know you wanted to go back, hoping there was a one percent chance that you would run into your mystery woman again."

"Truth be told, I thought about it, but what are the odds of running into her twice in one day in the same place? I'm not trying to stalk her. It would just be nice to solve the mystery of who she is. I swear I can't get her voice out of my head. It is just so familiar."

"I wouldn't care if she worked there and I knew exactly where she was. You saw the way those lights were flickering. Imagine what that old mall would be like at night. I would just wait until the next day."

"I laughed." What are you scared of? You think the mall is haunted?"

"Who knows. I just know I'm not trying to find out."

"I know you don't actually believe in ghosts, do you?"

"Just because you don't believe in something doesn't mean it's not real. Like I said, I'd rather not know."

"I can understand that. If you don't experience it, you don't have to acknowledge that it actually exists."

"Exactly."

"So, if one never experiences love, can one doubt its existence?"

Kaje rolled his eyes. "Okay Nietzsche, don't get all philosophical on me. I'm just saying, I've never seen a ghost, and I don't want to. You've never seen one, and I know you don't want to either."

"Well, that's not entirely true."

"What? Are you talking about that overexposed picture that Lori brought to work? The picture of her son with the thing in the background?"

I let out a small chuckle. "Not exactly. I had a weird experience when I was a kid. I mostly chalked it up to my eyes playing tricks on me, but the older I got, the less sure I became that that was actually the case."

"Oh, man. I'm starving, but I have to stay and hear this story."

I laughed at him. "Well, it's not a long story. So, once you hear it, you can get out and go get some fast food, and I can go to bed."

"Deal."

"Do you remember when I used to go to see my grandmother every summer?"

"Yeah, in Louisville, right? I remember you guys would always go to Niagara Falls and Louisville almost every summer."

"Yeah, well, one night we went out to dinner, but

my grandmother didn't go with us. It was pretty late when we got back. When we got to the door and tried to go in the house, the door was locked. We knocked on the door, but there was no answer. My dad ran around to the back of the house, but that door was locked as well. My mom looked in the window. It was dark, but she said she could see movement on the floor. She called out to my grandmother and heard a faint response. My dad opened the window, but he could only get it open a little more than half way. He told me to climb in and unlock the door.

"I looked in the window before I started to climb in. I could see a black shadowy figure standing over my grandmother. It slowly turned to look at me. The way it moved was unlike anything I had ever seen. I could feel my skin starting to crawl. 'There's someone in there,' I said, struggling to get the words out.

"My dad looked, but apparently didn't see what I saw. 'There's no one in there. Hurry up and get in, and go unlock the door,' he said. His patience had worn thin.

"I looked again, and the black figure was still looking at me. Its head seemed to shake in a deliberately slow fashion, as if it was telling me not to come in. I just stood there, terrified.

'Move!' My dad said as he pushed me aside.

"He used all his strength and lifted the window up. I'm pretty sure he broke the window frame. He jumped in the window and headed for the light switch by the door. When the lights came on, the figure disappeared from sight. My dad opened the door and let us in. My grandmother had passed out and fell to the floor. She had suffered a heart attack. The doctor said if we didn't get to her when we did, she would not have made it."

"Oh, boy! Okay, I am officially spooked," Kaje said.

"You wanted to hear the story."

"Yeah, and now I'm wishing I didn't. What exactly did the black figure look like?"

"Oh, now you want to hear more?"

"I'm just curious about what it looked like."

"It was weird. It was dark like a shadow. In fact, that's what my parents insisted it was after they checked the whole house and didn't find anyone there."

"You need light to create a shadow, don't you?"

"Exactly! That's what I told them. It had a thin, shiny outline to it. If I had to describe it, I would say it looked like that trophy that people get for best performance or something like that."

"A Golden Globe?"

"No, the other one, I think. The Oscar."

"Is there a difference?"

I laughed. "Nope, not to me. I get all of them mixed up. Anyway, it looked like that award, but all black."

"That's just craziness. I would have slept in the car that night."

"Oh, believe me, I didn't sleep anywhere. I was wide awake the whole night."

"So, what exactly do you think it was?"

"Honestly, and don't get all freaked out on me, but I think it was death. I think it was coming for my grandmother. The doctor did say that we got to her just in time."

"Dude, you saw death. That is the craziest thing I have ever heard in my life. I need to stop hanging around you!" Kaje laughed awkwardly.

"Whatever. I was a kid. I haven't seen anything weird since then."

Kaje made a spooky sounding noise and waved his hands up and down. "Except the ghost woman at the mall."

"Whatever. I'm sure there's a logical explanation for that."

Kaje laughed "I just told you what it was."

"Isn't it time for you to go? You heard the story. Now get out and let me get some sleep."

"Yeah, yeah. I'm going. I know you need all the sleep you can get. Maybe you'll get your butt up and get to work on time."

"I'll explain it to you again for the hundredth time. It's not the amount of sleep I get. It's the amount of times I hit snooze."

"I will never understand why you just don't get up."

"It's weird. It's like, sometimes my dreams are so vivid, I don't want to leave them until I absolutely have to. If you had snooze dreams like I have, you might just keep pushing snooze too. I don't know. Maybe I'm addicted to my dreams."

Kaje waved me off. "And on that note, I am out of here. I'll see you in the morning."

"Okay, see you in the morning."

Chapter 7 - The Path
Dreamscape
-Kaleb-

Slowly I come to. I rub my eyes and look around at this unfamiliar landscape. Where am I? A playground? What the heck is going on? I stand up and brush myself off. I feel lighter than usual. As my eyes begin to see things more clearly, I notice my shoes. I'm wearing what looks like kid shoes. I look at my hands. They appear to be much smaller. I walk towards the slide to attempt to see my reflection. I feel different. Nothing hurts. No nagging back pain. No knee pain. My steps are quick and effortless. I quickly run to the slide and look at the warped metal. The shock of what I see knocks me backwards and off my feet. I...am...a...kid...again.

    I struggle to get to my feet. I need to see it one more time. The reflection reveals the same thing. It also reveals something else. I am not the only one here. I turn to see a little girl standing behind me. Although she appears to be as confused as I am, she shows no signs of fear or panic. She looks around in wonder. Through her confusion, I can see a glimmer of glee on her face, almost as if she has finally escaped something to get here.

"What is going on? Where are we?" I say to her, but no sound comes out of my mouth.

She responds to me, but I can't hear anything she is saying. The only sounds I hear are the birds, the wind, and the clanking of chains as the swing sways back and forth. I survey the area. The grass is dead and the trees are withered. This place seems long forgotten.

Confused and scared, I sit down, pull my knees to my head, and begin to cry. She walks over to me. I look up to find her outstretched hand beckoning me to stand. I take her hand. She looks at me, smiles, and gives me a reassuring nod. She has a calming effect on me, and I trust her instantly. She seems to have a familiarity with this place, like she has been here before.

Still hand in hand, she leads the way and I follow. We make our way around the playground. It is a very old playground. The equipment is all metal and worn, almost to the point of rusting away. It is obvious that it hasn't been used in a very long time.

She leads me to the swings. She gestures for me to get on. I sit down. She smiles and swings back and forth. I rock back and forth gently. I am cautious. As an adult, just sitting on swings always made me dizzy. Since I am now in this kid body, I decide to give it a go. I pump my feet and swing myself back and forth. Before I know it, I am sky high. We look at each other as we swing in unison, and laugh uncontrollably. I feel as if I'm in elementary school again. The feeling overtakes me. She points forward and gives a sly smile. Before I can figure out what she's indicating, she launches herself into the air and flies almost twenty feet forward.

"Whoa!" I say.

She jumps up and down excitedly and waves her hands as if she is indicating a landing spot. I pump my arms and legs and swing as high as I can. Once I am certain that I can't go any higher, I let go and let the swing launch me forward. I soar through the air in what feels like slow motion. I feel close to the sky as the wind hits my face. I am flying, if only for this short period of time.

I can see the stunned look on her face as I soar overhead. I land hard, almost ten feet behind her. She rushes over to me with a concerned look on her face. She helps me up. I give her an indication that I'm okay and turn to wipe the embarrassment off my face.

She taps me on my shoulder. I turn around to see her laughing again. She reaches out, taps me on my arm, points to me, and runs towards the slide. I guess that means I'm it.

I start running and chase her around the playground. I am lightning fast, but she is too. We circle around the playground over and over again. Each time we circle, the entire area becomes more vibrant. The dead grass becomes green again, flowers bloom along the edges, and the trees become strong and full of life, blooming with vibrant pink cherry blossoms. The playground equipment, once old and rusty, regains the form of newly built equipment. I hear faint echoes of children laughing and playing. I give up my chase and marvel at what I am seeing.

She walks up behind me and smiles approvingly, as if things were finally how they should be. She takes my hand in hers and leads me away from the playground. I slowly follow, but for some reason, I am drawn to the playground. She gives me a little tug. I know it's time to move on.

We walk down a shaded path. It is familiar to her, but still seems to hold so much wonder. I stay close to her. She leads us to an old bridge surrounded by big beautiful trees. Only a few rays of sunlight dare to penetrate these trees. She leads us to a warm spot where we sit and enjoy the sound of the running water.

Butterflies of all different colors flutter about. Save for the birds and other small creatures, we appear to be alone in this world. We sit on the bridge, still hand in hand, dangling our feet over the side. She rests her head on my shoulder.

She points to an old shed and a pavilion that sit further down the path. I can tell these places hold meaning for her, and she can't wait to venture towards them. But, for now, we enjoy the warmth of the bridge, the sound of the water, the feel of the gentle breeze on our skin, and the solace of the moment. She grabs a stick and draws little hearts in the wet mud. She then draws one large heart around all the little ones. On one side of the heart she puts the letter I. On the other side she draws two stick figures. A boy and a girl. She smiles at me, then rests her head on my shoulder again.

After what seems like forever, she stands. I assume she is ready to venture further down the path. As we stand, she looks at me. She has a hint of concern on her face. I, in turn, look at her a bit curiously. Before I can gesture what I want to get across, she takes my hand and quickly pulls me down to the edge of the water. We look in. She puts her hands to her face in dismay. The reflection confirms what we both saw on the bridge. We have both aged a few years.

She shakes her head vigorously, almost in anger. She mouths what appears to be "Not yet. Too soon," but I can't accurately read her lips while her head is shaking. I gently put my hands on her shoulders in an attempt to calm her down. She is now crying. She buries her face on my shoulder and continues to sob. I hold her, hoping she would stop crying and attempt to tell me what's going on.

Seeing her so upset brings my fear back to the surface. She is the anchor and the glue that holds me together in this mysterious place, her mysterious place. If she is this upset, then something is definitely not right.

I lock my fingers in hers and attempt to lead her down the path. She shakes her head and refuses to budge. I try again. She snatches her hand from mine. I look at her with confusion. I make a shape of a shed and point down the path. Her face saddens even more. She slowly shakes her head and points.

I take steps to look more closely at what she is pointing at. She grabs my arm in an attempt to hold me back, but my curiosity will not let me be deterred. I slowly keep moving forward despite her protest. I look back at her and motion for her to follow. She cries, shakes her head slowly, and begins to take small steps backwards.

When I reach the top of the hill, the colors that once made up this area have faded to a washed-out appearance, like a colorful shirt washed too many times. The entire area in front of me appears to be waving eerily, like a mirage in a hot desert. The sounds I heard before are now a distortion of sounds. I look back. She is there, but barely in my view.

The shed is no longer there and the pavilion is in shambles. I slowly step a little further towards the phenomenon. I feel a pain in my knee. I look down to see I am no longer wearing any shoes and my feet have returned to their original size. The closer I get to the phenomenon, the older I become.

"Is this what she is afraid of? Is that what she meant when she said 'Too soon?'" I think to myself.

I turn to go back to where she was standing. The area is different. The trees that once blocked the sun are withered. The water has dried up and the bridge is nearly crumbled. Panicked, I run down the hill to where she was standing. The only things that remain are a black top, pink skirt with black polka dots, and little Mary Janes. The exact items she was wearing.

I fall to my knees. I look around in despair as this world unravels around me. I try to stand, I can't move. I feel like my very being is unraveling right along with this place. I...can't...move. Can't...feel. I—

Chapter 8 - Trouble and More Trouble
-Kaleb-

"Kaleb," a voice whispered, and I felt something touch my shoulder. I awoke suddenly in a panicked state. It took me a minute to get my bearings. "What the?" I mouthed.

My alarm was going off. I got out of bed and went into the bathroom. I turned on the faucet and splashed cold water on my face to fully wake myself up. I examined my adult self for good measure. I looked at the clock. My alarm had been going off for quite some time.

"Great! Just what I needed," I grumbled.

I was going to be late for work. I got myself together as fast as I could and hurried out the door, already trying to figure out the best excuse to use. That dream was still fresh in my mind, and I was having trouble concentrating.

I got to work about twenty minutes later than I wanted to. I tried to get to my desk as fast as I could. I was also trying to avoid being seen by anyone. I was totally out of sorts. I knew it was not going to be a good morning.

"Look who decided to join us. Good morning, sunshine," Brenda said as she looked over my cubicle wall.

"Morning," I grumbled. I was absolutely not in the mood for her.

I turned on my computer and immediately put my headphones on. I just wanted to be left alone. I decided that coffee would have to wait. There's something about when you walk in late all the time. You get that strange feeling that everyone is watching, waiting for it to happen, and taking bets on what time you will walk in.

I was settled into my chair with my music playing when Kaje walked by. "Dude, didn't you go to bed right after I left?" he asked.

"I did, but I had the craziest dream last night."

"Man, all your dreams are crazy."

"This one was different. I'll have to tell you about it at lunch. I'm still a little shaken up by it."

"Alright. If you don't start getting your butt here on time, you are going to have dreams you got fired, and they are going to come true."

"Yeah, I know. I even set my alarm to go off earlier. I had the—"

"The best intentions. I know. Let's go get some coffee. Not as many people as you think care about what time you get here."

Reluctantly, I agreed and followed him to the cafeteria. I really wasn't in the mood for coffee, but I thought it would be good to stick with the routine.

"Here comes trouble and more trouble."

"Good morning to you too, Tammy," I replied.

"Which one would I be?"

"Oh, you know exactly which one you are," she replied with a portentous grin."

"Sorry, Kaje, I guess that makes you 'more trouble.'"

"Yeah, right! You know exactly who she's referring to you as," Kaje said.

"He knows who he is. He is as much trouble as I am, and everybody knows I ain't no angel."

"Are you just in here to give me a hard time?" I asked.

Tammy laughed. "You know it, sweetheart. Now my job is officially done for the day. See you later, boys."

I shook my head. "That woman is crazy,"

"Yeah, and she's got a thing for you," Kaje said.

"Man, don't even go there. You say that about everyone. She is just overly friendly. We're cool like that."

"Yeah, okay. You can blind yourself to it if you want to."

"Whatever. I'm just going to get my coffee and try to survive this day. I actually wanted to call off."

"And do what? Dream some more? You and your crazy dreams are going to be the end of you one day. You should write them down and make a movie out of them."

"I'll get right on that. Right after I'm done filling out my spreadsheets. You can star in it and do the soundtrack."

"Maybe it's something you should think about. I told you I've been feeling like I'm bigger than this place. Maybe you should start feeling that way too."

"Right now, I just want to feel like I can survive and

not get fired from this place. Speaking of which, we better get back to our desks before Triple S makes his rounds up and down the aisles pretending like he isn't checking people's screens."

Kaje laughed hysterically. "I can't believe you have everyone calling him the Super-Secret Squirrel. You are a fool!"

I grinned. "I can neither confirm nor deny that I came up with that name. I'm heading back. I will talk to you at lunch."

"Okay cool. The path?"

Hearing Kaje say those words rattled me. It brought me right back to the unraveling path in the dream.

"Hello? Earth to Kaleb," Kaje said.

"Yeah?"

"We're walking the path, right?"

"Yeah."

"Dude, should I be worried about you?"

"I'm good. We'll talk later."

I headed back to my desk with my head down. I didn't want to chance making eye contact with someone and having to have a conversation with them. I just wanted to sit in my cube with my headphones on and keep to myself.

For the next few hours, I could not focus on anything except for that dream. Typically, I would think about the things that happened from the day before and analyze why I dreamed what I did. That one made no sense. That little girl. That path. That whisper, and the touch on my shoulder. It all felt way too real.

I managed to put it out of my head and focus on what I needed to get done. The music I listened to seemed to help with that. I was just about done with my current spreadsheet when Kaje popped his head over my cube wall. "I have a meeting right after lunch, so I'm headed to the door. See you there in a minute."

"Okay. I'm on my way," I replied.

I grabbed my jacket, met Kaje at the door, and we headed outside. It was a chilly day. We'd be lucky if we got back before the rain came.

"So, you want to tell me about this crazy dream?" Kaje asked.

"It wasn't so much that it was crazy. I've had crazier. It's just that it felt so real. It felt like it was actually happening."

"What was it about? Were you actually good at basketball?"

"No, it was about you actually showing up to play basketball, smartass."

"Touché."

"I will give you the short version because I know we don't have that much time. Who scheduled a meeting right after lunch?"

"I don't know. I didn't even look. I just accepted it. It's not like I had a choice anyway."

"True. So, anyway, I woke up on some playground. I have no idea where it was. I don't think I have ever seen it in my life. But get this, I swear I was like six or seven."

"Wait. Didn't you tell me you couldn't see yourself in your dreams?"

"Well, that's the weird thing. The first thing I saw was my shoes."

"So, you were wearing those old buddies that you used to wear? Pro-Sprint 1000s?" Kaje laughed. "Sorry, I couldn't resist."

I laughed. "Whatever! I was the fastest kid in the neighborhood with those buddies on."

"Says you."

"As I was saying, I went over to an old slide and saw my reflection. There was a little girl standing behind me. I think it was her childhood playground. I tried to talk to her, but neither of us could talk."

Kaje shook his head.

"What?" I asked.

"I swear, dude. Don't you ever just dream about normal stuff like hitting the lottery or something?"

"Sometimes. Those are boring though. Who wants to hear about those? Besides, those are the dreams that fade as soon as I wake up. I can barely remember them anyway.

"I don't remember my dreams at all."

"Maybe you hit the lottery every night. You should try to remember the numbers, so you can play them in the morning."

"I wish. Didn't you use to give your father numbers for the Pick 3?

"Yeah, on most nights."

"And he would win on most nights, right?"

"I don't know if it was most nights, but he won a lot."

Kaje shook his head. Dude, that is still crazy to me. So, tell me the rest of the dream."

"I'll skip to the crazy part. We were on this dark path and things got all weird. There was this distortion, like the world was unraveling. As I got closer to it, I got older. I think the world was ending."

"What the hell? Is that why you spaced out when I asked you about the path?"

"Yeah, pretty much."

"I see. So, what about the little girl?"

"She was freaked out. It almost seemed like she expected it to happen, but not as fast as it was happening. I lost track of her. I only found the clothes and shoes she was wearing. Soon after that, I couldn't move, and everything was going black. It was like I was dying or something."

"That's just crazy. I would just not sleep if I were you."

"That's not even the craziest part. After everything went dark, I heard a voice whisper my name and something touched my shoulder, waking me up."

Kaje stared at me. I couldn't tell if he was worried about me or if he thought I was full of it. I shot him a serious look. "You know I don't just make up crazy stuff. I'm thinking I was just sleeping really heavily and I touched my own shoulder."

"And the whisper?"

"I don't know. Probably just part of the dream."

"I have to stop hanging around you."

"Whatever."

"I'm not joking, man! That's two crazy stories in two days. You are going to give me nightmares."

"It won't matter. You won't remember them anyway. What was the other one?"

"The other what?"

"Crazy story."

"Oh, the golden globe, Oscar of death dude."

"Oh, yeah. Him."

"Yeah, him. He was probably the one in your dream unraveling the world. Did you see him anywhere?"

"I know you are joking, but maybe that's why I

dreamed that. I never even thought about that. But how would I explain the little girl?"

"Dude, the hell if I know. Maybe she's the mystery lady from the mall."

"Whoa! Look at you. Kaje Waters. Dream interpreter extraordinaire!"

He popped his collar. "Just another of my many talents. We'd better head back. I want to get something to eat before my meeting."

"Sounds good. Although I know you think I'm losing my mind, I do appreciate you listening to my crazy ramblings. I feel a lot better."

"No worries. That's what friends are for. Oh, and for the record, I thought you lost your mind a long time ago."

I laughed. "Gee, thanks."

"Now walk at normal person speed. I'm HAF"

"Hungry as Fred?"

"Yeah, him too."

Chapter 9 - Just One of Those Days
-Kaleb-

Kaje popped his head over my wall. "Yo," he said quietly.

"Yo. How was your meeting?" I asked.

"Very interesting."

"Oh? How so?"

Kaje's face filled with uncertainty. "Don't tell anyone I told you this. I'm not even supposed to tell anyone. They want me to strongly consider going for the Sr. Lead Analyst position."

"That's a good thing, right? More money?"

"Yeah, but it's also more responsibility. More responsibility that I'm not sure I want."

"Understandable. But are you really going to turn down more money?"

"I'm not sure. There is another issue that's weighing on me."

"You'll feel trapped if you accept the position."

"Exactly. I'm just not sure how long I want to do this corporate thing, and the more I make, the harder it will be to walk away from it."

"It doesn't close the door though. Just think about your options. We can talk more about it later."

"Okay. That sounds like a plan. Talk to you later."

If I was being honest with myself, I was a little jealous of him being offered that position. I knew I was more than qualified for it, but I couldn't expect to be offered anything when I couldn't even get to work on time. I wasn't sure I even wanted that position. That's what I tried to convince myself of anyway. Part of me really didn't like the job, but the realist in me knew that I didn't like what the job revealed to me about myself.

I refocused myself and tried to finish what I was working on. My headphones died, so I had to listen to all the office chatter. Sometimes I could tune it out, but there were certain people's voices that just pierced through everything. Brenda was one of those people. She was complaining to someone about how loud her neighbor's cat was. I'd heard of people complaining about dogs barking, but who actually complained about cats?

I tried to tune her out. I hummed a little tune in my head. It helped a little bit. It was always so odd that Triple S never seemed to make his rounds when Brenda was gossiping and complaining. It was probably because he was doing the same thing.

I decided to get up and go for a quick walk to escape the chatter, when I heard Brenda say something that caught my ear. I stopped and listened in.

"I tell you, she was just the cutest little thing. Wearing that little polka dot dress and the cutest little Mary Jane shoes."

My heart started racing. My head was spinning. I

wondered who she was talking about. It had to be the little girl. It felt like the room was spinning. I sat down and listened closer. Ron walked over to my desk. "D-D-Damn K-Kaleb. You look like you've seen a ghost."

"Shh!" I said emphatically as I vigorously waved him away.

Brenda continued. "She was just so adorable. I almost took her home with me, but Jeff is terrified of dolls. He would never let me bring one in the house."

"A doll?" I mouthed.

My heart rate began to slow. The room slowly returned to its stable position. I swore I was losing my mind. "What are the odds of her talking about polka dots and Mary Jane shoes the day after I had that dream?" I thought.

I got up and went to the water fountain. I saw Ron. "My bad. I thought she was gossiping about me."

"You looked like you were going to p-p-pass out."

"Nah, I'm okay. I just don't feel great today. Did you need something?"

"N-Not really. I was j-j-just going to sh-show you a picture of this girl."

"Dude, are you serious? You are killing me. I'll look at it later."

"Suit yourself. She is f-fine!"

As I walked back to my desk, I heard a voice call out. "Hey, Kaje."

It was Lori from the data team. She mixed me and Kaje up every time she saw us. "I'm Kaleb," I said.

"Oh, my God. I'm so sorry. You would think I would remember that. My sons are named Caleb and Cage, but with Cs."

I mustered a smile to make her feel at ease. "No worries. We look just alike, give or take fifty pounds, a bald head, about a couple inches in height, and eye color."

Lori laughed so hard, she snorted. "See! It's things like that. You two just remind me of my boys. You're both so funny. I'll get it right next time. See ya later."

"See ya later, Lori."

The work day couldn't be over fast enough. It was just too weird. I was on edge, and everything was getting to me. I needed to just get away so I could clear my head. I just had to survive a couple more hours.

I got back to my desk. Thankfully, Brenda was packing up her things and getting ready to leave. It didn't guarantee peace and quiet, but it was as close to a guarantee as I was going to get.

"See you bright and early in the morning, sunshine," she said facetiously.

I sighed heavily. She wasn't looking for a response. She just wanted to be her typical annoying self. I always told Kaje that if I ever hit the lottery, I wouldn't quit my job for about a month, just so I could tell a few people what I really thought of them.

I watched the clock for the next hour or so. I managed to finish what I needed to and started to pack up my things. I heard a boom of thunder. I looked outside. It had started to pour. Of course, the rain held off all day until it's time for me to leave. That's just how the day was going.

I was packed and ready to leave when Rob walked by. "Hey, what's up, man? You look like I feel," he said.

Rob was my favorite developer. He always kept things real with everyone. Whenever I needed a fresh perspective on life, he was the one I went to.

"It's just one of those days. I'm just glad it's over," I replied.

"Trust me, I know the feeling, man. So, real talk. You ever heard of Hammermill Friday?"

"I can't say that I have. What is it?"

"You'll see on Friday. Hey, man, I have to run. Hit me up sometime. We need to catch up."

"Okay. Talk to you later."

Rob was never in one place for too long. He could have a short conversation with ten people in five minutes. He would always make time to talk to me though. Sadly, I didn't always make time for him. I planned on changing that. I missed hanging out with him. We both had a childhood love of video games. We played games together here and there, but life just kind of caught up to us and we got too busy for each other.

I headed to the door. The rain was heavy and showed no signs of letting up. I thought about the huge umbrella I had in the car. I sighed, opened the door, and ran to my car. I got in and shut the door. I was completely soaked. I sat there and stared at the rain as it hammered the windshield.

My phone rang. It was Kaje. "Hello?"

"Are you home yet?" he asked.

"No, I'm sitting in the parking lot watching it rain."

"I'm headed towards your place. How long until you are there?"

"Probably about twenty minutes. I'm going to stop and get the biggest, juiciest, greasiest burger I can order."

"Don't forget fries and a milkshake."

"Oh, trust me. I won't."

"That's what I'm talking about. See you in about twenty minutes. I have some things I want to run by you."

"Okay. Sounds like a plan."

Chapter 10 - Come on in Monica
-Kaleb-

I held my stomach and looked at Kaje. "I ate that a little too fast."

"Dude, I haven't seen you eat like that in years. You are going to pay for that later."

"I think I'm already paying for it. I could crash right here."

"It's too early for that. If you think you are feeling it now, imagine how your stomach will feel in the morning if you go to sleep after drinking that chocolate milkshake."

"I'd rather not. Remember when we were kids and we could eat what we wanted, when we wanted, and it had no effect? I miss those days. I guess I have to stay up and deal with you for a while. What did you want to talk to me about anyway?"

"Just about life, really. What's going on at work, and where my head is at."

"Is this about that position?"

"Well, it's that and other things. Do you remember that guy that used to make beats for my music?"

"Dapp, right? He was kind of out there, but he was cool."

"Yeah, well he is still kind of out there, but he has been working with some high-profile people in the music industry, and he asked me if I was still serious about making music."

"Wow! What did you tell him?"

"I told him that I wasn't sure."

"What? Why did you tell him that? That has always been your dream."

"I don't know. I'm just not sure what I want to do. I'm not entirely happy with what I am doing now, but it's stable and it pays well. Going into the music industry involves taking a lot of risks that I'm not sure I want to take at this point in my life. It can be a dirty, dirty business."

"I get that. Let me ask you this though. Could you live with yourself, knowing that you passed up this opportunity?"

"That's the thing that's weighing on me. It's not a definite thing, but it might be as close as I'm going to get, and you don't see too many older rappers out there in the music game."

"When do you have to make a decision?"

"I don't, really. I am waiting for Dapp to get back to me. Which is good because it gives me more time to think about it."

"Yeah, but now that you know it's a possibility, you won't be able to focus on anything but that."

"Exactly! I just don't want to try it, fail, and then be SOL."

"Wow."

"What?"

"You are so torn by this, you are using regular, understandable acronyms."

Kaje laughed. "You are an absolute fool."

"Well, I think you should do it. I'll be your agent. I'll only take thirty-five percent of your earnings since I'm such a good friend."

Kaje was still laughing. "Good luck with that. More like zero percent. Better yet, you can pay me to be my agent."

"Yeah, okay. Are you sure you want to do music? You are a pretty good comedian."

We laughed. I was glad the seriousness of the day was washing away. Laughing with him like that reminded me of when we were younger and didn't have to worry about making such heavy decisions. While we were laughing, there was a hard knock on the door.

"Uh oh. Maybe we were laughing too loud? Does Liza live across the hall from you?" Kaje asked jokingly.

"Don't even joke like that. I would have to move. Although, I heard that outside of work, she is actually really cool."

"What? Who told you that?"

I smiled. "A source."

Kaje wore a suspicious look on his face. "A source my a—"

The knocking got louder. "Who is it?" I yelled as I walked towards the door.

"You know who it is. Open up," the voice demanded.

I turned to look at Kaje. We both sighed and said the same exact name in unison. "Monica."

I opened the door just enough to look out, but Monica pushed it all the way open and walked in. "You guys sound like you are having a good old time. You weren't going to invite me?" she asked.

"We knew you'd pop up sooner or later," I replied.

Monica popping up whenever she felt like it, was nothing new. She had lived in the apartment across from me since I moved in. In fact, she made herself at home while we were moving things in.

"Whatever. I just happened to be walking by, so I thought I would stop and see what was going on. Hey, Kaje. How's life?"

"I can't complain. How about yourself?"

"I can complain, but I won't."

"Man trouble?" I asked.

"Something like that," she replied.

Monica had been in an on-again, off-again relationship for the last couple of years. I used to give her advice, but I learned that she was always going to do what she wanted to do, so I just listened.

"Were we really that loud?" I asked.

"No, not really. I just got home, and I was going to knock on the door anyway. I heard you laughing as I was about to knock. What was so funny?"

"Kaje quit his job to become a comedian," I said.

"Whatever. What was really so funny?"

"Nothing. We were just talking about guy stuff," I replied.

"If you say so. You don't have to tell me. Keep your little guy secrets."

"It's not that they are secrets. Like I said, it's guy stuff. Women talk about women things. and guys talk about guy things. It's probably best that we don't mix the two, at least not tonight."

"I'm leaving it alone. Moving on, so, Kaje, did you have a good day?"

"I did, actually. It was a bit strange, but it was good." Kaje replied.

"Well that's good. How about you, Kaleb? Anything new and exciting going on?"

"New? Definitely. I'm not sure I would call it exciting though. What I am sure of, is that greasy fast food is not agreeing with me. I need to go to the bathroom. You two can chop it up while I'm gone."

"Oh, boy!" Kaje exclaimed.

I got up, went to the bathroom, and shut the door. I could somewhat hear them talking on the other side of it.

"Is he okay?" Monica asked Kaje.

"Yeah, he just ate too much of that greasy food. He'll be alright."

"I'm not talking about his stomach. I mean, is he okay, in general. He doesn't seem like himself. What did that 'at least not tonight' comment mean?"

"I'm not entirely sure what he meant by that, but I do see that he's not been himself. I know he has been having weird dreams."

"Well, that's nothing new. Hasn't he always had those?"

"Ever since we were kids. The one he had last night seemed to have a strange effect on him though"

"How so?"

"He said something about it feeling like it was real. It really shook him up. I'll let him tell you about it if he wants to tell you. He's probably tired of thinking about it."

"I won't press the issue. I just worry about him. He's

always listening and taking on other people's issues. It's sometimes easy to forget he has problems of his own."

"Oh, believe me, I get it. It's part of the reason I am over here now. It didn't seem like a good idea for him to be alone tonight. I'm glad you showed up too."

"Can I ask you a somewhat sensitive question?"

"What's up?"

"Has he told you why he still keeps the cat bowl and water dish out?

"Nope, and I don't ask. I suggest that you don't ask either. He's experienced so much loss in his life, and you know how hard it was for him when Titus died."

"Yeah, I know, but that was over a year ago. He needs to get a girlfriend and stop living this bachelor life. You too, now that I think of it."

"And you should be single and stop living that crappy relationship life," I said as I walked back in the room.

"Don't start. You know I'm just concerned about you."

"And I appreciate it, but I'm fine. The bachelor life suits me just fine."

"Maybe because you haven't given a true relationship a chance. All you've ever had was friends since you moved here. Who was the last person you were actually serious about?"

Kaje and I exchanged leery looks.

"What? What were those looks about?" Monica asked insistently.

"Don't look at me!" Kaje exclaimed. "I just returned his look."

Kaje was almost giddy with wonder. I'm sure he

was curious about how much information I would give Monica, and who I would give that information about.

"Her name was Julene," I said softly. "I met her on one of those dating apps."

Kaje shot me a peculiar look. He didn't know I was actually that serious about Julene. I just shrugged at him. I would explain things to him later.

"Wait a minute, you expect me to believe that you were using a dating app?" Monica asked surprisingly.

"I didn't actually use it. Well, I used it, but I was trying it to see what the buzz was about."

"Funny. That's what all the guys say."

"I don't say that. I used it, and I see what the buzz is about," Kaje said.

Monica sighed heavily and started to say something, but I cut her off. "We can talk about the morality of dating apps another time. Unless you want to talk about that and hear the story some other time."

Monica sighed. "They are sex apps. That's all I'm saying. Anyway, go on."

Kaje and I sighed heavily.

"As I was saying, I met this girl on the app. The weird thing was, she was the first person I saw. She was attractive, so I swiped. Apparently, she must have felt the same, because it told me she was interested."

"Sounds a bit shallow, but I digress," Monica said.

"Someone is in a mood. Are you sure you don't want to talk about your night?"

"I'm fine. Go on."

"Conversation started out small. I was a bit leery of the whole thing. I think she was as well. Each day, we got to know each other a little more. The conversation was easy. It flowed. After a few days it felt like we had known each other for years."

"You seem to have that effect on people," Monica said.

"Don't feed his ego. It's big enough," Kaje said.

"Whatever. I have no ego at all, and I think we clicked more because of her than me. Maybe it was both of us. I don't know. All I know is we got close very fast, and that was very unusual for me."

"Was she close by? Did you meet her in person?" Monica asked.

"Once. We met at a coffee shop. The thing about her was, she was secretive about her life. For as much information that she offered up, she held back just as much."

"Maybe she was married," Monica said.

"She said she wasn't married. I didn't get the impression she was. She was really religious and always talked about how she needed to get back to the church. I told her that she should, if that's what she wanted to do. She clearly had some demons she was dealing with. Sometimes I could feel her draining my energy over a text conversation."

Kaje sat up excitedly. "See! That right there would have been enough for me to be done with her. I don't know how you deal with that. Especially the whole energy draining thing."

"It's not like she was doing it on purpose. In fact, I think she was trying not to. She just didn't understand what she was doing. She once made mention that I was like her guardian angel."

"Did she know you're an empath?" Monica asked.

"If she did, I didn't tell her. It almost seemed like

she was fighting a battle with herself over whether she should have feelings for me or not."

"How long did this go on?" Monica asked.

"A couple of months or so. She would sometimes disappear for days. One day I went to message her to tell her I can't keep playing these games, and my messages wouldn't go through. When I searched for her, her name didn't come up."

"She blocked you," Monica said softly.

"Yes, indeed. No goodbye, no nothing."

Monica shook her head. "That's messed up. How hard would it have been to send a goodbye message?"

"It's not like a goodbye message makes things any better," Kaje said.

I knew what Kaje was hinting at. I shot him a disapproving look and a quick head shake, making it clear I didn't want him to go down that path.

"Sure, it would. It would at least provide him with closure," Monica said.

"I guess," Kaje said dismissively. He was clearly biting his tongue.

"She had issues anyway. After a while, I just felt like her dirty little secret. I told her that I didn't want to be that. She assured me that wasn't the case."

"I still think she was married," Monica said.

"That's my thought," Kaje said.

"Yeah, to the church. I think she was on a pilgrimage or something. You know, like the one Amish people go on to see if they want to live in our wicked world."

Kaje laughed. "Dude, you are crazy."

"I'm serious though. You know she had the nerve to message me again one night, telling me that she was sorry. She said she was going through some things."

"Are you kidding me?" Monica asked in amazement.

"Nope, but what's really going to blow your mind is, a few months after that, she messaged me and pretty much tried to pick up where we left off, like nothing changed."

"No way!" Monica said.

Kaje shook his head. "Whack job."

"I made small talk for about a couple of weeks, then one night, I went to reply to a message she sent earlier, and she had blocked me again."

"I don't know why you even talked to her again," Kaje said.

"I was trying to be nice, I guess. Sometimes people go through things. Everyone deserves a second chance. I won't make that mistake again with her. I blocked every possible way for her to contact me. She's basically dead to me."

"That's kind of harsh, but I understand it. She had issues. That's why you shouldn't date people from dating apps," Monica said smugly.

"Seriously? You think it happened because I met her using an app?"

"I'm just saying."

"You're just saying what? Honestly, how many people have you met that turned out to have all kinds of issues?"

"Quite a few, actually."

"And did you meet them outside of a dating app?"

"Yep."

"That's what I'm saying. People are people. It doesn't matter how and where you meet them. They are still going to be the same person."

"The wise sage has spoken," Kaje said.

"Good grief. Don't you start," I replied."

"I guess you're right though. I just know I couldn't date someone from a dating app," Monica said.

"Understandable. To each his or her own," I said.

"Every girl I met on there was weird and just sent RIMs," Kaje said.

Monica just looked at me with a puzzled look. "Don't look at me. I have like a thirty percent success rate figuring them out," I said.

Monica leaned in towards Kaje. "Okay. I'll bite. What is RIM?"

"Random idiotic messages," Kaje replied.

We all cracked up laughing.

"I swear, man, you and your acronyms. How do you just pull these things from nowhere?" I asked.

"No idea. They just come to me," Kaje replied.

"Both of you are crazy, and I'm done dealing with y'all tonight. I have some things I need to take care of. And for the record, Kaleb, don't think I'm stupid. You may have been interested in that girl, but you weren't all that serious. I'll get the real story out of you one day."

"It's funny how you assume there has to be a real story. Why can't I just like being a bachelor?"

Monica got up and walked to the door. "Because I know better. Call it women's intuition. Goodnight, boys."

"Goodnight, Monica," we both said in unison.

"Dude, for a minute there, I thought you were going to tell her about Marci," Kaje said.

"That's the last story I want to get into right now. I don't even want to think about it."

"I get it. Let's change the subject. So why didn't you tell me you were that serious about Julene?"

"Probably because I didn't think I was. It all seemed like a game. I mean, I felt like we connected, but I felt like I could disconnect at any time. Especially since she was so secretive and distant most of the time. It turns out she was just another one of those women who found me when they were going through something, then once I helped them through whatever they were going through, I was longer needed. I kind of knew she was going to vanish. It just kind of hit me like a punch when she actually did."

"I hope I never have to deal with crap like that. Hopefully Nandini stays normal."

"I'm sure she will since you didn't meet on a dating app," I said mockingly.

Kaje laughed. "Right! What was that about?"

"I think she caught her on-again, off-again boyfriend with that app on his phone."

"And there it is."

"Yep."

Kaje stood up and stretched. "I'm going to head out. Are you good, man? You had me kind of worried about you earlier."

"Yeah, I'm good. That dream freaked me out, but it has all but faded away now."

"Cool. I'll talk to you tomorrow then."

"Yes sir. Thanks for coming by. I think we both needed a night to just chill."

"Yep. Later."

"Later. Be careful out there. This storm is only getting worse."

It was still early, but I was exhausted and decided

I needed to get some rest. I was still full from all that food, so I decided to relax on the couch until I could build up the gumption to walk to my bed. I wasn't really looking forward to going to sleep. I lied to Kaje when I said the dream had all but faded. It was still pretty fresh in my mind and I was not looking forward to the sequel.

Chapter 11 - Fireflies Dreamscape
-Kaleb-

I find myself in the middle of nowhere. It is pitch black. I can't see anything. My hand is intertwined in a small, soft hand.

"Whatever happens, whatever you see, don't let go of my hand," a voice whispers to me.

The hand pulls me, and we begin to run. A loud crack of thunder shakes everything around us. We stumble, but do not fall. Our hands are still intertwined. The pace picks back up.

"What is going on? Where are we?" I manage to ask.

"Shh. It'll hear you," the voice whispers back.

"It?"

"Shh!"

Another boom of thunder. This one knocks us off our feet. I am quickly pulled up and we are running again. I have no sense of where I am or what we are running towards, but I somehow know that stopping is not an option.

In the distance I can see what looks like tiny sparkling lights. "Look," I whisper.

"Shhh!" the voice responds. Clearly more agitated than before.

As we near the sparkling lights, I notice that they are not lights at all. Everywhere I look, there are fireflies flying about, thousands of them. Instinctively, I slow down to look around. This time there is no tugging. The person leading me slows down as well. Suddenly, the person begins to hum a soft tune. Although the humming is faint, I can tell it is a female voice.

As she continues to hum, the enchanting song echoes majestically throughout the darkness. Slowly, the sky above us begins to fill with endless fireflies. I gaze upon them in astonishment as they dance in unison to this wondrous song. They slowly pulse their light in unison, creating a glorious light all around us.

As I catch my breath, I look around, examining my surroundings with the newfound light. It looks as if we are in an old abandoned city. The buildings I can see are crumbled, while others are completely destroyed. The houses that sit on the outskirts are old and withered. I feel a vague familiarity with this place, like I have seen it a very long time ago.

I feel a squeeze of my hand. I had almost forgotten I was holding someone's hand. I turn to look at my traveling companion. She has her finger up to her lips in what could only be anticipation of my reaction to her appearance.

My pulse starts to quicken as I see an almost translucent image of what appears to be a teenage girl. The image constantly shifts, as if it is being projected from several different sources to make one image.

I stare at her for several more seconds. The images

rapidly shift and form different versions of themselves. Young to old, then back to young again. It is as if they are cycling through stages of her life and then reversing the stages. As I watch in wonder, my hand slowly loosens from hers. The images all freeze on an image of an elderly woman before fading to complete blackness. The only thing that remains is a pair of sad, brown eyes. I open my mouth. I am not sure if I want to gasp in horror or cry out.

Her hand tightens around my hand. A faint, dark image of her other finger shakes, as she moves it to what should be a face, emphasizing the desperate need for silence. I close my mouth and stare terrifyingly at the image before me. As she pulls my hand and begins to walk forward, the image of the teenage girl flickers back into focus.

We follow the fireflies as they dance back and forth, shining their light on one thing after another as they light the path ahead. They illuminate an old wooden structure, then slowly move on to an old bicycle, an old car, an old wilted plant, and a large fallen tree. It looks as if they are searching for something. They hover over an old, broken park bench and pulse their lights a bit faster.

We slowly walk to the bench and begin to examine it, when we hear a long, low rumble of thunder. This time I see small flashes of lightning way off in the distance. The fireflies almost break formation, but continue to hold steady.

I can feel small drops of rain starting to fall. Still hand in hand, she quickly leads us on. Her pace is much faster than before, and I am struggling to keep up. The fireflies hover just above, still lighting the way forward.

The raindrops are now steadier. It is not a warm, summer rain. It is a cold, harsh rain. Each drop inflicts a measure of pain as it lands. The pace quickens even more, and I'm having a harder time keeping up. I want to look back, but I am afraid of what I will see. I hear a snapping and tearing sound, followed by the loudest thunder I have ever heard in my life.

The fireflies flutter away in terror, taking their light with them. We fall to the ground. Our hands almost completely separate. We are holding on by our fingertips. The image of the girl begins to fade to black. I pull her hand securely into mine.

There's another tearing sound, followed by a tremendous boom of thunder and several strikes of lightning. It sounds as if the sky itself is tearing apart. The lightning is becoming more frequent and starting to brighten the sky, almost as if it were daytime.

In the far distance, I can see a large tree. Above it, the sky has a weird ominous look to it. It looks as if it was ripped open just above the tree. Half of the tree is near the ground and the other half looks to be in the ripped, open sky. I can't tell if the tree has fallen from the sky or is being sucked up into it.

Boom! Another strike of lightning. This one hit right behind us.

"It is coming for us. We have to run!" the girl screamed.

She pulls my hand and we are now running at a frantic pace.

"Run where?" I yell back.

"To the tree! She needs you!"

"She? Who is s—"

Before I could finish my sentence, lightning begins to strike all around us.

"Faster!" she yells.

We are now running at such a dizzying pace, I can barely keep up. The wind and rain against my face causes my eyes to water, and I can barely keep them open. Everything is blurry now. I have no idea if we are any closer to the tree. The lightning strikes continue. The last one felt close enough to hit me.

"Just a little further!" she screams.

I feel a strong tug on my hand and we are running even faster than before. Everything around us appears to stand still while we are still moving. Lighting strikes continue to strike down in slow motion. We dodge them over and over again.

"Faster!" she yells.

I am having trouble keeping up, and I can't catch my breath.

"You can make it!" she insists.

"I...can't...breathe."

I can feel my lungs giving out, and my legs begin to slow down. I hear her let out an audible groan. She slows down to check on me when all of a sudden there's a deafening whip-crack and a blinding light. I feel our hands come apart. The last thing I hear is her scream.

"No!" she screams.

I open my eyes. I can't see anything. I slowly stand up. I feel my way around the darkness, but I do not dare to call out.

In the distance, I can see the fireflies floating about. I hurry towards them. I try to hum the song that she hummed earlier. Nothing happens. I calm myself and try again. The fireflies slowly begin to form something in the sky.

The numbers 1 4 3 appear in the sky above me. I stare at the numbers, trying to figure out what they could possibly mean. They begin to pulsate brighter and brighter.

"What does that mean?" I yell out.

The numbers continue to pulsate, getting brighter each time. I shield my eyes with my hand. The fireflies scatter, but 143 is now, even with my eyes closed, a lingering afterimage.

The fireflies retreat into the night. Suddenly it is quiet and calm. The rain is now a mist. I sit for a minute, hoping she would find me in the darkness. I try to blink away the image of 143 with no luck.

In the distance, I begin to hear a series of crackling thunder. I stand up and look around the darkness, hoping to see anything. I hear the crackling sound again, this time a lot closer. I feel as if something is right above me. I want to run, but there is nowhere to run. It is dark everywhere I turn. I feel trapped. It feels like it is closing in on me. Louder now, the crackling sound is all around me. I begin to run, when I hear a tremendous boom.

Chapter 12 - One Four Three
-Kaleb-

I jumped to my feet in a panic. I banged my leg on something in front of me. The pain quickly brought me back to reality, but I was still a little foggy. I rubbed my eyes into focus and looked around. The microwave in front of me was blinking something that was all too familiar. 1:43.

I shook my head in exasperation. "What the hell is going on with these dreams?" I mumbled.

At some point, the power had gone out and come back on. I looked out the window. It was still dark and rainy. I grabbed my phone to see what time it really was. 3:41. I sighed. "Of course, it is," I mouthed.

I slid the window halfway up. I needed the fresh air to clear my head. The dreams the past couple of nights felt more like out-of-body experiences than dreams. If they were just dreams, why did they feel so real?

I put the window down and walked over to the couch. I started to recall the weirdness of the girl in the dream and the things she said.

"She needs you? It will hear you?" I mumbled aloud.

Who was she, and what was it? I wasn't sure I

wanted to know the answers. I just wanted to clear my head. I wanted to wake up and not feel like I had just escaped death.

I slid the ottoman over to prop my legs up. I figured I might as well relax before it was time to get up for work. Truth be told, I was a little afraid of falling back to sleep. My legs ached as I moved them to the ottoman. They felt like I had run a marathon. My mind immediately flashed back to the dream.

The rain outside started to pick up again. Thunderstorms were normally my favorite time to sleep, but I wasn't quite ready to dodge lightning bolts again. I turned the television on and watched some sports highlights to occupy my mind. I saw a score on the screen. It was 143 to 141. I shook my head and turned the television off.

The sound of my alarm filled the room. I must have dozed off. I was thankful I didn't have another crazy dream, and if I did, I didn't remember it. One a night was more than enough. There was no point in hitting snooze, so I just got up and got ready for work. I wondered if I could get there early enough to catch Brenda reading. I wasn't sure that would even stop her from having something to say about me arriving early.

On the drive in, I noticed there were trees down everywhere. Most of the traffic lights were either off or flashing. That must have been one heck of a storm. Traffic was going much slower than normal. The drive took about thirty minutes longer than it would have taken on a normal day. I got to work about twenty minutes after I planned, but still much earlier than usual.

"Well, look what the cat dragged in. Good morning,

sunshine!" Brenda said, much too enthusiastically.

"Good morning, Brenda," I answered back, in a deadpan tone. I was not going to let her bother me.

I quickly got situated and put my headphones on. I was grumpy and would rather people not see me and make a big deal about me being there early. I already knew it was going to be a long day.

As the morning went on, I was so immersed in what I was doing, I didn't realize that it was well past the time that Kaje usually came by my desk. I checked to see if he was online. He wasn't. I sent him a text message to see if everything was okay. No response. It was unlike him to be late. Maybe he was stuck in traffic.

I decided to go get coffee. As I walked into the cafeteria, I saw Tammy talking to people I didn't really know. I decided to keep my distance.

"One four three! Can you believe it? One four three!" a voice from the group of people yelled out.

My mind instantly went to the fireflies and the dream. I felt weak and my legs began to ache. I stumbled a bit and used the counter to hold myself up. Tammy noticed and rushed over to me. "Are you okay, honey?" she asked.

"Yeah, I'm fine. Just got a little light-headed for a second."

"Maybe you'd better sit down for a minute. You look like crap."

"Really, I'm good. I just need some coffee and a little something to eat."

"That's not all you need."

"Oh, really? What else do I need?"

"We can talk about that later, when you aren't falling all over yourself. You're going to need all your energy."

"There you go again. And you call me trouble?"

She smiled. "Get your mind out of the gutter."

"Yeah, I wouldn't want to overcrowd it."

She laughed. "Such an ass!"

"But you love me."

"I do. I do. Hey, where's your sidekick?"

"I'm not sure. I haven't been able to get in touch with him. I'm sure he's probably in traffic and forgot to charge his phone."

"Hopefully he's okay. That storm was wicked last night. Did you see all that lightning?"

"Oh, yeah. I saw it. Up close and personal. Felt like it almost hit me."

"Tell me about it. That thunder was something else too. Felt more like an earthquake. It woke me up several times. I don't know how anyone could sleep through that."

"It was pretty crazy last night. I'm glad you didn't get struck by lightning."

She laughed heartily. "Oh, don't worry, honey, it'll get me sooner or later."

I couldn't help but laugh. "Trouble, trouble, and more trouble."

"That's me!" she said as she walked towards the door.

"Hey, Tammy. Quick question for you. What was that lady talking about when she said 'one four three?'"

"Oh, that was my friend, Mandy. She has been playing those numbers for as long as I can remember, and last night they finally came out. She won a lot of money. Or so she thinks." Tammy laughed. "Wait till she sees how much tax gets taken out. "Have a good day, honey. Glad I still knock you off your feet."

Tammy winked and walked away. I thought about the winning lottery numbers. That was just weird. There had just been way too many coincidences like that in the past couple of days. I felt like I was losing my mind. I grabbed my coffee and checked my phone. Still no word from Kaje. I headed back to my desk to see if he was online yet.

As I walked back to my desk, my phone vibrated. It was a text from Kaje.

Yo! I'm not coming in today. Everything is cool. I'm meeting up with Dapp. Fill you in later.

The day had just gotten a whole lot longer. That also meant I'd be on my own for lunch, but I was glad he was okay. That was one less thing I had to worry about.

Chapter 13 - Synchronicity
-Kaleb-

Work was a bore. Saying I couldn't focus would've been an understatement. All I wanted to do was get home and try to process what I had experienced the night before. I contemplated sleeping in my car at lunch, but I decided that still was probably not the best idea.

I decided to go for a walk instead. As I was walking out, I heard someone call my name. I turned around and saw Catherine standing there.

"Hey, Kaleb. Where are you headed?"

"Hi, Catherine. Just out for a quick walk. It's really nice out, now that the storms have cleared."

"Oh, I know. Isn't it beautiful out? Do you mind if I come with you? If you want to walk alone, that's okay too."

"It's fine. I would actually like the company."

"Oh, that's fantastic."

Catherine was my trainer when I first started the job. She was always very nice to me and had the patience of a saint. I could always talk to her about anything. She had knowledge of things that I didn't even know existed. She was probably just the person I needed to talk to that day.

"I really can't believe how this day turned out. Last night looked and sounded like the end of the world," Catherine said.

"It was pretty scary. I can't believe it either, but I'll take it. I'll take days like this every day of the year."

As we walked, a melancholy feeling washed over me. I looked around and took a few deep breaths. It was the end of summer. The leaves were still putting up a good fight. The air was a bit warm, but the breeze blew with cool hints of autumn. Autumn had always been my favorite season. The sounds of crunching leaves. The smell of burning wood. The sound of the wind through a cracked window at night.

I'd always believed that there was always one perfect day in autumn. A day where you felt things with more clarity and depth than you ever have. Thinking of that and how it would arrive soon, brought a warmth to my soul, and I found myself lost in the thought of it.

I began thinking of the girls in the dream again. Were they connected? I tried to remember the constantly changing images. I wondered if one of those images was the little girl from before, or if she was possibly the one that needed me. I wondered if I would ever dream of her again, if that was a dream.

"You okay over there?" Catherine asked.

"Not really." I said abruptly. I didn't know why it came out like that. I didn't know if I was upset that she interrupted my thoughts, or if I was upset that I couldn't figure out what the hell was going on with me lately. I could see she was taken aback.

"Catherine, I'm sorry. I just have a lot on my mind."

She smiled. "It's okay. Is there something you want to talk about?"

"Well, yes and no. I want to talk about it, but I also don't want you to think I'm losing my mind."

She smiled warmly. "Try me."

"Okay. You asked for it. Well, let's see. Where do I begin? Are you familiar with déjà vu?"

"Of course. I experience that from time to time."

"Well, lately I seem to be experiencing it a lot. Sometimes it's so strong, I feel like I can guess what happens next."

"I see. Have you ever guessed correctly?"

"No, not really. I actually think that would freak me out more than the déjà vu itself. I used to think it would be cool to guess, but if I were to somehow guess it, I'm not sure I can handle what that means."

"I know what you mean."

"Then there this thing that happens where I'll hear a phrase or a word for the first time, then later that day, I'll hear it a couple more times. It sounds silly, but the other night I was watching a TV show and there was an owl on the show. Later that night I was awakened by the sound of an owl on the tree outside my window. I could give you ten more examples of things just like that."

"You know, you should research synchronicity. You might find some useful information."

"Synchronicity? I've never heard of that."

"It basically means meaningful coincidences. Some people call them a wink from the universe. It means you are on the right path."

"On the right path to what?"

"Who knows. Maybe you have to just keep following it and see where it goes."

"Have you ever experienced synchronicity?"

"Not like you have. I do see 11:11 from time to time. Some people believe that is some sort of sign."

"That's interesting. I have had two dreams the past two nights that felt more like out-of-body experiences than dreams. Last night I saw the number 143 in my dream. When I woke up, the clock was blinking 1:43. I turned on the TV, and some team had scored 143 points. Oh, and get this, in the cafeteria this morning, one of Tammy's friends was celebrating because she hit the lottery last night."

"Let me guess. She played 143?"

"Bingo."

"That is fascinating. The universe is definitely winking at you."

"That's not all it's doing to me," I mumbled.

"We should head back soon. If you have time, some other time, I would love to hear about your dreams. I used to have nightmares as a child. I slept with a night light until I was fifteen."

"Wow. That had to be tough. I only remember having one really bad nightmare when I was a kid. The weird thing was, I could kind of control my dreams when I was younger, and somewhat change them to how I wanted them to go. That one, I had no control at all."

"I'm curious. Would you mind sharing? It's okay if you don't want to recall a bad memory. I would totally understand."

"It's no problem. I'll keep it short so that I can finish by the time we get back to the building."

"Great. I'm all ears."

"I was probably around three or four years old. I remember I was really sick. I think I had pneumonia. That night when I fell asleep, I dreamed that I was in my room, in my bed. The room was barely lit. The color of the light was this odd orangish, red color. People that I didn't know kept coming in and out of the room, but none of them acknowledged that I was even there. The weird thing was, I could not see their faces.

"I wanted to sit up to get a better view of what was going on, but I couldn't move. I called for my mom, but she never came. I turned my head to look at the door. It was open, but I could not see the hallway. It was almost as if nothing was beyond the door. I turned my head towards the window. It was covered up by a long curtain. The scary part was, there was something or someone standing behind the curtain. When I screamed for my mom, there was still no response. I called for my dad. No response. The people in the room started to make creepy laughing noises as whatever was behind the curtain started to slowly move. I screamed in horror. It felt so real, and I couldn't move. I couldn't run away.

"One of the people in the room walked over and began to pull the curtain away. I closed my eyes and screamed out for my mom. I woke up to my mother standing over me, hysterical. She held me and comforted me as she cried. She called my dad in the room and told him to get the car ready because I needed to go to the hospital. I was burning up."

"My word. That's a bit unnerving. I'm sorry I made you have to recall that."

"It's really okay. It was a long time ago. I can laugh

about it now."

"Oh, well that's good. I think dreams where you can't move or speak are the worst. It's like you are trapped in your own body."

"When you put it like that, I guess it did kind of feel like that. I learned my lesson though. No curtains in the house, ever."

Catherine laughed. "I guess that is a good lesson, although I really love my curtains."

"My mom took down the curtains in my room, and I haven't had curtains since."

"I see. Do you mind if I ask one last question about the dream, and then I'll leave it be? I understand if you don't want—"

"Catherine, really, it's fine."

"Sorry. I'll just ask. What did you think was behind the curtain?"

I pondered her question for a minute. That was the first time I had ever been asked that. "Honestly, I don't know. I guess I never gave it much thought. I just got the feeling that whatever it was, it didn't have my best interests in mind."

"I don't think so either. I'm glad you woke up."

"Me too."

We arrived at the entrance of the building. "That walk seemed to go very fast," I said.

"I was just thinking the same thing. Thank you for letting me walk with you. I had fun."

"You don't have to thank me. It was my pleasure. Thanks for letting me ramble on like a crazy person."

"You're not crazy. The universe is just sending you some strong signals. It's up to you to figure out what they mean."

"Yeah, but how do I go about that?"

"I'm sure you will figure something out. Here's an idea. You said when you were younger you could control your dreams, right? Well, next time you have a dream like the ones you had the past two nights, see if you can exert some measure of control. Maybe you will find some answers that way."

"Listen to you sounding all sage-like. You are pretty awesome. I appreciate all the advice. I'll definitely keep you posted on how things go."

"Oh, no problem at all. Sage Catherine is always here to help."

We both shared a laugh as we walked back into the building.

"Take care, Sage Catherine."

"Bye. Talk to you soon."

Chapter 14 - Listen to My Demo
-Kaleb-

I spent the last hour of the day watching the clock. I had just finished packing up my things when Tammy stopped by. "Hey, trouble. I just wanted to check on you before I left. Are you feeling any better?"

"Yeah, I just had a rough night. I'll be okay once I get some sleep."

"Me too. That storm kept me up half the night. I'm going to bed early tonight. I need my beauty sleep."

"At this point, I'll just take whatever kind of sleep I can get."

"Well, hang in there, darling. The week's almost over, and we have a long weekend coming up."

"That's right! We do. You just made me so excited, I could...never mind, we're still on the clock, I better be quiet." I winked at her.

"You are such an ass. I don't know what I would do without your humor."

"You'd be alright. Everyone who knows you, loves you. Just not like I do."

"You got that right. You are definitely one of a kind.

Goodnight, trouble. Go straight home."

"I'll try my best."

I packed up the rest of my things and headed to my car. It was still nice out. I considered going to the park, but decided against it. I needed to go to the gym. I could still feel that fast food weighing me down. I knew some cardio would do my mind and body good.

As I was driving, my phone rang. It was Kaje.

"Yo!"

"Yo! Kaleb, I got some big-time news!" he said excitedly.

"What's up? What's going on?"

"Dapp talked to some of his people, and they wanted to hear a more recent demo of my vocals. So, he needed me to come to the studio and record something ASAP. That's where I was today."

"No way, dude! So, this is really happening?"

"Kaleb, I'm starting to believe it can. I haven't even told you the crazy part. Dapp sent my demo to them, and they want me to fly out for a meeting this weekend."

"Oh, wow! Man, I am so pumped for you. I know you are so excited, you don't know what to do with yourself."

"I don't. I am just so fired up. I can't even relax."

"Do you want to come to the gym with me?"

"I actually think that would do me some good, but Nandini asked me if I was available tonight."

"Uh oh. The dreaded second date."

"Dude, I know. Save your little speech."

"I wasn't going to say a thing."

"Mmhm."

"Are you going to tell her about your big break?"

"I'm not sure. I have to tell her something. I just don't want to tell her before I know it's at least somewhat of a sure thing."

"Yeah, I know what you mean."

"We'll see. I'm just going to play it by ear. Anyway, what's going on with you? You sound tired as hell. Did that crazy storm keep you up? I almost turned around and drove back to your apartment. It was crazy driving home."

"I actually slept through most of the storm."

"What? Then why do you sound so tired?"

"Another crazy dream. I'll spare you the details, but it seemed to be a continuation of the previous night's dream."

"Dude, that's just crazy. Out of all the crazy dreams that you told me about, I don't ever remember you telling me that any were recurring. Except for the train dream." His voice trailed off as soon as he said it. It was probably not something he meant to bring up at that point. "My bad, man."

When we were kids, I used to have a recurring dream that my entire family was going on a train ride to some distant land. On the day of departure, the train left without me. I used to wake up crying, thinking it was real. The dream turned out to be more prophetic than I'd wished.

"No worries. You know, typically, my dreams aren't all that crazy. You just think they are because you don't remember yours. Yours would probably sound crazy too, if you remembered them. Again, the thing about these dreams are how real they feel. I swear I am really there. I can't really explain it. I'm not sure I even want an explanation. I kind of just want them to chill."

"Well, it's only been a couple of nights. Maybe that's the end of them."

"Hopefully. Enough about me though. I'm happy for you, man. I hope this works out. I could use that forty-five percent agent fee."

Kaje laughed. "Whatever! That number just keeps going up and up."

I laughed. "I guess you should have accepted my lesser offer."

"Yeah, I guess so."

"Okay, man. I'm home, and if I don't keep moving, I won't move at all. Let me know how the date goes. If it's late, just send me a thumbs up or thumbs down."

"Alright, I can do that. I'm not sure if I'm taking tomorrow off or not. I'll let you know that too."

"Okay. Sounds good. Congrats again, man. I'm really happy for you."

"Thanks. Later"

"Later days."

I sat in the car for a minute. I thought about what Kaje's news meant. It all happened so fast, I couldn't fully process it. I didn't know if it meant he was moving or if it just meant he would be around less. I didn't want to think about that.

The selfish side of me always wanted him to be around. I'd never even considered the fact that one day he would just not be there every day. The jealous side of me was envious that he was moving on to bigger things, while I was stuck in the same place, doing the same thing. It was another one of those situations that spoke more about myself and my unfulfilled potential. I wasn't sure exactly what I was meant to be, but I knew it had to be more than it currently was.

I went in, grabbed my things, and shoved them into my gym bag. I didn't even look at the couch. As much as I wanted to, I refused to fall victim to its allure. I knew that if I sat on it, I would not have not moved for the rest of the night. As I walked to my car, I could hear Monica in her apartment screaming at someone. It was not the first time that I heard heated arguing through her door. I shook my head and kept walking. I was sure I'd hear about it at some point.

Chapter 15 - Spring of Hope
-Kaleb-

I got home from basketball. I was exhausted. I showered and was just settled in for the evening when there was a knock on the door. I was pretty sure I knew who it was. I got up to open the door. A muffled voice penetrated the door. "Wake up, sleepy head."

I opened the door to find Monica with her knuckles out, about to knock on the door again. "Seriously? Was I supposed to sprint to the door?"

"You couldn't 'feel' that I needed to talk, through the wall?"

"Here we go again. You know that's not how it works."

"I know. I'm just messing around."

I walked back to the couch and sat down. "What's up? Who didn't call you back this time?" I asked. There was a bit of indifference in my voice.

"Why do you always have to go there? I can't just come over because I want to hang out and not talk about anything in particular?"

"Well, you can. You just typically don't. You always want advice on what to do about this guy or that guy."

"Well, maybe this time is different. Let's just talk

about life."

"You know and I know you didn't come over here to talk about life. You wanted me to 'feel' through the wall that you needed to talk about life?"

She sighed. "Touché."

"Nate again?"

"How'd you guess?"

"It always comes back to him. I wish you'd just be done with him. He doesn't deserve you. How many times has he left you for someone else, only to come back when it doesn't work out with that person? How many times has he just gone MIA with no explanation, only to come back when he needed something, and then had the nerve to act like nothing happened?"

"He's my soulmate."

"Soulmate. Right. What exactly makes him your soulmate?" I asked with a bit of exasperation.

She obviously picked up on my poorly hidden annoyance at her use of the term. "He understands me. He was there for me when I needed someone."

Besides the fact that I didn't believe there was such a thing as a soulmate, it took everything in me to hide my irritation at her assigning such a lofty title to someone like him. When she first met him, she was on the rebound. He was just doing what should be expected of anyone. Be there. Be kind. Listen. Care. I'm not saying he doesn't truly understand her, but the truth was, she was not that hard to understand.

I could feel the jerk in me coming on, so I carefully worded my next question. "So, if he is your soulmate, why doesn't his soul feel the pain it is causing your soul?"

"Maybe it does," she said. "We don't know that.

Everyone isn't like you claim to be."

She was upset, so I ignored her not so subtle jab. I started to make an analogy about him cutting himself with a knife while watching her scream in agony, but I decided against it.

She looked at me somewhat angrily. "Go ahead. Say it! I know you have something logical to say about my feelings."

"Nope, I just think you use the term soulmate a bit too loosely."

She rolled her eyes. "Whatever. It's my soul."

"Indeed, it is." I mumbled.

"How would you even know, anyway? Do you even know what it is to truly be in love and lose that love, Mr. Friend-zone?"

'Yeah, actually I do."

"Whatever. I'm talking about the real deal. Like, The Notebook, kind of experience. Not some weird, dating app, disappearing Amish chic."

"First of all, calm down. I know you are upset, but the little digs aren't necessary. Secondly, nobody has a story like that, but I do have a story. If you think you can handle it."

"Just tell me the story." she said

"Are you sure you can handle this?" I replied with a devilish grin while I fanned myself with my hand. It was an attempt to ease the tension in the room.

She stifled a laugh. "Whatever. Stop stalling and get to it."

"Well, back in the day, I was working at the corner gas station. It was a bitter cold Saturday morning in January, so it wasn't that busy. I can't even remember what I was doing, but I looked up and she was standing there. I never saw her come in. Never heard the door or felt the cold breeze that blew in whenever the store door opened.

'Oh, hi!' I said shyly. The words barely came out.

"She smiled back at me shyly. 'Hi.'

"She was something straight out of a dream. I felt an instant connection to her. Almost as if we knew each other from somewhere, but I am pretty sure I had never seen her before in my life. There were instantly so many things I wanted to say, yet nothing seemed to come out. I could tell she felt the same way about me. It was as if a thousand things lined up at the exact right moment for us to meet like that, and I couldn't bring myself to talk to her.

'Help you?' I stammered.

"She laughed shyly. 'A pack of Marlboro Lights, please.'

'In a box?'

'It doesn't matter.'

"She paid me for the cigarettes and put her change in her coat pocket. There was a long awkward pause as we both stood there wanting to say something to each other, but neither of us could come up with anything to say.

'Stay warm out—'

'Well, I better get—'

"We both nervously spoke at the same time. I'm not sure we even heard what each other said. I started to repeat what I said when another customer walked in. He was a bit flustered as he hurried in from the cold. "I need twenty dollars on pump eight, please and a large coffee."

'Will that be all for you, sir?' I asked, trying to hide

the fact that his mere presence was coming between me and the girl of my dreams.

'How about a few scratch-offs. I'm feeling lucky today.'

"I sighed and got the lottery tickets from the other side of the counter. When I turned back to hand him his tickets, I looked to where she was originally standing, but she was gone. I looked around the store, thinking maybe she went to the back. She was nowhere in the store. She left the same way she came in. No sound, no breeze, and no trace."

"Whoa! Did you ever see her again?" Monica asked.

"Nope. Fell in love from that little exchange," I said sarcastically.

"Whatever!" Just finish the story, smartass."

"Well you asked. Ask a silly question..."

"Oh, my gosh. Would you please just continue."

"Anyway, the next day I went to work, expecting her to show up. Every time the door opened, I thought it would be her. I figured she had to have felt what I felt. There was a definite connection there. There was no denying that.

"Hour after hour passed and she never showed up. I kept reminding myself that I needed to be patient and not overreact. I tried to convince myself that the 'connection' would lead her back.

"Nine hours went by and no visit from the mystery girl. I entertained thoughts of hanging around after my shift, but I had things I needed to take care of. The thing that bothered me the most was the fact that I was off the next couple of days. What if she came up one those days? It became nerve-wracking to think about.

"I talked myself into accepting the fact that it was probably just one of those moments. You know, like those times when you share a smile with someone in passing, or you share a few warm glances in an elevator, but when the doors open and you both go your separate ways, you are left wondering what the other person was thinking, or if you just missed out on 'the one.' This felt different though. It wasn't just a warm glance or a passing smile, it was the way we looked at each other, the way we seemed to know each other, the way she seemed to want to talk to me as much as I wanted to talk to her."

Monica feigned a romantic gesture. "That's so romantic. How long was it before you saw her again?"

"So, let's see, that was early January. The rest of January passed. February passed. I'm pretty sure most of March passed too. I remember it being really warm outside for the first time that year. I was actually working second shift that night. The manager had gone home, and I had figured out a way to hook my stereo up to the speakers that normally played the boring gas station music.

"Because it was such a warm Friday night, there was a certain energy in the air. The kind of energy that came from knowing that spring was really close and summer wasn't too far off. The pumps were full of cars. The people pumping gas had on light jackets. Some even had on summer gear. Most of them looked fairly young. They loudly exchanged playful conversations with each other while dancing to the music that I had playing through the overhead speakers. This gave me all the incentive I needed to play something a little more risqué from my music collection.

I put on one of those songs that made you want to dance as soon as you heard it. It was probably the most popular song out at the time. I turned the speaker volume up a lot louder than I should have, but I was caught up in the moment. I told my co-worker to watch the register so I could go outside and see just how loud the music was. I also wanted to feel the rhythm of the night and be a part of the energy.

"I walked outside and looked around. The air was warm and had a summer-like feel to it. The music was pumping. The crowd was excited. People who weren't even there for gas were just hanging out in the parking lot. It was almost as if it was a gas station party and I was the deejay.

"The crowd cheered as I walked towards them. In my mind I pretended the whole scene was in slow motion and everyone cheered for me like they knew I was the one responsible for the party. Truth is, they probably would have cheered for anyone who walked up at that point. I spoke to everyone that spoke to me. I danced a little bit, waving my hands in the air. It was one of those nights that I felt confident and loose. I felt like I could take on the world.

"As I walked back to the building, a little red car pulled up. Two females got out of the car. I didn't pay them much attention because I had to get back to work. As I opened the door to walk in, I heard a voice yell out with excitement. 'This is my jam!'

"I knew that voice. I had heard it once before. It seemed like forever ago. It was a voice I had given up hope of ever hearing again. I turned around. It was her. She was standing twenty feet away from me. My heart raced. A sudden wave of nervousness overtook me. I wasn't sure what to do or what to say. The one thing that played in my favor was the fact that I was still somewhat confident from the events of a few moments earlier.

"I looked her way and held my gaze so that she would know I was looking at her. She looked back and smiled guiltily. I shot back a scolding look. I pointed to the inside of the building. 'You need to come see me,' I mouthed slowly so there would be no doubt of what I said.

'Okay,' she mouthed back, then she flashed a big smile at me.

"After all that time, I had all but put her out of my mind. It had been at least a month since I thought about her. But now, every feeling I had from that cold January morning came flooding back to me. I couldn't contain my excitement as she walked towards the door. I stole a quick look in the mirror we kept by the register. My hair was freshly cut. I was clean shaven. There was nothing in my nose. I was good to go.

"I saw her at the door. I took a deep breath. She walked in with her friend. Her friend headed to the bathroom while she headed my way. 'So, that's how it is? You just keep me waiting for months?' I said playfully.

'It hasn't been months.'
'Oh, yes it has. Almost three.'
'I'm sorry.'
'It's cool. You're here now. So, are you going to finally tell me your name?'
'I'm Marci!' she said. She flashed that huge smile.

"The way she said it was so endearing. It was like she was asking to be loved because she was Marci.

'I'm Kaleb. Nice to finally meet you, Marci.'
'Come on! We have to go, Marci,' her friend said.
'That's Cheryl. She's a bit on the impatient side.'
'I can see that.'
'I better get going before she starts to spaz out.'
'Okay. So, can I call you or something?'
'Hmm, let me think about it.'
'Seriously? You have to think about it?' I said it with a bit of playfulness, but I was kind of put off by the fact that she didn't seem to feel for me what I felt about her. I mean, I'd waited months for that day. It was starting to seem like just another encounter for her.

'Give me yours,' she said.

"I wrote my number down and gave it to her. There was a large part of me that believed I would never hear from her or see her again. The crazy part about it was, I felt like I would've been okay with it. I really can't explain why. I just think the mysterious veil associated with the mystery of our first encounter may have faded since she was now actually a reality. Don't get me wrong, I was still totally into her. It just felt a little more grounded at that point.

"About a week or so after that day, she called me one evening. I'm not sure how, but I knew it was her.

'Hello.'
'Hi!'
'Who is this?' I said coyly.
'It's Marci!"

"There was always something about the way she said her name. It had the same effect on me as it did the first time she said it.

'I didn't think you were going to call me.'

'What? Why not?'

'I don't know. You just seemed kind of disinterested the last time I saw you. It seemed like I was a lot happier to see you than you were to see me.'

'I'm sorry. It was because Cheryl was there. She tries to act like my mom. She doesn't want me talking to any guys, unless it's the ones she picked out. I just didn't want to hear her mouth about it for the rest of the night.'

'So, you were happy to see me?'

'Absolutely!'

'I guess it was kind of okay seeing you too.'

"She laughed. 'Shut up!'

'Why did it take you so long to come back to see me?'

'That semester was killing me. I had so much to do. Then I went home for spring break. I did think about you a couple of times.'

"A couple of times, huh? Just two?'

'Maybe three.'

I laughed. 'Whatever!'

"The conversation continued into the wee hours of the morning. It felt natural talking to her. Nothing felt forced. It had a flow to it like we were old friends catching up. We talked about everything from family members to favorite foods. We discussed our plans for the future. We talked about where we saw ourselves in ten years and all the other silly things people talk about when they first meet someone they are really interested in."

"I can't believe this story doesn't end with you two together," Monica said.

"You can consider this a cautionary tale," I said.

"Duly noted. Now get on with it. I want to hear how you messed this up."

"Well, you are going to have to wait. It's getting late, and I have things to do. You know I don't stay up late like you do."

"Are you serious right now? You start a story and leave me hanging like that?"

I winked at her. "Dramatic effect."

"Whatever. You just want me to come back tomorrow."

"That would entail you leaving first."

"Smartass!"

Monica got up and slowly opened the door as if she was waiting on me to change my mind. I gestured my head towards the hallway as if to say "Keep going."

"You get on my nerves." she said jokingly.

"Love you too."

She walked out and closed the door. I sighed heavily. I hadn't thought about that story in years. Telling it to Monica had me feeling some sort of way about it. That's just what I didn't need before bedtime.

As I got ready for bed, I recalled Catherine's advice in my head about controlling my dream. I figured I would give that a shot. I wasn't eager to have another out-of-body experience. A dream where I was playing professional football or saving the world from bad guys would've been a welcome surprise. I set my alarm and turned off the light. As I was about to set my phone on the nightstand, it vibrated. It was a text message from Kaje.

Dude! I think I'm in love!

I smiled and put the phone down. I decided to wait until tomorrow to hear the story. I needed to try to get some sleep. I stared at the ceiling and tried to clear my mind. My body was exhausted, but my mind wouldn't shut off. I grabbed my phone and played Relaxation Sounds: Ambient Ocean Waves.

Chapter 16 - The Boat Dreamscape
-Kaleb-

"Mom! My room is clean. May I please go outside? They're all waiting on me."

"Did you put your clothes down the chute?"

"Oops. Doing it now."

"And don't just shove them all in at once. You'll clog it up again."

"Okay. I won't."

I look out the window and motion to my friends that I will be out in a minute. I rush to the laundry chute and shove the clothes in.

"Mom, I'm done. Can I go out now?

"Okay. Stay on the street, and don't forget to check in. I hope you did a good job on your clothes. I'm going to check."

"Okay!" I yell as I run out the door."

All my friends jump and cheer as I come outside.

"It's about time!" they all yell. "You ready to play?" Kaje asks.

"Let's do this. I have the first pick."

"Man, you always have the first pick," Kaje says

tersely.

I laugh. "Why do you care? I always pick you anyway."

"Maybe I want to compete against you."

"Oh? That sounds like a challenge. Okay. Kaje and I are the captains. He has the first pick."

We finish picking teams and get ready to play.

"Who has the football?" Kaje asks.

"I thought you were bringing it," I replied. "Can you go get yours?"

"Why? Your house is right there."

"If my mom sees that I stuffed the clothes down the chute, she'll make me stay in."

Kaje shakes his head and laughs. "Dude, why didn't you just do it right the first time? I guess I'll run and get mine. I'll be right back."

Kaje runs around the block and gets his football. We throw tennis balls at the streetlight while we wait. None of us are able to come close to hitting it. I try once more, the ball hits it square in the middle. The light turns on, flickers, then turns off. Everyone jumps up and down while they cheer.

"I'm back. Let's play. We start with a touchdown lead because I had to go get the ball."

"What? That doesn't even make sense."

"Kind of like you not getting yours when you live right there?"

Everyone starts laughing. "Whatever! Our ball. Let's go!" I say emphatically.

As we begin to play, ominous dark clouds begin rolling in. We only get in a couple of plays before rain starts to fall.

Kaje feels the rain and gets angry. "Great. Now we

won't be able to play. We could have at least gotten one game in if you hadn't taken so long. Come on. Let's go, guys."

As they all begin to walk away, I angrily stare at the dark cloud as the rain hits my face. A strange feeling washes over me. It's not déjà vu, but similar and just as odd.

"Wait!" I yell out to everyone. "Don't go. Don't leave me all alone. Kaje, please. Come back."

I squeeze my eyes shut. In my mind I replay everything that has happened up to this point. I think about the things that I wish were different. A feeling of stillness washes over me. I open my eyes. The rain is gone. The clouds are gone. It is a perfect sunny day, and my friends are waiting on me to play the game.

"Hello? Earth to Kaleb. You going to hike the ball or not?" Kaje asks.

I look around in confusion. I'm not quite sure what I did, but it doesn't matter. It's time to play.

"Hut, hut, hike!"

We play game after game. Kaje's team wins some games. My team wins some. After a while, we stop keeping score.

"One last game for bragging rights?" Kaje asks.

"Oh, yeah! I have to check in first. I'll be right back."

"Or you won't be, because you'll be in trouble."

"It's cool. I got it handled." I run home and open the door. "Mom, I'm checking in."

"Okay, honey. Good job on the chute, by the way. I'm proud of you for doing it right the first time."

"Thanks, Mom," I say guiltily. I run back to my friends and declare that I'm ready to play. Kaje looks surprised. I wink at him. "I told you it was handled."

We play until it starts to get dark. The streetlights come on and most of us have to go in. I squeeze my eyes shut. I attempt to add more daylight. Kaje's voice interrupts me. "Let's play some hide-and-go-seek before we all have to go inside."

Everyone cheers in agreement.

"Okay, but we won the game," I say.

"No way. How do you figure that?" Kaje replies.

"We used my ball, so we get an extra touchdown."

"What? What kind of crazy rule is that?"

"Isn't that your rule?"

Kaje looks confused. "Whatever. You're it. Count to twenty, and don't peek like you always do. Eyes closed and both hands over your eyes."

"Fine. I'm starting right now though. One. Two. Three." I pause. An eerie feeling takes over me. "No hiding near the spooky house on the corner. You'll be hiding there all night. I'm not going anywhere near it!"

Kaje laughs. "Man, what is with you and that house? Why are you so scared of it?"

"I'm not. Four. Five. Six."

"Yeah, you are. Scaredy-cat!"

I ignore Kaje. I can hear everyone else scatter and attempt to find a good hiding spot. As I'm counting, that strange feeling begins to wash over me again. It feels different from the earlier feeling, but all too familiar. My counting becomes slow and anxious.

"Seventeen...Eighteen...Nineteen...Twenty."

I open my eyes and remove my hands from my face. It is almost completely dark and I am no longer on my street. I look around me. Everything is still. Everything is peaceful.

I take a step. The ground underneath me illuminates. I take another step, the same thing happens. I look around. In the distance I see glowing colors in the sky and hear the sounds of crashing waves.

I close my eyes tightly and think back to earlier in the day and everything up to this moment. I open my eyes. Nothing has changed. I know that I am not in control anymore.

The ground in front of me lights up and goes out. I do not move. The ground flickers and then goes out again. This time I take a step forward. It illuminates. The next section lights up and then goes out. I step forward. The lights were obviously leading me somewhere.

Hesitantly, I follow. I can hear the sound of water getting closer. Everything else is quiet. There is an eerie calm about this place, and I begin to wonder what it looks like in daylight. I am startled by the sound of an owl in the distance. I stop for a second. The ground in front of me softly glows then fades to darkness. The soft glow gives me the feeling that everything is okay, so I continue onward.

The sound of the waves is closer now. Up ahead, I see spectacular glowing blue lights that span as far as the eye can see. It is as if there is a galaxy of stars in the water. It is mesmerizing and easily the most amazing thing I have ever seen. I quicken my pace in curiosity of what they could be. I come upon a long pier with a boat at the end of it. I somehow know the boat is there for me, but I am hesitant to approach it.

"It's okay. You are safe here," a soft whispering voice echoes from all around.

I wasn't sure if I heard it in my head or from someone around me. The lights begin to shimmer as I walk toward the boat. Each step causes a creaking sound on the wood. I stop just short of the boat and take a deep breath.

"She will guide you," the voice echoes again.

"Who will guide me?" I call out.

No response comes. I steel myself, step into the boat, and settle myself in. The boat begins to row itself. Astonished, I reach out my hands to feel the area where someone rowing would be sitting. My hands move freely through the air. I examine the boat closer. When the stars shine at just the right angle, I can catch a glimmer of an outline of a woman rowing the boat.

The sea of blue slowly pulsates as the boat moves through it. A calmness washes over me. I feel as if I am on a journey that's on its last leg. I lay back and take in the endless, peculiar shaped, twinkling stars in the sky, the beautiful glow of the northern lights, and the calming sound of the oars pushing the water.

I am not sure how much time has passed, or if time is moving at all. I sit up to examine how far the boat has traveled. The pier is no longer in sight. The blue lights that illuminated the water are dim and almost completely faded. I put my hand in the water and move it back and forth, creating ripples throughout the water. The blue lights fade completely.

As the water begins to calm, it is clear, with only the small remaining ripples from the soft rowing. I look into the water. It does not reflect me or the starry sky above. I lean over the boat to look closer. I am drawn to something I see deeper in the water. I rub my eyes and look closer.

There is a blurry projection of two little kids playing on a playground. They are swinging, chasing each other, and laughing to their heart's content. It feels as familiar to me as a memory from my own childhood. I keep watching as they walk along a path together, hand in hand.

The water suddenly begins to ripple and the projection fades away. I can feel the boat begin to move faster as I stare at the water, desperately wanting to see more.

I am startled by my own reflection that suddenly appears in the water. I fall backwards in the boat. When I lean forward and look in the water again, my reflection is gone. I can now see a blurry projection of two people, hand in hand, running swiftly towards what looks like a giant tree. I wonder to myself if this is the same couple that was on the playground, and wonder what they are running from.

The water ripples again, this time violently, and the projection fades. Before the ripples could subside, another projection appears in the water. I faintly see a woman writing in a large book. The image fades out and reappears. The woman is now arguing with someone. The image fades and reappears again. She is now sitting alone by a giant tree. Although I can't clearly make out her face, she appears to be crying.

The water ripples yet again. This time the ripples are tiny, as if being blown by a gentle wind. The projection begins to fade again, and another projection appears in the water. Two big doors open to a church. I see a full house of people waiting on a wedding to begin. A bride stands in the back room of a church being consoled by someone. She is scared and terribly upset. Strangely, I can feel her emotions. The projection fades, and all I can see is my own blurry reflection, but as I look closer, I notice it is not my reflection at all. I gasp and quickly back further away from the water. The boat starts to move faster, quickly moving us away.

The colorful lights in the sky begin to fade. Each bright star begins to dim to nothing, one by one. The rowing has reached a frantic pace, yet we are not moving. The darkness begins to swallow the night. My heart races as fear consumes me.

The boat begins to rock back and forth. One oar breaks, then the other one. The boat is no longer moving. In the remaining starlight, I can see what vaguely looks like a pier. It is close, but there is no way to propel the boat.

I am afraid to look in the water, let alone put my hand in it. I hold on to the sides of the boat and try to jerk my body forward, in an attempt to move it forward. It does not move. If anything, I moved it backwards, away from the pier. I take a deep breath and try to draw on my courage. "You can do this. You can do this," I keep repeating to myself.

I sit up and very slowly begin to look over the side of the boat. The water appears black and casts no reflection at all. I look up to the sky. It is almost starless at this point, as the last of the stars fade away.

I know I have to act fast or there will be no light remaining to guide my way. I take another deep breath and center myself in the boat. I slowly turn and get on my knees. "It's right there. You got this," I mumble to myself. I breathe deeply and try to will myself to put my hand in the water. I take one last deep breath, close my eyes, and put my hand in the water.

It feels warm, like an ocean during the hot summer months. I began to slowly swipe at the water, hoping to propel the boat forward. It barely moves. I put my hand deeper in the water and paddle harder. The boat moves forward. I paddle the water again. The boat moves, but starts to turn the opposite direction of the pier. I move to the other side and begin to paddle the water. The nose straightens back out and angles for the pier. The pier is so close, I can almost jump from the boat to it. Just a few more paddles and I'm there. I put my hand in deeper than before and paddle one last time. I relax and breathe a sigh of relief as the boat coasts toward the pier.

As I am pulling my hand out of the water, something grabs it and violently pulls me into the water. I shake my hand free, but something has a hold of my ankle, pulling me down into the depths of the dark waters. I panic and kick my legs, but I can't shake free. The water is now cold and everything is dark. I can no longer see the boat. I try one last time to break myself free, but I cannot free myself. It feels like a thousand hands have taken hold of me, and I am slowly being pulled deeper and deeper into the dark abyss.

Chapter 17 - Tammy
-Kaleb-

I woke up, coughing and gasping for air. My feet were hanging over the bed, touching the floor. It was as if I had been dragged out of bed. It took me a minute to fully gain control of what was going on. I sat up and sat on the side of my bed. I was more frustrated than anything. The dreams were getting to be too much, and if they had some kind of meaning, I didn't know what it was.

 I sat on the bed a little while longer. I felt like I slept for five minutes. I reached for my phone to see what time it was. The clock showed 6:55. My alarm was set to go off at 7:00. I debated on not going to work. The long week was catching up to me, and not getting good sleep wasn't helping matters.

 I got up and got ready for work. I was dragging and just couldn't seem to get going. I had some time before I had to leave, so I decided to sit down on the couch for a minute and rest my eyes. My phone vibrated. I picked it up and checked the message. It was from Kaje.

 Yo! Obviously, I'm not coming in today. I told them I had a family emergency. I'll fill you in later.

"Obviously?" I said groggily.

I replied with "Okay" and hit send. I closed the app on my phone. That's when I noticed the time. It was 9:15.

"Oh, crap!" I yelled in frustration. Resting my eyes turned into a full-fledged nap. I hopped off the couch, grabbed my keys, and ran out the door.

I drove faster than I should have. I was lucky I didn't get pulled over. As I pulled into the parking lot, I was greeted by flashing red lights. I parked my car and headed towards the building. An ambulance turned on its sirens and quickly drove away. Worry and sadness gripped me immediately. I stared in wonder as déjà vu washed over me. I was sure I had experienced the moment before.

"Tammy," I whispered softly.

I looked around the building for a familiar face. I saw Ron standing by the door. "Ron, what's going on?"

"T-T-Tammy passed out in the c-cafeteria."

"Oh, man. Did they say what happened?"

"Nope. Just that she w-wasn't br-breathing."

"Damn."

I slowly walked to my desk, deep in thought. I sat down and put my head in my hands. It wasn't the way the day was supposed to go. I was just laughing and joking with her the day before. She seemed fine.

I felt a hand touch the back of my shoulder. "She's going to be okay. She's a fighter," Brenda said quietly. "Just keep thinking positive thoughts."

I nodded. I had never seen that side of Brenda. A part of me expected her to be gossiping about it, but she was pretty shaken up. "Do you know what happened to her?" I asked.

"They said she was in the cafeteria getting coffee and the next thing they knew she was on the floor, unresponsive."

"Do you know what hospital they are taking her to?"

"I think she is going to Forestview. I'll let you know when I find out for sure."

"Thank you, Brenda."

I got my phone out and sent a text to Kaje letting him know what happened. I didn't get a response. He was probably busy with his new ventures. I just felt uneasy and wanted to talk to someone.

I put my headphones on and tried to concentrate on work. It proved to be an impossible task. I couldn't concentrate on anything, let alone work. I could feel the worry and sadness all around me. I thought about walking to the cafeteria, but decided against it. It seemed wrong to walk in there knowing Tammy wouldn't be in there cracking jokes. I got up and walked over to Catherine's cubicle. She always had a calming influence on me. "Cat, are you busy?"

"Hey, Kaleb. I have some time. It's a bit hard to concentrate. You heard about Tammy, right?"

"Yeah, I'm having the same problem. I figured I would come check on you and see how you are handling it."

"That's very kind of you. I guess I'm handling it okay. I'm just hoping we get news that she's going to be alright soon."

"I'm waiting to hear from Brenda. She said she would let me know when she heard anything. If I'm being honest, I kind of came over here for you to have that calming effect that you always have on me."

"That's sweet. All we can do is stay positive and hope for the best. Things will work out."

"I'm doing my best. Thanks for the talk. I know you are busy. I'll let you get back to work."

"Oh, you're welcome anytime."

I started to walk back to my desk when Catherine called out to me. "Kaleb, how did the dreaming go last night?"

"Oh, yeah. I wish I could say it went okay, but I had another weird one. It kind of started out like a normal dream, but it ultimately ended up feeling like another one of those out-of-body experiences. I won't bore you with the details. It's getting pretty frustrating though."

"I'm sorry to hear that. Try not to be frustrated. I'm sure the universe is trying to tell you something."

"It's trying to tell me that it doesn't want me to sleep."

Catherine stifled a laugh. "I'm sure it's not that, since that seems to be the chosen method of communication."

"Well, the universe has poor communication skills."

Catherine let out a full laugh this time. "Maybe it does. Just keep your thoughts open. Try to see a bigger picture."

"I'll try. Thank you again. You really are awesome."

"Oh, my. Well, thank you for saying that."

"Just speaking the truth. Now get back to work."

"Ha! Yes sir!"

As I got back to my desk, Brenda was waiting for me. She had a grim look on her face. I feared the worst. "You have an update?" I asked.

"She is in serious condition, but they said she is stable. They are running tests to see what's going on. That's all the information I have right now. Just keep her in your thoughts and prayers."

"I will. Thanks for the update."

I felt a little better knowing she was in stable condition. I sent Kaje an update on her condition, put my headphones on, and got some work done.

I got so engrossed in my music that I hadn't realized how much time had passed. It was almost 3:30. I stood up and stretched out a bit. I saw Rob heading my way. "Hey, what's up, man? I heard about Tammy. That's pretty messed up. Have you heard anything about how she's doing?" he asked.

"Last I heard, she was in serious, but stable condition."

"Crazy, man. She'll be okay. You look exhausted, man. You doing okay?"

"Yeah, just not getting good sleep. I'll catch up on the weekend."

"So, dude, check this out. Remember that little carnival thing we had here the week I started?"

I laughed. "Yeah, that's when we first met. You looked like you didn't know what you had gotten yourself into, coming here."

"Dude, it was crazy. No heads up about a circus at work the next day. I hadn't even met anyone in my group yet."

"I noticed you were just standing there by yourself. I know how uncomfortable that is. The same thing happened to me when I started. Actually, Tammy was the one that introduced herself to me."

"Well, you were the first person to come and introduce yourself to me. I won't ever forget that, man. All these other clowns just stood around and watched me suffer."

"Like you said, it was a circus at work."

Rob laughed. "Yes, it was."

"It still is," I said quietly.

Rob let out a hollow laugh. He walked around my cubicle and pulled something out of his laptop bag. "So, real talk, man. I found this picture in my desk drawer. It was from that day. I want you to hold on to it. Good times, man. Good times."

I took the picture from Rob. I looked at it and smiled. It was a picture of us with big goofy hats on. "Good times, indeed. You good, man?"

"Yeah, I'm good. I do have to run though. I'll talk at you tomorrow."

"Okay. Tomorrow's the day, right?"

Rob looked somewhat confused. "The day?"

"Hammer-time Friday, right? You said I'd find out on Friday," I said jokingly to try to lighten the suddenly sad mood.

"Hammermill Friday. Yeah, tomorrow. See you tomorrow, man."

"That got weird," I thought to myself.

I took the picture and pinned it to my cubicle wall. As I looked at it, that familiar déjà vu feeling began to wash over me again. I gave into it, letting it consume me, trying to predict what was about to happen. My phone started vibrating on my desk, snapping me back to reality. It was a text message from Kaje.

Chuck's Diner. Tonight. 6:00?

Sounds good.

I was looking forward to it. I just had to serve out

the rest of my sentence.

Chapter 18 - Chuck's Diner
-Kaleb-

I walked into the diner to find Kaje already sitting there. I nodded. "What's up, short-timer?"

"More like, no-timer." he said.

"What do you mean?"

"I told them I was leaving, today."

"You were at the job, today?"

"No, I called. I'll be up there tomorrow to fill out some paperwork and then that's it."

My head dropped a little. "So, it's official?"

"Like a ref with a whistle."

"I'm excited for you, man. I really am. I'm sad that you are leaving, but I'm more happy than sad."

"I know what you mean. I'm still trying to process it all. I had all but given up on this dream, then out of nowhere this opportunity popped up."

"Right! And now you're going to be that guy who makes those corny rap songs for those car air freshener commercials we always hear on the radio."

Kaje laughed. "Yeah, right. I'd rather stay where I am than do those cheesy commercials."

"I'm pretty sure they make them bad on purpose so people will remember them."

"I guess. I remember them when I choose the other product."

We laughed loudly. People in the diner looked at us. That was nothing new. It happened so much that we were used to it.

So, not to get all serious, but there is a very serious matter we need to discuss," I said.

"Oh? What's that?"

"You're in love, huh?" I said with a devilish grin on my face.

"Oh! Dude! I forgot to tell you about that! Man, this girl is perfect! We talked about anything and everything. We were on the same page with everything. We watch the same shows, enjoy doing the same things, and we like some of the same music. I really learned a lot about her. She told me a lot about Indian culture. It was pretty interesting."

"Does she know about your music endeavors?"

"I told her everything. I even let her hear some of my songs. She was kind of jamming to them. I was a little surprised."

"Because she is Indian? Or because you didn't think she was into air freshener songs?"

Kaje let out a loud laugh. "You are a fool, man! I'll be honest though, with her being Indian, I didn't know what kind of music she would be into. I didn't think it would be rap. She said she listens to all kinds of music, as long as it's good music."

"I like her already."

"Dude, you are going to love her. She is really down to earth. She was born in India, but her family traveled a lot, so she said she experienced a lot of different cultures. She's kind of the rebel of the family."

"That's pretty cool. I told you. A second date can be life changing."

"Yeah, I owe you one. I was probably going to give her another shot anyway, but what you said definitely helped me make the decision."

I laughed. "You owe me a lot more than one."

"I know that's right. Maybe I'll let you do a verse or two on an air freshener song."

I laughed. "Yeah, I can see that happening."

"Oh, I forgot to ask you. Have you heard anything about Tammy? That's pretty messed up."

My laugh quickly faded. "The last I heard was that she was in serious, but stable condition. I haven't gotten any updates since then."

"You know Tammy. She's too stubborn to stay sick. I'm sure the next update you get will be about her flirting with the doctor."

"You are so right! Knowing her, that's exactly what will happen. Then I will kick her ass for making me worry."

"She'd whoop your ass," Kaje said jokingly.

I smiled. "She probably would. I'm pretty sure she was a marine."

Our waitress came by the table. "Hey trouble and more trouble. You guys doing okay? Can I get you anything?"

Kaje and I exchanged looks. That was Tammy's pet name for us. "I'll just take a water," I replied.

"Yeah, same here," Kaje replied.

She laughed. "You know, if you two weren't regulars, I would have kicked you out by now for not ordering anything."

"We know, Nora. That's why we love you." I flashed

a charming smile.

"I'll be right back with your waters." She blushed and walked away.

"Flirting with the waitress. You seem like you are back to your normal self. Everything going okay with the crazy dreams?" Kaje asked.

"Not really. I'm just chalking them up to just that. Crazy dreams. I could spend all day trying to analyze what they mean, but at this point, I think I would just drive myself crazy."

"Have you actually sat down and analyzed them? Do you think they actually mean something?"

"Truth be told, I haven't had time. This week has just been crazy. And since when did you start believing dreams can mean something?"

"I just think maybe they mean something to you. Maybe something is just lingering in your mind or something. Weird stuff has always happened to you, even when we were kids. I've just never seen you flustered like this."

"I can only recall a few dreams like these. They just don't feel like dreams. They are just different. Anyway, I don't want to think about that. I'm sure they'll stop. I just need to get back to eating right."

"Eating right, huh? That's the cause?"

"It could be. You just never know."

Kaje laughed. "Whatever man. DBD! If eating bad causes out-of-body experiences, I would never be in my own body."

"Man, that is absolutely hilarious. It kind of puts it in a different perspective when you put it like that. I guess you're right. Wait a minute. Did you just tell me, don't be dumb, you jackass?!"

We laughed. Nora came back and set the glasses of water on the table. She smiled at us. "You two are always laughing at something. I don't even know what you all are talking about and it makes me want to laugh. As long as you aren't talking about me."

"No way. We would never do that. You're our favorite," I said.

"Aww. And both of you are my favorite customers."

"Shh. You better not say that too loud. Your other customers that you told that, might hear you." I winked.

"Oh, hush, you! I mean it. You both bring so much life and energy to the place when you come in. I couldn't imagine you two not coming in here."

"Well, thank you, Nora. I couldn't imagine it either."

Nora smiled and walked away. I looked over at Kaje. He had a bit of a guilty look on his face. "You alright over there?" I asked.

"It just feels weird knowing that so many things are about to change."

"Yeah, I get it. I don't think it's fully hit me yet either. I've been hesitant to ask, but are you actually moving? I thought maybe you would travel back and forth until everything gets finalized."

"I was wondering when you were going to ask that. I'm actually moving to an apartment in California. Everything is happening really fast. I fly out on Tuesday to finalize everything."

"Oh, wow. That seems so sudden. I mean, I know it's not, but it seems like it."

"Things are moving a lot faster than I thought they would. Once I get everything in order, I'll try to get back pretty often."

"In your fancy cars? All decked out with black rims, tinted windows, and a lifetime supply of air fresheners."

Kaje laughed. "I don't know about those air fresheners, but don't get it twisted, I am definitely getting a new Jeep."

"I am really happy for you. I know I keep saying that, but I mean it. Just don't forget where you came from."

"Oh, no doubt. I'm not leaving, just taking an extended vacation."

"Yes sir. Zonal in the house. The hit record maker. Let's go out and celebrate, tomorrow night."

"I can't, tomorrow. I have a date with my future wife."

"Oh, boy! Things are officially moving too fast now."

"I told you, man. She might be the one. Let's do Saturday night. Tell Monica to come out. We'll go out to Tankers. We haven't been there in forever."

"That sounds like a plan. I'll tell her that drinks are on you." I smirked.

"You can tell her that if you want. That won't make it true." Kaje laughed.

"Yeah, you know she can throw them down with the best of them."

"I know that's right."

A sappy song began playing over the diner speakers. I shook my head and responded to the song lyrics. "Nope. I guess nobody stays in one place anymore."

Kaje shot me a look. "Seriously, dude?"

I laughed. "Relax, I'm just messing with you."

"Yeah, you better be."

"Okay, man. It's getting late, and I know you have a lot of things to take care of. I'll check in tomorrow and let you know what's going on with Tammy."

"Cool, man. Keep me posted. I'll keep you posted on things too."

"I'm actually hungry now."

"Yeah, me too."

"One last Chuck's Rodeo Burger before everything changes?"

"Yes sir! Let's do it."

Chapter 19 - Summer of Love
-Kaleb-

I got home, quietly opened my door, inched inside, and quietly closed the door behind me. I didn't want to be heard by anyone in the building. Namely, Monica. I set my keys on the counter and plopped myself onto the couch.

I could've just fallen asleep right there. I played some relaxing music on my phone and casted it to the speakers. The initial volume was a lot higher than I expected. I scrambled to turn it down as fast as I could. I waited about thirty seconds, listening for movement. I didn't hear any, so I figured the coast was clear. I turned the music back up a little bit and laid back.

No sooner than my head hit the cushion, there was a small knock on the door. The knock was so light, I thought it may have been on a door across the hall. "I can hear your mood music playing in there. I hope I'm not interrupting anything," a muffled voice said through the door.

I got up and headed to the door.

"Do you really hope that? Because I don't think you really do."

"If you are busy, I can come back later."

I could feel a rush of sadness wash over me. This was not like Monica. Her voice was low. She almost sounded as if she was crying. I opened the door. Her eyes were red. Her mascara had run down her face. She looked weary, like she had just fought a battle.

She looked at me, still crying, trying to fake a smile. "Your 'pathy' sense wasn't tingling, huh?"

"You know—"

"Yeah, I know. It doesn't work like that." She sounded defeated. I pulled her close to me and hugged her. I knew that whatever she was going through wasn't going to be solved by standing in the doorway. I felt her face pulsating against my chest. She was bawling uncontrollably. She cried for a good three minutes or so. I just let her cry. I know she must have needed it.

I led her over to the couch. We sat down. "So, you want to tell me what's going on?" I asked.

"You were right about Nate. I ended it with him, for good this time. He told me that I would never find anyone like him."

"That's a good thing," I thought in my head. I knew it was probably not the best time to say that to her.

"He said a bunch of other nasty things that I won't repeat. Things that even if I wanted to get back together with him, I could never forget."

"I understand. A lot of the time the things said in anger are how we truly feel."

"Right. And that's why I will never go back. Guess you were right all along."

"Hey, don't think for one second that I'm taking any pleasure in this. I hoped I was wrong. I hoped that things would turn around and he would care for you like you care for him. I've just seen his kind before. Sadly, I was his kind at one point in my life."

"I highly doubt that."

"Yeah, well there is a lot you don't know about me."

"Speaking of which, you want to finish your story now?"

"Do 1 want to? No, not really. Besides, weren't we just talking about you? How did we get to my story all of a sudden?"

"You said there is a lot I don't know about you. You're right. I don't know the rest of that story. Besides, I could use the distraction."

"Hot mess. That's all I have to say."

"But you love me. So, finish your story."

I sighed. "Do you remember where we left off?"

"You guys were on the phone all night talking about getting married and starting a family."

I laughed. "Yeah, right. You are just remembering what you want to remember."

"Phone. Long call. 10 years. Got it. Just get back to it already."

"Okay, but listen. In all seriousness, I know you are going through something. If this gets to be too much for you, tell me, and I will stop. I don't want you crying and ruining my shirt any more than you already have."

She looked at the mascara stains and wet spots on my shirt. "Oh, my God. I'm so sorry. I'll wash it for you."

I rolled my eyes. "I know how to wash. It's not that

big of a deal. Just keep in mind what I said. I already feel bad telling you the happy part of the story while you are sad."

"I'll be alright," she said somberly.

"Famous last words."

"And again with the stalling."

"Well, remember how I told you how it was really warm that day I met her? Those warmer temperatures continued right into summer. I was still working second shift. Once school was out, she had a job working first shift. We spent every day we could together. Sometimes after work I would go over to her dorm. We would just lay on the couch and watch old movies. I remember just holding her and not really paying attention to the movie. She laughed a lot, and her laugh was infectious. Hearing her laugh at the funny parts made me laugh as well. She had no idea that I was watching her more than I was watching the movies.

"Other times, I would pick her up, and we would just drive around the town. I would drive by places from my childhood and share stories about them. I had an old convertible. She loved it when I put the top down. She would let her hair down, stand up, spread her arms, and feel the breeze flow through her as if she were flying through the air. I just loved watching her. She was from a small town, and sometimes it felt as if I was showing her a whole new world, and I got to share in each new discovery with her.

"There was a small park that sat back in the woods. It sat on private property, but I knew the way to sneak in without being noticed. Besides, in all my years of going there, I'd never seen anyone back there.

We called it 'The pond that time forgot' because the water was unusually clear. She absolutely loved that pond. She marveled at how clear it was and how the sun sparkled on its surface. There were two goldfish that always swam in the pond. She named them Echo and Narcissus. When we weren't in her dorm room or riding around the town, we were at that pond. It was our place, and that's how we referred to it."

"Aww. You guys were so cute. Did you ever go out to dinner or a movie?"

"We never went to dinner. We were both pretty introverted, so we did takeout. We did go to a movie once. I can't remember what we saw. That was about a week before she had to go home for the rest of the summer. Neither one of us were looking forward to being away from each other. I joked with her all the time about how much more time we would have had if she would have just given me her number that first day she met me. She would gently remind me that I didn't ask.

"The following Saturday was the day she planned on driving home. We made a promise to each other not to make it a big emotional thing. We knew it was only for a couple of months, and we would still be able to talk occasionally and write each other letters. She promised to write to me every single day, even if we talked that day."

"Did you guys keep your promises to each other? I mean, was the sendoff a small thing?"

"We actually didn't have a choice. All of her friends were there and they pretty much monopolized all her time. I remember being a little upset about it, but I think she may have planned it like that on purpose, so it didn't get emotional."

"Clever girl."

"Perhaps. Or perhaps her friends were just annoying."

Monica laughed again. It was good to see her smiling, if only for a little bit. I knew she had a rough road ahead of her. "So, no emotional goodbye. Did you at least get a hug and kiss?"

"Nope. Just a wink and a smile."

"And just like that, she was gone."

"Yep. Just like that."

"So, wait a minute. I don't remember you mentioning a first kiss. I know you guys had a first kiss."

"Oh, boy. Why does that even matter? I didn't know I needed to go into that much detail."

"Well, now you know. So, get to it."

I sighed heavily. "I know you are expecting some magical moment, but it wasn't like that. We had a few of those moments when things seemed to pause at just the right time, and it set up that first kiss. Sometimes it was at the end of a sentence. Sometimes it was the end of a night. Early on, I was always a little too nervous to seize the moment. I didn't want to miscalculate and mess the whole thing up. One night when we were in her dorm room watching some stupid movie, I asked her if she wanted a gummy worm. I knew she loved gummy anything because we talked about it on one of our walks. I put a gummy worm in my mouth and dangled the other end towards hers."

Monica busted out laughing. "Did she take the bait?"

"Really? You just couldn't keep that one to yourself, huh?"

"I couldn't. You set that up too perfectly," she said, still laughing heartily.

"As I was saying, she bit the other end. We chewed until there was nothing left. Our lips met, and everything around us ceased to be. We kissed like we were school kids enjoying the wonders of our first kiss. It felt so new, yet so familiar. I had played that moment out in my head a hundred times. None of those replays came close to the actual thing."

Monica didn't have a response to this. She just stared longingly into the distance. I'm sure she was recalling a memory of a similar situation. She was a hopeless romantic.

"Should I continue or do you need a moment?" I asked.

"I'm fine. Keep going."

"Well, she kept her promise. I got letters in the mail every day."

"Wait a minute. She actually wrote you love letters every day?"

"They weren't always long drawn out letters. Sometimes they were pictures of her with a few words written on the back. Sometimes she would send postcards with pictures that looked like places we visited. Other times she would send pictures she drew."

"Did you send letters back?"

"I told her that I would try my best to mail letters back to her, but I let her know that I hated writing letters. I told her if she writes the letters, I would pay for the long-distance calls. She agreed that was fair. I did write her a couple of poems though."

"You did what!?" Monica asked in amazement. "You

write poetry?"

"Yes, I write poetry. Why is that so surprising?"

"I don't know. You just don't see too many guys writing poetry these days."

"Sure, you do. Kaje writes poems all the time. Just because he raps them or sings them doesn't mean they aren't poems."

"Yeah, I guess I see your point, but this is different. You actually wrote love poems to her?"

"Something like that. Let's just say I did my best."

"Got any ones you want to share?"

"With you? Nope," I said sarcastically.

"Jerk mode activated."

I laughed. "Whatever. I'll share one with you that I sent to her as long as you don't get all mushy and start crying."

"Whatever! Women don't get mushy. Men just can't handle us showing emotions."

"If you say so."

I wasn't entirely comfortable sharing my poetry. I always thought it was a bit rudimentary, so I recited the poem with a bit of an English accent to give it a bit of panache.

"In silence you entered so softly
You made my world anew
In silence departed so swiftly
Leaving only fragments to view
Springtime blossomed with hope so real
A chance for love exists
A summer full of joy and laughter
First dates, first hugs, first kiss
Autumn blows its winds of change
Reunions cherished true

In time you will return to me
And I'll return to you."

"Wow!" Monica exclaimed. "Oh, my goodness!"

"I guess that means you like it."

"I just...wow. Why didn't this work out?"

"You want me to tell you or finish the story. I'll be happy to cut to the chase."

"No, finish the story. I just can't believe you two aren't still together."

I winked. "Maybe we are and I've been keeping it a secret."

"I would actually prefer that ending."

"It was nearing the end of the summer and she was coming back in a week. I remember there were days I didn't get letters. The ones I got were really short and had very little detail. They almost appeared to be unfinished. On our last phone call, she assured me that everything was okay. She said she was just stressed with the thought of leaving home and starting school again.

"I remember her last letter before she was supposed to come back. She told me about a local fair she went to. The letter described joyous things about the fair, but there was no joy in this letter. It felt like she was describing a fair that she would no longer be able to enjoy anymore. A fair that had run its course."

"Uh oh," Monica said with a worried look on her face.

"She just..." I responded sullenly. I felt memories begin to overwhelm me. "I'm sorry, Monica. Would you mind if I told you the rest another time?"

Although she was anxious to hear the rest of the story, she could tell by the look on my face that she should probably oblige. "Sure. Are you okay?" she asked

"Yeah. This next part just takes a lot out of me, and my 'pathy sense' as you call it, is already highly sensitive."

"Oh, yeah. Sorry about that."

"No worries. Just let me get some rest and I'll share the grand finale with you the next time I see you. I Promise."

We got up and walked towards the door. As I started to open the door, Monica stopped and gave me a big hug. "Thank you for tonight. You're a good friend. I wish more people were more like you."

"Well, thank you. You're absolutely welcome. You're a good friend too. Even though you ruined my favorite shirt."

"I really am sorry about that."

"I'm kidding. It's not like I'm wearing it out anywhere. Oh, speaking of, Kaje wanted to know if you wanted to join us for drinks Saturday night."

"Sure. What's the occasion?"

I looked towards the ground. "I'll let him tell you."

"Okay. Sounds like a good time. I'll get the details from you later."

We exchanged smiles and she headed to her apartment. Before she got to her apartment, she stopped. "Kaleb," she said sadly.

"Yeah? What's up?"

"I have something to tell you, but I..." Her words trailed off and the silence lingered for a moment.

"Hey, I'll tell you what, let's get some sleep, and we can discuss whatever you want, tomorrow. Sound fair?"

"Yep. Goodnight, Kaleb."

"Goodnight, kiddo."

I closed the door. I had never seen her like that. I was worried about her. I should have watched to make sure she made it into her apartment, but the day had completely drained me. I was mentally and physically exhausted. All I wanted to do was sleep and have a normal dream, or no dream at all. I walked over to the couch and let the full weight of my body just fall down on it. "I'll head to bed in a minute," I mumbled.

Chapter 20 - Land of Illusions Dreamscape -Kaleb-

"Do you take this man to be your lawfully wedded husband, to have and to hold, from this day forward, for better, for worse, for richer, for poorer, in sickness, and in health, until death do you part?"

"I...I do. A hundred times."

"And do you take this woman to be your lawfully wedded wife, to have and to hold, from this day forward, for better, for worse, for richer, for poorer, in sickness, and in health, until death do you part?"

"Well, I guess I have to now." He laughs smugly.

Several people on one side chuckle.

"I do, a hundred and one times."

From the crowd, I hear some sighs, some laughter, and a few whispers. A few people are crying and wiping away tears of joy. I stare on from the back pew. I occasionally look around, but I can't make out any of the faces I see. I lean forward to get a better view of the bride and groom. I can't tell who they are because their backs are to me.

I am suddenly overcome by deep melancholia. Tears begin flowing from my eyes uncontrollably. An elderly lady sitting next to me reaches her hand out to hand me a tissue. I reach for it, but my hand goes right through it. The tissue slowly falls to the floor. She flashes a wry smile and continues watching the ceremony.

"If anyone can show just cause why this couple should not be joined together in matrimony, let them speak now or forever hold their peace."

I feel an overwhelming need to speak up, but I don't. Everything about this feels wrong, but I don't know why. I don't even know who these people are. Why do I object to their wedding?

"Say something," a voice whispers to me.

I look around. Everyone was still looking forward, engrossed in the ceremony.

"Then, by the power vested in me—"

"Say something!" the voice yells.

I jump to my feet. "I object! I object a thousand times!" Sadness overwhelms me. I am embarrassed by what I just did. I hang my head low and speak softly. "She can't be with him. She's not in love with him. She's in love with me. And...and I'm in love with her."

A quiet calm falls over the church. Time seems to stand still for a moment. I exhale and slowly lift my head. Everyone is still smiling and crying as if I hadn't said anything at all.

"I now pronounce you husband and wife."

"No!" I scream. "I object! I object!"

"You may kiss your bride."

"No!" I yell. I can hear the voice from earlier, echoing my words. I begin to walk towards the front of the church. As I watch them kiss, my legs weaken, and I fall to my knees in grief. I cover my eyes. "This is all wrong. It's not supposed to be like this," I say as I sob into my hands.

My body begins to warm as I feel a soft embrace. It fills me with love and comfort. It feels familiar. I stay on my knees and let it envelope me for a while.

I rise to my feet. The church is empty. As I look around, it appears that no one has been in the church for quite some time. I head towards the front doors and make my way out. The church sits on the top of a hill that overlooks a beautiful countryside. The sun shines bright against my face as the wind tickles my remaining tears. The sky is as blue as I have ever seen it. Down the hill sits a large tree. A table and chairs occupy the shaded area underneath the tree. A little girl is swinging back and forth in a swing that hangs from the tree. A group of people dressed in white sit and talk at the table.

An elderly lady sitting at the table sees me standing there and motions for me to join them. I make my way down the hill and head towards the table. She smiles warmly at me. I recognize her from the wedding. She is the one who handed me the tissue. Her and the little girl look normal, while the other ladies at the table have an almost translucent look to them. They talk and laugh with each other without even noticing that I am approaching.

"Hello?" I say timidly.

The little girl smiles. She walks over to me and kicks me in the shin.

"Ouch! What was that for?"

"You're late, Mister!

"I'm late? For what?"

"You know!"

"I do?"

"Mhm. You're always late."

I look closely at her. There's something about her eyes.

"You don't recognize me, do you?" she asked.

"Should I?"

"Micaleah, be a dear and run along and play with your friends," the elderly lady says to her.

Micaleah shoulders slump as she pouts. "Okay." She sticks her tongue out at me, and then runs towards two little kids that are laughing and playing. They have the same translucent appearance as the ladies at the table.

The elderly lady approaches me. "Do forgive her. Not the most mature version of herself on display."

"Where is this place? Rather, what is this place?"

"Oh, dear. You're further than I thought?"

"Further?"

She gets up from her chair. She seems much older than she did in the church. "I'll be back, ladies. Just keep doing what you're doing."

The ladies keep talking and laughing, as if they didn't hear a word she said.

She reaches for my hand. "Walk with me, dearie."

I stare at her hand quizzically. She seems to know what my hesitation stems from. "Oh, don't worry about that, dearie."

She reaches her hand to mine. I reach out and take her hand. They connect. Her hand is lukewarm, bordering on cold. Something about it feels familiar. She leads me further down the hill. We walk through tall grass and flowers that sway with the breeze.

"You and Micaleah look alike. Is she your daughter?" I ask hesitantly.

"You could say that."

"What is your name?"

"Names aren't important here. I am called many things. You can call me Mother, if that helps you."

"Okay, Mother. Do you know where we are? I don't remember how I got here."

"No one ever does. It's just the way of things. They come, they learn, they leave. What they do with what they learn is up to them."

"I'm sorry. I don't know what any of this means. I have so many questions. Whose wedding was that? I loved her? I remember feeling so sad about it. Why don't I feel as sad now as I did then? Why does everything feel so foggy?"

"Well, that's a lot of questions, dearie. Which shall I answer first?"

"Whose wedding was that?"

"Oh, I'm sorry, dear. That's not my question to answer."

"Then whose is it?"

"Micaleah's, of course. She is the one who brought you here."

"Brought me here?"

"Why don't I tell you why don't you don't feel as sad as you did at the wedding. That is an answer I can give you. Look back at the church up there. Do you see how old and withered it is?"

I turn back and look at the church. "Yes."

"That is because that wedding happened ages ago."

"How is that possible? I just saw it."

"That you did. And I've seen it many times before. Funny thing, this is the first time I've ever seen you at it."

"I really don't understand any of this."

"In time, you will. In time. When your heart is ready. You are close. Oh, so very close."

"Close to what?"

"To the end, of course. You'll need all your strength if you are to make it to the other side."

I can feel myself getting frustrated. "The other side? How is any of this helping me? Why are your words so cryptic?"

"Oh? Are they now, dearie? I'm sorry. I've already said more than I should have."

"More than you should have? What have you told me?" I yell in frustration.

I hear footsteps in the grass running towards me. Micaleah runs up beside us. "Mummy! Can he play with me now?"

"I'm sorry, dear. He isn't quite ready yet. Soon, dear. He'll be ready very soon," she says. She has the same wry smile she had in the church."

"Aww! Okay, I guess I will wait." Her shoulders slump again. "I'm tired of waiting though."

"Remember what I told you about patience, love?"

"You said 'Be patient. I have all the time in the world.'"

"Very good. Now, shall we walk back up to the tree together?"

"Okay," Micaleah said softly. "Mummy?"

"Yes, dear?"

"Can I hold his hand this time?"

"Well, I guess that would be up to him. You did give

him a good kicking."

"Oh, yeah. I did." Micaleah looks at me with her big, brown eyes. "I'm sorry. Would you like to hold my hand?"

I look at Mother. She returns an approving nod. I reach out for Micaleah's hand. She grabs my hand and squeezes it. "Yay! Here we go."

When our hands touch, a rush of memories hit me all at once. The memories feel so vivid, it feels like I am reliving them over and over again. Some feel like memories of the past, while others feel like split second forecasts of the future. It is too much to take in. My legs give out and I stumble to the ground.

"Micaleah!" Mother says sternly.

Micaleah's face saddens. "Sorry, Mother."

Mother grabs my other hand and helps me up. "Are you okay, dearie?"

"I...I think so. What just happened?"

"I'm afraid Micaleah got a little impatient."

"Huh?"

"Micaleah. Your manners."

Micaleah puts her head down. "I'm sorry."

I take a minute to regain my footing. My mind is racing, trying to understand what I just experienced. As we begin to walk through the field, a strong wind begins to blow. The sun, which just minutes ago, was high overhead, begins to set behind the church. I begin to hear a gentle song starting to play.

"It would appear our time is almost up, dearie."

"What happened to me back there?"

Mother looks at Micaleah. Micaleah's big, brown eyes begin to water. She guiltily looks down at the ground. A single tear falls to the ground. A vibrant pink flower sprouts from the spot where the tear landed. Something feels very familiar about it. I look curiously at her, then look to Mother. Something about them begins to stir my memories.

"Have we m—"

"Listen, dearie. The path gets a bit rocky from here, but you mustn't lose hope. Though it may seem like it at times, you will never be alone. Her light will always guide you. Her light shields you from him. Love will always surround you."

"Him? The path? Whose light?"

Mother began to say something, but the music is now so loud that I cannot hear anything else. The world around us begins to break apart, like a completed puzzle being taken apart piece by piece. Mother stands there with a warm smile and one hand slowly waving. Micaleah jumps up and down excitedly waving her hand.

I feel confused, yet somehow comforted. I lift my hand to wave goodbye. They are the last remaining pieces of the puzzle. The rest is just a black void. Before the final pieces come apart, Micaleah puts both of her hands to her mouth and shouts to me.

"Don't be late!"

Chapter 21 - Monica's Decision
-Kaleb-

I opened my eyes to find Monica standing over me. "Don't be late!" she said sternly. "And if you are, don't blame me. I've been trying to wake you for the past 5 minutes. You need to change your alarm. How can you wake up to that soft music anyway?"

I sat up, rubbed my eyes, and tried to grasp what was going on. Monica stood there looking at me.

"What the? Have you been here all night?" I asked.

"Yep. Slept right on the other side of the couch. I put that blanket on you too. Warmed you right up."

I shot her a weird look. I lifted the blanket and looked down at my pants.

She rolled her eyes at me. "Seriously? Gross! You're like a brother. I left my keys in here somewhere, but you didn't answer when I knocked."

"So, you let yourself in?"

"Well, yeah. What was I supposed to do?"

"Sleep in the hallway!"

"Whatever! Can you just check? I'm pretty sure my keys are under you."

I reached around, grabbed her keys from underneath me, and held them out to her.

"Thank you very much." she said.

"You're welcome. Now get out, before you make me late."

"Rude! If it wasn't for me, you would have still been asleep."

"Says you."

"Whatever. I'm out of here. I'll see you later."

"Looking forward to it," I said with mock enthusiasm.

"I bet you are. Oh, and by the way, you talk in your sleep," she said. She winked and headed to the door.

"Hey!" I yelled. "Didn't you have something to tell me?"

Monica looked down at the floor. "Well, yeah, but now is probably not the best time for it."

"Why not? What's going on with you? You have me kind of worried about you."

"Didn't you say you were going to be late for work?"

"No, I said 'You were going to make me late for work.' Now if I'm late, it's on me. So, spill it."

She slowly walked over and sat on the couch. "Promise you won't hate me?"

"I could never hate you. Just tell me what's going on."

She took a deep breath. "Kaleb, I'm leaving."

"What do you mean, you're leaving? Where are you going?"

She began to cry. "I'm moving back home with my mom for a while. You were right. I need to get away from Nate. I need to get away from everything. I need a fresh start."

"I just meant you should be done with him. Break it off for good."

"I know, and I know you don't think so, but I have actually tried, but I just keep taking him back. This way, I don't have to be as strong. He can just be out of sight and out of mind."

"But that's not—"

"Kaleb, don't try to logic this into making sense. I have already made up my mind. I have to do this."

"I see that. So, when are you leaving?"

"Sunday," she said weakly.

"Oh, wow. I didn't expect that."

She cried harder. I walked over to the couch and sat beside her. "Hey, now. It's okay. It'll all work out. You're going to be alright."

"I know," she said softly. "You know what the worst thing about all this is?"

"What's that?"

"I feel like I'm losing a friend because of it."

I put my arm around her and pulled her close to me. "No way. You have a friend for life, no matter what. You have to take care of you. I get it. We'll still be in touch, and maybe hang out every now and then. Where does your mom live, again?"

"Portland."

"Oh, well, scratch that. I guess you are losing a friend," I said jokingly.

"You're such a jerk," she said. Laughter penetrated her sadness.

"Yeah, but you love me."

"Unfortunately."

I pulled her closer to me and rested my head on hers.

"Promise you don't hate me?" she whispered.

"I promise."

"Thank you, Kaleb.

"I am kind of pissed at you for another reason though."

"What? What did I do now?"

"You made me late for work."

Monica laughed. "Oh, no. I'm not owning that. You said it was on you if you were late."

"Whatever. Just get out, before you get me fired."

Monica got up and walked to the door. "I'm leaving anyway. Bye."

"Hey," I called out.

"Yeah."

I smiled. "I'm proud of you."

She smiled nervously. "Thanks. Me too."

As the door was shutting, I heard Monica say "And we're still on for later."

I rolled my eyes. "Of course, we are," I mumbled.

I grabbed my phone and checked the time. I quickly got up and hopped in the shower. I felt a sharp pain in my lower right leg. I looked down. My right shin had a huge bruise on it. It brought me back to the dream. The craziness of the morning hadn't allowed me the time to process it all. As I stood there and tried to let the hot water relax me, I remembered the wedding. I remembered how sad I felt, and how I yelled out in anguish. I wondered what Monica heard me say.

Something about that lady and that little girl felt so familiar, but I couldn't quite put my finger on it. It felt so strange to appear to have memories within a dream. It was all too much to handle, and I didn't want to think about it anymore.

I got out of the shower and got ready for work. I felt energized by the fact that it was Friday. All I had to do was survive this day, then I could enjoy a much-needed three-day weekend. As I walked out, I heard loud arguing coming from Monica's apartment. I shook my head. I was sure I would hear about it later.

It was a somber mood at work. I quietly walked to my desk and set my things down. I wanted to believe that if no one said anything, it meant that everything was okay. Brenda stood up and leaned into my cubicle. "Good morning, Kaleb."

Brenda never spoke to me like that. It worried me even more. "Good morning. How is she?" I asked.

"It's not good. They are still running tests. Her family has flown in. I'm hoping to know more as the day goes on."

"Have you gone to see her?"

"I tried. They are requesting that only family visit at this time."

"Oh, okay. Please let me know when you hear something. No matter how small the details."

"I will, dear."

"Thank you."

I sat down and put my headphones on. I just wanted the day to be over. I didn't want to think about anything heavy in this world or the stupid dream world, but something about the way Brenda called me "dear," brought back memories of the lady from the dream.

Why did she look familiar to me, and what did she mean when she said that I was close to the end? The question I should've been asking myself was, why was I giving any credence to nonsense that kept happening in my dreams? They were just that, dreams.

I got up and walked to the cafeteria. The place was quiet and felt empty. No one was in the cafeteria. I walked over to get coffee. Suddenly, I caught a whiff of the fragrance Tammy wears. Sadness washed over me. I could feel my eyes start to tear up. I made my way over to the window and composed myself. Luckily, no one walked in. As I stared out the window, that déjà vu feeling took over again, but it was much more intense than any of the previous times. I leaned against the wall and composed myself. I heard a muffled, but familiar voice.

"Smile, trouble."

I quickly turned around to find the cafeteria was still empty. "Yep. It's official. I am losing my mind," I said loudly.

I rubbed my temples. The feeling had passed. I got some coffee and went back to my desk. I pulled out my phone and texted Kaje.

I am losing my mind.

Chapter 22 - Unusual Visitor
-Kaleb-

I found it nearly impossible to focus on anything at work, so I decided to go to lunch earlier than I normally went. It was a cool day. It was gray and cloudy, but I decided to go for a walk anyway. I grabbed my jacket and quietly slipped out the side exit, making sure to avoid anyone. I really wasn't in the mood to walk with anyone.

As I walked along the trail, I thought about how quickly things were changing. Maybe it was just the fact that Kaje was moving on to bigger and better things, but I felt like everything around me was moving forward, and I was stuck in the same place. I wanted to make a move, but I didn't know what that move was. If I was being honest with myself, I depended on Kaje for support more than I cared to admit. I never truly considered a time where he wouldn't always be around.

I walked along the path, deep in thought. I noticed an elderly woman walking up ahead. She appeared to be laboring a bit. I quickened my pace and caught up with her.

"Are you okay, ma'am?"

"Oh, hello there. It appears my cane has reached the end of its journey before I've reached the end of mine." She held up a broken, wooden cane.

"Oh, no. We can't have that. Doesn't your cane know that you have places to be?"

"Oh, you're funny too. That's a plus," she mumbled.

"Pardon me?"

"Oh, don't mind me, dear. Just the ramblings of an old woman. Would you be a dear and walk me to my car? I would really appreciate it. I have a date that I cannot miss."

I held out my arm for her to hold on to. "Absolutely. Shall we?"

"And a gentleman as well. Perfect."

I smiled. "You set the pace. I don't want to go too fast."

"And such a beautiful smile. Thank you, dear. You are kind. People aren't as kind these days as they used to be. You have a good heart. I can see that."

"You can?"

"Oh, yes, but it is also a very troubled heart."

"How can you possibly know that?"

"It's the eyes, my dear. The eyes are a window to the soul. I can see you are dealing with many things."

"Yeah, something like that."

"You could always share your troubles with me. It may be good to let them all out."

"Thanks, but I don't want to trouble you with my issues."

She smiled. "Sometimes it's good to share your issues with a complete stranger you meet walking on a path."

I laughed. "Well, when you put it like that. You may

just have a point. If you think I'm crazy, it's okay. We'll probably never see each other again, so I won't have to worry about you calling me crazy the next time you see me."

She smiled lovingly at me. "I've experienced a lot of things in my time on this earth. I doubt you could tell me anything that would make me think that."

"I don't know. I'm not your average crazy person."

"I'm sure you aren't crazy at all, my dear. Maybe you just need a different perspective."

"I suppose so. Where shall I begin?"

"The beginning is always a good place."

I smiled. "If I started there, we'd be walking for a long time, and you have a date you can't miss, and I have to get back to work eventually."

"Fair enough," she said. "I suppose time is of the essence. Speaking of time, would you mind telling me the time, dear."

I pulled my phone out of my pocket. "It's 11:11."

"Oh, what a perfect time!" she said. Her face beamed with joy.

"What makes it the perfect time? The fact that the numbers are all the same?"

"Oh, no. 11:11 can have many meanings. Some say 11:11 is a sign that there is greater light and love searching for you, but you must open your heart and quiet your mind to become in tune with it."

"Funny you should say that."

"Oh? Have you found that special someone?"

"Well, not exactly."

"Oh, would you look at me. I'm sorry my dear, prying like an old woman. Please, go on with your story if you'd like."

I adjusted my arm and made sure she was comfortable. "My story, huh? How about I give you the CliffsNotes version?"

She smiled. "What's good for the goose is good for the gander."

"Okay, but just remember, you asked for it. So, let's see...I've always been a bit odd. Not to the casual observer, but I knew I was different from other kids my age. Although I didn't fully understand it as a child, I now know that I am an empath. Growing up, I always struggled explaining to my parents what exactly I felt at times, and why I felt happy or sad for no apparent reason.

"This may sound strange too, but I've always seen people in other people. If that makes any sense at all. It's almost like everyone has doppelgangers, and I can see the similarities when my friends can't. Or, if I see someone while I'm out, I always have the feeling that I've seen them before. Then there's the constant feelings of déjà vu. They were never something I paid much attention to. It was just a curious little feeling that went away as soon as it came. Lately, they have been more frequent and more intense. It kind of feels like I am experiencing the same thing over and over again, but I can't fully grasp hold of the memory, like it's not mine to grasp. And the more I try to recall it, the more it fades away."

"Very interesting."

"Have you had enough of my crazy talk yet?"

"Oh, not at all, dear. If you don't mind, I would love to hear more. It's quite fascinating."

"Well, then you'll love the rest. Lately, I have been having these crazy dreams. Except they don't feel like dreams. They feel much more real. They feel more like out-of-body experiences, and I can remember them vividly."

"Is that unusual for you?"

"Well, most of the time I can remember most of my dreams. I've always had really vivid dreams, even dreams that felt real, but there are always pieces and parts of my dreams that I can't remember, and the longer I take to recall them, the less I remember. I actually look forward to dreaming. Each one is like a new adventure. These dreams don't feel like that. I remember everything like it happened in real life."

"I see. And do these dreams have any similarities?"

"Well, I always feel like I'm trying to get somewhere, but I don't quite make it."

"Are you alone?"

"No, I'm not," I say slowly as the epiphany takes shape in my head. "There's always a girl there, but it doesn't always seem like the same one." My mind began racing. That was the first time I had really started to piece things together.

"So, it's just these girls and you, trying to get somewhere? Do you know where you are trying to get to?"

"It's always different, and I can never see a final destination."

"What stops you from reaching your destination?"

Although I knew the answer, I thought it was too grim to share. "I'm not sure. It's just darkness, I guess."

"I see."

"My last dream wasn't dark though," I blurted out, trying to lighten the mood. "There was a wedding and everything."

Her face brightened. "Oh, that's wonderful, dear.

Was it yours?"

"No, but I think I was supposed to stop it. I couldn't though. I think it was supposed to be mine."

"Oh, my word. Don't you see what this all means?"

"I wish I did."

"These dreams are no accident of circumstance. They are the universe telling you that you are about to meet someone very special."

"That's what you got from all that? I missed that part."

"That's exactly what I got, dear. As clear as a bell. Don't you worry. You won't keep missing signs from the universe. They'll just keep getting louder and louder until you hear them."

"That's exactly what I am afraid of."

"There's no reason to be afraid. This is a joyous occasion. You should consider yourself lucky. The universe doesn't speak to just anyone."

"Is that so? What makes me so special?"

"Perhaps you may be a healer. My guess is that smile and that kind heart of yours. Speaking of which, I think you've brought me far enough."

"You sure? I have no problem walking you to your car."

She smiled at me. "That's quite alright, dear. You've done more than enough."

"Well, it was a pleasure talking with you. Be sure to tell your friends about the crazy guy you met on the path today."

She chuckled. "I mostly certainly will. But don't you worry, they don't listen when I talk to them anyway."

"Doesn't sound like they are good friends."

"They serve their purpose."

I shot her a confused look. "What does that mean?"

She waved it off dismissively. "Oh, don't mind me, just more ramblings."

She walked closer to me and put her hands on each side of my face. I was a bit taken aback, but I did not move. Her hands had a familiar scent. A scent from childhood. "Listen to me, dear. Do yourself a favor. Get out this weekend and become one with nature. Let it clear your thoughts, and open your heart and mind. I'm sure the answers are out there. If you find yourself at a loss, just remember, love is the answer. It's always the answer."

She smiled at me and walked down the side path that led to the parking lot. I slowly walked at a distance, watching her walk away, to assure she would make it okay. She seemed to get along fine as she made her way down the small hill that led to the parking lot. Before I turned around, I noticed a small object gently fell from her person. I hurried towards her to pick it up.

"Ma'am. Ma'am. You dropped something."

I reached down and picked up a brownish-grey, striped feather. I had never seen that type of feather before. I held it up to the sunlight and examined it. It was fascinating. I continued walking towards the parking lot. There was another similar looking feather on the ground. I picked it up and examined it. It was the same as the first one. As I approached the parking lot, I noticed that it was completely empty. Yellow caution tape surrounded the entrance. The sign read "Closed for Construction." I shook my head. "Of course, it is," I mumbled.

Chapter 23 - Hammermill Friday
-Kaleb-

I was late getting back from lunch, but nobody seemed to care. It was Friday and everyone was looking forward to the long weekend. I looked over Brenda's wall, hoping she had an update on Tammy, but it looked like she was gone for the day. I sat down and tried to focus on what the lady from the path said, and not on her mysterious disappearance. I didn't need my weird dream world intersecting with my weird real world any more than it already had. I put the mysterious feathers on my desk. I planned on asking Rob about them. He always had knowledge on a lot of different things. I opened my instant messenger to ask him to stop by. His status showed as "Presence Unknown." That only showed for people who have been gone from the company for a while.

I grabbed the feathers and started to head to his desk when I saw him walking towards mine. He was carrying a box. My heart sank.

"Hey, man. Cool owl feathers." He had a somewhat sad look on his face.

"What's going on?" I asked.

He shrugged and pointed to the name on the box. It read "Hammermill." It had all his work belongings in it.

"Hammermill Friday, huh?" I asked, although I already knew the answer.

"Yeah, man. I have to get out of here. This place is killing me. I can't take it anymore."

"I see. Not exactly what I was expecting."

"Sorry, man. I wanted to say something earlier. I wasn't really sure I could. I'm kind of struggling a bit now."

"I know. I get it. Damn, that sucks, man. I was not expecting that. You have to do what's good for you though. I understand. Take care of yourself, man."

I put my hand out for a hand shake. He grabbed it and pulled me in for a hug. "I love you, man," he said. His voice started to give out. "I'll keep in touch."

Before I could respond, he grabbed his box and hurried out. I stood there and watched him leave. It felt like another chapter closing. First Kaje, then Monica, and now Rob. I hoped Tammy wasn't next. It just seemed like everyone I cared about was leaving me behind.

I clutched the feathers in my hand, sat down, and stared at my screen. I could feel my eyes starting to tear up. I glanced over at the picture Rob gave me. Looking back, it was clear what he was planning when he gave it to me. I was just too preoccupied to see it. As I stared at the picture, my eyes blurred. I couldn't hold back my tears. I covered my face with my hands and just cried.

"Why don't you take the rest of the day off, Barnes."

I wiped my face and looked up. Liza was looking over my cubicle wall. She always called me by my last name.

I sniffed. "But I still have a few hours to—"

"Don't worry about the time. Just go home and relax. Try to take your mind off of things."

"Thank you, Treve. I appreciate it."

She shot me a stern look for using her last name, then smiled and walked away. I quickly started packing up my things before she changed her mind. I reached for the picture Rob gave me, but decided I should keep it pinned up at work. I quietly slipped out the front door and headed to my car. It was much cooler outside than it was earlier, and it was strangely foggy. I could barely see where I parked.

I got to my car, threw my bag in the back seat, and closed the door. I sat back in the seat and rested. I was free. I made it to the weekend. I reclined my seat, took a few deep breaths, and tried to relax my mind. I couldn't help but to think about everything that went on during the week and what it all meant for me going forward. I thought about how this week may have been a sign that I should consider doing something different with my life. Maybe I was destined for more than a standard nine to five.

My phone vibrated. It was a text message from Kaje.

Wake up, slacker.

Whatever. I'm not sleeping. I could be though. I got out early

GTHOH. Nice! I wonder how you managed that. You at home yet?

Nope. On my way.

Cool. I'll see you tomorrow.

Later.

 I moved my seat up, put my seat belt on, and started the car. I was ready to officially get the weekend started. As I pulled out, the seat belt light began to flash. I double-checked that my seat belt was securely clicked in. It was. I glanced over to the passenger side. The airbag status light was on. "Great. If it's not one thing, it's another," I grumbled.

 I continued to drive home. The fog was something else. I drove very slowly. I could barely see in front of me. I hadn't seen another vehicle at all. Maybe everyone else was smart enough to stay off the roads. I turned on the radio, hoping to hear a traffic report, but the stations were all silent or full of static. Something didn't feel right. I decided to pull over at the next place I could. In the distance, all I could see was thick, dense fog. The kind you see in cemeteries during horror movies. There was no way I was going anywhere in that type of fog. I grabbed my phone to see if anyone else was experiencing what I was. The phone had no signal. Exasperated, I threw it into the passenger seat.

 I turned my windshield wipers on to see if I could see things more clearly. In the distance, there appeared to be someone slowly walking towards my car. I could barely make them out. I figured it was probably someone coming to see if I needed help. I flashed my lights a couple of times to let them know I was in the car. My lights did not shine onto the person. They just seem to absorb into them. I stuck my head out the window to confirm what I saw. The closer it walked, the less light I could see. Panicked, I pulled my head back into the car, rolled up the window, and locked the doors. It moved closer and eventually swallowed all of the light in front of me. I frantically tried to start the car, but it wouldn't start. I sat there, tightly gripping the wheel. Everything was quiet. There was an eerie feeling of nothingness. No sound. No movement. Just darkness.

Suddenly, I saw faint bright lights in the distance. In the blink of an eye, there was a blinding light, then nothing. I wasn't even sure how much time had passed. All I could hear was my labored breath and my heart beating. Eventually, I heard faint voices in the distance.

"He's not supposed to be here."

"Oh, my God. Is he alright?"

"Get up, Kaleb. Everyone is worried about you."

I heard a faint tapping sound.

"How long has he been here?"

"Kaleb, get up. You have to wake up."

"Kaleb, wake up!"

The knocking sound was now closer and louder.

"Kaleb! Kaleb!"

I turned towards the window. Two people with flashlights were standing outside my car door. One of them was banging her knuckles against the window.

"Sir? Are you alright?"

I sat up and rubbed my eyes. I felt groggy and confused. I rolled the window down. "I think so. What the heck is going on?"

"We were heading inside to clean the building and saw your car running. There aren't typically any cars here this late. We heard something in the car, so we came over to check things out," the man said.

"This late? What time is it?"

"7:42," the lady said.

I sat up quickly. My head was pounding. "Are you serious? It can't be that late."

She held up her phone and showed me the time. It showed "1:43."

Still a bit groggy, I rubbed my eyes and looked at her in confusion.

She noticed my confusion and looked down at her phone. "Oh, sorry about that." She slid her finger back and showed me the phone again. It read "7:43."

"Oh, man. I have to go."

"Are you okay to drive, sir? Is someone else in the car with you?" the man asked as he shined his flashlight in the back seat.

"What? No," I said, still confused.

"Kaleb? Is that your name? Are you sure you're okay?"

"Yeah," I said. I'm sure my tone was unconvincing. "I just fell asleep. It's been a long week. Thank you both. I should be fine. Wait, how did you know my name?"

"We have to get going. Please be careful. It's a bit foggy."

I was confused, but I nodded in agreement. They started towards the building. I took a deep breath and laid my head back on the seat. I left my window down. The fresh air helped with the grogginess. I could hear the couple talking in the distance.

"Amanda, did you hear another voice when we were walking towards the car?"

"Yep, sure did."

"A female voice?"

"Mmhm. Paul, let it go. It's none of our business."

They looked back towards my car, waved, smiled suspiciously, then walked in the door.

"A female? What the heck? I guess Monica was right. I do talk in my sleep, and apparently I talk like a female," I said to myself as I let out a little laugh. I immediately reached for my head. It was pounding.

I couldn't believe I fell asleep for that long. It's not like I was completely exhausted. Weird dreams or not, I had been sleeping. Apparently, my body just needed the rest. I took in several deep breaths of fresh air before deciding to head home.

I reached over and put my seat belt on. The seat belt light turned off. The airbag indicator light was off. I guess the problem worked itself out. At least one thing went my way that evening. I grabbed my phone and checked for new messages. Just one from Monica, wondering what time I would be home. I went to text Kaje to tell him the boneheaded thing I just did. The last message in the thread was a message from me to him.

I'm losing my mind.

No message from him telling me to wake up. No message saying he would see me tomorrow.

I thought about how apropos my last message to him was. I put both of my palms to my forehead and pressed hard. I just wanted one normal day. Was that too much to ask?

I sent Kaje a quick message.

What was the last text you got from me?

I didn't wait for a reply. I just headed home. The fog had all but cleared. I hadn't eaten all day, so I stopped and grabbed a bite to eat. I pulled into my building parking lot. There was a moving truck parked near my entrance. I turned the car off and headed inside. As I entered my apartment, my phone vibrated. It was a text from Kaje.

You are losing your mind.

"Sure am," I whispered.

I threw myself down on the couch, turned on the television, and started to eat. I barely took one bite, when I heard my toilet flush. I jumped to my feet and headed towards the bathroom. As I got to the door, Monica was walking out. "What the hell, Monica? You're just letting yourself in now?"

"You need new toilet paper," she said nonchalantly as she headed to the couch."

I just stared at her. "Seriously?"

She grabbed my sandwich and took a bite. "What? My apartment is a mess. I can barely get to my bathroom."

"You are unbelievable. After the day I had, I can't even deal with you right now."

I had never seen her act like this before. She had to see how frustrated I was. I was just about to ask her to leave, when I noticed she was crying.

She sat down next to me. "I'm sorry. I am not handling things very well right now. I was trying to just act normal like everything is okay, but I'm trying too hard. I don't know how to act anymore. I just want to be better, ya know?"

"Yeah, I get it. You just have to be patient. You have a long road ahead of you. Just be you. That's all you can be. The normal, annoying, you. Not this super-boosted, annoying version that breaks into my apartment and uses all my toilet paper."

She smiled, despite her best effort not to. "You're an

ass, you know that? You can always make me smile, but you're still an ass. How do you always manage to do that?"

I winked. "It's what I do."

"And for the record, you were almost out of toilet paper before I got here, so don't try to pin that on me."

I rolled my eyes. "If you say so. You probably broke in because you are all out."

"Wrong. And for the record, I didn't break in. I used a key."

I shook my head. "Should I even ask how you got a key to my apartment?"

"I got it so—"

"Never mind," I interrupted. "I don't even want to know. Just give it to me before you move."

"I guess I can do that. You know, if you came home from work at normal time, I wouldn't have had to let myself in. Where have you been anyway? You are normally home earlier on a Friday."

I sighed. "You don't even want to know, and I don't even want to talk about it."

"Come on. Tell me. Was it a hot date?"

"Yeah, no. Didn't I say I didn't want to talk about it? Let's talk about something else. Like, you going to get me another sandwich."

"Oh, please. I took one bite. You can have the rest."

"Oh? I can have the rest of the sandwich that I paid for? You're so kind."

"I know, right. You know, you could always finish your story. You did promise." She grinned sneakily.

"Yeah, I guess I did, and a promise is a promise."

"Yep! Sure is," she said as she took another bite of my sandwich."

Chapter 24 - Indian Summer
-Kaleb-

"So, where did I leave off?" I asked.

Monica's mood turned pensive. "She wrote you a letter about the fair, just before she was supposed to come back."

"Oh, yeah." I paused and took a deep breath. "Well, she came back on a Friday afternoon. I didn't hear from her until that evening. My phone rang at about 7:30.

'Hello,' I said. I tried not to sound like I had been waiting all day for her call. I was upset, but I thought maybe she had a good reason for waiting so long to call me.

'Hi, mister.'

I could hear the nervousness and forced excitement in her voice.

'Hi, Marcipants.'"

"Wait! Timeout! Marcipants?" Monica blurted out.

"What? It's what I called her," I replied.

"You never mentioned that before."

"I didn't mention a lot of things. Shall I continue? Or do you want me to backtrack and try to remember every little thing I left out?"

"Touchy, touchy."

"I'm sorry. I guess it still bothers me a bit. The fact is, I'm actually amazed it still has an effect on me at all."

"I'm sorry. I guess I didn't even consider that."

"It's okay. I don't think I did either. Anyway, the conversation continued.

'So how long have you been back?' I asked.

'I got here this afternoon. Around twelve or so.'

'I thought I would have heard from you by now. Were you just getting settled in?'

'Something like that.'

'So, can I come see you?'

'Can we wait until tomorrow? I'm really tired.'

'How about I just stop by for a minute? I've been waiting for this day all summer.'

'And you can't wait one more day?'

'Why do you want to wait one more day?' I said, somewhat angrily. 'Look, I know something is going on with you. There is something you aren't telling me. I don't want to worry about us all night. I'd never fall asleep. All I'm asking is twenty minutes, then I'll let you rest. Is that fair?'

'Yeah, I guess that's fine. Just buzz the door when you get here. I'm in a different room this year.'

"I jumped in the car and headed to her dorm. I was worried and didn't know what to expect. My stomach was a mess. I wanted to be happy that I was finally seeing her. I wanted to believe that she was just tired from getting settled in, but I knew better. She had been distant for a couple weeks.

"The fifteen-minute ride felt like it took hours. If you asked me about what I remember seeing during that drive, I could only tell you flickering streetlights and broken white lines. Everything else was a blur.

"I got to the dorm and she buzzed me in. I waited in the vestibule for about a minute or so. I fiddled with the bag of gummy bears I had in my pocket, debating on if I should give them to her right away or see how things went. I was sad that I even had to think that way.

'Hey there, mister,' she said, with that big smile that always made me smile.

'Marcipants!'

"We embraced, and for those long seconds that we held each other, everything seemed like it was going to be okay again.

"I slowly pulled back from the embrace. I looked her in her eyes. Her face wore a smile, but her eyes couldn't hide her sadness and uncertainty. I moved to steal a kiss. She returned the kiss, but not with the same passion I was hoping for.

"She took my hand and pulled me towards the stairs.

'Come see my new room.'

'Oh! You aren't on the first floor anymore. Moving up in the world.'

"She laughed. 'Second year. Second floor.'

'How many floors are there?'

'Four, silly.'

'Ah. I'd hate to see what they did with the fifth-year seniors.'

'Ha! Not many of those here.'

'Maybe there are, and you just don't know what they do with them,' I said, mocking a menacing tone.

"She laughed. 'Shut up!'

'Okay, just better hope you aren't one of them,' I said with a devilish grin.

"She continued to laugh all the way up the stairs. I was a prisoner to her smile and her laugh. Everything in the world felt right when she was happy. I felt right. We felt right.

"She opened her door. 'Home sweet home.'

"I looked around. It looked exactly the same as her previous room, except there was no couch.

'Where's our couch?'

'Still downstairs. I guess sophomores don't need couches.'

'Guess we'll just have to intrude on whoever's room it is now when we want to watch old, corny movies.'

'Hey! I thought you enjoyed those old movies.'

"I just flashed a big smile so I wouldn't have to confess anything. 'Check it out. I bought you gummies.'

'Nice deflection, mister.'

'What?' I shrugged.

"She hesitantly took the bag of gummy bears and set them on the table. She looked sad as she accepted them. She had a nervous energy about her. It felt as if, if I didn't lead the conversation, there wouldn't be one.

'Hey, you want to go to our place tomorrow? I have something I want to share with you.'

"I thought she would light up at just the mention of our place, but she seemed indecisive.

'I'm not sure if I'll have time. I have some things I need to take care of, plus Cheryl is supposed to come over.'

'Okay, look, I don't want to pressure you, but is there something you need to tell me? You've been acting strange since before you got back. I understand you are a bit stressed with school starting and everything, but I feel like you are shutting me out. I wish you would just talk to me about whatever is going on.'

'It's nothing. I'm just tired. Can we talk about this tomorrow? I don't feel well.'

'Of course. I'm sorry. I stayed much longer than I said I would. Get some rest. We'll talk tomorrow.'

"I gave her a hug and a kiss on the cheek, then headed for the door. The whole night had a sense of finality to it. I didn't know how things had come to this. With any of my past relationships, I would have just walked away from it, but she was different. I felt something deep for her that I never felt before."

"Love?" Monica said softly.

"Yeah, love," I replied back sadly.

"Did you tell her that?"

"Well, I'll get to that."

"Sorry. Carry on."

"So, the next day I called her and she didn't answer. I figured she was busy. I left her a message to call me back, but I didn't hear from her. I called a few more times only to get the same results.

"I was beyond upset. I got in my car, turned the radio up as loud as it could go, and just drove around the city. At some point during the drive, I made up my mind that I was just going to go to her dorm and demand answers. So, I drove to her dorm, parked the car, and sat there trying to talk myself out of what I was about to do. Maybe she just needed space, and I was about to give her the exact opposite.

"I didn't manage to convince myself of anything other than the fact that I wanted to know what was going on. I turned the car off, got out, and headed towards the main doors.

'Kaleb,' an unfamiliar voice called out.

"I looked around and saw Cheryl walking towards me. Almost as if she was expecting me. 'Have you seen Marci? I'm worried about her. Is she okay?'

'She's fine. She wanted me to give you this.' She handed me a folded-up letter.

'What's this? Why couldn't she give it to me herself? Did you have something to do with this?'

'I was just asked to give it to you. I don't even know what it says. I just got back today.'

"I could feel the tears welling up. I wanted to get back to my car as fast as I could.

'I'm sorry. Thank you.'

"I turned to walk to my car. I kept a steady, but brisk pace, even though I wanted to run. I just wanted to be away from there. I wanted to be alone. I was in no hurry to read the letter. I'd seen this movie. I knew how it ended.

"I sat in my car. Tears rolled down my face. I opened the letter, but did not read it right away. A bit of anger had taken hold. I welcomed it. It would help me deal with the sadness.

'This was her loss. She just threw away the best thing that ever happened to her,' I thought to myself.

"I lifted the letter to read it. It was not a long letter. Short and straight to the point. Certain words had wet spots on them. I remember hoping they were her tears. At least then I would know she felt something for me.

'Hello, My Love,

I'm sorry to do this in a letter. I just didn't know how to tell you in person. I just can't do this anymore. I'm just not ready. I need to keep my focus on school right now. Please know that I cherished every moment we spent together and I will never forget you.

All my love,
Marcipants'

"I read it about fifty times. I don't know if I was looking for understanding or hoping that each time that I read it, the words would change."

"Oh, my God. That is horrible," Monica said.

"Yep. It kind of was," I replied.

"I'm sorry. I don't even know what to say."

"You can say whatever you want," I said with a somewhat fake laugh. "That was a long time ago. I'm over it."

"You sure? Your eyes tell a different story."

I wiped my eyes. My hand was a little wet. "I'm good. I guess I just got caught up in the story."

"Mmhmm. So, what did you do after you finished reading it?"

"You know how when something really bad is happening, you try to come up with reasons why it's not true. You try to convince yourself that it has to be a dream? I sat in the car for about an hour, convincing myself that I would wake up soon.

"Finally, after I accepted reality, I steeled myself. I told myself that I wasn't going to let this get the best of me. I neatly folded the letter up, rolled my window down and tossed the letter out. I started my car, drove away, and didn't look back."

"And how long were you able to hold up that facade?" Monica asked.

"Facade? What makes you think it was a facade?" I

replied.

"Seriously? Are you really going to waste time going down that road?"

"Well, I suppose there's no real point, since you already know everything."

"About some things." She winked.

"For the next few weeks, I was surprisingly good. I kept myself busy during work, and I was always doing something after work. She rarely crossed my mind at all. I had a friend that I would hang out with after work. She went to the same school as Marci, but she didn't really know her, so I did not have to worry that she would bring her up in conversation.

"One day she invited me to the campus to hang out with a few of her friends. Something inside of me knew it was not a good idea, but there was a large part of me that felt that everything would be okay, and that was just the test that I needed to prove I had moved on from Marci."

"I can already guess how that went," Monica said worriedly.

"It actually went well for the first couple of hours. It was a chilly night and someone had one of those portable fire pits, so we all hung around drinking and talking. I wasn't totally comfortable being in the crowd, but I wasn't uncomfortable either. I had only thought about her walking by a couple times, and when I did, it was more along the lines of her seeing me happy and doing fine without her.

"At around eleven o'clock, I told everyone that I had to go. I lied and told them I had to work in the morning. The truth was, I was just ready to go home. The fire had dwindled and wasn't keeping me warm anymore. Plus, I had given up hope that Marci would show up.

"As I walked to my car, I heard playful laughing and loud talking. It was pretty dark where I parked. I couldn't make out exactly where the laughter was coming from. As I got closer to my car, I saw four figures laughing and joking. I knew that laugh. It was unmistakable. I heard two male voices and two female voices. The one male voice said something jokingly to me as I got closer to my car. I couldn't quite hear what he said. Marci busted out laughing. As I walked into the light, I could clearly see all of them. Marci realized it was me and her laughter stopped instantly. She just stared at me. She had no idea what to say."

"Well, what did you say to her?" Monica asked impatiently.

"Nothing. I just stared back at her.

'What are you staring at, fool?' the guy standing next to her blurted out.

"I turned my gaze towards him. My fists were balled up so tightly, I could feel my knuckles about to explode.

'Rico, don't. Just leave him alone,' Marci said.

"I stared him down. I couldn't bring myself to say a word. I just knew I had never felt what I was feeling at that moment, and I was about to tear him apart.

"I don't know if it was just rage, heartbreak, betrayal, or all of the above. All I knew was, the best thing for me to do was to get in my car and drive home. So, I did just that.

"I made it home, went to my room and paced the floor. I was not supposed to be feeling like that. I was over her. I had moved on. She wasn't supposed to be happy and enjoying life, like nothing happened between us. How could we share the whole summer and it mean so little to her that she could just move on? And who the hell was that ugly, homely looking guy she was with? She broke up with me for him? Seriously?

"I could feel the tears running down my face. I couldn't stop pacing. I didn't know what to do with myself. I wanted to drive back over there and demand answers. I wanted to punch that guy in his face. I wanted to disappear."

My fists were clenched pretty tightly, and I could feel my face getting warm. Monica placed her hand on my fist. I was trembling. I could feel that she was upset.

"Kaleb, relax. We can stop it right there. I think I can piece together the rest."

"It's fine. We're almost to the end, and that was probably the worst part to recall."

Monica's touch relaxed me, but her sadness only deepened mine. I took a few calming breaths, but I knew I needed more than that. "Actually, I'm sorry. I do need a minute. Give me a second. I'll be right back." I got up and walked to the bathroom. I felt I needed to compose myself. I didn't want Monica to see me like that.

Chapter 25 - Too Perfect
-Kaleb-

I plopped back on the couch next to Monica. "I'm sorry. I'm good now. Where was I?"

"You sure, Kaleb? I was serious when I said we can stop."

"Really. I'm good. I just really wish I would have punched that guy in the face!"

Monica laughed. "I kind of wish you would have too. So, you drove home and paced around. Then what?"

"Oh, well, I finally managed to get some sleep. My dreams were nothing but a cruel reminder of that night's events. My clock radio alarm also decided it wanted to get in on the cruelty as well. You know, I once heard a quote that said 'The song is only as sad as the listener.' I can't even remember what song was playing, but at that moment, it was the saddest song I had ever heard in my life. Strange though, I didn't turn it off. I invited it in. I almost felt like, since I was at rock bottom, if I took it all in, there would be nowhere to go from there but up.

"Despite the fact that all I wanted to do was lay in bed, I managed to get myself to work. It was a gray, gloomy day. Fittingly, there was no hint of the sun."

"Oh, my goodness. That had to be horrible, especially since you met her there," Monica said.

"It was unbearable. Everything was a constant reminder of her. I was not doing well. The worst part about it was, I was the person who always did my best to make my customers smile and be positive about their day. I'm sure a lot of them looked forward to seeing me each day. Now I had to fake it and act like I cared about what was really going on with them when all I wanted to do was crawl under my blankets."

"I honestly don't know how you held it together all day," Monica said.

"I didn't. Around noon or so, the Muzak system decided to pay me back for unplugging it that spring night."

"Uh oh. What song came on?" Monica asked.

"Now before I tell you, I want you to keep in mind, Muzak never played anything remotely current. It was always songs from yesteryear."

Monica laughed. "This should be good."

"It was that song by Boyz II Men where they sing about how they are doing fine after being dumped."

"Are you serious? That song is sad when you aren't going through a break up."

"Exactly! So, you can imagine the effect it had on me. I was not doing just fine, and it was the last song I needed to hear that day."

"It's one of those songs you can only listen to once you are truly over the person."

"I guess. I mean, I like the song, but how ironic are love songs about being over someone? If you are truly over them, why did you write the song?"

Monica busted out laughing, "You've got a point."

"Anyway, that damn song was playing, and I was weakening by the moment. The tears I had been holding back, fought for their release. I headed outside to check on things.

"Luckily for me, the skies opened up. I stood in the rain and let my tears flow down my face. I let the warm autumn rain envelope me for what seemed like minutes. There was no distinguishing where my tears started and the rain ended."

"That might be the saddest thing I've ever heard," Monica said sadly.

"Well, that was how I made it through that day and the rest of the week. The Muzak taunted me and the rain shrouded me."

"And nobody knew what was going on with you?"

"Oh, I'm sure they did, but nobody said anything. There was this one customer that said 'Hang in there. It gets easier.' The odd thing about that was, I had never seen her before."

"Maybe she was your guardian angel."

"Well, then where was she when I really needed guarding?"

"Maybe you needed to—"

"Please don't tell me I needed to go through this for some reason or another. I think I would've been just fine if I hadn't."

Monica made a gesture as if she was zipping her mouth shut.

"Sorry. Jerk mode deactivated," I said.

Monica smiled. "So, I'm assuming you never saw Marci again, and you just slowly got over her?"

"Not exactly. Although the next couple of weeks were nowhere near as bad as the first week, I felt stuck in a rut. I didn't feel like things were getting any worse, but I didn't feel like I was getting any better. I was just numb. I didn't find pleasure in the things that normally brought me pleasure.

"One day, my apparent fairy guardian angel came in and asked me how I was doing."

"See, I told—"

"Nope. Don't even. Bring that zipper back out," I said, pointing to her mouth. She once again made the zipping gesture.

"I told her I was hanging in there, but I couldn't seem to move forward.

'Did you get closure?'

'Well, I thought I did because she closed it.'

'But do you know why?'

'Apparently, I wasn't ugly or homely looking enough for her.'

'You're obviously still bitter about it, so I won't press you for details. Just find out the real reason, and you'll have your closure.'

'I'm not sure how I'll get that. She won't speak to me.'

'Have you tried?'

"Well, not really.'

'Then you'll never know. Give it a try.' She winked at me and vanished into thin air, leaving nothing but white smoke."

"What mode did you say you deactivated?" Monica scowled.

"Oh, yeah. Sorry. Anyway, I knew she was right, but I didn't know if I could reach out to Marci and take the chance of being rejected again. That would set me back to square one. And even though I wasn't that far from it, I was much better off where I was. I figured I would sleep on it and make a decision the next day.

"The next day I decided to give her a call after work. My stomach was in knots. I could barely bring myself to push the right numbers. I ended up just hanging up the phone. I took deep breaths and steadied myself. I had recited what I planned to say to her over and over in my head. I wanted to make it short and sweet.

"I recited it softly one last time for good measure.

'Hi, Marci. Sorry to bother you. I know you made it clear we were finished, but I just wanted to know if I did or said something wrong that made you feel like we couldn't be together. I'm not looking to change your mind. I just want to know so I can finally move on.'

"I took one more deep breath and dialed her number. The phone rang about seven times. Everything inside me wanted it to just keep ringing, so I could say I tried.

'Hey!' She answered cheerfully as if she was expecting it to be someone else.

'Hi, Marci,' I said nervously.

'Who is this?'

'It's Kaleb.'

'Oh, my God.'

"There was a rustling sound and the phone hung up."

"Are you kidding me?" Monica asked in disbelief.

"Nope. That's exactly how it happened."

"Ugh. I'm really starting to not like this girl. Did you call back?"

"I called back a couple of times. Each time there was no answer. The next day I tried once more and it said my number had been blocked."

"You have got to be kidding me."

"For some reason, her blocking my number put me in a state of despair. If I was at square one before, I was at square zero at that point. Not only was I not going to get the closure that I desperately needed, I was being treated as if I was this horrible person that did some horrible thing.

"The next day, I struggled through work. I was hurt and angry. I had no idea what to do next. Even if I wanted to call again, I would just be blocked. I couldn't use the work phone because it was in the manager's office. As I stared out the window, pondering, I caught sight of the pay phone in the parking lot. I decided that I was going to use it to call her.

"After my shift, I made my way to the pay phone. I was defeated. I had no hope that it wouldn't be a repeat of my last attempt, but it was all I had left. I put the quarter in the phone and dialed her number.

"The phone rang at least seven times. I was just about to hang up when the ringing stopped.

'Hello?' she answered.

"My heart was pounding through my chest. I could barely breathe. What was left of the dam that held my emotions, broke.

'Marci, please don't hang up. Please. I can't...I just need...I just...I adore you. I...I love you. I think I always have. And I understand...I understand that you...don't love me...And I can't say that I understand that, but I have to be okay with that. But please...please, Marci. If I meant anything to you at all, please tell me what

I did wrong. Tell me how I messed us up. Tell me why my love wasn't enough for you. Tell me I can—'

"My voice faltered, and I stood against the pay phone, crying. After about a minute of silence, I could hear what I thought was crying on the other end of the phone, but no voice to explain away my pain. No comforting words. No reciprocation of my love."

'Kaleb...I can't. I just can't, okay? Why can't you just let me go?' she said behind her tears.

'Because I'm dying inside, Marci!' I bawled. 'How am I supposed to just let you go and keep acting like I'm okay when you are destroying every single part of me? Every part of me hurts, every hour of every day. Do you know how hard it is to sleep with a broken heart? Do you know how it feels when the person who makes you the happiest in this world is also the greatest source of your pain? I thought we were perfect together. I thought we could—'

'Stop! Please just stop,' she cried out. 'I broke up with you because of you. Because you are perfect. You are forever.'

"I stood in stunned silence. Confused as to what I just heard. 'I'm...I'm too perfect?'

'I was never expecting to meet anyone like you. Most of the guys I meet are either jerks, or are just out for one thing. You were different. You cared about my feelings. You put me first. We never fought. We never argued.'

'It sounds like you are giving me reasons why we should be together.'

'You just don't understand. I'm not ready for all of that. I'm not ready for perfection. I'm not ready for forever.'

'So, why didn't you tell me that you just wanted to slow things down? And for the record, I'm far from perfect.'

'You're perfect to me. That's what scares me. You make me want to be someone that I don't think I am quite ready to be. I still have a lot of messing up to do, and I didn't want you to be a part of that. I couldn't stand the thought of you thinking less of me.'

'Oh, Marci. I wouldn't—'

'But you would. You just can't see it now. I always let people down.'

'Why couldn't you just tell me this before?'

'I was scared. I was just waiting on you to lose interest in me. I figured you would meet someone else while I was home. When that didn't happen, I tried to mess it up by being standoffish and writing less. I thought that would push you away, but it didn't.'

'I see,' I said somberly. 'And the guy I saw you with?'

'He's...He's just safe.'

"That answer didn't sit well with me, but I wasn't going to press her any further. Although I didn't like it, I believed she was telling me the truth about everything. I just had to deal with the fact that I was too perfect or whatever. And although her words made me feel a little better, I was still barely holding it together. I was sad, angry, and defeated. I needed time to process everything I just heard.

'Well, I guess there's nothing left to say, huh?'

'Kaleb, I'm sorry.'

'Yeah, me too. I wanted closure, and I guess you gave me that. Thank you. I have to go now. You take care of yourself, Marcipants.'

"I hung up before she could hear my cry out in anguish. That was the last time I ever talked to her."

"Damn! Punished for being too good of a guy. That's just so messed up. Did you ever see her again?"

"I don't think so. There were times when I saw someone that may have been her, but I could never say for sure."

"Can I ask one last question before we close the book on this story?"

"Can I say no?"

"No."

"I didn't think so."

"Remember you said you felt love for her?"

"You want to know why I didn't tell her back then?"

"Perfect, and a mind reader!"

"Very funny. Well, for one, I believe that when something is felt as deeply as what we felt for each other, it is known, and proclaiming it is just a symbolic gesture. However, I also believe that there is one perfect day in autumn where everything just feels right. The breeze, the sun, the birds, the leaves, the scents. They all come together to form a feeling of euphoria. That is the perfect day to proclaim your love."

"That is absolutely beautiful. You are something else, Kaleb Barnes."

"Thanks. I try."

"So, now what?"

"Um, you leave, I go to bed, and we never talk about this story ever again."

"Come on. The night is young, and this is probably the last night we'll be able to hang out together for a while."

"Seriously? You're going to play that card?"

"Okay, not entirely fair, but it's true."

I was exhausted, but I knew she had a point. I didn't know exactly why she didn't want to go home, but I knew she hated being alone. I also knew that I would miss her annoying visits when she wasn't right across the hall any longer.

I laid back on the couch. "One more hour. Then you have to go. I'm not a night owl like you. But, no more stories. Let's watch television or something."

"Deal! Let's see if there are any romantic movies on."

I shook my head. "You are killing me."

"What? It's our last night."

"And you want to spend it watching a romantic movie?"

"What can I say? I'm a hopeless romantic."

"Yes, yes you are. I doubt I will stay awake for a movie, so if I fall asleep, I trust you can let yourself out. We can touch base about tomorrow, tomorrow afternoon.

"Tomorrow?"

"Going out with Kaje. Remember?"

"Oh, yeah. I forgot all about that."

"Well, consider yourself reminded."

"Does he know I'm leaving?"

I took a deep breath. "No, and you don't know he's leaving either."

"What? Where's he going?

"Well, this is between us, although it won't be much of a secret soon. He signed with a record label, so he'll be across the country for a while, working on his music."

"Oh, my gosh! That's great! How exciting!"

"Yeah, it is."

Monica's excitement quickly subsided. "Oh, but we are both leaving you. Oh, my goodness, that's so terrible. I'm so sorry."

"Don't be. I'll be okay, really. I'm happy for both of you. Besides, it's not like it is permanent."

"Yeah, but still."

"Trust me. I'll be okay. If it comes to the point where I'm not, I'll just move in with you and your mother."

"That would be so much fun! My mom would love you. She's just like me."

"Oh, great. I'm sure she—"

"Ooh, look! The Notebook is on. I love this movie."

I sighed heavily. "Make sure you lock the door when you leave."

"Shh! I love this part."

"Goodnight, Monica."

Chapter 26 - At First Sight
-Kaleb-

I woke up around 10:30 to the sound of a gentle wind blowing. My window was cracked from the night before. The cool night breeze always helped me sleep. Monica must have let herself out at some point during the night. For the first time in a very long time, I couldn't really remember my dreams. It was odd, but at the same time, it was a welcomed break from what I had been waking up from.

I rolled off the couch and headed towards the window. The neighborhood was bustling. I could hear people laughing, dogs barking, children playing, and birds singing what would sadly be some of their final songs until spring came around again. I smiled, took it all in, and let it wash away all my worries. It made me nostalgic for my childhood, when everything was so much more simplistic, and I didn't have a care in the world, other than who to play with when I got outside.

When I was a child, I had a little toy box in my room. It had little stick figures and funny looking birds painted on it. I remember thinking how happy the stick figures looked as they threw their ball to each other and played on their simple looking playground. It was as if that was all they needed to make their life complete. I used to stare at it and pretend I was playing with them. I remember using a red crayon to draw myself on to the playground by the stick figure that was standing alone. I often wondered what ever happened to that toy box. Hopefully, some kid was getting the same joy from it that I did.

I turned some music on, then headed to the shower to get ready for the day. In the shower, I was usually in deep thought or singing. I could get through five to six songs if the hot water held up. I never really considered myself a good singer, but I liked to sing, so I did. I thought about how Marci would always say "If it feels good, do it!" I always loved how she said it. At some point I thought back to the old lady's advice about getting out and becoming one with nature. It was the perfect day to do just that.

I got dressed, ate a little something for breakfast, and headed out the door. It was one of those autumn days where you just had to be outside. It was warm with a light breeze. Leaves fell slowly from the trees, almost as if they were asking me to catch them and soften their final descent. The smell of burning wood filled the air. Summer had finally given up its fight.

I decided to take a walk in the park near my old neighborhood. Growing up, that was always one of my favorite places to visit. It was my first walk in that park in quite some time. It had changed quite a bit over the years. A hospital now sat in the distance beyond the trees, but the main parts were still intact. I went to sit on my favorite bench just to think, relax, and enjoy the day. The past few days seemed like the longest, strangest days of my life. The downtime was just what I needed to unwind and let it all go, if only for that moment.

As I sat on the bench, I closed my eyes and took in everything around me. The sun on my face was warm and pleasant. The wind felt familiar as it blew childhood memories across my face. I inhaled deeply. In the autumn air, beyond the smells of the leaves, I felt a strange feeling I had not felt before. I took it in, nonetheless. It was pleasant, and at the same time, sad. I exhaled my worries away. Butterflies fluttered about, all over the park. I didn't recall ever seeing that before. I clutched my hands on the bench as I inhaled again and took in my surroundings again. Between the feel of the bench, the warmth of the sun, the feel of the wind on my face, and the butterflies, I felt completely immersed in everything around me. I felt like a child experiencing something for the first time. I was lost in a place that I never wanted to leave.

A woman's voice in the distance brought me back to reality.

"Hey, I hope you aren't ignoring me. I'm really sorry about yesterday. You'll never believe where I am. I really wish you were here with me. I miss you. Hopefully I'll see you tonight. I really want to tell you about— Hello? Hello?" She held the phone up and looked at it closely. "Great, not another one."

I slowly walked towards the bench across the way. A lady sat there clutching her necklace. She was covered in sadness. It was the kind of sadness one doesn't recover from easily. I walked towards her hesitantly. That familiar sense of déjà vu enveloped me. I didn't give in to it. Whatever she was going through was really none of my business, but something beckoned me to her side. It wasn't like the normal feelings I feel from other people. It was almost as if I could feel her sadness deep inside me.

"Hello," I said quietly. "Is something wrong?" It was a stupid question. Of course, something was wrong, but I was unsure of what else to say.

She stared at me for a few seconds. "I'm fine," she replied.

I handed her a tissue. "You don't look fine."

She took the tissue and wiped her eyes. "Really, I'm okay. I'll be fine."

I could tell this was not a good time to try to break down her defenses. "Hey, if you want to talk about it, I'll be right over there." I said, pointing to the bench underneath the large maple tree."

She looked at me. Her light brown eyes were doing their best to hold back more tears. "Thank you. You're sweet, but really, I'll be okay," she replied.

I smiled. "Okay, but I'm going to sit on that bench until I know you're okay, and I have lots of time. At least a day or two."

As I hoped, this penetrated her defenses.

She smiled at me. "Okay, maybe I'll see you tomorrow then."

My knees quivered at the sight of her smile. She was the most beautiful woman I had ever seen in my life. There was something about her eyes. I would have waited on that bench for as long as it took. "Alright then, tomorrow it is. Good thing it's warm out. Does it count if I run home and grab a pillow?" I asked jokingly.

Against her will, she laughed. "Thank you."

"For sleeping on a bench? No problem. I've always wanted to see what that was like."

"No, silly. For making me laugh. It's been a long time since I've heard my own laughter."

"It's what I do." I smiled. "Hey, I know you are going through something, so I won't keep bothering you. You obviously came here to be alone. I kind of did the same thing, but If you ever need someone to talk to, I think I'm going to relocate my home to that bench over there."

She laughed. "Is that so?"

"Well, at least until winter. I don't do cold very well."

She winked at me. "Well, maybe you won't have to wait that long."

At those words, my face began to feel warm and my heart felt like it was beating twice as fast. I wanted to say more, but I felt frozen in the moment. It was as if we were alone in the park, the leaves halted their descent, and the breeze paused to observe that moment.

I took the moment to steal another glimpse of her. She was stunning in every way. Her long flowing hair, her soft, smooth skin, and her smile. Oh, that smile. It was enough to make anyone want to be their best self. But it was her eyes that weakened me. I would swear I saw distant worlds in them.

She looked at her phone and sighed in disgust. "I'm sorry. Would you happen to know what time it is?"

"Battery died?"

"Something like that."

I pulled out my phone. The numbers caught me off guard. I paused and shook my head.

"Everything okay?" she asked.

"Yeah, sorry. It's 1:43," I said slowly.

"Oh? That's interesting."

"You're telling me. I've been—"

"I'm sorry. I have to go," she said sadly, realizing that reality beckoned.

"Okay. Well, hopefully we'll meet again. If not in this life, in another," I said, trying my best to say something clever. "Oh, my goodness. That was so corny," I thought to myself.

"Perhaps we will," she said, hiding her rediscovered worry behind a smile. "I'd like that. Same time, same sandbox. Don't be late."

Before I could say anything else, she gathered her things and quickly walked towards the entrance of the park. I watched the wind gently blow her hair as she walked away. I stared on, still lost in the moment, when a sudden gust of wind shook the giant tree and released its hold on its leaves, creating a wall of yellow, orange, and deep red. By the time they had all fallen, I could no longer see her. She was gone.

"Wow! She was absolutely amazing," I said softly. I stood in utter amazement that she even talked to me. She almost seemed too good to be true. I couldn't wait to see her again. What were the chances that we just happened to be in the same park at the same time? Whatever the chances, I knew I planned on going to that park more often, with the hopes of running into her again. "Hopefully it's in this life and not another," I said to myself, mockingly. "Yeesh! What a cornball."

I walked around the park for a little while, before I headed home, I replayed our brief encounter in my head over and over again. I was on cloud nine. I was so happy, I wanted to sing out loud. I smiled and spoke to everyone I passed. Some of them smiled back at me. Some of them looked at me strangely, not understanding why I could possibly be so happy. If they only knew. I just met the girl of my dreams.

Chapter 27 - Beginning of the End
-Kaleb-

As I approached my apartment door, I saw Monica carrying things out of her apartment.

"Going somewhere?" I asked sarcastically.

She rolled her eyes. "Shut up!"

"Need any help?"

"Nope, I got it covered." She looked at me with her eyes squinted. "What the heck is going on with you?"

"What do you mean?"

"You know what I mean. You are glowing."

"Am I? Maybe it's just a beautiful day."

"Yeah, whatever. I'm not stupid. I want to hear all about her later," she said. She made her way down the hallway. "Don't forget to text me the time and place."

I smiled. I was glad I had a glow. I wanted to share this feeling with everyone. I opened my door and walked to the couch. I pulled out my phone and texted Kaje.

> *Man! You are never going to believe what happened to me today. Text me back when you can. Oh, and what time are we meeting*

up tonight?

The phone vibrated almost immediately after I sent the message. It was Kaje.

What happened? You got somewhere on time? LOL! JK. It better be something good. Tankers. 7:00. Don't be late.

I rolled my eyes. Kaje always had jokes. It was all good. Nothing was going to affect me on cloud nine. I texted Monica the time and place, then straightened up my apartment.

When I was satisfied with how the apartment looked, I sat on the couch and thought about the mystery woman from the park. I never even asked her name. I was always so bad at that. Not that it mattered. I'd just have to wait till I saw her at the park again to ask her.

I got up, made something to eat, and decided to chill until it was time to go. The window by the couch was open. The aroma of autumn and the blowing breeze relaxed me once again. I thought about everything that went on during the week. I thought about the crazy dreams. I thought about Tammy and wondered how she was doing. I thought about Rob leaving. I even thought about the old lady on the path. Then I began to think about how things would be different without Monica and Kaje around, and how I would be alone. A twinge of sadness began to wash over me, but I quickly dismissed it and replaced it with thoughts of the mystery woman. I allowed myself to believe that I would meet her and we would live happily ever after. I closed my eyes and played out the whole illustrious fantasy in my head.

I was startled by a knock on the door. I got up and opened it. Monica stood there looking at her phone.

She held it up to show me the time. It was 6:20.

"I guess you changed your mind and don't want to go?" she said.

"Very funny. Your clock isn't right. I just sat down a few minutes ago," I replied.

"Well, you must have dozed off, because it's now 6:21 and we are going to be late. Check your phone if you don't believe me."

I grabbed my phone and looked at it. "What the heck? How is that even possible? I swear I just sat down to relax."

"Don't ask me. I've been waiting for you to text me and tell me you were ready."

"I'm assuming that means we are going together."

"Yes sir."

"Why didn't you just let yourself in like you normally do?"

"Because I was busy and didn't want to bother you."

"Really? You didn't want to bother me? Since when?"

"Since today. Now hurry up and get ready."

I shook my head. "Girl, you are an enigma."

"Says the guy who took a three-hour long, two-minute power nap."

"Whatever. I'll be out in a few minutes. Stay out of my refrigerator."

"Whatever!"

I hurried up and showered, then got dressed. Monica was sitting on the couch with her head in her hands. "Hey, you okay?" I asked.

"Yeah, I'm good."

"Are you sure? You aren't acting like yourself."

"I'm just tired. It was a long day of moving things.

Let's just go. We may actually make it on time if you speed and run every light."

I knew something else was bothering her, but I chose not to press the issue. We arrived at Tankers at exactly 7:01. I parked the car and we got out. Monica started walking quickly towards the entrance.

"Hurry up. We're already late," she yelled back to me.

"Late? We're here. Relax," I yelled back.

I heard a voice softly say. "You're too late."

I looked around me. There was no one around except Monica. I picked up my pace and caught up with Monica.

"Did you hear that?" I asked.

"Hear what?" Monica responded.

"You didn't hear that—. Nothing. Never mind. Let's go."

We walked in. Kaje was sitting at a table near the bar. He waved us over.

Kaje laughed. "I knew I should have told you 6:45."

"Whatever. I'm like three minutes late."

"One of these days, three minutes are going to cost you."

"You done preaching? I'm thirsty."

"Yep, I'm done." Kaje turned to Monica. "What's up? Did he tell you what we are celebrating?"

"He did! Congratulations! I am so happy for you! You must be so excited," Monica said.

"I am. Probably more nervous than excited."

"That will pass, I'm sure. It's just all so new to you now."

"Wait till he starts touring," I said jokingly.

"Yeah, right. I just want to get this one album out. I

can't even think that far ahead," Kaje said.

"Just don't forget where you came from," Monica said in a somewhat sad tone."

"Oh, I won't. I could never do that."

Kaje looked at me, then kind of looked towards Monica, like he was wondering if something was wrong with her. I just gave him a little shrug.

"You okay over there, Monica?" Kaje asked.

"Sorry. Yeah, I'm okay. I was just having a moment. Did Kaleb tell you that I was moving back home to Portland tomorrow?"

"Oh, wow! No, he didn't. I've been so busy we haven't had much time to talk."

"Yeah, I just need to get away and take care of myself for a while. It's not permanent."

"I hope not. Kaleb might not be able to survive on his own."

I laughed. "Whatever. I'll be fine. I'll just replace both of you."

"There's no replacing us. There's nobody like us," Kaje said.

Monica chimed in. "I know that's right, and don't even try to replace me. I'd have to come back and wreak havoc."

"Yeah, and we all know how good you are at that," I said.

"I swear you two act like a married couple," Kaje said.

Monica scowled. "Oh, my God. I just threw up in my mouth."

"Whatever! Don't try to act like you don't want to marry me," I said jokingly.

"You wish. You're like a—"

"I know. I'm like a brother to you. I was joking. Relax."

Kaje just stood there laughing. "He can't marry you, anyway. He met the girl of his dreams today."

"Oh, yeah! He was glowing this afternoon! Alright, dream-lover, tell us all about her, and don't leave out a single detail," Monica said giddily.

I blushed. Just the thought of her made me feel like everything was going to work out.

"Look at him. He is blushing. Aww, isn't that cute," Monica said. "I thought Marci was the girl of your dreams?"

I shot her a disapproving look. "Really?"

"What? Too soon? My bad. Please continue."

I shook my head at her. "I'm not going to go through all the details. That would take too long and this night isn't about me. I'll just tell you that I went for a walk in the park from the old neighborhood and there was a lady sitting on the bench, crying. Hands down, the most beautiful woman I have ever seen in my life. I'm talking Hollywood pretty."

"Get outta here. And you went up and talked to her?" Kaje asked.

"I did. I can't even explain to you where I got the courage from. Everything just felt right. I felt drawn to her."

"So, how did it end? Did you get her number? What's her name?" Monica asked.

Well, I don't know her name because I didn't ask."

"What!?" Monica exclaimed.

"I was enthralled. I am surprised I could even talk at all."

Kaje laughed. "Were you fumbling all over your

words? I've seen that episode before."

"Believe it or not, I played it pretty cool. There was a calmness in the air. She had a calming effect as well."

"So, if you didn't get her name, I would assume that means you didn't get her number," Monica said.

"Nope."

"Then how are you ever going to see her again."

"I know how." Kaje laughed. "He's going to be spending a lot of time at that park, in the future."

"I won't even have to do that. She'll be there waiting on me the next time I go."

"Yeah, okay. Keep dreaming. You know it never works out that way."

"This time is different. Everything about it felt different. You'll see."

Kaje laughed. "Dude, you aren't ever going to see that woman again, unless it's in one of your crazy dreams."

"Oh, I see you got jokes. You'll see. I'm going to find her, and I might even marry her."

"Whoa! Slow down, tiger," Monica said.

Kaje laughed. "And be late to your own wedding."

"Shut up, jackass!" I said jokingly.

Monica stood up with a surprised look on her face. "Wait a minute. Are you guys arguing? I have never heard you two argue, unless it was about who was better, Lebron James or Michael Jordan. And for the record, I think Lebron is way better than Jordan."

I rolled my eyes at her. "Have you ever even seen Jordan play?"

"Well, no. I saw Space Jam though."

Kaje and I both laughed hysterically. Monica's scowled and waved both of us off. "Whatever, jerks!

I'm done with both of you! I'm going to the bathroom," she said as she walked off.

Kaje reached his fist out for a fist bump. "My bad, man. I didn't mean to give you crap about your future wife. I'm kind of feeling some sort of way about leaving you behind, and I guess I'm trying to hide it. Seriously though, I hope you do find her."

"It's all good, man. I've kind of been acting the same way. Going around pretending I'm all good, even though my best friend is leaving and I'm stuck here behind a desk. I wish your future wife could have made it. I would love to meet her."

"I kind of wish she could have too. You'll meet her soon enough though. And for the record, dude, you are crazy talented. You can be whatever you want to be. You just have to find your niche."

"I hear what you are saying. I just don't know where to start. I have no idea what I would even do."

"Make a movie or something. I've told you that before. Better yet, write a book about those crazy dreams you always have. That's gold right there."

I laughed. "That's so true. If only I knew how to write."

"Learn. Take a class. If you want to get from behind the desk, do whatever it takes."

"You're right. I'll give it some thought. If all else fails, I'll just hang out in your entourage and live off your earnings."

Kaje laughed. "Good luck with that!"

"Let's head up to the bar. I need something to drink," I said.

"A Grolsch?"

"A what?"

"A Grolsch!"

We both started cracking up. It was another one of our inside jokes. "Let's go."

As we headed to the bar, a sudden wave of sorrow washed over me and stopped me dead in my tracks. I had a harder than normal time trying to shake it off.

"You good, man?" Kaje asked.

"Yeah, I think so. Sorry," I replied.

I walked slowly and looked around me. The place had started to fill up and get livelier. Across the bar, there was a ruckus. There was a huge guy with fully tattooed arms as big as tanks and a crazy looking haircut. It wasn't quite a mohawk. It almost looked like a shark's fin. He spoke obnoxiously loud and commanded the attention of everyone around him. He looked like he had a few too many already. He was involved in an altercation with some other guy.

"Damn! Don't get in that guy's way," Kaje said.

"I know, right!" I replied.

"That hair though. Talk about FUBAR."

I laughed. "Better not let him hear you say that."

"Right?"

From the side of him, I could see someone's hands reaching out, pulling his arm, trying to get him to walk away. We moved to the other side of the bar, trying to avoid it all. It was when we approached the bar that I noticed who the hands belonged to.

I grabbed Kaje's arm. "It's her!" I said excitedly.

"Who?"

I pointed to a woman standing in the area we were avoiding. "Over there on the other side of the bar. That's the woman from the park!"

"No way! No way! Get the heck out of here! That's

the woman you met at the park?"

"Yep! I told you she was stunning, didn't I?"

"You didn't say she looked that good. And she actually talked to you?"

"Yeah, she did, jackass!" I laughed. "And I described her to you the best I could with words."

"Dude! She is way out of your league!"

Monica walked up and lightly smacked both of us on the back of our heads. "Thanks for leaving me, punks. Who are we ogling at?"

Kaje pointed. "Kaleb's future wife."

Monica let out a loud, obnoxious laugh. "Yeah right! Dream on. Who is that, really? Someone famous?"

I felt like I was in a bit of a trance. I canceled out everything around me and focused on the lady from the park. She looked even more beautiful than she did in the park. She also looked just as sad. I wanted to reach out to her. I wanted to make her smile again. I wanted her to always be happy.

"Hello! Earth to Kaleb. Seriously, who is that?" Monica asked.

"That's the lady from the park," I said slowly.

"Oh, my God! No way!" Monica exclaimed.

"That's what I said," Kaje said.

"Aww. She looks so sad,"

"She does. She looked that way in the park. I was able to make her smile a couple of times though."

"Well, maybe you should go try to again. Poor thing. She looks miserable."

"Maybe I will." I said somewhat confidently. "You know what, I'm absolutely about to."

I straightened my shirt and began to make my way

over to the bar. I could hear Kaje and Monica saying something as a voice came out of the speakers near the dance floor.

"Ladies and gentlemen, we got one of Cleveland's own in the house tonight. Show some love for Zonal! You'll be hearing that name a lot in the upcoming months. Remember you heard him here first at The Tank!"

Cheers erupted from all over the club. The deejay started playing "In the Zone." It was one of Kaje's songs that he made when we were younger. It was always my favorite. I looked back at Kaje and pointed to him in excitement. He smiled back as people surrounded him, shaking his hand, and patting him on his back. It was his moment, and I was as happy as I'd ever been for him.

In all the excitement, I lost track of the woman from the park. I looked around feverishly, but she was nowhere to be found. The place was crowded. I knew there was no way that I was going to find her. I began to make my way back to Monica and Kaje. My face was visibly distraught. I felt a hand grab my wrist. It was Monica.

"I found her. She's over there," Monica said. "But I don't think you should go over there."

"Why not?"

Monica pointed near the exit. "She is standing with some dude. He is huge. Like, the size of two of you."

I looked over. She was standing near the big guy we saw earlier near the bar.

Kaje popped up behind us. "What's up? Did you talk to her?"

"Nah," I replied. My head was down.

"Why not? What's wrong?"

Monica pointed to her and the guy standing by the door.

"Oh, boy! Yeah, probably not a good idea if she is with him," Kaje said.

"Yeah, probably not. Oh, well. It was a nice dream," I said, trying to sound more chipper than I really was.

"Don't worry about it. There are plenty of other fish in the sea," Monica said.

"Warning. Warning. Cliché alert!" Kaje and I both said in unison, then laughed.

Monica rolled her eyes and held her hands up to our faces. "Nice. Double jerk mode activation. Whatever!"

"Let's go get something to drink, y'all. I'm sure if we say we're with Zonal, they'll be on the house, or on him." I smiled.

"Good luck with that," Kaje said. "Hey, Monica, you want a Grolsch?"

"A what?" Monica replied.

Kaje and I looked at each other and laughed.

Monica rolled her eyes. "I hate both of you."

As we walked towards the bar, the lights seemed to quickly flicker. That all too familiar déjà vu feeling washed over me.

"Did you guys see that too?"

"The lights? Yeah, we both saw it," they said.

The lights flickered again, and this time there was a sound like something was sparking. We turned and looked back. The exit sign was sparking and blinking off and on.

"What the heck is going on back there?" I asked.

"Um, I don't know what all the sparking and flickering is about, but your future wife is in a heated argument with her dude," Monica said.

"What? I moved Monica out of the way.

I began to take steps towards them. I needed to see what was going on. I could see them arguing. He was blocking the exit so she couldn't leave. I could hear Monica and Kaje yelling for me to wait.

"Do something," a familiar voice called out.

A familiar, long forgotten feeling deep inside me began to take over. I turned and looked back at Monica and Kaje. "She needs me," I mouthed.

"Kaleb! Hold up! Just wait!" Kaje yelled out.

"Kaje! Wait! I'm going to get security," Monica screamed.

I turned and ran towards them. He had grabbed her arm and was twisting it. She screamed out in pain.

"Do something!" the voice called out.

He raised his hand as if he was going to hit her. I ran towards him, jumped in the air, and kicked him right in his face, knocking him off his feet. "Leave her the hell alone!" I yelled.

She looked at me. She was as surprised to see me as I was to see her again. But there was something else about the way she looked at me. She seemed more surprised than I would have expected. She mumbled something about a story.

We exchanged smiles, and for a moment, we were lost in each other's gaze. Everything about the moment felt familiar, felt right. I reached out my hand to hers. She instinctively reached out to mine.

"The hell? Who the hell is this? Is this your mystery guy?" The big guy laughed as he reached out and grabbed my shirt, pulling me away from her.

"No! You don't know what you're talking about. Let

him go, Shark!"

"Didn't I tell you he'd better be a big motherf—"

"Shark, leave him alone!" She screamed.

The lights began to flicker more rapidly than before. People in the crowd panicked and started heading for the exits. I grabbed his hand and tried to pull it off of me. It wouldn't budge. I took a swing at him. It landed square on his jaw. He didn't budge. He looked at me, laughed, and punched me square in my face. I fell to the ground. My head throbbed.

I could hear Monica scream out. "Kaleb!"

"You messed with the wrong dude!" Kaje yelled.

Out of nowhere, I saw Kaje fly in and hit the guy with a flurry of punches. The big guy stumbled. I struggled to my feet. My vision was blurry, but I had to help Kaje. I took another swing at the big guy while he was stumbling, but I missed. I felt a punch to the side of my head. I heard screaming. I tried to get up, but I couldn't. I saw Kaje get hit again and again. I wanted him to go down, but he just kept trying to fight back.

The lady from the park jumped on his back. "Shark, stop it. You're killing him!"

He flung her off his back and continued whaling on Kaje. I watched punch after punch land on Kaje. I tried to crawl towards him, but to no avail. The punches finally stopped, and over me loomed a large figure. I heard a deafening scream, felt a thump, then saw nothing but darkness.

Chapter 28 - Fait Accompli Dreamscape
-Kaleb-

I blink my eyes into focus. I turn to look around me. There is darkness all around, but I can see clearly. There is nothing above me, nothing below me. I feel weightless, yet anchored to something, or someone. I am neither warm, nor cold. I am not scared. I feel welcomed and safe. I look around again to get my bearings. There is a dim light shining from something in the distance. It is moving closer to me. It is an outline of someone. It is her. I can feel her presence.

This place...it feels so familiar. It is nowhere, yet it is everywhere. It is our place. Our place we share within each other. It is the place we know there is no escape from. A place there is no surrender, yet we journey here freely.

Is this really happening?

I make my way to her. The dim light enhances her beauty. She has never been more beautiful to me than she is in this moment. I move to steal another glance, but my nerves do not allow an effort worthy of success. I smile to hide my nervousness. She returns my smile with a soft inviting smile of her own. We speak, but not in words, in love. Who is this lovely creature? Why do I adore her? Why does my soul feel so connected to hers?

In what seems like no time at all, I am committed to her and her to me. As we dance our dance of love, we move in effortless agreement. Our bodies are so closely intertwined that we are one with everything around us.

Is this happening? Can she feel how nervous I am? Can she feel my heart pounding? Then, as if she was guiding my hand with hers, I reach for her face and gently turn her gaze to mine. Her skin is soft against my hand. My goodness, is this really happening? She slowly opens her eyes and looks up at me. Consumed by her essence as our eyes truly meet in what feels like the very first time...again, it is then that I truly know, this is really happening.

A warm light emanates all around us. Is it starlight or her light? It makes no difference. It envelops me and I invite it. There is nothing she could offer that I would not gladly accept. The feeling is overwhelming and yet I want, no, I need more.

How much can I consume? How long has it been? How long until it swallows me whole. Time has no meaning anymore. For what seems like forever, we stand, looking over this vast star-filled void in time and space that belongs to us alone. I hold her in my arms, feeling her warmth, mesmerized in her glow, lost in her being.

In the far distance, a light slowly begins to appear. Suddenly, I can feel her warmth slowly start to dissipate. As I reach to hold her closer to me, she is there, but she is not. I reach for her again. My hand strangely goes right through her. Panicked, I look at her as the darkness seems to melt her away. Her face fills with angst and worry. She reaches for me, to no avail. She is slowly fading away. We are no longer one. We are no longer two. She is gone, and I am lost.

Part Two

Chapter 29 - Despondence
~Penny~

*I look in the mirror through the eyes
of the child that was me.*
- Judy Collins

"Penny, what do you remember about that night?"

"How many times do I have to tell you? There is nothing to remember, only cold and darkness. I don't want to remember anything about that night. There was nothing but pain. You want me to grieve? I don't grieve. I don't like grieving. Grief doesn't bring me memories. Grief is just my losses. Grief is all of my unexplained failures.

"I don't even know why I'm here. You can't possibly understand me. Nobody can. Have you ever just wanted someone to understand all of you? Just forget it. I don't even know why I'm here. Please just leave me alone. Leave me alone!"

Chapter 30 - Josie Knows Best
~Penny~

"Oh, bollocks!"

"Penelope Johnson! You mind your mouth."

I hated my name. I hated even more when she used my entire name.

"Josie, please stop acting like my mother. I am a grown woman."

"Then maybe you should start acting like one."

"And what does that entail again? Going out on a date with a different guy every night?"

"I'll have you know, who, and how often I date, is none of your concern. How about you dump that so-called boyfriend of yours, find someone who treats you right, and go out and enjoy your life every now and then."

"He's not my boyfriend, and I enjoy my life plenty."

"Bollocks!"

"Josephine Marie Adams! Who needs to mind their mouth now?"

Josie just waved me off. "I'm the older one. I can talk like that. Besides, you are just mimicking me and things you saw on television. You were too young to even remember England."

"That doesn't make me any less English. I remember enough."

"No, Penny. I suppose it doesn't, but stick to your American foul words. It's what you grew up on."

My father was born and raised in the United States. My mum was raised in a small county in southeast England. They met at a writers conference a few years before I was born. They both said it was love at first sight. Mum knew she would never get the family's blessing to marry Dad, so they eloped a month after meeting each other. When Mum's family found out, most, if not all of them disowned her for marrying outside of her race. Dad's family wasn't too happy with it either. Not so much because of Mum's race, but because of the problems they thought it would bring.

Mum would always say, "There's no question that love can't answer, no problem that love can't solve."

After the accident, my half-sister Josie went to live with her biological father in Devonshire. I bounced around from family member to family member here in the states. After all of them decided that they couldn't deal with me any longer, Josie moved to the States to look after me.

My memories of my childhood were scattered. While I remembered some things, other things escaped me, only showing themselves as cruel, fading glimpses every now and then. Josie was my only constant, and she did her best to help me remember things from our childhood.

She walked over and stood over me. "Have you been sleeping? You look tired. You know you need to sleep. What are you going to do today? You plan on sitting around and doing nothing? Why don't you get out and get some sun? You're starting to take on my complexion, you know."

"Nag much? I don't need sleep, and there's sun coming through the window," I replied dryly. "Besides, I'll never look that pasty."

Josie scratched her nose with her middle finger. "You know bloody well the sun is not doing a thing for you while you sit in here. You don't need to be so difficult, you know. I'm just trying to help you."

"I know. I just need a break from people telling me how I should live my life. Besides, you've been here all weekend. Now you're here again straightening up, and the house is already clean. If you want me to get out of the house that bad, I will. If it will stop you from nagging me."

"First off, I do not nag. And secondly, this house is never clean. Or else I would not be here."

"Is that the only reason you're here?"

"Penny, stop it. You know I worry about you. You can't go on like this. You have to get out there and live your life. You're young, talented, and not to mention, beautiful. Which you obviously got from Mum."

I shot her a cold look.

"I'm just saying, Penny. You're wasting your life away, sitting in this house day after day."

"It is what it is."

"Why do you always say that? Of course, it is what it is, until it isn't."

"I'm fine. I manage."

"That's the problem. You're just managing. You could be doing so much more. Are you even writing anymore? You know your father would want you to write."

"Don't mention my father!" I shouted angrily.

Jose's expression changed to a worried one. She grabbed her phone and examined it. She breathed a sigh of relief.

"Calm down, Pen. You know I'm right. Just think about it, okay?"

"I do write," I said dismissively.

"Oh, come off it. You know what I mean, Pen. Real stories, like the ones you used to write. Not those dark, sad, confusing snippets that you write these days."

"Yeah, okay," I responded, knowing I had no plans on changing a thing.

Alexandria walked in from the living room and plopped down next to me. "Aunt Penny, how come you don't have a television?"

"Well, Alex, you see—"

"Alex, let's let Aunt Penny rest. She has a long day ahead of her. Isn't that right, Penny?"

"Yep, sure do," I said dismissively.

"Okay," Alexandria said. "Can I have my tablet back now?"

Josie responded. "Soon, lovie. Wait till we get to the car. Go grab your things."

"Okay, Mummy."

Josie shot me a disappointed look and shook her head. I shrugged my shoulders. I knew she hated when I did that.

Alexandria returned from the other room with her things. Josie knelt down to help her put her backpack on. She whispered something in her ear.

Josie smiled. "We're off, Penelope. Have a lovely day."

"Aunt Penny, will you write me a story next time I come over?" Alexandria said.

I shot Josie an evil look. She knew exactly what she was doing. She smiled back with a devilish grin and winked. She knew I couldn't say no to Alexandria. "Sure, Alex. I can do that."

"Promise?"

"I'll promise if you promise to help write it."

"Yay! We'll write the best story ever!"

Josie reached her hand out to Alexandria. "Come along now, Alex. Mummy has errands to run. Oh, and I left you some flowers on the kitchen table, Penny. Your favorite. Cheers, love."

Chapter 31 - Mood Rings and Sunnies
~Penny~

I needed to clear my mind, so I headed down to the fitness room. Lifting weights was the only thing that really seemed to clear my mind. There was no thinking. It was just me, my music, and my weights. I had only been lifting a few months, mainly just following routines that I found in magazines. My bench press was 125 lbs. My deadlift was 250 lbs. Not bad for someone who had just started lifting.

I spent more time in my fitness room than I spent in any other room in the house. It was my sanctuary. I tried to do the gym thing once, but that just led to drama that I didn't need, and I don't deal with humans particularly well, so I had a gym put in at home.

After I finished up, I came upstairs. Josie was waiting for me in the kitchen.

I looked at her with disdain. "Seriously?"

"We need to get you out of this house. How about we go do a little shopping?"

"How about, I don't want to do any shopping."

"Oh, come on, Penny. It'll be like old times. Let's

buy whatever we want."

"Really, Josie? Why must you constantly do this? Why can't you just leave me alone?"

"Because you're my sister, and I love you. I want us to be able to talk and laugh like we did before—"

"Before what? Before the flashbacks started?"

"You don't know that those aren't completely accurate, Penny."

"I do know that, and you know it too. I'm just the one who is willing to accept it. So, you can keep living in your fantasy world, thinking everything is okay, and I'll keep living in my world where things are real, and will never be okay again!"

Josie approached me and attempted to hug me. I turned away from her and walked away. "Just leave me alone, okay. I just want to be alone."

I turned back and looked at her. Her face saddened as she stared at me. I could see her eyes had begun to water. She always tried her best to act strong. She always struggled showing emotion or watching people get emotional. I knew I hurt her this time, and I immediately felt like crap because of it.

"Well, I guess I'll check on you later. I put your flowers in a vase for you," she said. She walked to the door and opened it.

"You pronounced that wrong. It's vase. There's no z in it," I said. My face cracked the smallest of smiles.

She looked up at me and smiled. "Screw you, Penelope Johnson. Did I pronounce that correctly?"

We hugged and held the embrace for quite a while. She always wanted to hug all my troubles away. If only it was that simple.

"So, does this mean, you'll go to the shopping

centre with me?" Josie asked.

"Josie, you know what happened the last time I—"

"Don't worry about it. That was a long time ago. You're much stronger now. Just remember what we practiced."

"And the other thing?"

"Pfft. When was the last time that happened? It doesn't affect me or Alexandria. Maybe it doesn't happen anymore."

"You're right. It doesn't. Why do you think that is?"

"I don't know. Maybe we're just immune to you."

I sighed. "I guess, but at the first sign of it, I'm out of there."

"It'll be fine. Oh, that reminds me. I left something on the table for you."

I glanced over at the table. "What the hell is that ugly thing?"

"It's a mood ring. It'll help you see when you're being a grumpy old fart."

"I'm not wearing that."

"Come on, Penny. Give it a go. Better safe than sorry."

I grabbed the ring off the table. "I can't believe you think this thing would even work."

"Of course, it works. It's science. Put it on and let's see."

"Fine," I said. I slid the ring on my index finger.

"See! It's working!" Josie said excitedly.

"What are you talking about? It didn't even change. It's still black."

"That's because of your current mood. Here let's look at the chart. Black means that you are tense or nervous."

"It also means that the crystal is broken. Oh, and look at that, it can mean I'm being harassed. Maybe it is working after all."

Josie rolled her eyes. "Well, I guess you'll just have to get in a better mood so we can see if it changes."

"Doubtful," I said dismissively.

"Stop being so negative, Pen."

"You know I hate when you say that. I'm just being real."

"Real negative," she mumbled.

"Then how about I just don't go. I can keep my negative self right here and not bother anyone."

"Penny, stop. Let's just go back to the part where you agreed to go to the shopping centre with me."

I stifled a smile. "So, was that before I agreed to put this ugly ring on?"

"Penelope Johnson! Was that a smile I saw trying to break through?"

"Nope."

"Liar. Your ring almost turned blue." She winked and looked down at the chart. "See there. The color of optimism. Oh, and flirtatious! Fancy meeting a real bloke at the shopping centre, do you?"

"I don't know what a bloke is, and my current friend suits me just fine. He serves his purpose."

"Friend, huh? Still going with that? And exactly what purpose does he serve?"

"He's low-maintenance. He lets me be me. There's no pressure to be anything I don't want to be."

Josie shook her head. I could tell she was holding back a lecture that I've heard a hundred times before about what she rescued me from, how much more I could be doing with my life, and how much better than him I could be doing.

"Maybe you can find another man for your collection," I said facetiously.

She smiled devilishly. "You never know."

I shook my head at her. "I'm going to get ready. Try not to straighten up anything. I'm sure the maid will be here tomorrow too."

She coughed really loudly. "Smartarse!"

"I heard that."

I got ready and came out to the living room. Josie was straightening the pillows on the couch. I cleared my throat to let her know I was ready. She looked me up and down. "I said we were going to a shopping centre, not a bloody funeral."

I looked her up and down. "I thought you said we were going to a mall, not a strip club."

"Oh, you're such a wanker. Can we just go?"

"I'm waiting on you."

"Alright then. We're off. Grab your sunnies. It's bright out there. Not that you would know, with all these dark curtains drawn."

I rolled my eyes. "I'll grab my sunglasses," I said, really emphasizing the word, just to get under her skin.

Chapter 32 - The Shopping Centre
~Penny~

"This traffic is ridiculous. Why did I agree to this again?" I asked.

"Because you know it's a good idea," Josie said, clearly annoyed with me.

"It was a good idea to sit in traffic?"

"Oh, hush, Penny. If you don't have anything positive to say, don't say anything."

"I'm just saying."

"Saying what? There you go with those silly American phrases again. How can you be just saying when you already said it?"

"Damn, you're old."

She waved me off. "Only as old as you make me out to be."

"Why don't we just go to the other mall? There's no traffic going that way."

"Bite your tongue. I would not be caught dead in that rubbish mall. What would we even do there? Count the number of closed stores?"

"All the stores will be closed at Northern Summit

because it will be closed by the time we get there."

Josie let out a hefty sigh. "Fine. The rubbish mall it is. Let's hope they haven't closed the few good stores they had left."

"We could always just go back home."

Josie quickly changed the subject. "Do you remember the time we went to Niagara Falls and you wouldn't get too close to the rails because you were scared you were going to fall in?"

"Nope. No memory of it at all." I lied. I just didn't want to talk about it.

"When you eventually overcame your fear, it was the first time I realized how special you are. All those people you affected. It was amazing to watch it—"

"Can we change the subject, please?"

"What shall we talk about? Your love life? Or lack thereof?"

"I have no love life. True love doesn't exist."

"Oh, come off it, Pen. You know it exists. You just have to find it. Or hope it finds you. It'll never find you if you keep hiding from it."

"I'm not hiding from anything."

"Of course, you aren't. That's why you stay holed up in the house all day," she said sarcastically.

"How about we talk about your love life? Is that what you call what you have going on?"

"Oh, blimey, let's not go there. I'm just having a bit of fun. I don't have time for love. It's too messy."

"But I should have a love life? Why wouldn't it be messy for me?"

"It absolutely would, but nowhere near as messy. You don't have the baggage I have. You're still sweet, innocent, and unjaded."

"I don't know about that. You know, you aren't helping your case with all this."

"I'm just saying you should keep your heart open to the possibility of it. If he's the right one, it will be worth the mess."

"If you say so. Hey, whatever happened to that guy you were dating a while back? He had an animal name."

"Wolf?"

I snickered. "Yeah, him."

"You're one to laugh at a boyfriend's name."

"At least his is actually a nickname. Don't try to get out of answering the question."

"It turns out Wolf and I weren't right for each other."

"And why is that?"

"He's married and I'm a crap 'other' woman."

"Was he your number one?"

"Hell no."

"Then why did it matter?"

"Because I'm too competitive, and I have to be number one."

"How long did you know he was married?

"For a while."

"So, what took you so long to end it?"

"I don't know. I kind of liked the bloke."

"So, you knowingly continued to be the other woman?"

"Don't be so absolute. You can be the other woman without being made to feel like the other woman."

"I guess."

"Anyway, just make sure you are never the other woman. You deserve so much more than that."

"So do you, Josie."

Josie flashed a half-hearted smile. "Well, shall we go and show this dump what style is all about?" She looked me up and down. "Well, at least one of us can."

I shook my head. "You're such a snob."

"Oh, please. I'm nothing of the sort, although, this place would make anyone feel like a snob."

We walked in through a department store. Josie wanted to avoid as much of the mall as possible. I did as well, so I didn't complain. She tried on outfit after outfit. Each time she came out and asked for my opinion, I just gave her a thumbs up. I knew that she was going to buy them no matter what I said.

"Can we go soon?" I yelled over the dressing room door.

"We just got here. Aren't you going to try anything on?" she yelled back.

"Wasn't planning on it."

Josie walked out of the dressing room. "Come on, Penny. You've got to try something on."

"I was going to get some leggings from the fitness store."

"Ugh! Don't you ever feel like wearing something other than workout clothes? Wait, don't answer that."

She handed me all her things and headed towards the dresses.

I rolled my eyes. "Don't worry about your things. I'll just hold on to them."

She examined a dress, then forcefully swiped it to the side and looked at the next one. She picked up an all-black dress with pink flowers, held it up to the light, and then held it against me.

"Perfect! You've got to try this on."

I stared at her.

"Please, Penny. For me?"

I put her stuff down and snatched the dress from her. "Just this one thing," I said.

"Oh, stop being so mardy."

I got undressed and slipped into the dress. I could hear Josie fussing on the other side of the door. "Has the body of a goddess, but wears nothing but workout clothes. If I had that body, I would—"

"I can hear you, ya know."

"I'm just saying," she said mockingly.

"Whatever."

"I'll be right back. I'm going to go pick out the perfect boots for that dress."

"Can't you just wait?"

I heard the door in the next stall close. I sighed as I turned back to the mirror. The dress was really pretty, and for some reason, it had a scent that smelled really lovely. It reminded me of happier times. In the mirror, I noticed my ring changed to an amber color. I let my hair down and twirled around. I smiled. I felt carefree, like I was a kid again. I grabbed the bottom of the dress, twirled, and smiled. It was such a foreign feeling. I could hear the person in the other dressing room laughing with glee.

As I spun around, I noticed the reflection in the mirror was not my own. A beautiful little girl twirled along with me in tall beautiful flowers. She was in some sort of beautiful countryside. She mimicked my movements with exact precision. I stopped and looked behind me, then looked back at her. She smiled and waved. I slowly put my hand up and waved. She smiled at me. I studied her for a few seconds. She studied me back. There was something very familiar about her. She turned and looked behind her. Her smile immediately turned to worry and she quickly ran off. The mirror returned to normal, and I saw my own reflection again.

You would think I would have been a bit freaked out, but for some reason I wasn't. I wasn't sure what just happened. My first thought was that I was on one of those prank shows. I quickly changed back into my clothes, set the dress down, and started to walk out. I turned and looked back at it. It was almost like the dress was calling out to me. I picked it up and smelled it again. The scent was heavenly, but I had no recollection of what the scent was and why it invoked such strange feelings.

Suddenly, the mirror began to vibrate and fill with eerie black smoke. A feeling of uncontrollable fear began to take hold of me. I opened the door as fast as I could. The lady in the stall next to mine screamed in horror. Everything appeared to be going dark.

I screamed out. "Josie! Josie, where are you!? I need you!" I ran out of the store as fast as I could. I could hear someone yell something to me, but I kept running. I was in full-fledged panic mode. I slowed down and walked past each store, looking for Josie, occasionally calling her name. I couldn't find her anywhere. I felt like I was suffocating. It felt like all the walls in the mall were closing in on me. I had to get out of there, so I started running again. I felt like something was coming for me and it was close.

I ducked into one of the abandoned stores and hid, clutching the dress. I cried out for Josie, but she didn't come. My breathing became labored and I couldn't catch my breath. I closed my eyes and sat in the darkness. I faintly heard Josie calling for me, but I couldn't catch my breath enough to respond.

"Penny! Penny!"

"I'm...here..."

Josie placed her hand on my shoulder. "Oh, Penny. Breath, love. It's okay. Just relax."

I was panic-stricken and struggling to relax. Josie wrapped her arms around me and whispered.

"Mother's earth."

"F—"

"Come on, Pen. You have to calm down. Mother's earth."

"Father's...heaven," I said reluctantly.

"Mother's earth."

"Father's heaven."

Chapter 33 - The Whole World Smiles
~Penny~

Josie sauntered into the kitchen. "Good morning, sunshine! Up all night again?"

I sat there and stared at her. I was still angry from the day before.

She smiled as if everything was fine. "You know, they say company goes great with a cuppa."

"You know what else goes great with coffee? Silence."

"Oh, Penelope. Don't be like that. You can't stay mad at me forever, you know. Besides, you really shouldn't be mad at me at all."

"You left me!" I shouted.

"I did nothing of the sort. I walked away to get you some boots. And for the record, I found the cutest thigh high boots for you. You were going to look amazing. Any-who, when I walked back, you were clutching that dress and running out of the store like a bat out of Hades. I called out to you, but you just kept going. You nearly gave that poor, overweight security guard that was chasing after you, a heart attack. Took me a good minute to convince him to leave you be and let me take care of it. So, I paid for the dress, and sadly, not the boots. Did I mention how cute they were? Then I walked up and down that terrible mall looking for you. I barely heard you calling out to me. Lucky for you, I have great hearing."

I just kept staring at her. I wanted to stay mad, but after what she explained to me, I really couldn't.

"Penny, I'm sorry. I shouldn't have walked away. I thought everything was fine. You seemed to be doing fine."

"Actually, I was. I was doing better than I'd been doing in a while. That ugly ring even changed colors."

"Is that so?"

"Yeah, it was goldish."

She grabbed the little chart off the table and examined it. "Hmm, mixed emotions or surprise. Were you surprised at how you were feeling?"

I hesitated before answering. I wasn't sure I wanted to give her any more reasons to be concerned about my mental status. "I kind of experienced something in the dressing room."

She leaned closer. "Experienced something?"

"Yeah. Something in the mirror. It was a reflection."

"Well of course it was, silly. That's what mirrors do."

"Do you want to hear the story or not?" I griped.

She made a gesture of zipping her lips, locking them, and tossing away the key.

"Well, I tried on the dress. I liked it. It reminded me of the dresses we had when we were kids. It had this scent to it. I'm not sure what the scent was, but it brought a rush of memories or something. When

I looked into the mirror, the reflection was not my own. It was a little girl mimicking my movements."

"Perhaps a younger version of yourself?"

"I don't think so. She didn't look like me. I thought the store was playing some sort of prank on me."

"What happened next?"

"She ran off, then a black smoky substance filled the mirror."

"The black stuff? Is that what triggered everything?"

"It is. I hadn't felt fear like that in a long time. I just had to get out of there. That's why I ran. You probably think I'm crazy, don't you?"

She reached over and hugged me. "Well, of course I do, but not because of that. I'm just sorry you had to experience that all by yourself."

"Can I ask you a silly question?"

"Of course."

"Did you spray something on the dress? Like, Mum's old perfume or something?"

"Oh, heavens, no. I wouldn't spray that on my worst enemies. You don't remember it? We all hated it. Dad used to call it 'old woman's perfume.'"

Josie got a good laugh out of that. I smiled and thought about all the things I wished I could remember. "Can I ask you another question?"

"Of course, love."

"Why don't you think I'm crazy? If you told me that happened to you, I would think you were crazy."

"Let's just say, I've seen my share of crazy things, and that doesn't even scratch the surface. This world isn't always what it seems. You've been through a lot. I'm just here to help you get through it all."

"And to keep the house clean."
"Well, you are a bit of a skiver."
"What? You hussy!"
"Twit!"
"Ass-clown."
"What? What the hell does that even mean?" Josie rolled her eyes. "Americans."

She put her arm around me and pulled me close. I rested my head on her shoulder.

"Penny, do you remember when we were on holibobs, and Mum and Dad took us to that fair on the beach? You wanted to wear your dress, but Dad told you it wasn't a good night for a dress. When we got to the fair, you pouted the whole time. You didn't want to ride any of the rides or play any of the games. You were being just downright awful. Dad wanted to leave. None of us were having a good time, and the fair just seemed boring and lifeless. Then, all of a sudden, Mum had an idea. She took you to the car. When you came back, you had the biggest smile on your face and the prettiest dress I had ever seen.

"You walked around the fair, smiling and waving at everyone. You laughed as you skipped along the boardwalk. We rode the carousel, the Ferris wheel, and the giant slide. We played games and ate all the sweet food Mum and Dad would let us eat. There was excitement in the air everywhere you went. The entire fair was full of laughter and happiness. The lights shone brighter, the air felt lighter, and everything felt perfect.

"The best part of the night was when that band started to play and you ran over and danced. You lost yourself in the music and danced to your heart's content. Then, the most amazing thing happened. People from all over the fair flocked to the area just to dance with you. Hundreds of people surrounded you, and you all danced like there was no tomorrow. Dad said it was the most phenomenal thing that he had ever witnessed."

Tears streamed down my face. "Why are you telling me this?"

"Because I want you to know the power you have. I know it sounds cliché, but when you smile, the whole world will smile with you."

I wiped the tears from my face. "I'm sorry, Josie. I know I've been such a pill lately. I just feel lost. Half the time I don't even know which direction I'm facing. Sometimes I feel strong enough to push forward, and other times it's a battle just to get out of bed. I try to put on this brave face, but inside I just feel like I'm falling apart and just trying to keep up with life, when all I want is a quiet place to somehow figure out how to turn off my mind."

"It's okay, Pen. The brave face is what matters. It means that you're trying. Everything we do as humans is all a front. It's the juxtaposition of public and personal personas. At some point in our Venn diagram, we overlap. In the moment we are one thing, upon reflection, we are another, and we constantly tell ourselves stories to make sense of it all."

I shot her a confused look. "Well, I'm just going to say Okay because you aren't making any sense."

"Oh, you are such an arse! Did you lose the plot? Do I need to break that down for you?"

"No, smartass. I get it. I just don't know what to do with that."

"I'm sure you will when the time is right."

"I guess. Cryptic much?"

"Oh, whatever. You're the queen of cryptic. Speaking of, I see you got the book I left out for you. Did you open it?"

"I opened it and read a few pages last night. It was rather...interesting, to say the least. Looks like Mum's writing."

"Interesting is one way of putting it. Proper weird, if you ask me. That was Mum and Dad's book. I remember they used to write in it together, but no one else was allowed to touch it. Dad used to hide it away when they were done."

I held the book up and examined it. It was a really old book. Much larger than a normal book. The cover was leather with a golden emblem of a tree, and six spots where it would appear some sort of jewels went. The edges of the pages were gold, like an old Bible. The pages seemed to go on forever. "I've never seen a book like this before. Where did you find it?" I asked.

"It's called a tome. I found it in Dad's study. It was a bit hidden. Nowhere near where he kept his other books, but I saw him hide it a few times."

I carefully flipped through the pages. "It seems a bit random. There's no page numbers or chapters. It looks more like a journal than a novel. It is only half finished."

Josie's head dropped. "I guess they never got to finish it. I thought maybe you could—"

"Josie, please don't do this again. I'll write when I'm ready. I just haven't been feeling it."

"Okay. I won't press the issue any longer."

"Thank you."

Her voice got softer. "Have you been to see Dad?"

"No."

"And Mum?"

"No."

"Maybe you should. Maybe drop off some flowers or something. You need to make peace with everything. You need to grieve. Maybe it will give you some clarity."

"Josie, I'm just not ready yet."

"Just give it some thought. That's all I'm asking. That's the last I'll say of it."

"I will. I promise."

"Well, I'd better be off. I've got to pick up the munchkin from Himself.

"Do you ever call him by his name?"

"For what? He knows who he is."

"Give her kisses for me."

"Of course, I will. Think about getting out of the house and enjoying the weather. It's a beautiful Indian summer."

"It's no spring," I said somberly.

"No, it's not, but it has a beauty of its own."

"I suppose it does."

Josie smiled. "Penny, I'm proud of you."

I smiled back at her, but didn't say anything. Josie pointed to my ring. "Oh! Would you look at that? Bluish-green. Someone is content and at peace. Cheers, love."

Chapter 34 - Discovered Treasures
~Penny~

I finished my workout. I hated leg day. It was hell. I probably overdid it, but that's what I told myself every workout, and yet, I kept coming back for more. I deemed it a necessary evil for my sanity.

I laid on the bench and stared at the ceiling fan. I locked on to one blade and watched it circle over and over again. I found myself mesmerized by its spinning and drifted into deep thought. I thought about the incident in the dressing room. I questioned if I even saw what I thought I saw. I thought about some of the things Josie said and how things had started to feel a little better. Things had felt so abnormal for so long, I wondered if life could ever feel normal again.

I felt melancholic, but not sad. Melancholy was a feeling that I invited in. In an odd way, it helped me feel present. It allowed me to think of things on my own terms. To be happy that things, sad or not, actually happened. It was cathartic for me in a way, reflective more than anything. It was like I was looking back on my life like a movie and choosing what parts I want shown in the montage while the music played. I used to use music to try and simulate that feeling, but I found that the true essence of the feeling came from just being in the moment.

As I drifted deeper in thought, I heard a pounding on the door. Anger quickly took hold of me. I knew exactly who it was. The pounding started again. I charged upstairs and forcefully opened the door.

"What up, babe? Miss me?" He leaned in to kiss me, but I shoved him away.

"Why were you pounding on my door?" I said angrily.

"I figured you couldn't hear me."

"Did it ever occur to you that I may not have been home?"

"Come on, babe. When are you ever not at home?"

I hated that he was right. "That's not the point. You don't bang on my door like that."

"Well, excuse me. It's not like I can text or call. I just figured I would come see how things were. You don't come to the boxing gym or my fights anymore. I'm really missing your energy at my fights, ya know."

"That was a long time ago, and you know I hate boxing."

"Yeah, so you say. I remember when you couldn't get enough of it."

There was a time when I tried to get into whatever it took to dull my pain. I met Joey at the local boxing gym. He was a local up-and-coming boxer. That was before he shattered his hand in a street fight. His career went downhill pretty fast after that. Now he only fights in underground street fights. He spiraled out of control and took me right along with him. The sad truth was, I willingly went down the spiral with him. I thought I could fix him, but I couldn't even fix myself. It was Josie who rescued me from that whole mess.

"Is there a particular reason you're here?" I asked.

"I just missed you. That's all," he replied.

"Okay, now what's the real reason?"

"Well, the boys are coming to town this weekend and I was wondering if you wanted to come celebrate with us."

"Celebrate what?"

"You'll see. It's a surprise."

I sighed. "I don't like surprises. Where is this celebration supposed to take place?"

"One of the local clubs. Not sure which one yet."

"You know that's not my scene anymore."

"I know. I'm just putting it out there. I have a feeling you'll change your mind."

"I'll let you know."

"Cool. You're looking all swole. What did you work today?"

"Legs."

"You still working? I could go for another leg session."

"No, I'm done and you need to go. I have things I need to do."

He moved really close to me. "You sure you don't want company, babe?"

I moved away. "Yes, I'm sure. I'll catch up with you later."

"Sure thing, babe."

I hated when he called me that. It made my skin crawl. I opened the door and sent him on his way. I could feel a cold chill from outside and dark clouds loomed in the sky. I decided to stay in and relax. I would have to enjoy autumn another day.

    I grabbed my notebook and a pen. I wasn't really in a writing mood, but I'd hoped to rekindle that melancholic feeling from earlier and write a few lines. I jotted down a few sentences, then quickly crossed them out. I sighed and closed the notebook in frustration.

    I headed to Dad's study. I hadn't been in there in a while. Since Josie found that tome, I was curious to see what else I could find. I rummaged through papers on his desk. Some looked like unfinished chapters. Some were just papers with his name written in cursive over and over again. He used to do that when he was bored or when he couldn't concentrate. He used to tell me that I should always use pen and paper to write. It would help me become one with the story. I never knew what he meant by that.

    Underneath the papers was Dad's first novel. I turned it over to look at the picture on the back. He looked so happy. I remember trying to read it as a child and not being able to understand any of it. I set it aside and continued to rummage through things. I looked around the bookshelves. One shelf had all his books and the other had all of Mum's. The lowest shelf was empty, save for a little book of silly stories I wrote in elementary school. It laid flat on the shelf. It was just notebook paper stapled together. Dad would always say "I'm saving this shelf for you, so you better get started." I grabbed the book and slowly flipped through it. I smiled as I read all the silly little stories. Half of them made no sense at all. I used to illustrate my own stories with little crayon drawings. Dad said that maybe I'll follow in Mum's footsteps and write children's books.

I flipped to the end of the book and noticed that a page was torn out. I couldn't, for the life of me remember what story used to be there. I set the book aside. I thought that Alex would get a kick out of it seeing my old stories when she came over again. On the shelf, underneath where my book was, was another small book. It looked somewhat similar to the tome that Josie found. I flipped through the pages of the book. The stories were identical to the ones in the tome. There was a Polaroid picture nestled between the pages where the story ended and the blank pages began. I flipped the picture over. It was an old family picture of Dad, Mum, and me standing by a tree. I wondered why Josie wasn't in it. I couldn't recall seeing a picture without her in it. I made a mental note to ask her when she came back.

Chapter 35 - Slumber Party
~Penny~

I laid in my bed and flipped through Dad's first novel. Josie quietly slipped into the room. "I see someone has been rummaging around Dad's study," she said.

I quickly sat up and shoved the book out of sight. "What are you doing here?"

"I was wondering if you were ever going to try reading that again."

"You know, one of these days I'm going to change the locks."

"Oh, please. Do you really think that would stop me from getting in?"

"It would at least slow you down. Where is Alex? Is she downstairs? I have something I want to show her."

"Can you believe it? The little bugger wanted to stay with Himself for a couple more days."

"That's new."

"Sure is. I'm not complaining. I just wish he would have told me over the phone, so I didn't have to see him. He's such a bell-end."

"You are terrible."

"I know, but I'm okay with that."

"He still has an effect on you, huh?"

"He nearly broke me, you know. First time I've seen him in a while. Got a bit emotional."

"How did he react to seeing you?"

"He spilled his coffee down himself. It was priceless. I loved it!"

"I bet you did."

"Enough about me, love. How are you enjoying that book? Pretty wild, isn't it?"

"It's fascinating. Dad had a pretty vivid imagination."

"You know he used to always say 'This book is based on real life events,' then he would wink and give that little smirk he always gave."

A sad expression crossed my face. "Yeah, if only."

"Well, that's enough reminiscing. I see you didn't make it outside today."

"It was a bit chillier than I thought it was going to be."

"You attempted. That's a start."

I couldn't hide the guilty look on my face. "Yeah."

"You didn't attempt to go out, did you, Pen?"

"I was going to. I had my mind all made up. Out of the blue, Joey showed up, banging on the door."

"Oh, for fu—"

"Language!"

"For Frank's sake! Have a bit of a chinwag, did you? What the hell did he want?"

"I don't know. Nothing important. He just said he had a surprise for me and wanted me to come out and celebrate with him and the fellas."

"Of course, you told him no, right?"

"I told him I would think about it."

"Penelope!"

"I told you how he is. It's hard to tell him no. He just keeps insisting. It's like he only hears what he wants to hear."

"Penny, you know him and his lot are not good for you. You've come a long way from that."

"I know. I'll handle it. It's not like I want to go."

Josie shot me a look of disbelief. I couldn't be upset, because I wasn't quite sure how I was going to get out of it, myself. "Whatever! Don't look at me like that." I yelled.

"I'll look at you whichever way I please. Nutter!

"What the heck was that for? You heifer!"

"Trollop!"

"Wench!"

"Scrubber!"

"Thirst-trapper!"

"Thirst what? What the bloody hell does that mean? Seriously, do Americans just make things up on the go?"

"It means, I win, again."

"You did not win. You just made up a word and declared yourself the victor. I win by disqualification."

"Hmph."

"Anyway, just keep in mind what I told you. You are stronger than you think you are."

"Thanks, Josie."

"Anytime, love. You want me to leave you be, so you can finish up the book?"

"Wow! You're actually offering to leave? Must have a date or something."

"I'll have you know I canceled my date to spend time with you. This storm is supposed to get even worse, and I didn't want you to be alone. I also know that I've been a bit intrusive lately, and I wanted to give you space, if you wanted it."

"I don't even know who you are right now."

"Oh, shut up. Do you want me to go or not?"

"Actually, I was kind of hoping you would stay. This crazy storm does have me a bit on edge. Maybe you could share another story with me. One like yesterday."

"It's bloody dreadful, ain't it? Of course, love. I'll stay as long as you'd like. What would you like to hear about?"

"I don't know. Surprise me."

Well, let's see. Should I tell the story of your fear of water, or the one about the little boy you fancied in school?"

"What? I never liked any boy at my school. All the kids picked on me and called me dumb names."

"I'm not so sure about that. You always came home with stories to tell about this boy and how much fun you had on all the adventures you would go on together."

"You are obviously making this up. I don't remember any of that."

"It's the truth. Every word of it."

"Then what did he look like?"

"Hell if I know. It's not like you could bring him home. You weren't old enough to even think about having a boyfriend. Dad didn't even like you talking about the lad. Mum thought it was cute. Dad clearly wasn't amused. He even told you to stop writing stories about him."

"I think you are just making this up. I don't recall writing any stories about a boy I liked."

She laughed. "Maybe next time you go snooping around Dad's study. Perhaps you will find a few of them."

"Shut up. I wasn't snooping. Technically, it's my study anyway."

"Relax. I was kidding. I'm glad you went in there. Maybe it will help with some of your memories."

"Bad memories," I mumbled.

"Come on. Don't be like that, Pen. There are some good memories in that room. You'll find them."

"I guess."

We heard the raindrops pounding on the roof and loud thunder boomed in the distance. I got up and nervously paced back and forth. I could see the streetlights flickering from across the room.

"Do you want me to put the window down?" Josie asked.

"No," I replied nervously. "The breeze actually feels good."

"Penny, relax. You should rest. When was the last time you had a good night's rest?"

"What month is it?"

"Oh, Penny. You need to sleep, love. You can't keep going on like this. Lord knows you need your beauty sleep."

"He also knows you could use a tan."

"Oh, aren't we a cheeky little bugger. We weren't all blessed with caramel skin. It's a shame no one can see it though, since you stay in the house all day."

"Weren't you supposed to be telling me a story?"

"I already told you a story and you thought I was lying. So now it's your turn."

"My turn? I don't have any stories that you haven't

heard already."

"Well, go grab Mum and Dad's medieval tome, and I'll go get some tea and biscuits. We can have a...what do you Americans call it? Ah, yes. A good old-fashioned slumber party."

"Are you serious?" I asked in an exasperated tone.

"Absolutely. It'll be fun. Just like old times."

I hesitantly got up to go get the tome. Josie bounced up and down on the bed like she was a child. I shook my head. "You need help," I uttered.

Josie jumped up and headed downstairs. "I'll be right back with the tea and biscuits."

"I'll pass. And they're cookies, not biscuits."

"Don't start."

"I'm just saying. They're cookies."

She blew me a raspberry and kept walking. I sighed. I knew it was going to be a long night. I didn't want to be alone, but I didn't want a slumber party either. Just the fact that she was there was comfort enough. I wasn't going to tell her that though. Then she would never leave.

Josie returned from downstairs. "Are you sure you don't want anything? I could make you some hot chocolate. You used to love that."

"I'm fine."

"Suit yourself. Can you believe this storm? That last crack of thunder damn near shook the whole bloody house down. Good thing you already have candles lit. So, which story are we reading?"

"I don't know. Just pick one. They all seem pretty random," I replied in an exasperated tone.

As Josie slowly flipped the pages, a gust of wind swept into the room and turned a bunch of pages.

"Well, I guess the universe wants you to read this one. 'No Wind. No Rain, Can Stop Me.' Hmm, that seems apropos."

"Whatever. I'll read. You can stuff your face."

As I read through the story, I could hear the storm getting worse. I looked out the window. All the streetlights had gone out. Josie had fallen asleep. Her head rested on my thigh. I shook my leg in an attempt to wake her. She mumbled something I couldn't understand, then started snoring. I rolled my eyes, annoyed by the fact that this was her idea and she fell asleep twenty minutes into it. I adjusted my pillow, sat back, and turned to the next page in the book.

I was nearly done with the chapter when another gust of wind blew out most of the candles. Thunder and lightning shook the room again. Josie continued to sleep right through it. I gently moved her head onto the bed. I got up to close the window. A large bolt of lightning lit up the entire night sky, followed by several more strikes. As I closed the window, I looked back at Josie. Something about her looked weird. She laid there, still, and barely breathing. She almost looked doll-like. My heart stopped for a moment, and I felt like I couldn't breathe. I rubbed my eyes. Lightning and thunder boomed again. Josie turned over and mumbled. "Penny, you okay?"

I let out a sigh of relief. My heart raced. "I'm fine. Go back to sleep." I sat on the bed next to her, as close as I could be. I rubbed my temples, then rubbed my eyes. I looked her over once more. She laid there peacefully. I ran my fingers through her hair. "I don't know what I would do without you, sis," I said softly.

Chapter 36 - Ride of Darkness
~Penny~

"Penny, what do you remember about that night?"

"It was dark. The only light I saw was the occasional flash from the streetlight as it whooshed by. Raindrops danced as they trickled down the side of the window, fighting with the wind to maintain their grip. I was tired, but not enough to rest. Mum and Dad spoke to each other in hushed whispers. I held Josie close to me for comfort. All I wanted to do was get home to my soft, comfy bed.

'You okay back there?' Mum asked. I could see her eyes looking at me through the rear-view mirror.

"I nodded 'Mhm.'

"The hushed conversation between Mum and Dad continued.

'We'll be there soon, sweetheart,' Dad said.

"I smiled. Daddy always had a way of making me feel safe, no matter what the situation was. I sat back in my seat and relaxed. The rain began to pick up. Mum and Dad's conversation became louder than whispers. I held Josie's hand a little tighter.

"It was a lot darker than it was before. I hadn't seen light from a streetlight in a long time. I caught occasional glances of Mum's eyes in the mirror. Though she tried, she could not hide her worry. She began to hum softly. I closed my eyes and hummed along. The sound of the rain on the roof of the car became louder.

"I opened my eyes and looked around. All I could see was darkness. I looked into the rear-view mirror. I could not see Mum's eyes. I called out to her. She did not answer. I called out to Dad. He did not answer. Panicked, I began to shake Josie. She would not move. The car was moving at a dizzying speed. I removed my seat belt and crawled to the front seat. They were both empty. I screamed out in horror, then everything went black."

Chapter 37 - I Heart You with Me
~Penny~

Josie yawned as she walked into the kitchen. "Good morning, Penny. How did you sleep?"

"I didn't. But you sure did. Didn't take very long either."

"I was knackered. How long did I last?"

"I think we read through a half a story before you started snoring."

"Bollocks! I do not snore. That must have been someone else you heard."

"Right. That's it. It must have been."

"I see you're eating. First time I've seen that in a while."

I rolled my eyes and held up the muffin in my hand. "Blueberry muffin. Breakfast of champions."

"Ah, yes. Always was a favorite of yours. I never knew what you saw in those things."

"The morning's young. I might even make some bacon."

Josie frowned. "Carnivore."

"And proud of it."

"Is that blueberry tea?" Josie asked. She had a horrified look on her face.

"Yeah, so what?"

"Stand in the corner and have a very firm word with yourself!"

"Why? Tea is tea."

"English breakfast, Tetley, PG Tips, or Yorkshire tea. That's it. Yorkshire tea, one sugar and milk. Simple. Toast. Farmhouse loaf with butter. Yum."

I sipped my tea and just stared at her.

"You've forgotten where you come from. But I suppose you always were your father's child."

"Oh, would you look at the time. What's on your agenda today?"

"Smartarse. Anxious to get rid of me?"

"Nope."

"Just my usual. Country dancing. Garden partying and generally dicking about."

"What's with the sassy attitude?"

Josie laughed. "Sassy? Such a silly little word. Makes me want to click my fingers. Well, if you must know, I have a few errands to run. I was going to get flowers for Mum and Dad. Then maybe do a bit of shopping. I need to buy a new outfit. I want to look my best in case Himself calls and wants me to pick Alexandria up."

I sighed heavily. "Seriously? How long did it take you to move on from that?"

"Oh, please. I'm so over that. I just want to see the look on his face when he sees what he is missing out on. I could never go back to that. I wasn't myself when I was with him. I felt compartmentalized and one dimensional. I am anything but that now. I have sides, edges, and depths that need to be touched, felt, and explored. I need more than he was willing or able to give."

"I'm sorry I asked."

"Smartarse. Maybe one day you'll understand what I mean."

"Hopefully not. I don't want to deal with that."

"You ever wonder if you've ever come across your soulmate already?"

"Oh, Geezus! Don't start that again."

"I'm serious, Pen. You may have been in the same room or right next to each other, and you didn't even realize it."

"Don't you have country dancing or something to get to?"

"Think about it, Pen. He could be out there just waiting on you, but you keep yourself locked up in here like Rapunzel."

I faked excitement. "Or maybe it's the little boy from school!"

"There ya go. Now you're thinking."

"It would seem that ship has sailed."

"You never know. The universe has a way of course correcting itself," she said with a devilish grin.

"The universe has screwed me enough already."

"Better watch what you say. The universe is always listening. Hence words are so bloody powerful. Pagan rituals work. Intentions are cast. Powerful stuff."

I sighed heavily. "You done? I have cardio to do."

"Right then. I'll leave you to it. You stay in and build that perfect body that nobody sees, and I'll go outside and enjoy this lovely weather. It's cleared up quite nicely."

"Sounds like a plan."

Josie sighed. "Cheers, love."

As she walked towards the door, I remembered something I wanted to ask her. "Hey, Josie. Did the numbers 143, mean anything to Mum and Dad?"

You mean besides the obvious?"

"The obvious?"

"I love you. 143 means I love you. Mum used to teach us that in different languages. Even sign language. She said it was important to know how to express love in as many languages as possible. She said you never know when you may need it."

"I vaguely remember that."

"You used to always sign it wrong. No matter how much I tried to correct you, you would always sign the same thing."

"What did I sign?"

She made several gestures with her hands. The last one was her pointing to herself. "Fancy a guess?" she asked.

Something about it seemed very familiar to me, but I couldn't quite remember it. "I love you, me?"

"Close. But when you sign it that way, it means I heart you with me. Mum and Dad always found it so very charming."

"I heart you with me," I said out loud very slowly. Something about those words brought back a flood of random memories. The words begin to sing over and over in my head, like a song from a dream that you can't recall when you wake up.

"Penny? You okay?"

"Love is the answer. Mum used to always say that."

"You're right. She did. You remembered that just

now?"

"Not that, specifically. It was more like I remembered a bunch of little random things that added up to that."

"You had a flashback. That's great, Penny! Are you okay? Do you want me to stay? We could talk about it."

I was still a bit lost in my head. "No, I'm fine. Go run your errands. I think I need some alone time to process it."

Josie smiled. "Okay. I'll be back a little later. By the way, yellow looks good on you."

I looked at her curiously. She looked down at my hand. The mood ring was bright yellow. "Oh, I forgot I had this ugly thing on."

She winked. "Sure, you did. Cheers, love."

Chapter 38 - Crystals of Hope
~Penny~

My workout was supposed to be high intensity cardio. It was anything but. My mind was completely preoccupied. All I thought about was that phrase and the memory fragments it brought to life. I wanted to remember more, and though I tried, memories seemed to evade me. That's the funny thing about not being able to remember things, the more you try, the more you can't recall them. The mind begins to insert fake puzzle pieces to complete the puzzle. It's only when my mind was truly preoccupied with something else that it tended to recall what I was trying so hard to remember.

I sat on the floor and hugged my knees into my chest. I rocked myself back and forth. I was angry and frustrated. I didn't feel human. I felt empty and sad. I was happy once upon a time, but I didn't know how to get that back. I was tired of faking my way through life.

I wasn't sure how long I sat there. It felt like hours. I got up and went upstairs to the kitchen. I was half expecting Josie to be upstairs waiting for me. I called her name, but there was no answer. It was probably for the best. I was better left to my own devices. I was in a pretty dark mood and I knew how she felt about that.

The sun shone through the window in the living room. I walked over and gazed outside. It was so beautiful out. The trees were beginning to turn. I could feel the warmth of the sun through the window warming my skin. I wanted to go outside. I really did, but the sadness had me, and it wouldn't let me go. I quickly closed the curtains and ran to my room.

I sat on my bed and cried. I wondered where Josie was. I laid back onto something hard. I reached back and grabbed the tome. I opened it to the story I read the night before and turned a couple of pages. I closed the book. My mind wasn't in the right place to read anything. I reached over to the nightstand, grabbed my notebook, and began to write. I wrote down a couple of the memories from earlier, then I began writing down those dark, gritty thoughts that I shared with no one, not even Josie. I especially did not share them with her. I wanted to write myself out of the darkness. I wanted to write away my demons.

A noise downstairs startled me. I looked at the notebook. I had written two pages. I felt like I wrote two sentences. Josie always told me that I zoned out when I wrote. I closed the notebook and walked down to the kitchen. Josie was sitting at the kitchen table.

"Where have you been?" I asked.

"Afternoon, love. I told you I had errands to run. Aww, did somebody miss me?"

"That's not the point. You are normally back by now."

"Well, I stopped and got a few things done. I got a deep tissue massage as well. My shoulder was killing me. The masseur was a charmer. We flirted outrageously. Had to let him down easy though. Couldn't have the poor bloke falling in love with me."

I rolled my eyes. "Of course, not. Couldn't have that," I said sarcastically.

"What can I say? I have charisma." She held out her hands. "Got my nails done too. They were shite. You like? You absolutely should have come with. What's the point of being posh buggers if we don't spend any of it?"

As I looked down at her nails, I caught a glimpse of her lips. "Geezus! Did you have something done to your lips?"

"What? How very dare you! I did nothing of the sort!"

"Mmhm. If you say so."

"I say so."

I rolled my eyes. "Your word is law."

She smiled. "Not law. More like gospel. Any-who, what did you do with yourself today? I see you haven't left the house."

"I wrote a couple of pages."

"Did you? And how did that make you feel?"

"Really? Are you shrinking me now?"

"No, arse. Just asking a question."

"It felt like writing."

She waved me off. "Fine. Be difficult. I don't suppose you want to share it either."

"It's dark. You wouldn't care for it."

"Be careful, Penny. If you walk in the dark too long, you will lose the light that guides you out."

"I wish you could understand what it's like to walk in my shoes, and to feel the things I feel. I wish you could understand what it's like to feel happy and normal one minute, then overcome by sorrow the next, for no apparent reason."

You don't think I feel sorrow? You don't think I feel pain? Loss? You aren't the only one that lost someone, Penelope. I replay that night in my head every day. And yeah, it will always hurt, but Penny, that was a long time ago and life has to go on. That's what they would want for you. It's what I want for you."

"I...I just can't seem to put the pieces together. I don't want to replay that night over and over in my head. I'd be content with seeing it once and understanding everything."

"Pen, we've gone over that night, hundreds of times, what more do you need to see?"

"It just doesn't add up. It's like something is missing and I can't wrap my mind around what it is. Like, today, I got these little memory fragments, but I can't make heads or tails of them. It's like they are not my own, but I feel the emotions of them. I can't really explain it. I just know they make me feel lost. Like I'm living a life that's not my own."

"Of course, it's yours. You just need to claim it. Stop letting tragedy define you. You have so much to offer this world."

"I tried that, remember? You know how it goes. I eventually push everyone away or they just leave. I'm not the easiest person to deal with."

"Oh, Penny. If only you saw yourself the way I see

you."

"With rose-colored glasses?"

"Funny you should mention that. I picked up a pair of those." She dug into a bag and put on a pair of rose-colored glasses. "You like?"

"They're okay. They seem a little beneath you."

"Yeah, they were cheap as chips. But I'll wear them with attitude."

"You do everything with attitude."

"I try! I got you a little something special as well. It's in the box on the table. Have a look."

On the table there was a very old metal box with a strange design on it. I picked it up and examined it. "What the heck is this?"

"Well, you have to open it and see, you nutter."

I slowly opened the box. Inside was a beautiful necklace with one large black crystal in the middle. It was encased in what looked like an old tree. The tree had seven branches. Each branch had its own colored crystal. I held it up and stared at it in amazement.

Josie came and stood next to me. "You like it?"

"It's beautiful," I said, still gazing at the necklace.

"I had to pull quite a few strings to get that for you. Those crystals are supposed to help you control your energy. The black one in the middle, that's supposed to shield energy. I guess that's why it's the biggest."

"What are the other ones supposed to do?"

"I can't remember what all of them do. Let's see, I know this bluish green one is Labradorite. It protects you from fear and chaos."

"So, you're saying it will protect me from you?"

"Ha! Very funny, cow-bag. Anyway, the violet one will reduce your anxiety and give you a sense of control over things. I'm not even going to tell you what the smoky one does because I don't want to hear anymore smartarse comments out of you."

"Oh, come on. I promise I won't say anything."

"Bollocks!"

I put my hand over my mouth. Josie stared at me, unconvinced. I put my other hand on top of my hand already covering my mouth."

"It provides a sort of invisible cloak. Allowing you to go undisturbed." She rolled her eyes at me. "Don't think I can't see you smiling underneath your hands, you wanker! It's okay. You're going to miss me when I go back home."

"Go back home?"

"Well, yeah. I've got to go back eventually, now don't I?"

I hung my head. "Yeah, I guess I never really thought about it."

"Don't worry, love. I'm not going anywhere, anytime soon." She winked. "Besides you'd be lost without me."

"Whatever."

"Any-who. Pay attention to this last one. It's important. The smaller black one is obsidian. It will cleanse you of negativity, but it reflects it back to the source. So, you have to be careful. If you are the source of the negativity, you will create a continuous loop of negative energy. That will render all of the other crystal powerless."

I gave her a skeptical look. "And you really think this will work?"

"Of course, it will. It's science."

"For someone who is always talking about the universe, you sure do reference science a lot."

"What's wrong with that? It's simple. Some things can be explained by science. Some things can't."

"Yeah, okay. If you say so. Can I ask you a question?"

"Yeah, sure. Crack on."

"Where did you get this from? It doesn't look like something you could pick up at a store."

Josie paused and let out a deep breath. "It was Mum's."

"What? She had the same—"

"Yeah, she did. She kept her secret well. I'm not even sure if Dad knew."

"But that doesn't make sense. I don't remember seeing her with jewelry on. And I don't remember ever seeing it happen."

"I don't know. Maybe she learned how to control it somehow. Either way, it's yours now. You should try it on and see if it works."

I held it tight in my hand. "I'll try it on later. I'm tired."

"Penny, come on. It'll work. You just have to try. Think about how nice it will be to get out of this house and not have to worry."

"I will. I promise. Just not right now."

Josie sighed. I knew how much she wanted me to try it on. She so badly wanted to believe that this necklace was the solution to all my problems. I had almost no faith that it would help at all. And even if it did help me, I knew it wouldn't change the past. It wouldn't help me remember those lost fragments. It wouldn't help me understand why I feel like the memories I do have aren't my own.

"Okay. I won't pressure you. Whenever you're

ready."

"Thank you, Josie."

Josie laughed. "Besides, between the necklace and that ring, you'll look like a proper gypsy."

"Shut up. You harlot."

"What the!? You knob-head!"

"Jezebel."

"Thot."

"What? What the hell is a thot?"

"You, over there."

"Whatever! It's about time I bugger off. You know, I stopped by and saw them today. I really think you should too."

"And say what? What's the point of talking to them if they can't hear me?"

"Oh, for Frank's sake, Penelope. Why must you be so stubborn all the time? It could be cathartic for you. Did you ever consider that?"

"I'll think about it," I said dismissively."

Josie gathered her things. I could see she was annoyed with me. "I'm sure you will. You have a lovely evening. I'll check on you tomorrow."

"Bye," I said as the door slammed shut. I hated when she was upset with me.

Chapter 39 - The Great Owl
~Penny~

I stood there staring at the door. I knew she was still standing on the other side. I felt like if I opened the door, she'd feel like she won. In my mind I could hear her calling me stubborn. I reluctantly walked over and flung the door open. Josie stood there crying. "Josie, I'm sorry. I can't—"

"You can't what? Can't stop being stubborn? Can't stop giving up? I don't want to hear what you can't do. I want to hear what you plan on doing."

"I know. I'm sorry."

"What's being sorry going to solve? Do you even want to get better?"

"Of course, I do! How could you even ask me that? You think I want to be like this? You think this is easy for me?"

"No, I don't think it's easy for you. I also know that change isn't easy. But you have to try, Pen. Take the first step."

"I am trying," I said angrily.

"See, that's what I'm talking about." Josie shook her head. "Just saying that you're trying is not trying."

"But I am trying."

"Are you?" Josie reached out her hand. "Then walk with me."

"What?" I staggered backwards.

"Walk with me. Just around the block."

"Sh...should I go grab the necklace?"

"Forget the necklace. It'll be fine. I promise."

"Okay," I said nervously."

It was a cool night. The sky was clear. All the stars were shining brightly. It was getting late, so there was nobody walking around. That made me feel a little less anxious. Josie held my hand tight. I think she was worried that I would run back towards the house.

"The sky is beautiful, isn't it?" she asked.

"Mhm."

"Can I ask you a question? You don't have to answer if you don't want to."

"I guess."

"What happened to you while we were apart? What brought out all of this anger and bitterness?"

"You said I don't have to answer, right?"

"I did. That's fine. Can I ask you why you have so much bitterness towards Mum?"

"Seriously?" I yelled. "You really don't know?"

Josie looked up at the pulsing streetlight. "Penny, calm down. Let's change the subject. Do you remember the playground we used to play on?"

"No."

"We would play there for hours. You and Mum loved the cherry blossom trees. You would swing on the swings for hours just looking at them. You used to say you loved the way the wind felt against your face. Everyone at the park thought you were the prettiest thing in the world. You would laugh as you ran around the playground.

"One windy day at the park, all of the cherry blossom petals were blowing in the wind. You danced in the falling petals, twirling and spinning to your heart's content. Then suddenly you stopped. Dad asked you what was wrong. You said 'my visitors are here.' Dad didn't know what you meant. He told you to let them dance with you. You told him they didn't want to dance. They wanted you to follow them. Dad told you that he didn't think that was a good idea. He told you to stay put. You, being stubborn as usual, slowly made your way towards the path that led into the woods. You kept yelling 'Olly olly oxen free!' Each time it grew fainter and fainter. When Dad looked for you under the tree, you were nowhere to be found. Mum and Dad looked for you for hours. At some point, Mum heard a scream from inside the forest. She rushed into the forest, and after a few minutes, she came out holding you in her arms. You were absolutely terrified. You never told anyone what you saw that frightened you so much. After that day, we never went to the playground again. You'd have none of it."

"Why are you telling me this story?"

"I'm telling you because I want you to realize that hiding from your fears won't heal them. You have to conquer them, love, or you'll be hiding from them forever. What happened to Mum and Dad was tragic. But whatever sorrow you are dealing with, whatever anger you are holding in, you are only hurting yourself. Let the sorrow let you go."

I stared at the sky, pondering Josie's words. "Streetlight," I said sadly.

Josie looked up at the light. "Yeah? It's fine."

"Streetlight. That's what my nickname was. That's what my so-called friends called me. Not in a mean way, just in a way that made me feel more like a novelty than a friend. Once they knew what I could do, I became nothing more than a cheap parlor trick. I've done things I'm not proud of. At first it was just a bit of fun, then things became more dangerous. I used the boxing gym as a way out. I needed a way to channel my anger. That's where I met Joey. I know how you feel about him, but he was the only person that treated me decently, and wasn't just out for my money."

"He just used you for other things."

"It wasn't like that. You wouldn't understand."

"Then make me understand."

"It doesn't matter. It's in the past."

"You can't change your future, if you haven't dealt with your past."

"Can we head back now?"

"Tired of hearing the truth?" Josie sighed. "Blimey! Sometimes I don't even know why I try."

"I didn't mean it like that. I hear what you are saying. I really do. I just want to go back to the house."

"Fine! Let's go."

"Josie, don't be like that."

"No, it's fine. I need to be on my way anyway. I could go for a swift half. I'll check in on you tomorrow."

"Okay. I guess I'll see you then."

Josie walked up to me and ran her hand down the back of my head like Mum used to do. "You don't have to do things all by yourself. Just remember that."

"I know. I will."

"Cheers, love."

"See ya."

I closed the door, hurried up the stairs, and went into my room. I flopped on the bed and let my head fall back onto the pillow. I felt safe inside. Not safe from anything outside, safe from myself. As I laid back, I stared at the constellations glued to my ceiling. I always loved how they would just take me away. I could hear my dad's voice telling me each star's name. There was one star that shone brighter than all the others. Dad said that it was officially my star as of my birthday. At the time, I didn't know what he meant. I picked up the old tome. I was determined to read it all. I thought maybe I could rekindle some old memories in the process. I flipped through the remaining pages to see how many stories were left.

It was warm inside, so I got up and slightly opened the window. The night air was crisp, and I welcomed the cool breeze. I could hear the soft hoot of a great horned owl off in the distance. It had a soothing familiarity. I searched the tree branches, but it was nowhere to be found. I took a step from the window. I heard the soft hoot again. This time it sounded much closer. I scanned the branches again. I noticed a large set of yellow eyes staring back at me. An owl stood on the branch just above my window. It appeared to wink at me. Its gaze held such wonder. The stunning, yellow eyes studied me as I studied them. It almost looked sad. I held my hand up, as if to wave. It gave a soft hoot. Its gaze seemed to intensify, drawing me in deeper.

A weird feeling washed over me. I felt anxious, yet calm. Almost as if I was in danger, but being closely watched over. I felt light, but I couldn't move on my own. I felt as though I was being moved by something. I kept staring into the eyes of the owl. I felt like I was outside of my body looking back at myself, but through someone else's eyes.

I began to recall small fragments of things. I wondered if the lost memories were from a distant past. They felt so familiar, yet so foreign. I felt loved, scared, confused, and angry. The feelings grew more intense by the second. They were overpowering and too much to handle. I closed my eyes, but I could still see everything. I saw a vision of a sad, lost little girl, hopelessly trying to escape to somewhere I couldn't see, while constantly looking backwards. I reached out to her, but I could not reach her. She was close, but just beyond my reach. She was scared. I called out to her. "Hello?" She looked around. She couldn't see me. "Over here," I called out again. It felt like she heard me, but she couldn't find her way to me. "I'm here," I said desperately. She looked around feverishly. Unable to find me, she ran into the darkness. Everything turned dark. "Don't go! I'm here! I'm here!"

Chapter 40 - Losing Time
~Penny~

"Of course, you're here, love. Where else would you be?"

I felt a jolt, like I was just hit by a truck. I was suddenly standing in the window staring outside at an empty tree. The sun was almost blinding.

"Penny? You okay, love?"

I turned to see Josie standing in the doorway. I was totally confused. "What are you doing here?"

"What the hell are you on about? Why wouldn't I be here? Aren't I here every morning?"

"But you just left," I said, still confused.

"I think your lack of sleep is finally catching up to you, love. And it's a good thing, too. I was beginning to worry you'd become a vampire. Come sit down. You look like shite. Have you been standing there all night?"

I started to gather my senses. "No. Just a couple of minutes, I think. I swear I was just standing there looking outside. There was this owl, and I was looking at it. Next thing I knew, you were in the doorway."

"Well, it definitely wasn't a few minutes. Maybe you fell asleep standing up. I came in and expected you to be in the kitchen. I called out to you a few times. You yelled for me not to go. You told me that you were here. Which was a bloody relief. I was really worried that you were out and about again."

"Shut up. I don't need your crap this early."

"You mean, this late. It's the middle of the night in your world."

"I hate you."

"Ha! You wish. Get yourself together and meet me downstairs. I'll make you a midnight snack." She winked.

I went into the bathroom and splashed cold water on my face. I still felt a little like I was in a trance or something. The cold water helped. I dried my face and walked down to the kitchen.

"So, you want to tell me what that was all about?" Josie asked.

"What?" I asked nonchalantly.

"Oh, don't be daft. Please don't tell me you were up all night staring out the window, talking to a bloody owl. I think I may be a bit jealous."

"I wasn't talking to the owl. And I don't think I was up all night. I could have sworn it was only a few minutes."

"Blimey! Losing time, are you? Tell me what you remember about last night."

"Well, after you left, I went upstairs. I sat down with Mum and Dad's old book and looked at a few pages. I was warm, so I got up to open the window. There was a fascinating looking owl in the tree, so I looked at it for a minute."

"And then you called out to someone?"

"I did." Confusion washed over me again. "It was

me."

"Oh, for Frank's sake! You called out to yourself?"

"It was a younger me, from the past, I think. I remembered things, Josie. I can't tell you exactly what I remembered, but I could feel that they were my memories. They were all fragmented. Like pieces of a dream."

"That must've been some owl."

"You don't believe me?"

"Of course, I believe you. Some people say that owls represent all kinds of things. Like, wisdom and helpfulness. Nan loved owls. She used to say they have powers of prophecy."

"Really? What do other people say?"

Josie sighed. "That they are a sign of evil and impending doom. But you know what they say, Nan knows best."

"Yeah, well this owl didn't seem evil. The way it looked at me had a strange familiarity to it that I couldn't place."

"That's interesting. Maybe it was both."

"What do you mean?"

"Perhaps the universe is warning you of impending doom, and the owl was there to help you avoid it."

I shook my head. "You and your superstitious nonsense."

"Ignore it if you want to. One of these days you'll wish you listened to me. I'd love to hear your explanation for why you thought I had just left. And while you're at it, explain what happened in the mirror while you were trying on the dress."

"I...I'm sure there's an explanation."

"Exactly. But you don't have one. So, stop being a

stubborn know-it-all. You'll end up old and lonely."

I became frustrated with her and didn't want to discuss it any further. I considered the fact that she may have been right, but I didn't find it helpful since I didn't know what to do with that information. "Whatever! It's the universe," I said mockingly.

"Knob-head."

"Hussy."

"Numpty."

"Heifer!"

"Spoon!"

"Chubnuggle!"

"Oh, bloody hell! Couldn't just accept defeat. You had to make up the most ridiculous word that you could come up with."

"Look it up."

"I'll do nothing of the sort. I'm not sure I even want to know what it means, if it means anything at all. Just eat your breakfast. I got your favorite, with extra blueberries."

"Thanks."

"You're welcome. Any big plans for today?"

"Just my usual. Survive and advance. What about you? Any big dates?"

"I'm actually supposed to meet my masseur for dinner."

I shook my head. "So much for letting him down easy."

"What? I did. At least I thought I did. I had a few conversations with the bloke. That's all. He is all over the shop. He thinks we have this soul connection, which is literally not possible. I do love our conversations though. We get very deep."

"I bet you do. I may need to go grab my boots. What does he look like? What's his story?"

"Looks a bit like you. If you know what I mean."

I grinned. "Interracial love."

"Yeah, so what. Surely, you fancy who you fancy. Seems a bit old-fashioned for it to even be mentioned. Anyway, so, here's the thing. He doesn't want to be 'just another one of my men.' He can't handle that I don't want to settle down. He feels at this stage in his life, he wants to be everything to someone. All this I understand, but he thinks we have a shot at a deeper connection, beyond the physical connection. Which, by the way, is very strong."

"And how do you feel about him?"

"Eh. He is quite fascinating, and I like the depth. He said he wants a meaningful connection, but then the conversation gets hot and risqué. Then, out of nowhere, he pulls back and feels remorseful."

"My head hurts just listening to all that. You're going to lead the wrong guy on, one of these days."

"I am not leading him on. It's just dinner. Nothing else. You know me. I get bored. What I'll do is just disappear. Besides, I have to pick up Alexandria tonight."

"Good. I can't wait to see her."

"I'm sure she's missed you too. I may not be over tonight though. We'll stop by tomorrow. I need to get going. I have some things I need to do. Try to have a good day. Have you tried your necklace out?"

"Not yet. But I will."

"Oh, Penny. Nothing ventured, nothing gained. Cheers, love."

Chapter 41 - A Mum's Love
~Penny~

I finished my workout. Back and biceps were always my favorite things to work on, but I couldn't stay focused at all. I was exhausted. I laid on the floor and watched the fan blades turn. I played with the thoughts running through my head, trying to make sense of them all. I thought about the owl, the book, the fleeting memories, and even Josie's nagging. I grew frustrated. I just wanted something solid that I could wrap my brain around. I felt like I was losing myself.

I put a towel over my face and laid there in silence. I just wanted to rest. My body was tired. My mind was tired. I felt like my life compass was damaged, and I didn't know how to proceed. For some reason, Josie telling me that I would be old and lonely really got to me. I wasn't sure why. Maybe there was a part of me that believed she was right. I'd pretty much lost everyone I loved and drove those away that may have cared for me.

I heard movement upstairs in the kitchen. I figured Josie had come back for some reason. I yanked the towel off my face and headed upstairs. I walked into the kitchen. Something smelled great. It smelled like...childhood.

"Oh, there you are, Penny. Wash your hands. It's almost time for dinner."

I stopped dead in my tracks. My heart raced. "M-Mum?" I stuttered.

"Well, who else would it be, my love? Are you feeling okay? You look as if you've seen a ghost."

I stood there staring at her in disbelief. "What are you doing here? I mean, how are you here?"

"What has gotten into you? Did you bump your noggin? Come here. Let me feel your head."

I slowly took a few steps towards her. My heart raced, and my head was foggy. I couldn't grasp what was going on.

"Blimey. You're burning up. Sit down. I'll get you a cold compress. You've probably run yourself ragged. I told you not to push so hard. The body can only take so much."

As her hand touched me, I was overcome with emotion. Tears streamed from my eyes. How could she be here? She walked over to the sink. As she ran the water, she calmly sang a little song.

My grandfather's clock was too large for the shelf, so it stood ninety years on the floor.

"I remember that song," I said softly.

"What's that, my love?"

"Nothing. Where's Josie?"

"I don't know. Where did you put her?" Mum winked. "It wasn't my turn to watch her. I'm sure she'll turn up." She smiled warmly. She put the cold compress against my forehead and held me close. "There, that should help."

"Mum?"

"Yes, my love?"

"Where's Dad?"

"Oh, I'm afraid he won't be joining us."

"Why not? Where is he?"

Mum paused and stared out the window. "I'm not sure. I haven't been able to reach him."

A deep sadness washed over me. Mum was here, but Dad wasn't. That could only mean one thing. "Can you try to reach him again?"

"I've already tried several times. Don't worry. I'm sure he's fine. How about you eat a little something? It might make you feel better."

I got frustrated and more confused. "I'm not hungry."

"Well, you'll need to eat something soon. How's your writing coming?"

"I..."

"Remember, writing is your gift. Never forsake your gift. It can take you anywhere you want to go. It can also guide you through the darkest of places."

"My gift? I don't understand."

"One day you will. Have you been reading?"

"Reading what?" I said in a surly tone.

"The book we gave you, silly. You really should finish it. You really are acting strange today. Perhaps I should get you in to see the doctor."

"I'm fine. I'm just a little confused. Why can't I talk to Dad?"

"Maybe you should lay down. You'll feel better after some rest."

"I don't need rest. I want to talk to Dad!" I yelled.

"Penny, please calm down. You are getting yourself all worked up."

Tears streamed down my face. I was angry and frustrated. "I am calm. I just want to talk to Dad. Why can I talk to you and not him? Why won't you tell me what's going on?"

Mum walked over and hugged me. "Shh. It's okay, my love. Just relax. Everything is going to be okay."

"I don't understand any of this."

Mum gently caressed my hair. "Perhaps you should rest. You have a big day ahead of you, tomorrow."

"I do?"

Mum put the cold compress over my eyes and began to sing a song.

Father's earth. Mother's heaven. Father's earth. Mother's heaven.

I felt a sense of calm. I relaxed and allowed my mind to go free. Through the window, I could hear birds chirping and children playing. The sunlight was warm and the gentle breeze was pleasant on my skin. I could smell the flowers through the window. I just wanted to lay there forever and be a kid again. I longed for a time when life wasn't so heavy, complicated, and cruel.

I suddenly realized that Mum's song was a bit different than I remembered it. "Mum. Isn't it Mother's earth? Father's heaven?" There was no answer. "Mum?" I removed the towel from my face and opened my eyes. The fan blades spun around and around, welcoming me back to a cold reality.

I ran upstairs to the kitchen. It was exactly how it was when I went downstairs...empty. Although I didn't feel like it, I figured I must have fallen asleep. I looked at the time. Only a couple of minutes had passed since I finished my workout. I sat at the kitchen table and cried. I couldn't explain what was happening to me lately, but I suddenly felt trapped in this world. I really needed to talk to Josie. I wanted her to help me make sense of it all.

I glanced over at the necklace across the table. I figured it was as good a time as any to see if this thing really worked. I grabbed it and put it on. I walked over to the drawer and rummaged through the phones in it, looking for one that would turn on. After a few attempts, one finally turned on. The screen buzzed and flickered, but it stayed on. I anxiously dialed Jose's number. There was no answer. I dialed again, no answer. I became frustrated. Of all the times for her not to answer. I dialed the number one last time. This time, I got her voicemail. "Hey, Josie. I need you to call me back. I talked to M—. Just call me back."

I hated talking to her voicemail. I was angry that she didn't just pick up. I slammed the phone onto the desk in anger. The screen flickered, then turned off.

Chapter 42 - Renewed Vigor
~Penny~

The house seemed more quiet than usual. The days grew shorter and shorter. Through the window, I could see the sun had already set. I was curled up in a ball on my bed. A position I was all too familiar with. The events of the day had me emotionally spent. I didn't know what to do with myself. Everything felt right in Mum's arms, but I knew that I would never feel that again, at least not in any real sense.

I thought about how angry I had been with her. I needed someone to blame for everything, and she was the easiest one. Now I'd give anything for some more time with her. Even in my daydream, hallucination, or whatever you want to call it, her words carried so much meaning. Maybe they were things I've known all along, but I needed to hear that gentle reminder from her.

I dried my wet eyes, sat back on my bed, and read the tome. Each page read like a distant memory. I stopped and played out each scene in my head. I wondered if the stories were real stories or made up adventures that Mum and Dad shared.

Hours passed, and I read story after story. Some of

them sparked memories, while others were as foreign to me as an unread book. I made a note of things in stories that I planned on asking Josie about. I thought back to her story about me and the park. Something clicked in my brain. I flipped the book back to one of the first stories I skimmed over. It was about a little girl on a path. I wondered if the story was about me. I was fascinated by the idea that it might have been. I began reading it and each subsequent story again. I couldn't help but feel a twinge of excitement. I couldn't wait to tell Josie.

"Maybe some of these stories are bringing back memories because they are stories about me," I thought to myself.

I flipped to what I remembered being the last story. I had folded the top of the page so I knew where I was going to begin my writing, if I ever got around to it. There was a story there that I didn't recall seeing. It confused me. I knew for certain that the story was not there before. I thought of a time when Josie could have written it. I wondered if perhaps she wrote it while I was downstairs working out. Or, maybe I just folded the wrong page. Whichever it was, my eyes were burning, and I had read all I was going to read for the night. I sat the book down and walked over to the window. The sky was showing signs of light in the distance, and a few birds had started chirping already. I scanned the branches in search of the owl that I knew was not there. It was probably for the best. I had had my share of weirdness for the week.

I stared out at the sky. The sun was beginning to rise, and with it, the hope of a new day. I began to think about my life and what I'd done with it. A somber feeling set in. I thought about a quote I read in Dad's book. "Every moment in your life is a moment to change the course of your life." A tear slowly trickled down my face. I knew he would hate how I was living my life.

"Why not today? Why not use this day to change the course?" I thought to myself.

I dried my eyes and took a few deep breaths. My ring displayed a deep orange color as it glistened and reflected the light of the early morning sun. I closed my eyes and took in the sunlight. I thought about Dad and what I would say to him if he appeared the same way Mum did. I opened my eyes, stood up tall, and prepared to attack the day with a renewed vigor.

Chapter 43 - Indecent Proposal
~Penny~

I showered, got dressed, straightened up the kitchen, and made coffee. I even put my necklace on. My ring flashed a brilliant orange color. I was a bit anxious for Josie to arrive. I had so many questions for her.

An hour or so passed and she still hadn't arrived. I paced the kitchen, peeking out of the window every so often. I didn't recall her saying she wasn't going to stop by in the morning. I began to worry. Worry turned into anger, which was my typical defense mechanism. I took my necklace off and headed to the workout room. I put weights on the bar and started lifting. I needed to completely clear my mind of things. I put on plate after plate, going heavier and heavier. At some point, I stopped keeping track of what I was adding and just lifted.

I'm not sure how long I had been lifting when I heard a noise upstairs. "Oh, now she shows up," I said to myself. I kept squatting. "She can wait like she made me wait," I grunted between reps.

"Yo! You down there?" a voice called out. Joey made

his way down the stairs, holding a bag in his hand. "There's my girl, killing it as usual."

I let the weights drop to the floor. "What the hell are you doing here?"

He moved towards me. "I came to see you, babe." His lips puckered.

I held him back. "How the hell did you get in here?"

"I was knocking forever. The door was unlocked, so I thought I would see what you were up to."

I toweled myself off. "Not cool, man."

"What? I told you I'd let you know about this weekend, babe."

"Please stop calling me that."

"What's up with you? Why you acting all angry?"

"What? It's nothing. I'm fine."

He walked over and picked up the barbell with one head. "Whoa, this is some serious weight. Something piss you off, babe? You sure you don't want to get it off your chest?" He looked at me with a sinister grin.

"I told you I'm fine. And how many times do I have to tell you to stop calling me that?"

He moved closer to me. "Oh, I love it when you get feisty like that."

"Okay, it's time for you to go. If my sister comes home and catches you here, she will not be a happy camper."

"Oh, right. The mysterious sister. Maybe I should stick around so I can finally meet her."

"Or, maybe you shouldn't. What exactly are you here for, again? What are we touching base on?"

He turned his back, picked up a plate, and put it on the rack. "On the celebration this Saturday."

"What exactly are we celebrating?" I asked. I was

completely exasperated.

He turned around. In his hand was an opened box with a huge diamond ring in it. "Our engagement. Would you marry me, babe?"

I stood in stunned silence and just stared at him. I didn't know whether to be flattered or completely annoyed. I had no idea what on earth would make him think I would want to marry anyone, let alone, marry him. "I—"

"I know it's out of the blue, but you know we've always had this connection, babe. We click, you know. We have that energy. I figured, who else you gonna find that with, right? It may not be like Romeo and Julia, but we can make it work."

I shook my head. "It's Juliet," I mumbled in anger, trying my best to hide my annoyance. I was nauseated. I couldn't bring myself to say anything else. I just stared at him. He was so full of himself, so annoyingly confident. Energy? What energy? That energy was all mine. I didn't want to share it with him. Of course, I didn't want to marry him. I stood there quiet and numb. I opened my mouth to express my disdain at the fact that he even asked me to marry him. "I—"

"You will? Oh, babe. That's friggin awesome! He grabbed my hand and slid the ring on my finger. "Oh, man! How great does that look? I had to win a few fights to pay for it, but it's cool. Plenty more where that came from. You excited as I am?"

I stood there, shocked. I couldn't believe what was actually happening. "Smug bastard," I thought in my head. But "Yeah" was the only thing that came out of my mouth.

"I'll pick you up Saturday, babe. Around 6:30. Oh,

man! It's gonna be so lit. I better sneak out before the mysterious Josie comes back," he said in a mocking tone. He leaned in and kissed me.

I watched him strut up the stairs. I heard the door shut. I grabbed my stomach. I was nauseated. I turned and vomited on the floor. I was angry and disgusted. I was mostly angry with myself for not telling him no right to his face. I was disgusted with the fact that I still couldn't just tell him no. I knew I was going to have to tell him eventually. There was no way I was going to marry him.

I took off the ring and put it in the box. I headed upstairs to get something to clean up the mess. I tucked the box in my pocket, in case Josie showed up. I was no longer in a good place. I found myself navigating to that dark, lonely place again. I just wanted to disappear.

Chapter 44 - The Darkness Within
~Penny~

It was early in the afternoon and there was still no sign of Josie. I thought about calling again, but I figured I would just get her voicemail again, and I knew leaving her another message would have been pointless. I knew when I asked her about it, she would say, "Voicemail? I can't be arsed with checking that."

I made my way upstairs to my room. I grabbed my notebook and sat on the bed. I stared at the blank page. A tear fell onto the page. I felt lost and alone. I grabbed my pen and started to write what came to mind.

A dark mist shrouds my vision. The way forward is as dark as a moonless night. It comes for me. I cannot hide. It resides in every nook, around every corner. It hides in plain sight, watching, waiting. I barely have the strength to run.

It's now everywhere. It consumes my days. It haunts my nights. I cannot escape this faceless enemy. I fear it already has me, and I run in vain. I am trapped in this endless nightmare. My cries are no longer audible, my thoughts are no longer my own. I reach out, but nothing reaches back.

It has come for me. I no longer have the will to run. It has claimed me as its own, erasing me from myself, completing my nothingness. Why fight the inevitable? Why not embrace this darkness? I don't fear it any longer. It feels familiar. It feels effortless. Maybe I should stay here. Maybe I belong here.

The hints of light tease me with cruel uncertainty. Make your intentions known or leave me to my darkness. I don't need you anymore. I don't want you. Save your hope for someone who wants it. Save your light for someone who sees it. I am where I belong now. Where l will stay. Where I am free.

I heard rustling downstairs. I tore the page out of the notebook, opened the tome, put the page in it, and closed it. I straightened up my face, grabbed the tome, and headed downstairs. I walked into the kitchen and set the tome down on the counter. Alexandria came in from the dining room. "Aunt Penny!" She ran over to me and gave me a big hug.

"Hey, doll face! It's about time you came back to see me. I missed you. You're going to have to tell me about all the fun you had while you were away."

"Okay. I missed you too. You didn't write the story without me, did you?"

"No way. I couldn't possibly write an awesome story without you."

"Yay! I can't wait to get started." Alex pointed behind me. "Can we write it in that book Mum has?"

I turned around to see Josie standing there with the tome open. "That old thing? We'll see," I said nervously.

Josie walked over to us. "Alexandria, sweetheart. There's pen and paper in the dining room. Why don't you go get started on that story while I have a little chat with Aunt Penny."

"Okay, Mum. See you soon, Aunt Penny."

"See you soon."

Josie stood there, holding the page I just wrote. "You care to explain this to me?"

"It's nothing, just an anecdote."

"Bollocks. This is no anecdote. When did you write this?"

"Today."

"This is bloody deep and dark," she said angrily."

"Yeah, well, I feel bloody dark. Trust me, the things I don't detail are the dangerous parts I keep tucked away."

"What happened today? This isn't you, Penny."

"Oh, baby, my soul is coal black."

She stared at me and shook her head. "You know, Penny, you can't stay hidden behind this veil forever. It's just not healthy. You stayed holed up in this house day after day. You still sleep in your childhood room, for Frank's sake. There's a whole world out there just waiting for you. Get out there and explore it. Maybe you're just afraid to remember. Have you ever thought of that?"

"I'm not afraid of anything. Why do I need to go outside? Because you want me to? What if I want to stay inside? What if I don't want the world to see what a freak I am?"

"You're not a freak, Pen."

"Easy for you to say. You're not the one who affects electricity with your mood. You're not the one who is an emotional contagion, or whatever the term is that you all came up with."

"Penny, stop it. You say it as if it's a bad thing. You have the power to make people happy. Is that such a bad thing?"

"I'm not happy! I can't make people happy when I can't even make myself happy!"

"You have to try, Pen. Depriving yourself of sleep, and keeping yourself locked up in this old place isn't helping matters."

"Do you want to know why I don't sleep, Josie? Because I don't know what to do about night terrors so vivid, they make me sick, and nightmares so strong, I'm up for hours trying to figure out where I am. I can't call anyone to validate that I'm not actually dying, so I just stay up and wait for the sun to rise."

"Oh, Pen. You know you can call me."

"Yeah, I tried that," I said dismissively.

"I know. I'm sorry. I—"

"Don't be sorry. It's not your fault. I don't know how to explain the place I'm in right now. It is thick, gritty, and dark. I don't want to fight for my life, so I don't understand why anyone else would want to bother to do so on my behalf."

"I really wish you wouldn't talk like that."

"Why not? Because words are so bloody powerful? Because the universe is listening? Pagan rituals? Blah blah blah."

"Now you're just being an arse."

"Hmph."

"Not because of any of those things. Because your life is worth fighting for. I want you to fight for it. I want to fight for it. We are one. Without you, there is no me."

"What does that even mean?"

"It means get your shite together, and stop blaming the world for your problems."

"I'm not blaming anyone. I'm fine. It was just writing. It wasn't some semi-suicidal depiction or cry for help. Nobody told you to look in the tome anyway."

"Really? You know what? Whatever! I'm just going to go. I can't deal with this right now."

I stood there and seethed with anger. There were so many things I wanted to scream at her. My body was shaking. She grabbed her purse and walked towards the dining room to get Alex. "Joey asked me to marry him. I told him yes."

"What!?" she screamed. "You did what!? Oh, for Frank's sake!! Please tell me you are kidding! Because if you are trying to piss me off, you have thoroughly succeeded!"

"I'm not trying to piss you off. I'm just letting you know. I was hoping you would be happy for me."

"Happy for you!? Happy for you!? For what? For throwing your life away by marrying a complete and utter numpty that you have absolutely no feelings for?"

"He doesn't judge me. I can be myself around him. He makes me happy."

"Oh, bollocks! He coddles you and doesn't challenge you to be anything more than what you are now."

"Oh, really? And what's that?"

"The truth is, you blow hot and cold, and you rarely open up and talk about anything you are going through. You are like clay. One minute you are all squishy and easy to handle, and I can get right into you. The next minute you go hard, and I feel like you are ready to crack. Sure, you're going through a lot, but it's like you don't even try anymore. You just wallow in your own self-pity. The world is not going to feel sorry for you. Sure, I can keep coming over here, trying to help you, and you can keep lying to me and telling me you are trying to help yourself, but are you really? Or are you just telling me what I want to hear so you can crawl back into your pit of despair as soon as I leave?"

"So, that's how you see me?"

"Penny, how can I see you any other way? You don't open up to me. When you do talk, you barely say anything. You're negative all the time. You aren't writing anything except for dark, negative snippets that are barely understandable."

"I don't want to not talk to you. I miss being able to freely express details and daily things, but if you cannot see me as more than my dark places or accept that sometimes I truly just can't bring myself to push through, then I don't know what to say. I do my best, but I fail sometimes. I want light, but the dark comforts parts of me you just don't understand. It's not always negative, unforgiving nonsense. Sometimes it is just me being me. I feel like nothing I do is right, and that happy-go-lucky inner child that you are waiting for to come back, is dead. I'm just not anything I intended to be. I can't live up to what you need from me as a sister or a person, and I don't know how to fix it."

"Oh, bollocks! That's just a bloody cop out, Penny, and you know it. You fix it by trying. By doing everything you can. And if that doesn't work, then you can say that you don't know how to fix it."

"You just don't get it."

"No, Penny, I guess I don't. But I guess your new fiancé does. I'm sure he has all the bloody answers. Good luck with that. I hope he makes you as happy as you claim he does. Maybe he's exactly what you need."

My blood boiled. Tears poured down my face. "Get the hell out!" I yelled.

"Oh, is that how you want to be? Kicking me out, are you? Don't worry, I was leaving anyway!"

"Good!"

"Alexandria, grab your things. We are leaving."

"But we just got here, Mummy. Aunt Penny was supposed to write a story with me," Alexandria said."

"Sorry, Alex. We have to go. Tell your Aunt Penny goodbye."

"Aunt Penny, why are you crying?"

"Alex, please just tell your Aunt Penny goodbye. We have to go," Josie said. She was trying her best to keep from crying.

Alex ran over and hugged me. "Bye, Aunt Penny." She handed me a piece of paper. "I wrote a story just for you and him," she whispered.

As they walked out the door, Alexandria stopped and turned towards me. Her eyes wet with tears. She signed five words. "I heart you with me."

Josie grabbed her hand and they walked out the door. As the door slammed, I dropped to the floor and cried. I was completely broken.

Chapter 45 - Aunt Dulce-Ella
~Penny~

In the darkness, I sat on my bed, rocking, while hugging my knees. My eyes were dry. I had no tears left. I knew I had really messed up this time. Josie was tired of dealing with me. I was, for all intents and purposes, engaged to someone that I had absolutely no feelings for, and I lacked the courage to get out of it. I didn't know what to do. I considered just staying home, keeping the door locked, and hoping he would just get the hint. But I knew that was just childish and dumb. I knew I would have to face him and tell him.

I turned over, buried my face in the pillow, and sobbed. A warm touch caressed my hair. "There, there, my love. It's going to be okay. You don't have to do this alone."

"Mum?" I rolled over. "You're here again. How did you know?"

"Oh, my love. A mother is only as happy as her saddest child."

"I've really messed up this time. I've gotten myself in too deep, and I don't know what to do. I don't know how to get out."

"What have I always told you, Penny? There's no

question that love can't answer, no problem that love can't solve."

"I don't think it can answer this. There is no love here, just a tremendously stupid mistake."

"So, undo the mistake."

"It's harder than it sounds. Sometimes I feel like it would be easier just to live with the consequences."

"Will that make you happy?"

"Not at all."

"Then choose what makes you happy."

"Lately, I feel like I don't know what happiness is anymore. How did you know when you were happy? I mean, with Dad? How did you know it was love?"

"There were so many different things. The butterflies. Oh, those butterflies." She shuddered. "He had this way that he made me feel. It felt like I had been waiting for him my entire life. The way he looked at me. The way I felt when he smiled at me. The way I felt when I knew I was going to see him. When he looked into my eyes, I felt like he could see every part of me. I felt like there wasn't anything we couldn't conquer as long as we had each other. When he held me, I just knew everything was right with the world. There are other things that are not so easily describable. Some things you must experience yourself to fully grasp. And when you do experience them, you will know beyond the shadow of a doubt, it's love."

"I don't think I will ever experience that."

"Of course, you will, my love. You just have to open yourself up to it. Life is full of hidden boundaries, and if we are willing to step just a little further, we open ourselves up to a world of possibilities."

"Is that what you did?"

"In a sense, yes. But my story has been told. It's time for you to write yours."

"What if I don't have one?"

"Everyone has a story, and every story finds its writer. You have been given gifts that one could only dream of, and when you are ready to use them, there will be nothing you can't do."

"I wish I could share in your optimism. I feel like my gifts are more of a curse, right now.

"I promise you, if you keep your mind open to experiencing new things, you'll find your way."

Tears began to flow down my face. "I miss you, Mum, and I miss Dad. I miss how things used to be. I wish we could go back and be a family again."

Mum continued to caress my hair. "I know, my love. I wish the same thing. But sometimes we must let go of the past, for the sake of our futures."

"I don't want to let go of either of you."

"Oh, no, my love," She pressed her hand to my heart. "We'll always be here, always with you. But we cannot guide you through this darkness because it is your darkness, and you must find your own way through it."

"I...I can't. I can't do this alone."

"Penny, my dear child. Everyone has their own journey that divides at some point. It's the path you take that defines your future. Search for the light, and you will never walk it alone."

I leaned in closer to her. "I'm scared, Mummy."

She hugged me tight. "Oh, Penny, my brave little girl. All of your wildest dreams are already true. Follow your heart, and everything will be as right as rain."

"My wildest dreams?"

She kissed me on the forehead. "See you soon, my love."

"Mum. Don't g—"

"Shh. Sleep, my love. It's been such a long time. Sleep."

"Mum," I said. I didn't want to let her go. "Before you go, would you tell me a story?"

"Okay, my love. But only if you promise to try to get a good night's sleep and treat tomorrow, and each day after that like the blessing it is."

I yawned. "I promise, Mum."

"Well then, let me tell you the story of my Great Aunt Dulce-Ella. She was the reason that I became a writer. This old story, passed down through the years, tells the story of Dulce-Ella the great writer who wrote love stories that so perfectly captured the essence of love, that whoever read the stories together, would fall in love and go on to live out their days in love, for all of eternity. Sadly, she never had a love to call her own.

"One day she met a young man while writing out in her garden. He slowly approached her. He was wounded, tired, thirsty, and barely standing. He wore a royal air force uniform. She rushed to his side and helped him into the house. He was in bad shape. He collapsed onto the bed and passed out.

"Over the next four days, she nursed him back to health. Each day he got better. She wrote and read to him every night, not entirely sure if he could hear her or not. She would tell people that he smiled in his sleep.

"On the fifth day, he woke. She heard him call out.

She rushed into the room to find him sitting up in the bed. Their eyes locked, and he smiled at her. She explained to him what happened and how he came to be in her home. He smiled and thanked her profusely. They both agreed that he should rest for one more day, and the next day she would make arrangements to have him taken back to his base.

"When he woke the next day, she had already prepared breakfast for him. She set his cleaned uniform on the chair by the bed. They shared breakfast and conversation well into the early afternoon. When the time came for him to leave, he was hesitant. He knew he had to go, but something held him back. She didn't want him to leave either, but she knew his duty was to his country, first.

"They walked to the door. They smiled lovingly at each other and shared a long embrace. He told her that he could hear every story that she read to him. He told her that they were the most beautiful things he had ever heard. She cried tears of joy, and they shared one last embrace. He promised her that he would come back for her after the war was over. He made her promise to keep writing stories of all the adventures they would share together.

"Several months passed with no word from him. Whenever an aircraft flew overhead, she waved her paper in the air to let him know that she was still writing him stories.

"In the coming months, when it was clear the war was coming to an end, she became excited at the prospect of seeing him once again. One late spring morning, she decided to relax in her garden and enjoy the day. From a distance, she could see a young man walking towards the house. He was dressed in all black. She stood up. He approached her and handed her an envelope, nodded, then turned and walked away.

"Seeing as though she was not a spouse, she was hesitant to think the worst. She opened the envelope. It was a letter indicating that her husband had been killed in action. She stood there for hours, refusing to believe the letter in her hand. When she finally accepted it as real, she gently folded the letter, walked back to the garden, looked to the sky, and thought of him. She couldn't help but to gleam some happiness at the fact that he listed her as his wife.

"She arranged to have his body, along with all of the stories she had written, buried in the catacombs. Upon her eventual death, she was buried beside him, where they could finally be together, in love, for all eternity.

"In the following decades, the catacombs experienced a rash of grave robberies. Some of the grave robbers eventually found their way into the coffins of Aunt Dulce-Ella and her husband's. The bodies were not harmed, but all the letters were stolen. They were never recovered. It is said that, if you walked the grounds of the catacombs at just the right time of night, you could hear Aunt Dulce-Ella crying ever so softly.

"When word of The Lady of the Catacombs started to spread, it is said that the townspeople would roam the grounds of the catacombs at night to hear her cries. Eventually, people from all over the globe would travel to the catacombs to hear her cries. As the tragic story of why she cries began to spread, people began to write love stories to replace the ones that were tragically stolen. Your nana told me that even Queen Elizabeth, herself, wrote a story in a special book and left it in the empty vault next to Aunt Dulce-Ella and her husband's vault. The strangest thing is, throughout history, it is said that no one has ever been able to find any records of her husband's actual existence. But you know how stories go. Things get added and removed every time they are told."

"That was a beautiful story, Mum. You still got it," I said sleepily. "I'm going to rest now."

"Goodnight, my love. Remember. Be brave. You are your only limit."

And just like that, she was gone again.

Chapter 46 - Imagined Darkness
~Penny~

"Penny. What do you remember about that night?"

"It was late. I was exhausted. We were on our way home. I don't remember where we were coming from. We had been in the car for a couple of hours. I sat in the middle. Josie sat behind Mum. Her doll sat behind Dad. Daddy always told her that she was too old for a doll. Mum couldn't care less.

"The sky was grey. Dark clouds were quickly rolling in. The car was silent, with only the intermittent sound of the windshield wipers screeching across the windshield.

"Dad grunted. 'You're going to ruin the windshield wipers.'

"Mum looked over at him. 'No. I won't. They're fine. There are enough raindrops.'

"I hated when she looked at him while she was driving.

'I've only counted one so far.'

'It's been steadily drizzling for the last few minutes.'

'Except, it hasn't. That's why the windshield wipers are screaming in pain.'

'Whatever.'

"I sighed loudly.

'Shh,' Josie said quietly.

"They always argued. It always ended in them yelling at each other.

'Let's ask the girls, then. Windshield wipers on or off?' Dad asked.

"Mum huffed. 'Leave them out of this.'

'Off!'

'On!'

"Josie nudged me and gave me a scowl. She always took Mum's side.

'Welp, I guess I was right.'

"Dad always liked to say that. Mum sighed, rested her head on the headrest, and began humming. Josie joined in and began humming as well.

"Dad sighed. 'I see how it is. Ignore me all you want.'

"Mum just kept humming. Dad never joined in on Mum's nursery rhymes. He always said English nursery rhymes were corny and silly.

"Low rumbles of thunder could be heard in the distance, and huge drops of rain began to fall. I sat up in my seat. Josie held my hand. She always comforted me whenever I got scared.

"Dad leaned over to Mum. 'You should pull over.'

"Mum turned and looked at him. 'It's fine. I can still see.'

"He pointed to the windshield. 'Stop looking at me and watch the road, then.'

"Josie tightened her grip on my hand. I think she was as scared as I was.

"*Boom!* There was lightning and thunder so loud, the car shook. Josie and I both let out a loud scream. Daddy reached his hand out and placed it on my leg. He yelled to Mum to pull over.

"*Boom!* This time it was louder and more violent than before. Mum would not pull the car over.

'We can make it!' Mum yelled.

"Josie leaned over and held me tight. 'Close your eyes, Penny. You just have to think happy thoughts and everything will be fine.'

'I'm too scared.' I replied.

'I'm scared too, but you still have to try. Let's do it together.'

"I closed my eyes and tried to think of my favorite things, but I couldn't. I was too scared. I looked out the window, all I could see was rain smashing against it. It felt like it was hitting hard enough to break the window. I closed my eyes and tried once more. That's when everything went black."

Chapter 47 - New Beginning
~Penny~

I woke to the bright morning sun shining in my window. I slowly blinked my eyes as I watched the dust particles dance in the rays of the sun. I got out of bed, walked over to the window, and opened it. A soft, warm breeze lightly ruffled the curtains. I slid the curtains open as far as they could go. I stood there and let the warmth of the sun envelope me. I took a deep breath. I felt rejuvenated. I felt like a new person. I was ready to take on the world.

The sunlight hit my ring. It revealed a bluish green color. I couldn't remember what that meant, but that didn't matter. I knew how I was feeling inside. I showered and got dressed. I even put on a little makeup. I stood in front of the mirror. "Be brave," I told myself.

I headed downstairs to the kitchen. For the first time in a long time, I was starving. On the kitchen table sat a large blueberry muffin. The withered cherry blossoms were replaced with fresh new ones. Draped across the chair was the dress from the mall. I smiled. "Josie," I said softly. I wished she was with me. There were so many things I wanted to say to her, so many things I wanted to take back.

After I was finished eating, I headed upstairs and changed into my dress. It had that familiar smell to it. I welcomed it. I loved the way I felt in that dress. I smiled at myself in the mirror, took a deep breath, and secured my necklace. It was time to attack the day.

"Be brave," I whispered. I knew exactly where I wanted to go. The park Dad used to take us to when I was younger. It had been so long since I'd been there. I had always avoided going there. I just didn't want to face the heartache of being there without him. I thought it would be the perfect place to test my new-found bravery and to be with Dad again, if only in spirit.

I grabbed a phone out the drawer, checked it, and put it in my bag. I grabbed my notebook and pen. I opened the door and took a hesitant step out. The reality of the moment hit me harder than I expected. I steeled myself and began my personal journey. As I exited beyond my gates and walked to the park, I took in all the sights and sounds around me. It had been so long since I just walked around the neighborhood. So much in the area had changed, yet so much was the same. At least, the same as I remembered them.

I watched two little boys rake leaves in a pile. One of them was angry at the other for jumping in too soon. As I walked past them, they smiled and began throwing leaves in the air. I walked past a little girl who was making leaf angels in the scattered leaves in her front yard. She smiled and waved at me. I smiled and returned the wave.

"I like your necklace. Are you an angel?" she asked.
"Thank you. No. No, I'm not." I replied shyly.
"Do you want to make more angels with me?"
"I'm sorry. I can't today. Maybe tomorrow?"
"You can't tomorrow."
"I can't?"
"No. You have to s—"
"Hailey." The girl's mom quickly approached. "I'm sure this nice lady has somewhere to be." She smiled at me. "I'm sorry."

I smiled back at her. "It's okay. She's adorable." Something about the way the little girl said that gave me an uneasy feeling inside. I ignored it. I wasn't going to let anything affect my good mood.

"Thank you. That's odd. She doesn't usually talk to strangers. You must have had quite the effect on her."

"Maybe she just really wanted me to play in the leaves. Autumn can have that effect."

"This is true. She'd play in them every day if I let her."

I smiled. "I kind of miss playing in them myself."
"Simpler times, right?"
"Much simpler."

"Well, sorry to keep you. Take care. I love your dress, by the way."

I blushed. "Thank you."

The little girl waved to me as I walked away. I thought about how much I would have loved to make leaf angels all day, instead of doing what I knew I had to do later on. "Stay positive," I whispered to myself. I pulled out my phone and checked the time. I quickened my pace a little bit. I was almost at the park.

I reached the entrance of the park. My heart was

racing. Each step I took was measured as I walked towards the giant tree in the center of the park. The tree was glorious. It was a lot bigger than I remembered it being. Or maybe I was just smaller. Dad would say that it was the tree that grew in the center of everything.

I made my way to the bench near the tree. I took a deep breath and sat down. I took my notebook out and sat it down. A butterfly landed on it and slowly flapped its wings. I reached my finger out to it. It flew away and rejoined its other friends that fluttered about. I closed my eyes. I just wanted to be present in that very moment. It was quiet. All I could hear was the wind and the rustling leaves. Emotion after emotion began to well up inside me. "Daddy," I called out. I wasn't sure if it felt like life was being sucked out of me or pumped back in. I gripped the sides of the bench tightly. The intensity of each emotion seemed to amplify. Memories began to overflow my mind. It was almost too much to consume. I took a deep breath. It had no effect. I took another deep breath. I held it for a few seconds, then let it out. There was silence. I opened my eyes. Everything was calm.

I began to cry profusely. I was extremely sad for what I lost, yet happy for the memories I had just gained. I reached into my bag and grabbed my phone. I really wanted to tell Josie what had just happened. I called her number. It went straight to voicemail. I hung up the phone. I called again. It went straight to voicemail again.

"Hey, I hope you aren't ignoring me. I'm really sorry about yesterday. You'll never believe where I am. I really wish you were here with me. I miss you. Hopefully I'll see you tonight. I really want to tell you about—. Hello? Hello?" I moved the phone from my ear and looked at it. It flickered, then turned off. "Great. Not another one," I mumbled. I sighed and clutched my necklace. "At least you somewhat work," I said. My eyes began to tear up.

"Hello. Is something wrong?" A man asked.

I saw him approach out of the corner of my eye. He caught me off guard. I didn't see anyone else around. He was handsome. There was something about his eyes. There was something strangely familiar about him. "I'm fine," I replied. I lied, but I wasn't about to dump my problems on a complete stranger. No matter how handsome he was.

He handed me a tissue. "You don't look fine."

"Really. I'm okay. I'll be fine."

He smiled. His smile was warm and inviting. He was shy and doing his best to hide it. He pointed to the bench that sat adjacent to the bench I was on. "Hey, if you want to talk about it, I'll be right over there."

"Thank you. You're sweet, but really, I'll be okay,"

"Okay, but I'm going to sit on that bench until I know you're okay, and I have lots of time. At least a day or two."

He was charming, and there was something about his smile that drew me in. I smiled at him. "Okay, maybe I'll see you tomorrow, then."

"Alright then. Tomorrow it is. Good thing it's warm out. Does it count if I run home and grab a pillow?"

It was at that moment that I did something I hadn't done in a very long time. I laughed. "Thank you."

"For sleeping on a bench? No problem. I've always wanted to see what that was like."

"No, silly. For making me laugh. It's been a long time since I've heard my own laughter."

"It's what I do," he said. He flashed that warm smile. "Hey, I know you are going through something, so I won't keep bothering you. You obviously came here to be alone. I kind of did the same thing, but if you ever need someone to talk to, I think I'm going to relocate my home to that bench over there."

"Is that so?"

"Well, at least until winter. I don't do cold very well."

I winked at him. "Well, maybe you won't have to wait that long."

With all the talk of time, it got me thinking about what I had to do in a few hours. I looked at my phone and sighed. "I'm sorry. Would you happen to know what time it is?"

"Battery died?"

"Yeah, something like that."

He pulled out his phone and looked at it strangely. He seemed a bit exasperated.

"Everything okay?" I asked.

"Yeah, sorry. It's 1:43," he said.

I thought about the odds of meeting him at that time. I also didn't realize it was that late. "Oh? That's interesting."

"You're telling me. I've been—"

What I had to deal with in a few hours quickly started to weigh on me. "I'm sorry. I have to go," I said sadly.

"Okay. Well, hopefully we'll meet again. If not in this life, in another."

In my head I thought it was cute. A little on the

cheesy side, but he pulled it off. I figured that maybe I would catch him there the next time I came. "Perhaps we will. I'd like that. Same time. Same sandbox. Don't be late." I winked.

I grabbed my things and hurried towards the entrance. Out of nowhere, a strong gust of wind blew, slowing my steps. I quickened my pace and exited the park. My anxiety was starting to get the best of me, so I made my way back home.

Chapter 48 - The Shark Tank
~Penny~

I was dressed and ready to go. I made sure the door was locked. I didn't want any surprise entries. I sat at the kitchen table, waiting. I was hoping that Josie would show up and possibly get me out of this mess, but I knew what she would say. "It's your mess, buttercup. Clean it up yourself."

I thought I had built myself up. I convinced myself that I was ready to tell him, but as the time drew closer, I found myself getting more and more anxious. I paced the floor for almost an hour. I rehearsed what I was going to say to him. I wasn't sure if he would understand or not, but technically, I never told him I would marry him. I sat down at the table again. I stared at the clock, hoping to slow it down. I grabbed my notebook and tried to write. All of the thoughts in my head translated to nothing but my name written in cursive over and over again. I turned the page and tried again. I found myself just staring at the blank page, thinking of nothing. Out of nowhere, thoughts of the guy from the park gathered in my head. I thought about his smile. I allowed myself a smile at the thought of it. I closed my eyes and visualized his face. There was something so familiar about his eyes. Something so familiar about him, like, someone you know you know, but you don't know where you know them from.

I kept my eyes closed. I visualized us together, walking in the park. We are holding hands. We are happy. We are light as feathers. All of our worries are behind us. The birds serenade us as the wind gently blows leaves from in front of us, revealing a path for us to walk on together. He pulls me closer. He puts his arm around me. He is warm. I melt into him. "We found each other," he says. I smile and stare into his eyes.

A knock on the door snapped me back to reality. "Yo! Babe! You in there? It's time to celebrate!"

Anger and frustration quickly built up in me over what he just interrupted. I swiped my hand to the side, knocking everything on the kitchen table onto the floor. "Crap!" I exclaimed, realizing that I knocked the tome to the floor. I knelt down and picked it up. All the loose pages flew out.

"Yo! I hear you in there. We're going to be late."

I looked at the clock. "You're early! I'll be ready in a minute." I checked the front of the book. Everything was still intact. I quickly straightened out each page before putting it back in. I grabbed the last page and straightened it out. I looked closely at it. It was the missing story from my old story book. My face lit up with excitement. I remembered the story.

The knocking started again. "Babe! We're gonna be late! What are you doing?"

"I said give me a minute! Just go to the car. I'll meet you there."

"The boys are waiting for me. Two minutes! I'll leave you if you don't hurry up. I'm serious."

"Yeah, right. I wish I could get so lucky," I mumbled. I heard him walk away. I stood up with the old page and began reading the story of the girl who fell in the big fish tank and was rescued from a shark by her hero. I flipped the page over to find a drawing of the girl and her hero hand in hand. I looked closer at the picture. A strange feeling washed over me. It felt similar to the feeling in the park.

There was a pounding on the door again. "WE...HAVE...TO...GO!"

"Fine!" I yelled. I carefully put the page back in the book, grabbed my purse, walked over to the door, and flung it open. "I told you to wait in the car."

"I just couldn't wait to see you, babe." He looked me up and down. "Whoa, nelly! Looking good, babe!"

"I asked you not to call me that."

"What's the big deal? Stop giving me a hard time. It's our night to celebrate."

I just stared at him blankly.

"Hey! Where's your ring?"

"It's in my purse. I was working out. I didn't want it to get messed up."

"Well, put it on. I want everyone to see it on you."

I sighed, grabbed the ring out of my purse, and slid it on. "Happy?"

"Hell yeah! We better head out before I want to stay here. Just the two of us."

We walked out and got in the car. As he drove, I sat in the passenger seat, staring out the window, mesmerized by the reflection of trees on the window. I watched people walking up and down the sidewalk.

I saw people standing in their yards conversing with one another. I wondered about their lives. I wondered if things were as carefree as they looked from the outside.

"...and your family on the other side. Wanna know what I want to say when we accept? It's going to be awesome! Hello? Are you listening to me?"

The annoying sound of his voice snapped me back to reality. "What?"

"Check this out. You should say 'I do. A hundred times, yes.' Or something like that. That'll show everyone how much you love me. You know what I mean, babe?"

I felt a single tear roll down my cheek as I stared out the window. "Yeah."

"You okay, babe? You been kinda quiet."

"I'm okay. Just nervous about being around all these people. Where are we going, again?"

"Tankers. We're almost there. The place is a dump, so It shouldn't be that crowded. All the boys are already there, so it's gonna be lit."

We pulled into the parking lot. He pulled into the closest parking space. I put my hand on the engagement ring. "Can we talk about something before we go in?" I asked.

He leaned over the seat and got really close to me. "What up, babe? You wanna fool around a bit, before we go in? I'm down."

I pushed him away from me. "Stop it! Would you just listen to me? I...I...don't think we should—"

I was interrupted by a pounding on the window. "Open up, lover boy! You two lovebirds gonna come in or stay out here making out?"

Joey rolled down both windows. "What up, man?! I thought you guys were inside already." He turned to me. "Let's go. Everyone is waiting for us." I nodded reluctantly, and we both got out of the car.

"Streetlight! It's been forever. You still looking mighty fine. How the hell are you?"

"Hey, Pike." I said in a perturbed tone. "I don't go by that name anymore."

"Well excuse me. How would you like me to address you? Your highness? Your grace?"

"Penny is fine. Smartass."

Pike frowned. "I see the attitude hasn't changed."

"Bro, leave my fiancé alone or I'll clean your clock."

"Please! I taught you everything you know. I'd pound you and then take your girl."

"Ha! You wish. The student has become the teacher."

"Yeah, you're probably right. Look at you. What the hell have you been eating? Whole cows? Let's get in there. I'm sure the boys can't wait to see you guys."

We walked in and headed to a table near the bar. As we approached, I saw faces that I hadn't seen in a very long time, faces I would have been fine with never seeing again. We were greeted by cheers, shouts, and clanging bottles. I felt so anxious, I wanted to just disappear.

I said my hellos, then found a chair to sit in, somewhat away from the crowd. Joey was too busy drinking to even notice I slipped away. I was kicking myself. I knew the car ride was my best chance to break it off. There was no way it was happening inside the club. I just had to sit and endure this agony until it was time to leave.

"Hey there, Streetlight," a quiet voice from behind me said. "Never thought I'd see you again, let alone see you with that big moron."

I turned around to find Char standing behind me. I stood up and gave her a hug. Char was older than all of us. She kind of ran in the same bad crowd as I did back in the day. She was smart enough to break away. She always told me that I was foolish for hanging out with them, and that I was meant to do much greater things. It took me longer than it should have for me to realize that she was right. Well, at least about half of it. "Hey, Char. I didn't expect to see you here."

"Well, when I heard the news that you were actually going to marry that jackass, I figured someone better come and knock some sense into you."

"Yeah. I—"

"What are ya doing, kid? You don't love him. You couldn't possibly love him. Hell, with the way he acts, I doubt if his own mama loves him." She put her hand out and opened it. "Well, anyway, you better let me see it."

"See what?"

Char lifted up my hand. "The ring." She examined it. "It's real, alright. Never thought I'd see the day where he spent money on anyone besides himself. Better be careful with that. Looks like it's a few sizes too big."

I nodded. Tears flowed down my face. Char grabbed me and hugged me tightly. "I never actually said yes, you know. He asked me. I was stunned that he even thought I would want to. Before I could get a whole sentence out, he just assumed I was going to say yes. You know how he is."

"Yes, I do. He's an arrogant SOB. You gotta tell him,

honey. The longer you put this off, the harder it will be."

"I know. I tried to tell him in the car, but Pike interrupted."

"Jackass number two."

"Yep."

"Come on, honey. Let's get you some good ole liquid courage."

"You know I can't drink."

"Oh, that's right. The whole loss of control thing. Speaking of, how are you even able to be in a place like this?"

I reached in my shirt and pulled out my necklace. "Science." I winked.

"Well, look at you! That must be some wicked science. Come on, honey. Let's get me a drink, then." She grabbed my hand. My ring almost slid off. "Oh, for crying out loud. Put that thing in your pocket. Last thing you need is him going berserk over a lost ring that I'm sure he didn't insure. Everyone here knows you're engaged. His big mouth made sure of that."

She took the ring off and put it in my pocket. We walked over to the bar. She ordered a beer. I ordered a glass of water. As we made our way back to where we were sitting, some guy walked up beside me. "Hey, beautiful, how about I buy you a real drink?"

"I'm good, thanks," I said quietly.

"Oh, come on baby. I know just the thing."

Out of nowhere, Joey came over and shoved the guy into the bar, hard. "You talking to my girl, punk?"

The guy hit the bar hard, but stayed on his feet. "The hell's your problem, man?" the guy said.

"You talking to my girl. That's my problem."

"Man, how the hell was I supposed to know she was your girl? You need anger management, man."

"What I need to do is teach you a lesson. Hey! Everybody! Who wants to see me teach this punk a lesson?"

All of Joey's boys began cheering and raising their beers. Joey began advancing on the guy. I grabbed his arm and attempted to pull him back. "Stop it! He didn't know!" I yelled.

"He knew! He saw that ring on your finger!" As he said it, he looked down and noticed that the ring was no longer on my finger. His face turned a dark shade of red. "Where's the ring, babe? He said in a slow, deep, sinister tone that I had never heard from him before.

I was frightened. I never believed he would hurt me until that very moment. "It's...I...put..."

"Leave her alone, you big lug head. I took the ring off and put it in her pocket. The damn thing is three sizes too big," Char said.

"Stay out of this, Charlotte." His eyes never moved from me. "That's the second time you took it off. Something you want to say to me? I hope it's not someone else. Because if it is, he'd better be a big MFer!" he said in that same sinister tone.

I knew it was an opening, but I was frightened by the look on his face. He grabbed my wrist. "I asked you a question!"

Anger instantly boiled up inside me. "Let go of me! Now!" I saw the lights flicker, and I began to panic. I pulled my arm out of his grip. "I'm leaving!" As I walked away, he began yelling things at me. An announcement began playing over the speakers and drowned him out. I didn't care. I didn't want to hear it anyway. Before I could reach the exit, I could hear him swearing at me, calling me all sorts of names. "You're nothing without me anyway! Freak!" he yelled.

I turned to him, reached in my pocket, and threw the ring at him as hard as I could. It hit him right in his forehead. I'm not sure what angered him more, the fact that it hit him or the fact that I threw it back. He rushed towards me and pushed me to the floor. I sat there for a minute. I looked at him. I was angry. Tears rolled down my face. I moved to get up, I heard a crunching sound. I looked down, my necklace was broken and lying on the ground. He laughed at me. I stood up. I was enraged. All the lights began to flicker. The exit sign flickered and started to spark. I walked towards him. "Move!" I yelled.

He stood there, blocking the exit. He looked up at the sign. "What's wrong? Afraid everyone's gonna see what a freak you are?"

"You are such an ass! Get out of my way!"

"I'm not going anywhere. You had your chance. I'm the best thing that ever happened to you. Nobody else is gonna want you. You are going to die old and lonely in that house all by yourself."

I cocked back my arm and punched him right in the jaw. He staggered backwards. I could hear cheering and laughter in the crowd. He thumbed the side of his mouth. He was bleeding. He grunted and took a step towards me. I went to hit him again. He grabbed my arm and twisted it. I screamed in agony. He raised his hand to hit me. I desperately tried to pull away. Out of nowhere, I saw someone fly in and kick him square in his mouth. The force of the kick knocked him backwards and off his feet. I stumbled and fell to the ground.

"Leave her the hell alone!" the guy yelled. I quickly sat up and gathered myself. He looked at me. My heart raced. I could hardly catch my breath. "You? From my story." My mind was swirling. I couldn't fully grasp hold of what was happening. It was him. The same guy from the park. He smiled at me with that warm smile. I smiled back at him. It was as if time itself stood still, the room was empty, and it was just us. I wasn't sure why it all felt so familiar, but it did. It felt perfect.

He reached his hand out to help me up. I reached my hand out to his. In an instant, we were no longer alone. Loud voices and flickering lights filled the room. Out of nowhere, Joey grabbed his shirt and pulled him away. "The hell? Joey looked at him curiously, and with disdain all over his face. "Is this your mystery guy?"

"No! You don't know what you're talking about! Let him go, Shark!

He sniveled. "Didn't I tell you he'd better be a big motherf—"

"Shark, leave him alone!"

I could feel myself losing control. The lights began flickering more rapidly than before. People in the crowd started yelling and running towards the exit. Joey hit the guy from the park so hard, he fell to the ground. Out of nowhere, another guy started throwing punches at Joey. The guy from the park somehow managed to get to his feet and threw another punch at Joey. He missed and Joey hit him again, this time even harder than before. He went down in a heap. Joey turned his attention back to the previous guy. He just kept landing punch after punch. The guy was strong. He kept fighting back, but he appeared to be out on his feet. Joey just kept hitting him over and over again. I jumped on his back and tried to get him to stop. "Shark, stop it! You're killing him!" He flung me off and continued to pound on the guy.

    I slammed up against the wall, hitting my head. I stood up and looked around the club. The crowd was actually cheering. It was complete chaos. Joey had turned his attention to the guy from the park. He walked over, stood over top of him, and raised his foot. I knew what he was planning to do. Fear and anger overtook me. I grabbed the fire extinguisher off the wall, ran over to Joey, and with everything in me, I let out a scream and swung it at his head with strength I didn't know I possessed. He went down in a heap.

    As I stood there in the darkness, crying, and unable to move, a moment of intense clarity washed over me. Everything was now clear to me, as if I knew it all along. My body weakened as my mind processed the information. I began to shake. I no longer felt control over my own body. My legs gave out. I fell to the ground next to the guy from the park. With my remaining strength, I moved his head to my lap and held his face, as I rested my head on his. The faintest of light illuminated the room. I sat there, holding him, while staring at the ceiling fan. It spun slower and slower, until it completely stopped. Despite my best efforts, my eyes slowly began to close. The darkness swallowed me.

Chapter 49 - The Day Everything Changed
~Penny~

"Penny, what do you remember about that night?"

"It was very late. We were almost home. We had been in the car for almost ten hours. I sat behind Mum. Josie sat behind dad. Her doll sat in the middle. Daddy always thought it was odd that a doll had a doll. Mum thought it was clever.

"The sky was ominous. Dark clouds were quickly rolling in. The car was silent, with only the intermittent sound of the windshield wipers, screeching across the windshield.

"Dad laughed. 'You trying to clean the windshield in preparation for the rain?'

"Mum pointed to the windshield. 'It's raining now.'

'I've counted two drops so far.'

Mum softly laughed. 'Oh, come off it. It's been steadily drizzling for the last few minutes.'

'It has, has it? Is that why the windshield wipers are screaming in pain?' Dad laughed.

"I quietly laughed.

'Shh,' Daddy said jokingly. 'You know she hates

when you encourage me.'

"They always playfully argued. It always ended in them smiling and staring into each other's eyes. Sometimes they even shared a kiss in front of me.

'Let's ask Penny. Windshield wipers on or off?' Dad asked.

'Off! Josie and Alexandria say off too.'

'Welp, I guess the home team wins again.'

"Dad always liked to say that when we were in the states. They both laughed and interlocked their hands. Mum smiled, rested her head on the headrest, and began singing softly.

My grandfather's clock was too large for the shelf, so it stood ninety years on the floor.

It was taller by half than the old man himself, though it weighed not a pennyweight more.

"I always loved when Mum sang that song. I jumped in and began singing along. Dad chuckled. 'I see what you did there, stealing back the home field advantage. Well played.'

"Mum just smiled and kept singing. Dad never joined in on Mum's nursery rhymes. He always claimed it was too late for a grown up to learn new nursery rhymes, but every now and then we could hear him humming along.

"Low rumbles of thunder could be heard in the distance, and huge drops of rain began to fall. I sat up in my seat. I grabbed Jose's hand. I always held her when I was feeling scared.

"Dad leaned over to Mum. 'Do you think we should pull over?'

"Mum turned and looked at him. 'I think we should be fine. Let's at least get over the bridge.'

"Dad nodded and pointed to the windshield. I tightened my grip on Josie's hand.

"*Boom!* There was lightning and thunder so loud, the car shook. I let out a loud scream. Dad reached his hand back and placed it on my leg. I heard him tell Mum that she should probably pull over.

"*Boom!* This time it was louder and more violent than before. Mum pulled the car over and parked under the nearest street light. She looked at me through the rear-view mirror and gave me an affirming nod. I leaned over and held Josie and Alex tightly. 'I'm really scared,' I said.

'Close your eyes, Penny. You just have to think happy thoughts and everything will be fine,' Mum said.

'I'm too scared.'

'I'm scared too, but you have to be brave. Remember the phrase? Let's say it together. Mother's earth.'

'Father's heaven.'

'Mother's earth.'

'Father's heaven.'

"I closed my eyes and thought of my favorite things. I felt a calm wash over me. Everything was now still. I opened my eyes. The skies were clear. The rain had stopped. Mum was softly humming and driving along the road.

'All better now?' Dad asked.

"I nodded. 'Mhm.'

"Mum looked at me through the rear-view mirror and smiled. As I looked into the rear-view mirror, the clear sky became dark again, and the rain began to pound on all of the windows. I could see a large, black figure approaching the car. I screamed in horror at what I saw.

'Mummy! It's coming! Go! Drive! It's coming!' I yelled.

'Penny, calm down. What's coming?' Dad asked frantically.

"Instinctively, Mum began to drive faster. Dad turned to Mum. 'Honey, slow down.'

"Mum kept driving faster and faster. I looked out of the back window and saw that it was still coming. I screamed again.

'Penny, you have to calm down. You have to go to your happy place. Penny, you have to calm down,' Mum said frantically.

"The car was moving so fast, the street lights appeared to shimmer. I remember the look of terror on Dad's face as he looked out the back window. He turned to Mum to tell her to speed up. I looked in the rear-view mirror again. The black figure was closer than ever. I let out a loud scream. That's when everything went black.

"When I came to, everything was hazy. Mum was out cold. Daddy was writhing in pain. The car was leaning over the side of a bridge. He tried to sit up in his seat. The car started to rock from side to side. He sat still, took deep breaths, and then looked around the car. He reached over to Mum and tried to wake her. 'Sweetheart, can you hear me? Wake up!'

'Daddy?' I called out.

'Oh, my goodness. Penny are you okay, honey?'

'I think so. My head hurts really bad.'

'I know, honey. Hang in there. I'm going to get you guys out of here.'

"The reality of what he said didn't register with

me at the time. The car rocked back and forth again. I could hear the sounds of sirens off in the distance. 'Daddy, are they coming to help?'

'They are, honey. Try to stay still.'

'But I can't reach Josie and Alexandria.'

'Just sit tight. I'll get them.'

"As Daddy reached for my dolls, the car shifted and leaned over the edge a little more. Mum let out a moan. She opened her eyes and slowly began to look around. 'Honey, what's going on?' she asked. She was in really bad shape. 'I think I'm stuck.'

'Just sit tight. Don't make any sudden movements. Help is on the way.'

"The thunder and lightning continued. With each bolt of lightning, I could see just how perilously close the car was to going over the edge. The sound of the sirens never seemed to get any closer. The car rocked again and tilted over the edge a little more. I wanted to scream, but I was too scared.

'They aren't going to make it in time,' Daddy said quietly.

'Andre what are you doing?' Mum yelled out.

'They aren't going to make it,' he said. This time, not so quietly. 'I...I have an idea. It's a weight thing.'

Mum cried. 'Andre! Please tell me what you are doing!'

'I need you to trust me, baby.' He turned to me. 'Can you be brave for Daddy?'

"I nodded my head. He took his seat belt off and slowly began to climb onto Mum's seat. The car began to lean more towards the road. 'Penny, I need you to lean back as much as you can towards your door. Can you do that for me?'

'Mhm.'

"As I leaned, the car tilted ever so slightly. Dad laid there, exhausted, and in obvious pain. 'Okay. We should be good for a while.'

'Daddy, I still can't reach them.'

'Honey, you may just have to—'

"Mum spoke through her pain. 'Keep being brave, sweetheart. We'll be out of here soon.' She turned to Dad and spoke softly. 'See what you can do. You know that doll is like a sister to her.'

"Dad tried to maneuver his body in a way that would allow him to slide my dolls up to me with his feet. Each time he tried, he got closer and closer, but his pain got greater. 'Okay. Last try. This is it.' He moved his feet down and squeezed them together around both of the dolls and slowly brought them within my reach. I grabbed them and hugged them tightly.

'Thank you, Daddy!'

'You're welcome,' he said. His breathing was labored. 'Now, to get back to—'

"As he moved his body back to his previous position, the car shook violently. He lost his grip on the seat. He slid down towards the passenger door, forcing it open. He grabbed the seat belt and held on tightly. His legs dangled out of the car.

'Daddy!' I screamed.

'Andre! Oh, my God. I'm coming, honey. Hold on.'

'Baby, wait! Don't move. You have to stay on your side or the car will tip.'

"I reached my hand out towards him. 'Daddy!'

'Lean back, honey. I need you to lean back. It's all going to be okay.'

"I leaned back and watched as he dangled from the car. Lighting continued to strike, and the rain continued to pour down. The car teetered back and forth. The street light above us dimmed and flickered. The sounds of the sirens could no longer be heard. I looked down at my father as he struggled to hold on. He looked at me. He had tears in his eyes. He gave me a look of resignation.

'I want you two to know something. I love you both very much. You both are my world, my sunrise, and my sunset. You both make my life complete. You are the reason I breathe. I want you to know that I will always be with you.'

'Andre, no!' Mum cried out.

'Shh. It's okay. Everything happens for a reason, right? Take care of Penny. Show her how to use her light to make the world a better place.'

'Andre, no. please don't leave me.'

'It's just for a little while. Find me again.'

"Mum cried as she reached out for Dad. 'I love you, Andre'

'I love you too, honey. All the world and then some.'

"Mum's cries got louder. Dad turned and looked at me. 'Hey. Chin up, buttercup. You are a very special girl, you know that?'

I nodded. 'Mhm.' Tears poured down my face.

'You are more special than you can ever imagine. Always remember that. You are going to go on and have a wonderful life. Whatever you do, be brave, and know that I will always love you.'

'Daddy, I hear the sirens. Just hold on.'

"He looked me in the eyes and smiled a sad smile.

'Goodbye for now, honey. I love you.'

'Daddy....'

"He smiled and let go of the seat belt. I screamed as I watched his body fall further away from the car. Mum let out a cry of anguish. The car shifted sideways, closer to the street side of the bridge. Mum reached back and held out her hand. I reached out to her. She closed her hand around mine. We sobbed together as the deafening sounds of the sirens approached.

"I sat in the back of the ambulance and stared at the spinning red lights. Through the blinding lights, I watched them take Mum away. I had no tears left to shed. I grabbed Josie and Alexandria, squeezed them as tight as I could, and closed my eyes."

Part Three

Chapter 50 - Back to Reality
-Kaleb-

The doctor walked in the room. He examined the monitors and wrote something down on the clipboard. This was a different doctor than the one that normally came in. He wasn't mean, per se, but his bedside manner left a lot to be desired. I figured I would take a shot at getting some information out of him. "Doc, how ya doing? Shouldn't he have woken up by now?"

"Mr. Barnes, your friend suffered massive trauma to his brain. I cannot give you a timetable of when he will wake up. We just have to—" He walked out of the room and motioned for me to follow him. Once we were both in the hallway, he closed the door. "Listen, with the amount of trauma he suffered, we have to accept the fact that he may never wake up again."

"No, I can't accept that. He has to wake up. This is my fault. I have to make it right."

"With all due respect, Mr. Barnes, every man is responsible for their own actions. Unless you were the one throwing the punches at him, I wouldn't say that you were at fault."

"He was trying to protect me. So, yeah, it is kind

of my fault." I could tell the doctor wanted to say something, but I spoke again before he got the chance. "Why did you bring me in the hallway to tell me that he may never wake up? Can he hear us?"

"I can't say for sure, Mr. Barnes. However, some recent studies have shown that patients in comas can sometimes benefit from hearing stories from the familiar voices of loved ones. It may help awaken the unconscious brain and speed recovery."

"Really? So, I should tell him stories?"

"Tell him stories. Continue to tell him things about your everyday life. Tell him anything. Hearing those things in a familiar voice is said to exercise the parts of the brain responsible for long-term memories. That stimulation helps trigger little signs of awareness, and as a result, coma patients can wake more easily." The doctor looked down at his pager. "I'm sorry. I have to go. Excuse me."

I walked back into the room. I couldn't stand to see Kaje laying there helpless. He was on his way to fulfilling his dream. Now, because of me, he was stuck in this bed. Why couldn't I just leave it alone? Why didn't I just walk away? Why did I risk my life for a woman I barely knew?

I leaned over Kaje. "Why did you have to jump in? Why didn't you just let me fight my fight?" Tears streamed down my face. "Why couldn't you just—"

The nurse entered the room. I quickly wiped the tears from my face. "Visiting hours are almost over, Mr. Barnes." She smiled warmly. "I just have to check a few things, then I'll be out of your hair."

"I know. I was just getting my stuff together."

"Take your time. You still have some time. I'll get

out of here so you can say whatever you want to say. I'll see you tomorrow, right?"

"You know it, as soon as I get off work."

"You're a good friend. I know you don't believe that, and I know you blame yourself for him being here, but you have been here to see him every day, without fail. That's amazing. That's what good friends do."

"Thanks, nurse Nicole. I appreciate it."

"Would you stop with that 'nurse Nicole,' silliness. You can just call me Nicole."

"I'll stop when you stop calling me by my father's name. He's Mr. Barnes. I'm Kaleb."

"Very well. Kaleb it is."

"Thank you, Nicole."

"I'll see you tomorrow, Mr...I'll see you tomorrow, Kaleb. Get some rest. You look like you could use a good night's sleep."

"I'll try. Goodnight, Nicole."

She walked out and closed the door behind her. I moved the chair closer to Kaje's bed. "Dude, don't look at me like that. I was not flirting with her. She was flirting with me. I was just being nice. She is kinda cute though. Nice tattoos. A little too young. Well, maybe not. Whatever. I can't even think about that right now. Yeah, yeah, I know what you are thinking. No, I haven't seen her since that night at Tankers. That's old news now. I'm not sure she would even want to see me again. I'm not sure what I would even say to her anyway. 'Hi, remember me? The guy from the brawl that tried to save you, but ended up getting knocked out?' Besides, I wouldn't even know where to find her. Not that I have had time to look anyway.

Want to hear something crazy though? Every now and then, I feel like I can feel her presence. Like she is close, but not close. You know what I mean? Of course, you do. Of course, you don't think I'm crazy. Why would you think that? You've always known my life to be perfectly normal and uneventful." My tone dripped with sarcasm.

I started gathering my things and putting them in my bag. It was almost time to go home. "I'm outta here, man. I'll be back tomorrow. Doc said I should tell you stories or something to help you wake up. I'll fill you in on all the exhilarating things going on at work. It's really boring without you there. Every day seems the same. I would tell you about my dreams, but ever since that night, my dreams are filled with a bunch of nothingness. Like I'm just floating in space or something. That doesn't make for very good storytelling. Maybe I'll bring a book of fables." I laughed a bit, thinking about what he would say to that. "Seriously, do me a favor and wake up, so I don't have to tell you bedtime stories."

I headed for the door. I stopped and looked at him for a moment. Sadness began to set in as I replayed that night in my head for the hundredth time. I still wasn't sure how I could have handled it any differently. I couldn't have just walked away from her. Maybe I should have just kicked that dude harder.

I walked out of the hospital and headed to my car. It was unusually warm outside. I guess autumn was still holding on. You'd never hear me complain about that. I drove home to my apartment. As I got to my door, I stopped and took a long look at what used to be Monica's door. I sure could have used her company, no matter how annoying it was.

I opened my door and headed straight for the couch. I turned on some new age music to help me relax. The doctor said that I was lucky to be alive, and not because of the fight. He said my blood pressure was so high, I was a ticking time bomb. The music also helped me fall asleep, which had been hard to do since that night, between the headaches and the flashbacks. I replayed that night over and over in my head. I had convinced myself that the harder I tried, and the more times I replayed it, the possibility of changing the outcome would increase. Of course, it didn't.

I started to doze off. My dreams, which used to be things of wonder, were now blank empty canvases. They made me feel more alone than I felt in my awakened state. Either way, I couldn't fight it any longer. I closed my eyes, lost myself in the music, and let sleep overtake me.

Chapter 51 - Awakening
~Penny~

Sometimes the pain of knowing the truth is too much to push through. I'd lost track of the days and nights since that night that changed my life, for a second time. The visions in my head, the memories that flooded my mind with such precision, the harsh reality, and the cruelness of the timing was too much for me to bear. I didn't know what was real anymore. I didn't want to know. My pain was real, and it was the only thing I could count on. My days consisted of lying on my bed or curled up in a ball, crying.

I made my way to the bathroom. I splashed cold water on my face and stared into the mirror. I didn't even recognize my own reflection. I was a shell of myself, wasting away in sadness. I covered my face and wept for what felt like hours. The sound of the water hitting the floor brought me back to reality. I quickly turned the water off and watched as the water slowly ran down the drain. I grabbed a washcloth, dipped it in the water, and rang it out. I threw it over my face and washed the tears away. The cool cloth felt good on my eyelids, so I left it there for a minute. I removed the cloth and stumbled backwards, taken aback at what I saw in the mirror. A reflection of a sad, little girl stood in the mirror staring back at me. It was the same girl from that day in the dressing room.

"I'm sorry you're sad," she said.

I stood there, quiet. I wasn't sure what to reply with. "Who are you?" I asked, after a long pause.

"That's a silly question. You know who I am."

"I guess I do. Why are you here? Why now?"

"You know why."

"I don't know what—"

"Open your heart."

"Open my heart?" I said angrily. Do you realize that everyone that I have ever held dear to me is gone? Open my heart? Open it to what? To more fantasies of love and happiness, to more heartache and pain? Yeah, I'll pass."

"Not everyone," she said. Her big, brown eyes started to tear up. Her image in the mirror started to fade.

"Hey! Don't go!" I shouted. "I don't want to be here alone. Don't go!" Her image faded away. I found myself looking directly into my own eyes. I covered my face and wept again.

I walked into the hallway. The house was eerily quiet. It almost felt like a tomb. I felt trapped in an endless cycle of sadness. The house that once held so much love and so many joyous memories was now just a black hole of despair. All of the good memories were devoured by all the bad ones, and there was nothing I could do about it.

I made my way around the house, searching for anything, anything that would give me hope. I walked downstairs to the kitchen. It was a mess. On the table sat my broken necklace, my mood ring, and the old tome. I hadn't touched them in ages. The desire to read or write anything was gone. I'd had moments of thinking I wanted to write something, but nothing ever came of them.

I walked down the stairs to the workout room. The place that was once my sanctuary, and my escape from my dark thoughts, was just a dusty, cobweb infested room that served no purpose. I stared at the room. Sadly, that had become an almost daily ritual. Part of me was hoping that by looking at the room and remembering my old routines, it would rekindle my passion. It did nothing of the sort.

I walked back to my bedroom, slid open the curtain, and looked outside. The sun had already begun to set. Time really had no meaning for me anymore. Ever since that night, everything seemed to run together. I looked off into the distance. The full moon shone brightly. A strong, steady wind rocked the trees back and forth, causing them to creek like old rocking chairs. Amazingly, through it all, the trees still held onto their leaves of bright red, orange, yellow, and gold. As the wind blew the large tree in front of the window, the branches violently swayed back and forth. It seemed to be the only tree that had lost all its leaves. Inside, a part of me wondered how the tree felt about that.

I closed the curtain and headed towards my bed. I heard the soft hoot of an owl. I rushed back to the window and looked out. It was the same owl as before. Although, it looked much older. Its feathers were ruffled and mangled. It looked weary, as if it flew a great distance to get here. Its eyes were nowhere near as bright as before. It looked at me. I looked back intently. That familiar calm began to wash over me again. Although, not as vivid as before, I felt as if I was outside of my body, looking at myself. It was different than looking in a mirror. It felt like I was looking at all aspects of myself. Like, I could see my physical, emotional, and mental status as something that I could reach out and touch. I saw parts of me that I didn't know existed anymore. I saw a child surrounded by light, by strength, by hope, and by love.

In an instant, I felt as if I returned to my own body. The owl, still looking at me, its eyes now bright as ever, seemed to smile at me. On the branch that the owl stood on, I noticed one single leaf still hung on. I hadn't noticed it before. It had endured all of the wind and rain. I wondered why it hung on so tightly. Was it scared to let go? Did it not know how to let go, or did it not want to let go? I remember my dad used to say, "Sometimes what we perceive as an act of cowardice, is actually an incredible act of bravery." I wondered if he knew just how prophetic he was being.

I wiped a tear from my face. "Stay strong, little leaf," I whispered.

The owl let out a soft hoot. Its now brightly lit eyes pierced right through me. I looked deeply into them. It was like I was looking beyond this world into an endless void. In an instant, everything was still. I looked around me. There was nothing but darkness. I called out, but my voice just echoed into the void. I began to panic. I closed my eyes and took deep, steadying breaths.

"Mother's earth. Father's heaven. Mother's earth. Father's heaven," I recited repeatedly. My body began to feel light as a feather as I felt myself move further and further into the void.

Chapter 52 - The Void Dreamscape
-Kaleb-

"Hello? Is someone there?" I call out.

I am somewhere dark, with only small glimmers of light appearing and disappearing. Everything feels hazy. I am not standing. I am not sitting. It would feel like I am floating, except I don't feel like I have a body.

"Hello? Is anybody out there?"

There is no response. The little glimmers of light appear again, then quickly fade away. I look around. More glimmers appear, then slowly fade away. In the distance, a soft warm light begins to shine. It pulses as it moves about. It leaves little traces of its light along its path as it draws closer.

"Hello?" The light stops and everything is still, as if frozen in time. The only movement is the dim flicker of lights from the hundreds of glowing flowers that now cover the ground. The flowers have a calming, pinkish light.

"Hello?" a voice in my head responds. It is a young girl's voice. Something about it sounds familiar.

"Hi, can you hear me?"

"Yes. Who are you?"

"I...I'm..." I don't answer. It's not that I don't want to tell her my name, I just can't recall it. "What's your name?"

There's a long silence. "M—" She doesn't finish. "Where are we? Why can't I see you?"

"I'm not sure. I was hoping you would know," I reply.

"I'm sorry. I don't."

"Are you afraid?"

"No. Are you?" she asks.

"I feel like I should be, but I'm not."

"So, we are alone here, together?"

"It would appear so."

"Do you know how you got here?" I ask.

"I don't know. The same way you did, I guess," she replies.

"Are you sad?"

"No. Why would I be sad?"

"I don't know. I just feel sadness. And since we are the only two here, I just thought maybe you were sad."

"Maybe it's you."

"Maybe. Either way, I'm glad I'm not here alone. I'm glad you are here with me, wherever this is. Things were hazy at first. Now they seem to be a little clearer."

"Hazy?"

"Yeah, kind of like how you feel when you just wake up from a deep sleep. But now I'm starting to sense and feel things."

She doesn't respond, but I can still feel her presence. Whether she wanted to admit it or not, there was sadness all around her.

"You are quiet. Have you closed yourself off from me?" I ask.

"No, I haven't."

"Yes, you have."

"No, I haven't."

"Uh huh!"

"Nuh uh."

We go back and forth like children. The odd thing is, it feels completely natural. I wonder if I sounded like a young boy to her.

"Yes, you have."

"Did not."

"Did too."

"Did not."

"Then prove it."

There is silence for a few seconds. Then all of a sudden, I begin to feel her presence all around me. Not like she is next to me, but like she is everywhere, everything, and everyone. The future, past, and present. Then as quickly as the feeling started, it stopped.

"Whoa! What did you just do?" I ask.

"What do you mean?"

"Did you just feel that?"

"Feel what?"

"That thing. That feeling?"

"I—"

And just like that, I can't feel her presence any longer.

Chapter 53 - A Time for Reminiscing
-Kaleb-

"Good afternoon, Nicole."

"Good afternoon, Kaleb. You're a little early today."

"Yeah, I got out of work a little early."

"Must be nice. I'll be out of your hair in a minute. I'm just finishing up a few things."

"No worries. Take your time. How's he doing today?"

"Unfortunately, the same as yesterday. He'll come around though." She headed towards the door. "Keep the faith." She smiled and walked out.

I put my bag down and sat down in the chair. "What's up, man? You still faking this coma? I know you are just milking it. Don't worry, I won't tell anybody. How was my day, you ask? Oh, you know, another day, another dollar. I'm still dealing with the same old stuff at work. Everyone asks about you." I leaned in closer and spoke quietly. "I really hope you can hear me. I would feel so stupid talking to you and you're not hearing a word I say. I guess we'll find out when you wake up."

I reached into my bag and pulled out a portable speaker. I pulled the chair close to Kaje's bedside and put the speaker down on the bed. "I figured I would play some music for you. Keep you up on the latest songs. That'll keep your skills sharp so you can jump right back into the game when you wake up. Although, I think half of this new stuff is trash or some overproduced remix of older songs anyway. But that's how it works though, isn't it? Whatever version you heard first is the best version, and all other versions are compared to that one. It's like our minds are programmed to not allow a new version, however better it might be, to take the place of our first love."

I brought up a playlist on my phone and played it through the speaker. "I'm going to stop rambling and just let you listen for a bit. I'm going to take a quick power nap. I'm exhausted. I actually had a crazy dream last night. I guess things are getting back to normal. I'll tell you about it before I leave."

I leaned back in the chair and put my feet up on the bed. "You don't mind, right?" I let out a little laugh. "That was a jerk move. Who does that remind you of? That's Monica all day. I know she wishes she could be here, probably more for the free Lorna Doone cookies. Man, I miss how things used to be. Hurry up and wake the hell up."

I yawned. "Quick power nap, and I'll be right back." I closed my eyes and tried to make myself comfortable in the chair. Every way I moved felt less and less comfortable. I finally just sat up. "Who am I kidding? I can't sleep in that chair. And truth be told, I don't know how anyone, even coma patients, sleep with that constant beeping. I swear I hear that beeping even when I'm not here. I know it's driving you crazy. Maybe I should ask Nicole about it when she comes back in. And no, that's not just a reason to talk to her. But TBH, as you would say, it's kind of cool when she is in here. It reminds me of sitting around the apartment with you and Monica. You would like her. You will like her, I should say."

I got up to close the blinds. There was a tree with a white trunk, white branches, and dark red leaves. It looked odd, almost like it was picture perfect. "Huh? That's interesting. Never seen one of those before," I thought. "At least you have a room with a great view," I said. I was trying hard to hide the sadness in my voice. "Remember that mulberry tree in Mr. Bergis' backyard? Man, that dude was mean. We would always sneak back there and eat the mulberries when we saw him leave. Remember that one time we thought he left, so we climbed up on his garage and had a mulberry feast. Then you saw him in his window, walking towards the back porch. We dropped down and laid on our stomachs. We probably stayed up there for five hours, telling stupid jokes, deciding which super hero we should be, making songs, wondering what was beyond the sky, and at what point was the sky not the sky anymore. Do you remember us contemplating the meaning of life? Like, what would eight-year-olds know about the meaning of life? How long was my punishment for missing two check-ins? A week? Not to mention how mad my dad was because I didn't get him his Pick 3 numbers for the night. And as usual, you tried to take the fall for it. That was a great day, man. It was worth the punishment. That was the day I knew we would be best friends for life. You know, sometimes I wish I could be a kid just one more time. It was all so simple then."

I closed the blinds and sat back in the chair. I could feel my sadness starting to overwhelm me. "I'm going to get out of here, man. I'm starving. I know I said I would tell you about my dream, but it was just really more of a weird dream, than a crazy dream. I'm not sure what it even meant. I just know I woke up feeling really sad. I'll tell you about tonight's dream, if there is anything worthy of telling."

As I was walking out, Nicole was just walking in. "Leaving so soon?" she asked.

"Yeah, I'm going to head out. I need to eat something and get some fresh air. Today was a rough one."

"I completely understand. You go take care of you. I'll tell him a story for you."

"You are awesome. Thank you. Should I leave the book of fables I brought?"

She laughed. "No, that's okay. I'll share one of the stories that I wrote."

"Oh? You're a writer?"

"I dabble. I write a few things here and there, as they come to me."

"That's great. I'd love to read some of them one day. That is, if you don't mind sharing. Kaje will just share them with me when he wakes up, so you'd be better off just bypassing the middleman."

She blushed. "Maybe I will. We'll see. You go home and get some rest. I'll see you tomorrow."

"Okay. Thanks again. I'll see you tomorrow."

I left the hospital and headed home. I was hungry and exhausted. I knew it was definitely going to be an early night.

Chapter 54 - Blueberry Muffin

Dreamscape

-Blueberry-

I find myself in a field surrounded by glowing flowers that are outlined with a pinkish hue. Tiny lights pulse as they move about. There is what looks like an outline of a large tree. The flowers and the tree sway back and forth, but I cannot feel the wind.

"Hello," I say softly. I know you're there. I can feel you. I'm really glad you are here with me again. This place is much better when you are here."

"Hi," a quiet voice responds.

"You left so suddenly last time. What happened?"

"I...I'm not sure."

"I see. Well, you are here now. So, I have another question."

"I have one to ask you first," she says.

"Okay, shoot."

"How is it that you can feel me?"

"I'm not exactly sure. It's just a feeling that I have. It doesn't feel like my own. When you were sad, I knew I wasn't sad, so I knew that it was you."

"I see."

"You can't feel my presence?"

"Not really, no."

"Before you disappeared, I felt something. Like intense feelings or something. Did you do something?"

"Not really. I just tried to focus my energy on not closing myself off. What did you feel?"

I want to tell her everything I felt. Instead, I decide that may be too much to divulge. "Just really intense feelings."

"Hmm."

"So, what should we call each other? Should I call you 'M?'"

"M?"

"When I asked you your name before, you said 'M,' but you didn't finish."

There is silence for a few seconds. "Muffin. Call me Muffin."

"Hmm, Muffin it is. Let's see. I guess that makes me…Blueberry. Nice to meet you, Muffin."

"Blueberry. I like that." She lets out a small giggle.

As she giggles, there are ripples across the void, and more flowers appear. Parts of the tree that were outlined, fill in with color.

"Hey! What just happened? Do you see that?" I ask in amazement.

"See what?"

"The tree. Some of the color filled in."

"Did I do that?"

"I think so. It happened when you laughed. You felt happy."

"You could feel that?"

"Yep."

"Hmm, I guess I did do that."

"I guess I have to make sure you are happy, then."

"And how do you plan on doing that?"

"I don't know. I can tell you riddles. Let's see...okay, here's one. What's big and blue and eats rocks?"

"I don't know. What?"

"A big, blue rock eater."

She laughs. The void ripples again. This time filling in grass, flowers, and more of the tree. "That was corny," she says.

"But you laughed."

"Not because it was funny, because it was corny."

"As long as you're happy. That's all I care about."

"That one just caught me off guard. You're going to have to come up with better riddles than that."

"Let's make a deal. You keep meeting me here, and I'll do my best to make you laugh. Is that a deal?"

"I guess so."

"You guess so? I would make you pinky promise, but I don't think we have pinkies."

She laughs again. The grass fills in with a lush green color. The tree trunk fills with a deep brown color. The flowers explode with bright pink. The lines that once outlined these things expand and outline new areas of the void.

"Wow, Muffin! This is amazing!"

"It is! I'm not really sure how I'm doing it."

"Maybe whenever you laugh at my great jokes, the void fills in."

"It can't be that, because you haven't told any great jokes yet."

I laugh. "Whatever. You love my jokes and you know it." I look around in amazement. "If I could, I would pick a bunch of these flowers and give them to you."

There is silence. Then like before, I feel that intense feeling again. As I look around, everything for as far as I can see starts to fill in as if they were being perfectly painted on a canvas. In the distance, the sun begins to rise, and trees fill with rich green leaves. The sky turns a magnificent blue. Puffy white clouds begin to float by. All of the trees near me fill in with vibrant pink flowers. The tiny lights that move about, blossom into butterflies of all colors and flutter all around me. I can see a playground in front of me.

I begin to feel a feeling of weightiness. I feel my feet touch the ground. I look down to see a line outlining my shoes and making its way up my legs and body. I hold my hands in front of my face and watch in amazement as the outline slowly fills in.

I feel a tap on my shoulder. I turn around to see an outline of a young girl, hovering slightly above the ground. She is covered in a light so spectacular that I can barely see anything else. As she lowers, the light begins to dissipate, and the rest of her starts to fill in. She lands in front of me with a smile on her face. I stare at her in a state of wonderment. She reaches out to me with her pinky out. "Hey, Blueberry. Pinky promise?"

"You!" I say in astonishment, as I reach out and seal the promise.

Chapter 55 - My Safe Place Dreamscape -Blueberry-

I walk over to the slide. My reflection confirms what I already know. I am a kid. Muffin's reflection appears on the slide, next to mine. I look around and take in the familiarity of the place. It looks exactly the same as it did the first time I was here. Only this time, it feels more alive.

"Do you remember this place?" I ask.

She nods. "Mhm."

"We couldn't talk to each other then. Why was that?"

"I don't know."

"So, what exactly is this place?"

"I'm not entirely sure. I know I feel happy when I'm here."

"Maybe it's your safe place, or something like that."

She shrugs. "Maybe. Want to go play?"

"Absolutely!" I shout as I take off towards the swings. "Last one there is a rotten egg!"

"Hey! No fair. You got a head start!" she shouts.

As I run from the slide, I feel a gust of wind blow

past me, almost knocking me down. I look up. She is standing by the swings smirking at me. I shoot her a look of disbelief. She sticks her tongue out at me and climbs onto the swing.

"Hey! That's a lot faster than before. How did you do that?"

She shrugs her shoulders. "I don't know. I just thought about it and kind of did it."

"Cool! What else can you do?"

She swings back and forth. "I don't know. I haven't tried anything else." She points to the swing next to her. "Aren't you going to swing me with?"

"Okay, then you have to teach me how to do that."

We swing and laugh together. We jump out of the swings, going further and further each time. We climb the jungle gym, play on the teeter-totter, and spin around the merry-go-round until we are too dizzy to stand. We laugh at each other every time we try to stand, but fall over. The dizziness starts to wear off. We run around the entire playground, chasing butterflies until we tire ourselves out.

We walk over to a grassy hill, sit down, and stare at the sky. The butterflies still flutter about. Birds fly from tree to tree, chirping as the warm sun shines down on us. Everything feels like it is exactly how it is supposed to be. Everything feels perfect.

"We should stay here and play all day and all night," I say.

She smiles. "I'd like that."

"You hungry?"

"Nope."

"Thirsty?"

"Not really."

"Me neither. What do you want to do next?"

She shrugs. "I don't know. What do you want to do?"

"Maybe you can show me how to do what you did earlier."

"I told you. I don't know how I did it. I just did it."

"Maybe you can fly too!" I say excitedly.

"Maybe I can. You want to go for a ride?"

"I would, if we really could fly. Flying is kind of cliché though, don't you think?"

She giggles. "Are you scared to fly, Blueberry?"

"No! I'd just rather, um, stay down here and see what else is around."

Upon hearing me say that, her face takes on a worried look. I recall the last time we were here. I get goosebumps just thinking about it. "We don't have to go there," I say. She shoots me a half smile and nods her head. I can tell she is still worried. I slowly move my hand closer to where hers is. I want them to touch, but I want it to seem like an accident. I lean back and watch the sky. She leans back with me. As she leans back, our hands make contact. We don't look at each other. We just keep looking at the sky as our hands slightly touch.

"Muffin."

"Yeah, Blueberry?"

"How do you think we got here?"

She shrugged. "I don't know."

"How do you think we leave?"

"I don't know that either. Do you want to leave?"

"I don't. It's nice here."

"Well, let's just stay here."

We lie there and watch as the sun begins to set. Time feels strange here. It seems like no time at all

has passed, but the day is starting to fade. As it gets darker, the birds fly away, and the
flowers begin to glow softly. All of the butterflies that flutter about, transform into fireflies.

Their slow pulsing light fills the sky with a calming glow.

"Hey, Muffin."

"Yeah, Blue?"

"Are you getting sleepy?"

"A little. Are you?"

"Yeah, just a little though. I'm just going to rest my eyes a bit. Then maybe we can play some more, okay?"

"Okay. Me too."

I close my eyes and move my hand a little closer to hers. "Just going to rest them a bit. Just for a..."

Chapter 56 - Continuum
-Kaleb-

I walked into Kaje's room. He laid there peacefully. The blinds were open. Someone must have visited before I got there. It was a cloudy day. The leaves on that strange looking tree, swayed back and forth in the wind, but still hung on. Thankfully, there was no snow in the forecast any time soon. There is nothing quite as unnatural as snow on leaves.

I walked over to Kaje's bed and pulled up a chair. "What's up, sleepy-head? Ready to wake up and join the world? I could really use someone to listen to my crazy stories. I mean, someone who will listen and not want to have me committed." I reached into my bag and pulled the speaker out. I had just started to play some music to drown out the beeping when Nicole walked in.

"Hey, Kaleb. Don't mind me. I'll be out of your hair in a minute. How was your day today?"

"Hi, Nicole. It was okay. Same as yesterday and the day before that."

"I hear ya. I can't wait for the weekend."

"Big plans?"

"Not really. Just looking to break the monotony.

I'm just going to chill and love on my puppy."

"Nice. What kind?"

"She's a pug. How about you? Any pets?"

My heart sank a bit from just hearing the question. "No...I had a cat."

"Aww, I'm sorry. Crossed the bridge, huh?"

"The bridge?"

"The Rainbow Bridge. Where our pets go once they pass on."

"Oh, yeah. I guess he is there."

"It gets easier. You just have to find a way to make peace with it."

"Thanks. I'll keep that in mind."

"You're welcome. So, how about you? Any upcoming plans? Maybe you should get out and enjoy this extended autumn. It'll be snowing before you know it."

"I...I don't want to take the chance of Kaje waking up and I'm not here."

"I understand. Well, I'm out of here."

"See you tomorrow?"

She smiled. "You know it. Same time. Same sandbox."

"Hey, quick question for you. Do you dream?"

"Eh, if I do, I don't remember them. Why? Are you dreaming about me?" She winked.

I blushed. "I...no. I was just—"

"I'm just messing with ya. I have to head out. See you tomorrow."

"Bye."

I looked at Kaje. "See, I told you she was flirting with me. I'm just an innocent bystander. Anyway, remember those crazy dreams I had a while back? The one with the playground and stuff? I had one again.

It wasn't exactly the same. It's like a continuation of that dream. I would share all the details with you, but it's all a bit foggy. The longer the day goes on, the less I remember the little details. Sometimes I'll have a quick recollection, then it fades away. Here's the weird thing, it's like I'm watching a movie of myself as a kid. Oh, and get this. The same girl is there with me...him or however you want to see it. It's just weird. It's like, in my dreams, my memories are those of the person I am in the dream and not my actual memories. That's why I, he, me, whatever—" I palmed my face. "You know what I'm saying. That's why he doesn't know he is dreaming, because he doesn't know what I know or remember what I remember. So, while I'm him or he is me, I can't control what he does. I can only observe. But I feel what he is feeling. Clear as mud, right? I think I gave myself a headache just explaining it. I'll be honest though. It's kind of cool. There's something about the girl in the dream. I...he kind of digs her. I woke up feeling like I had an elementary school crush."

For a second, I swore I saw him smile. It was probably because I wanted so badly for him to wake up and make fun of me for digging a girl from a dream. "I know you are in there laughing. It's all good. Keep laughing. Maybe I should remind you of the girl you liked in elementary school, but you were scared to walk her home because someone told you that a green lady lived in the woods behind her house. Come to think of it, that's the only thing I remember you being afraid of."

As the evening wore on, I told a few more stories about old girlfriends and other adventures we shared, growing up. I caught him up on all the current events and sports. I didn't know if he was tired of hearing me or not, but I was tired of hearing myself.

"I'm going to put on some music and chill for a bit. Maybe tomorrow I'll see who I need to badger to get a television in here. I'm sure you'd rather hear that, than me babbling on all the time."

I relaxed in the chair for a while. My alarm went off, alerting me that visiting hours were almost over. I stopped the music and gathered my things. "Alright, man. I'll be back tomorrow. You'll wait here for me, right? I'll take your silence as consent."

I walked over and closed the blinds, then headed out the door. I couldn't wait to get home and sit on my comfortable couch. I walked out of the front doors of the hospital. The evening air was a bit crisp, but still unseasonably warm. I hopped in my car and made my way home.

My apartment was an empty, lifeless place. I was barely home anymore. I was either at work or at the hospital. All the fun and laughter that once took place here was gone. As I stood in the doorway, I thought about Titus and how he would always greet me at the door, purring and circling my legs. "Oh, what I wouldn't give to have you around right now," I thought to myself.

I went into the bathroom, took my blood pressure meds, got myself ready for bed, then sat on the couch. I took a deep calming breath. I swore I could hear that annoying beeping sound again. I put on some music, closed my eyes, and laid back on the couch.

Chapter 57 - Our Creation Dreamscape
~Muffin~

I'm walking through a field of glowing, pink flowers. Each one flickers as I walk past. The sun begins to rise on the horizon. The fireflies transform back into butterflies. I walk through a grassy field. The golden rays of the sun warm the air as the grass sways back and forth. I lie down on the grassy hill and stare at the sky. This place seems so familiar. It's not like a memory. It is more like a feeling or an emotion. I don't know how it is that I came here, or how it was created, but I feel safe and at peace here.

The butterflies flutter about. A cool gust of wind blows, blowing flower petals everywhere. When the petals land, Blueberry is sitting next to me, smiling. His smile always makes me smile. "Hey, Blue."

"Hey, Muffin," he responds. It was just some silly name I chose, but I love when he calls me that.

"Miss me?"

"Maybe."

"You miss me?"

"Maybe." He feigns looking at a watch. "How long

has it been?"

"Oh, maybe a few months or so."

He laughs. "Well then. I absolutely missed you. Any less time, and I would have had to seriously think about it."

Despite my best efforts, I blush. "Good, I missed you too. You look a bit older than before."

"You do too. Still just as pretty though."

I blush again. "Thank you."

He smiles. "You're welcome."

I stand up. "So, what should we do today?"

"I don't know. We can go for a walk. We can play on the playground again. We can play hide-and-go-seek. Is there water? We can swim."

"Oh, I suppose we could," I say timidly.

"Uh oh. Are you scared of water, Muffin?"

"I'm not scared of it. Water and I just don't see eye to eye."

"I get it. Swimming is cliché, right?" He winks.

I wink back. "Yes! That's it. We'll go with that."

"Okay, so no swimming and no flying. We should go for a walk."

"I'd like that."

"Lead the way."

We head the opposite direction of the path we walked down before. In the distance we see a bright light. It sparkles magnificently. As we walk, the area in front of us seems to materialize right before our eyes. With each step we take, trees with bright pink flowers sprout up on each side of us, creating a natural path. We pick up the pace a bit and head straight for the sparkling light.

Blueberry turns to me. "Are you scared?"

I shake my head. "Not really. Are you?"

"Not as long as you're with me."

I smile. He just always seems to know how to make me smile. I put my hand out to his. "Let's go."

We approach the edge of a beach. It has the whitest sands I have ever seen. The blue water sparkles like diamonds as it reflects the bright sunlight. Several waterfalls flow from a large mountain into the body of water. We stand in awe, staring at the area we stumbled upon.

I gently tap him on his shoulder. "Ha! You're it!"

"No fair! I thought we weren't playing. Besides, you know this place better than I do," he yells as I run away.

The mist from the waterfall gently sprays us. "You know it just as well as I do," I say as I run through a waterfall.

"I do?"

I sneak up behind him and tap him again. "Of course, you do, silly. We created it." Before he can fully turn around, I run away.

"Hey! Wait. No fair. Get back here! How did we—"

I laugh and run into the far waterfall near a grassy hill. I turn and look at him.

"We created this?" he says. He looks around in stunned silence, marveling at the thought that he could have possibly had a part in the creation we are both witnessing.

I walk over and stand next to him. "You okay, Blue?"

"This place. How did we create this?"

I was so excited to play, I didn't take the time to truly appreciate the beauty in front of me. The sky is bluer than I have ever seen it. The mountains have lush green trees for as far as the eyes can see. The sun is shining brilliantly. The water from the numerous waterfalls glistens and sparkles like diamonds. The mist from the waterfalls creates countless little rainbows all around us. Birds fly gracefully through the sky, singing beautiful songs.

We watch as the birds fly to an area so high up the mountain, it looks like it is suspended in the sky. A single waterfall flows from that part of the mountain, as if it was the water source of every other waterfall below. A majestic blue bird circles the waterfall again and again as it makes it way up the mountain.

"Whoa!" Blueberry says.

I tap him again. "Hey, this is our place, you know. We can stare at it whenever we want."

"This is true. I just got caught up a bit. You said that we created this? How?"

"I'm not entirely sure. It's weird, it's just something I know inside. I know what parts are from me, and the rest must be from you."

"I see. So, we have super powers?"

"Maybe. I mean, I know I do. That's why you can't catch me."

He laughs. "Oh, is that so? We'll see about that."

I run into the nearest waterfall. Each one seems to bring me out of a different waterfall. "We haven't got all night, silly," I yell from across the beach.

"Then why don't you stop running. Are we playing hide-and-go-seek or tag?" he yells back.

I laugh. "We're playing 'You can't catch me.'"

"Okay. I see how it is. Game on! Nothing like a good challenge."

Chapter 58 - Waterfalls Dreamscape
-Blueberry-

I look at all the waterfalls around me. I run into the closest one. The water is warm and exhilarating. I come out of the water under a completely different waterfall. Muffin is standing and laughing by the waterfall across the beach. I run back into the waterfall. I am now right back where I started. I survey the area again. She appears to be standing by each waterfall with her hand over her mouth, giggling.

"What the!?"

"Ha! What's wrong? Can't catch me in your own creation, huh?" she says smugly.

"Our own creation," I shout. "And don't worry, I will catch you."

"How do I catch someone that is everywhere, yet nowhere at the same time?" I wonder aloud. I quickly dash though one waterfall. I look back. She is now standing in front of the waterfall I just ran into.

"Yoo-hoo! Blueberry. I'm over here." She smiles from ear to ear.

I dash through the waterfall as fast as I can, taking

all the water with me as I head to the next waterfall. *Whoosh!* Through another one I run. By the time I get through the last one, I realize that I am completely submerged in water.

"Well, that's not fair," she says.

I quickly turn around. She is behind me trying to get away. I reach out for her. She is fast, but this time I am faster. I catch up and embrace her. I pull her close. We laugh and share a smile.

"I guess I'm it, huh?" she asks quietly.

"I guess you are," I quietly respond as I look into her eyes.

Our smiles fade into something more like longing breath as we lose ourselves in each other's embrace.

"Look at us. We are flying and swimming," I say softly.

"I guess we are," she replies softly. "How cliché of us."

The water begins to fall from around us, returning to its natural place on the mountain, but we stay suspended above everything, locked in each other's arms. As I stare into her eyes, she suddenly begins plummeting towards the beach. I swoop down and catch her. "Muffin? Are you okay?"

"I...I am now. You saved me." She smiles.

I wink at her. "Falling for me, huh?"

She blushes. "I...I..." She doesn't finish the thought.

Being here with her feels so natural. We rest our foreheads against each other. Our noses touch and we smile warmly at each other. Still locked in each other's gaze, we slowly start to descend. We land softly on the beach. The sand feels nice beneath our feet. We shyly pull back from each other as if we had crossed a line too soon.

"That was amazing," I say.

She nods. "Mhm."

I look up at the sky. The sun is getting low on the horizon. Muffin slowly walks up the beach. Her head is down as she kicks the sand. "Hey, Muffin," I call out. "You think we should head back to the playground?"

"Yea, we probably should."

"You okay? You got kind of quiet once we—"

"I'm fine, just a little tired."

I can feel that something is weighing on her, but it would be a bit intrusive to ask her about it. I figure when she is ready to tell me, she will.

The walk back is a quiet one. A cool breeze blows, bringing a slight, but enjoyable chill to the air. Pink petals line the path back to the playground.

"Muffin, are you cold? I can stand in front of you and block the wind?"

"No, I'm fine. It actually feels nice."

"Same here. It reminds me of something, but I can't quite place it. I'm sure it will come to me. Have you noticed all the petals are falling from the trees?"

"Yeah."

"Are you doing that?"

"Not that I know of."

"Maybe it's just their time."

"Maybe."

We are almost back to the playground. The moon is visible and bright. We use it to guide us. We can see the playground in the distance. The cherry blossom trees that normally surround it are now maple trees with brilliant red leaves. A giant maple tree now stands in the middle of the playground. "Muffin, do you see that? The trees have changed, and that tree wasn't there before we left."

"Mhm. I think you may have done that."

"Did I? I'm still not sure how. Are you upset?"

"No, silly. I love it."

"Hey, back there on the beach, I'm sorry. It's just that I felt something, and I thought you felt it too. I should have—"

"Don't apologize. I felt it too. It was...beyond words. I just...I have this feeling inside of me that I can't explain."

"What sort of feeling?"

"That I don't deserve to feel like this."

"Oh, Muffin. Of course, you do. Everyone deserves to be happy. Why shouldn't you?"

"I don't know. I just—"

"Come here. I have something for you."

She slowly makes her way towards me. "Yeah?"

I reach out and wrap my arms around her. I hold her as close as I can. I have trouble feeling what she is feeling. It is odd. It feels like I am feeling some of her emotions and the emotions of someone else. "You deserve this and so much more. Never forget that."

She wraps her arms around me. "Thanks, Blue. I'm really glad I met you."

"And I'm glad I met you, Muffin. Even though you cheat at hide-and-go-seek."

She laughs and pushes me away. "Whatever! You're the one that cheated. Next time, maybe we should just race. Let's see who wins that."

"Be careful what you wish for. I might have learned a few tricks today."

"We'll see about that."

"Sure will. But in all seriousness, I am really glad that I met you. I'm glad we are here. Wherever here is. Hey, if for some reason we ever lose each other, let's always meet here. It'll be our home base."

"Okay. I like that idea."

We hold hands and head to a grassy hill. We lie down and stare at the sky. Bright stars begin to appear one by one. Each time one appears, it moves to a spot in the sky, so that the next star can appear and find its place.

"Whoa! Am I doing that?" I ask.

She smiles. "No, that's me."

"That's amazing. Can you make them go wherever you want?"

"No. Every star has its rightful place in the sky. No one should mess with that."

"I see."

"What about shooting stars?"

She winked. "Those are fair game."

"Gotcha. I'll keep that in mind."

"Blueberry?"

"Yeah, Muffin."

"Did you know that you're fantastic?"

I try to hide my smile. "I know that I try to be the best I can be."

"You do well."

"Thank you." I can't hide my smile any longer. "Today was amazing, Muffin."

"Mhm. We should do it again, soon," she says through a yawn.

"You sleepy?"

"Mhm."

"I'm getting there. I'm just going to stare at the stars

a little while longer."

"Okay."

I turn to look at her. She is slowly drifting off to sleep. I let go of her hand and rest my hands on my chest. I yawn and turn back to look at the stars. Suddenly, a deep rumble of thunder booms in the distance, followed by a crack of lightning. I turn over to check on Muffin, but she is gone. I stand up and look around. "Muffin!?" I call out. There is no answer.

I hear another loud boom of thunder. This time it sounds much closer. More lightning strikes off in the distance. I feel a drop of rain. I look up at the sky. Each star begins to fade one by one. The entire area is getting darker. The flowers no longer glow. The bright light of the moon has all but faded. The only light that remains is the random pulses of fireflies. The rain picks up. Frightened, I run and take cover under the giant tree.

After a while, everything is quiet. The only thing I can hear is the sound of the rain. I want to get up and look around, but it is too dark, and I am afraid. As I sit on the ground, I hear a strange beeping sound. I stand up, hug the tree, and peek around it. In the distance, I see a house with eerie red lights on the inside. My skin begins to crawl. My fear overtakes me. I fall to the ground and black out.

Chapter 59 - Stay in the Light
-Kaleb-

I walked into the room. There were a couple of doctors in the room that I hadn't seen before, discussing something. I walked past them and sat in the chair. When they noticed me, they walked outside and continued their conversation outside of the room. I felt a pit in the bottom of my stomach.

I unpacked my things. I set the speaker on the table by the bed. Nicole walked in the room. She shot me a half smile. "Hey, is something wrong?" I asked.

"I don't want you to freak out. Kaje had a small seizure last night. They were able to stabilize him and everything is status quo."

"So, was that just a fluke thing, or should I be concerned?"

"Well, he's not out of the woods yet. But I wouldn't worry about it. It's rare, but those kinds of things can happen in coma patients."

"You know, it's weird. I had a bad feeling all day that something was going on with him."

"You guys are good friends, and you seem to be in

tune with him. Maybe it's just a sixth sense or something. Like I said, I wouldn't worry."

I put my head in my hands. "Okay. I'll try not to worry, but that's not my strong suit." I sat back in the chair and let out a hefty yawn.

"Oh, my. Someone is sleepy. Didn't get much sleep last night?"

"I actually did. I just woke up pretty abruptly."

"Nightmare?"

"I'm not sure. I remember feeling wonderful. Then I remember seeing something that scared me, something from my childhood."

"Those are the worst kind of nightmares. Well, you're awake now. Try not to let it linger."

"I'll try."

"I'll be out of your hair in a minute. You can take a nap if you want. Just don't sleep past visiting hours."

"Thanks, Nicole. Like I told you before, you can take all the time you need. The company is a welcome addition."

"I know, but other duties call. I'll stop back in and check on you before I leave. Keep your head up. He'll be okay."

"I will, and thank you." I wiped my face. Just any case any tears escaped without me realizing. "Getting closer to the weekend though. Detox just to re-tox!" I said, quickly trying to brighten the mood.

"I know that's the truth. See you in a little bit."

She walked out of the room and closed the door. I was still a bit shaken by that dream, and hearing about that seizure only made things worse. I pulled the chair close to the bed. "Man, didn't you read the rule book? It specifically stated that there were no health scares allowed. How about not doing that crap again? You are going the wrong way. Take the path that leads back to you being awake. 'Stay in the light Carol Anne!' Or whatever she said in that old spooky movie you made me watch when we were kids. I had nightmares for weeks after watching that. But that was a perfect impression of that old lady, wasn't it?"

I reached in my bag and grabbed some water. "Man, speaking of nightmares, I dreamed of that house on the corner again. Well, it wasn't entirely about that house. I just remember it being there, along with a bunch of other crazy things. You'll laugh, but I'm still not going anywhere near it. As an adult, if I was on my old street, today, I wouldn't go near it." I chuckled. "But that girl was there again. And I'm not even going to lie to you, I wake up feeling some kind of way. I can't really explain it. If you can hear me, I know you're making fun of me, but I'm so into her. This feeling, it's like the bridge of a beautiful song. I just want to keep rewinding it over and over again. Anyway, I'm done with the sappiness. With my luck, my next dream will be about the Browns losing the Super Bowl on a missed field goal or something crappy like that. I just want to take a nap, but I know if I do, I'm not going to wake up until the morning. I barely made it through work. I'm taking your advice and writing my dreams down. Maybe I'll make them into a movie script one day, then I can quit my job and live on the beach. Hell, I may do that anyway."

I turned on some music, sat back in my chair, and began to jot down little snippets of whatever I could remember from my dreams the last couple of days. It was odd looking at the dreams in writing. It gave me that all too familiar déjà vu feeling.

"Knock, knock," Nicole said as she entered the room. "I'm just checking in to see how you're holding up."

I reached over and turned the music down. "I'm doing okay. Getting ready to head out soon."

"Whatcha writing over there? Writing me a story?" She winked.

"I...no...I was, um—"

She laughed. "You are so easily flustered. I'm just teasing. I know you aren't writing me a story."

"Well, actually I was," I said with an embarrassing look on my face.

Her face turned a rose-colored shade of red. "Oh, my goodness. Seriously?"

I winked at her. "Now who's easily flustered?"

"Well played Mr. Barnes. Well played. So, what are you really writing?"

"Well, Nurse Nicole, I was just jotting some things down from some of the dreams I've been having. My dreams have always been crazy. Kaje once told me that I should write them down. Maybe someday someone will make a movie out of them or something. I'm finally taking his advice."

"Good for you. Set your goals above the sky. If you reach the sky, that ain't half bad."

"Absolutely! Great advice."

"Thanks. Well, I should be getting out of here. I have a hungry pup waiting at home."

"That's right. What's her name?"

"Pandora, because she is full of surprises."

"Interesting."

"Kaleb, can I ask you a personal question before I

head out?"

"Sure."

"How long ago did your cat pass away?"

"It's been a few years now. He died in my arms."

"Aww, so you were there for him and did all you could. That's what matters."

"It's just that sometimes I don't feel like I did everything I could."

"Is that why you haven't made peace with it?"

"I guess so. I can't ever make that right."

"Have you tried telling him how you feel?"

I shot her a confused look. "Um."

"Go to where he is and say it out loud. Let him know how you feel. He'll hear you. You'll be amazed at how much better you'll feel."

"I guess I could do that."

"Just consider it, okay?"

"I will. Thank you, Nicole. You are wise beyond your years."

She laughed. "How old do you think I am?"

I shook my head. "Nope, not falling for that trap."

She laughed harder. "You have a good night, Kaleb."

I smiled at her. "You too. Go straight home."

She was still laughing. "Yeah, I'll get right on that. Goodnight, Kaje," she yelled as she walked out of the room.

I packed up my things and put on my coat. "Man, if she didn't remind me of a less obnoxious Monica, I would entertain the possibility of that, but I'm sure you already know that. Oh well, I'll catch you tomorrow, man."

Chapter 60 - The Flower Meadow Dreamscape
~Muffin~

I'm standing at the bottom of the grassy hill. A pond materializes in front of me. The crystal-clear water reflects the sky. The sunlight makes the cherry blossoms sparkle. I stare at my reflection in the water. Two goldfish swim close to the shoreline. A red leaf falls gently onto the surface of the pond, causing it to ripple.

"Muffin?" Blueberry calls out.

"I'm down here," I reply.

He joins me at the bottom of the hill. "Hey there. What are you up to?"

"Just enjoying the water and waiting on you. You're late."

"What!?" I'm not late, am I?'

I giggle. "I'm just kidding, silly."

"Oh." He smiles, and breathes a sigh of relief. "That's a beautiful pond. Yours?"

"No."

"Mine?"

"I think so."

"Hmm, I have a question. What do you see when I'm not here?"

"Usually, the same things I see when you are here. Your red maple leaves growing on the cherry blossom trees are new. Also, it's a bit cooler now. Why do you ask?"

"The last time we were here, you left before me. There was a little bit of thunder and lighting," he says.

I get the impression he isn't telling me everything.

"Maybe you called a storm. Do you like thunderstorms?"

"I do, but this was no ordinary storm. Everything kind of went dark."

I sit up and look at him quizzically. "What do you mean?"

"Well..." He pauses for a minute. "Everything that shined light, just kind of stopped shining. The moon, the stars, even the flowers. The only thing I could see was the fireflies. Weird, huh?"

"Yeah," I say quietly. I wonder if he is feeling the worry that I feel. I quickly stand up and dust myself off.

"Time to head out?" he asks.

I nod. "Mhm."

"Where to?"

I reach my hand out and smile. "Wherever the journey takes us."

"Judging by our reflections, I would say we are a little too old for the playground now"

"You're never too old for a playground. But let's go somewhere else. It doesn't matter where we go, as long as we're together."

He takes my hand and we set out. I have no idea where we were going. All I know is where we aren't going, just thinking about that path still causes me angst. We walk until we come across a field of tall open grass. It is as tall as we are. Blueberry lets go of my hand and runs through it gleefully. "This is a perfect place to play hide-and-go-seek," he yells.

I shake my head. "Boys are so immature," I mumble playfully. "You're going to get lost and be lost in the grass forever," I shout.

"That's okay. As long as you're lost with me," he yells back from a good distance away.

"Are you really going to make me find you? You know I could, easily." There is no response. "Blue? Blue?"

I run through the grass at lightning speed, searching every inch of the grass. He is nowhere to be found. I can hear him laughing. It sounds further away than before. I close my eyes and elevate myself just high enough to see above the grass. I can see him hiding behind a thick patch of tall grass. "Olly olly oxen free!" I call out. "Last chance to—" Before I can finish my sentence, I fall to the ground. Blueberry races over to check on me.

"Muffin! What happened? Are you okay?"

"I...I think so," I reply. My mind is racing, and I am having trouble gathering my thoughts. "I just need a moment."

"Take your time. Did you hit your head? Does anything hurt?"

"Yeah, my butt!" I let out a small laugh. "I fell right on it!" Blueberry has his hand over his mouth trying to cover the fact that he is laughing. "Go ahead and laugh it up."

"I'm not laughing at you. I'm laughing with you."

"Uh huh. Nice save."

He gently helps me to my feet. "Are you sure you're okay?" he asks.

"I think so."

"I saw you levitating. What made you fall like that?"

"I'm not sure why I fell, but while I was up there, I called out 'Olly olly oxen free.' Then all of a sudden, I got an intense feeling of déjà vu or something. I remembered something for a split second, then it was gone."

"What does that phrase mean? I've never heard it before."

"I don't know."

"Well, I'm thinking you shouldn't say it again. And you might want to keep your feet on the ground. That's the second time that's happened."

"You are probably right."

He puts his hand out to mine. "Shall we, Ms. Muffin?"

I smile at him. "We shall, Mr. Blueberry."

He smiles back. "This way. I have a surprise for you."

"Oh? I can't wait to see it."

We walk through the grass until we come to an opening at the bottom of a small hill. On the top of the hill is a wild flower meadow with rows of beautiful flowers that seem to go on forever. On the horizon, the sky emanates a golden, blue hue. Golden sunrays rain down on the field. It is the most beautiful thing I have ever seen. "You did this?" I ask in amazement.

"I did, for you."

I stare on, still in amazement. "But how?"

"I'm not sure how to describe it, but I'll try," he says. He takes both of my hands in his and looks deep into my eyes. "In the past, when I closed my eyes and thought of what I wanted to happen, nothing really worked. Now, when I close my eyes, and I think of things, I also think of you. That's when things happen. It's not always exactly what I'm thinking, but it is pretty close. It's like, this place is a canvas, and our thoughts paint the picture. I didn't understand it before, but now I realize that you are the brush."

"I don't know what to say."

"You don't have to say anything. Just keep your promise and stay by my side, so I can continue to create beautiful things for you."

"I will. There's no place I'd rather be."

We walk into the middle of the meadow. Thousands of butterflies grace us with their presence. "Can I share a fear with you?" he asks.

"Of course," I reply.

"Of all the things here, you are by far the most beautiful of them all. I just hope you aren't a beautiful creation of mine."

"You are so sweet. I can assure you that I am not a creation of yours. I'll be honest with you. I always thought you were too good to be true, and I worried you were a creation of mine."

He pulls me close. Our foreheads rest against each other. Our noses gently touch. "I guess we'll just have to hold on to each other and see."

"I think you're right," I close my eyes and melt into his arms. When he holds me, I feel like he holds every part of me. I love the way he makes me feel vulnerable, yet safe. He awakens parts of me I didn't know existed. There is just something about him that sets my soul ablaze. I feel like he is the one I have always longed for, yet he has been right here all along.

"Muffin," he whispers.

"Yeah, Blue?"

"I'm really glad I met you."

I slowly open my eyes and look deeply into his. "I'm really glad I met you too."

Chapter 61 - Still Spring Chickens Dreamscape -Blueberry-

In her eyes I can see the reflections of butterflies fluttering about. I am pretty sure she sees the same in mine. We turn and look around us. Hundreds, if not thousands of butterflies are all around us. Their wings tickle us as they fly close. Muffin giggles as she steps back from me with her hands raised to the sky. She tilts her head back, smiles, and spins around. I stand and watch as she spins around in the rays of the setting sun. It feels like everything is in slow motion. Seeing the joy that she has at this very moment brings me a sense of joy that I have never felt before. I feel everything she is feeling, so deeply, it flows through every part of me. She is everything. Her happiness makes me happy. I want to make sure that she is always happy, so we can always share this feeling together.

"Do you feel this?" she asks, still spinning around.

"I do, two-fold. It's the most amazing thing I've ever felt."

She stops spinning and walks over to me. "I love how you can feel what I'm feeling. I didn't know how to feel about it at first, but now I want you to feel everything. I don't want to hide anything from you."

I put my hand on the side of her face. I caress her cheek with my thumb. "I wish you could feel what I am feeling right now and all of the pure joy I feel when we're together."

She looks at me and motions something with her hands. I'm not quite sure what it means. "You heart me with you?" I ask? She stares at me and appears to lose her balance. I reach out and hold her up. "Muffin, you okay? It happened again. Something I said?"

"That phrase. I've heard it somewhere before. I got that weird feeling again. I'm okay now."

"You're kind of scaring me. Maybe I should just keep my mouth shut."

"No, silly. It's fine. I'm alright. You better not stop talking to me."

"Then you better stop passing out on me."

"I did not pass out. I just got a little lightheaded."

"Mmhmm. If you say so. The sun looks like it's ready to set. Shall we start heading back?"

She nods. "Mhm."

The sun slowly descends on the horizon. The sunset is a brilliant shade of pink and purple. The usual cool, evening wind blows. I put my arm around her as we walk back. The sun has finally taken refuge for the night. The fireflies sparkle in the trees as we pass.

We arrive back at the playground and sit on the swings. Our feet no longer dangle above the ground. We lightly push off the ground to start ourselves in motion. I can feel that she is worried, but before I can say anything, she stops the swing and looks at me. "Blue, what happens if we just keep getting older?" she says. Her face is full of worry.

"I don't know. I guess I never thought about it. I guess all we can do is make the best of each day that we have. I'm not overly concerned about it. Are you?"

"Not overly."

"Good. Watch this." I rock the swing backwards, pump my legs a few times and then jump twenty feet forward. "See! We are still spring chickens!" I yell.

Muffin smiles, pumps her legs, and rocks the swing. She lets go of the swing and launches herself ten feet over my head. "Yeah, I guess we are."

I roll my eyes. "Showoff!"

She puts both of her hands over her mouth and laughs. I turn my head and stifle a laugh. I walk over to her with a serious look on my face. "I have something I need to tell you. You aren't going to like it."

Her laughter subsides instantly. "Blue, what is it? What's wrong?"

"Are you sure you want to hear this?"

"I'm sure. Just tell me."

"Well...you're it!" I reach out and tag her on her shoulder, then run away.

"Oh, you are such a butt!" For a moment, she looks angry. Then she laughs and takes off after me. I run as fast as I can. I circle the trees, run up the slide, and run down the slide. I even jump over the jungle gym. I can't shake her. No matter how fast I think I am running, she is always right behind me.

I run over to the grassy hill. It is covered in red and pink leaves. I stop and stand there, huffing and puffing. "Okay, you win. I'm exhausted. How are you so fast?"

She smiles. "I don't know. Maybe you are just slow."

"Ouch!"

"You deserve that for making me worry."

"Touché." I try to catch my breath. "Well, this is new."

"What's new?" she asks.

"I'm actually thirsty."

"Interesting. I've been a little thirsty as well."

We lie back on the hill and stare at the sky. The stars are as bright as I have seen them. I close my eyes for a few seconds, then open them. I tap her and point to the sky. "Muffin, watch this," I say excitedly. Several falling stars shoot through the sky in unison. "Did you see that!?"

"That was amazing! Who's showing off now?"

I blush. "Hey, Muffin. I was thinking about something. I don't care how much we age in this place. As long as I can do it with you, that's all I need."

She turns and looks at me. Her big, brown eyes penetrate right through me. Overcome by emotion, she seems to be at a loss for words, but I feel everything she wants to say.

"Hey, watch this," I say. I begin flapping my arms and legs in the leaves. I stand up. "Look. A leaf angel. You make one now."

"A leaf angel?" she says quizzically. "I...I need to lay down and rest."

"That feeling again?"

"Mhm."

"Let's rest together. It's been a long day, and we'll always have tomorrow. Goodnight, Muffin."

"Night, Blue."

As I lie there with my eyes closed. I feel a gentle wind blow the leaves. I smile and enjoy the moment before it's gone. I hear a low rumble of thunder in the distance. "Muffin, did you hear that?" She doesn't answer. I sit up and open my eyes. There is nothing but darkness. There is another rumble of thunder. This time, louder and much closer. I try to stand, but I stumble. I scoot away from the direction I hear the thunder. The next boom of thunder is tremendous. In terror, I scoot faster. My back hits up against something hard. An incredible flash of lightning illuminates the entire sky. I struggle to my feet. I can barely breathe. The lightning strikes again. As it lights the sky, I see a large, black shadowy figure that seems to be as large as the sky itself. I close my eyes and yell out in horror. When I finally open them, everything is quiet.

Chapter 62 - Confusion and Despair
-Kaleb-

I arrived at the hospital. There were a couple of doctors outside of Kaje's room. I immediately feared the worst. I quickly walked towards the doctor I recognized. "Hey, Dr. Mada. What's going on?" I asked.

The doctor whispered something to the other doctor and then turned to me. "Good evening, Mr. Barnes."

"What's going on with Kaje?"

"Mr. Waters had a series of seizures last night. We were able to stabilize him, but—"

"Wait. What does that mean? Is he going to be okay?"

"As I was saying, we need to perform a procedure called hyperventilation. I've scheduled it for tonight. I need to relieve some of the pressure on his brain. Hopefully this will eliminate the seizures."

"Hopefully? What if it doesn't? And is this a dangerous procedure? What are the risks?"

"There are risks with any procedure, but I don't expect there to be any complications."

"How can you say that if there are risks?"

"Mr. Barnes, I am the best at what I do. Now if you will excuse me."

"Smug bastard. You better be," I mumbled as he walked away. I opened the door and walked in the room.

"There he is," Nicole said. "Running late today?"

"No," I said sadly. "I was talking to Dr. Smug in the hallway."

She laughed. Oh, Dr. Mada. He's not that bad once you get used to him. So, I assume you heard about the procedure?"

"Yeah."

"I wouldn't worry about it. It should be an easy procedure. And I am sure you've heard that Dr. Mada is the best at what he does."

"Yep, I was informed. I have a silly question. Will he need to go under for this procedure?"

"That's not a silly question. Yes, coma patients are still given anesthesia in the event that they are fully aware of what's going on."

I put my face in my hand. "You mean, like he could hear us now?"

"Yeah, just like that. Oops," she whispered. "Trust me. He's going to be fine."

I smiled and nodded at her. I sat in the chair next to Kaje. I put a hand on his shoulder. "Hang in there, man. Follow the light."

"Nicole do you believe in synchronicity?" I asked.

"I can't say that I know what that is," she replied.

"It's basically when weird things happen that seem related, but there are no real explainable connections. Like, when you hear a word for the first time, then you hear it all the time."

"Isn't that just a coincidence?"

"I suppose so. But what if that kind of thing keeps happening? That can't just be a coincidence."

"No, I suppose you're right. I can't say that I've ever experienced that. Are you experiencing that?"

"Currently, no. It was something I kind of experienced throughout my life. Now, not so much. I've just been having weird dreams lately."

"Nightmares again?"

"Not really. It was kind of like the other night. Everything was fine. They were more than fine, actually, then things got kind of scary, and I woke up."

"Well, that was the night Kaje had his first seizure, and then there were the seizures last night. I'm not a big believer in all that mythical stuff, but maybe your dream was trying to warn you. That would be synchronicity, right?"

"Possibly, or just a coincidence," I said sadly. "I hope I don't ever need a warning like that again. It's not like I can do anything to help anyway."

"I'm sorry. I didn't mean to—"

"It's fine. I know. I just miss him, and I feel so helpless."

"I'm sure he misses you too," she said softly. She walked over and put her hand on my shoulder. "Hang in there, Kaleb."

"I will. Thanks." I stood up and walked over to the window. "Nicole, do you mind if I close these blinds? I'm kind of tired of seeing this same old, weird looking tree every day. So, I know you are tired of seeing it."

She chuckled. "No, I don't mind. I don't even notice it anymore. I guess it has just grown on me. I'm just about finished, then I'll be out of your hair. I'll give you guys some time."

There was something about the way she said that. It made me feel weird inside. I couldn't quite explain it. It just felt different from the other times she's said it. "Earth to Kaleb. Are you still with me?"

"Huh? Yeah, sorry."

"You okay over there?"

"Sorry, just a lot on my mind. Thinking about how I can cut down this tree without getting caught."

She laughed and headed for the door. "Good luck with that. See ya later."

"Later."

I pulled a chair up to the usual spot, and pulled out my speaker and my notepad. "Well, I've gone and done it now. I'm pretty sure I have feelings for the girl in my dreams. Don't ask me how, because I won't be able to explain it. It's just weird, and I'm just weird. All things you've known already. It used to feel like I was watching myself in a movie. Now, more and more, it feels like I'm the main character. I mean, I might as well be, if I'm feeling what he's feeling in the dream. I don't know, man. Maybe I am just lonely and screwed up."

I rested my head in my hands. "You know, you could just wake up and tell me that I'm crazy. Tell me that I'm not making any sense. Tell me to get my crap together. If I'm being honest though, I've been feeling a lot happier in my dreams than I have when I'm awake. And I know that's selfish, and I know that sucks, but it's the truth. I miss the way things were. I miss you. I miss Titus. Hell, I even miss Monica. Never thought I'd be saying that out loud. I'm sorry for getting all sappy on you. It's just been a rough day, I guess. I'm sure tomorrow I'll be alright."

I played some music and wrote a bit about what I remembered about the dream I recently had. From the moment I woke up, all I could think about was Muffin. I felt bad that all I wanted to do was go home and sleep. In my head, I started rationalizing all the reasons why it was okay for me to leave a bit early and go home and sleep. One side thought that leaving a bit early wasn't going to matter in the grand scheme of things, but the other side disagreed. I decided that I wasn't going to keep having the internal argument that always ended with me thinking that somehow, I needed to be there or Kaje wouldn't wake up.

I needed to get something to eat and probably a change of clothes if I was going to be camping out in the waiting room all night. I started packing up my things, when Nicole walked in. "Leaving early, huh?" she asked.

"Yeah, I'll be back. I have some things I need to take care of."

She grinned at me. "Hot date, huh?"

"What? No! I just—"

"Relax. It was a joke. Besides, no one would blame you if you took some time for yourself and maybe got out and enjoyed the weather. You know, someday autumn will end, and all its beauty along with it. You'll have to wait almost a whole year for it to come back."

"I know. You're right. I do need to take some time for myself. I'm sure Kaje would understand."

"I'm sure he wouldn't want you to sit around being sad and lonely. If there is something you want to do, seize the moment. You never know when you'll have the opportunity again."

"Thanks for the words of encouragement, Nicole. I'm going to get out of here and grab something to eat, and a change of clothes. Maybe I'll take some time to do a little something I enjoy before I head back. We'll see how that goes. I'll see you tomorrow?"

She smiled. "If you're lucky."

I packed my things up and headed towards the door. Nicole called out to me before I walked out. "Hey, I'll pull a few strings and get you a rollaway. I don't want you to have to stay in the waiting room all night. Just come back in here when you get back."

"Really? You are awesome. Thank you so much. I've been told that I talk in my sleep. I'm sure that wouldn't go over well in the waiting room."

She laughed. "You're welcome. Hey, I know this is a bit forward, but would you like to go out for a drink or something."

Her words caught me by surprise. The truth of it was, I liked her and had considered asking her out a few times, but didn't have the nerve to do it. But now, I just wasn't sure. It was crazy of me to turn down something real and tangible, standing right in front of me, for something that was nothing more than a fairy tale. But, oh what a fairy tale it was, and no one had ever made me feel the way Muffin did. That's not something you just throw away, and I wasn't about to.

"I'm sorry, Nicole. I can't. I think I'm in love with someone."

Chapter 63 - The Rainbow Bridge Dreamscape -Blueberry-

I open my eyes to an unfamiliar place. I look all around me. The playground is nowhere to be found. "Muffin?" I call out.

"I'm here, Blue," she responds in a soft, sweet tone.

"Where is this place? What happened to the playground?" I whisper as I look around in amazement.

She is looking around. She is just as amazed as I am. "I don't know. I did not bring us here."

"I did?"

"Mhm."

We stand at the beginning of a bridge that overlooks green pastures that seem to go on forever. A rainbow showers the bridge with dazzling colors so bright and intense, they look like you can reach out and touch them. I find myself filled with a sense of wonder, but also sadness. A rush of memories flood my mind so abruptly, I fall to my knees. Suddenly, I know why I brought us here. Muffin rushes to my side. "Blue! Are you okay?"

I slowly stand up. Sadness grips me. "Yeah, I'm okay. I think I know why we're here."

"Is there someone you want to see across the bridge?" she asks.

I don't know how to answer. I want to, but I'm not sure I should. I'm not even sure I am ready. "I think so," I say hesitantly.

"Come on. It'll be fine," she says as she reaches out her hand.

I slowly reach my hand towards hers. I stop just short of holding it. Tears fill my eyes. "I can't. I can't face him, not after how it ended. I could have done more. I should have done more. I was distant. I thought it would be easier for me to deal with. I should have held him more. I should have had the vet try everything they could. I could've afforded it. I let myself accept it was his time before I knew that for sure. I let him wither away. I let him die in my arms."

Muffin moves towards me and puts her arms around me. "I don't think this is a place of guilt or grudges. It doesn't feel like a place of sadness. It feels like a place of peace and incredible happiness." She smiles gently, looks me in the eyes, and gives me a reassuring nod. "Shall we?"

She always has this way of making everything feel like everything is going to be okay. "We shall," I say softly. My voice chokes up. We make our way across the bridge towards the pasture. I see animals of all species running and playing together. A warm feeling begins to take over my body, almost as if the rainbow itself was providing warmth. I feel like I am a kid in a pet store for the first time, only I know exactly the pet I am looking for. I scan the area. Pets frolic and play with each other to their heart's content. There are no elderly pets. They all seem to be the age they were at their most playful.

"I'm going to play," Muffin says. She begins chasing a puppy that nibbled at her leg.

"Wait. How will I find him?"

"You won't," she says. Her voice trails off as she runs away.

"I won't?" I say curiously. "Then why did I come here if I won't find him here?" I say quietly to myself.

"Because he'll find you," a young boyish sounding voice says.

As I look around to see where the voice is coming from, I feel soft fur rubbing against my legs, and I hear purring that I have not heard in a long time.

"Titus!" I shout! I kneel over. He stands on his hind legs and puts his front paws towards me. He always did this when he wanted me to pick him up. I always found it fascinating. It was very similar to what a toddler would do when they see a parent. In his later years, he didn't have the leg strength to do it anymore.

He looks at me. His eyes show signs of worry. I pick him up and let him relax on my shoulders, leaving my arm up as a perch. "I've missed you so much, little buddy!" I say excitedly.

"I've missed you too!" he replies.

"You can talk here?"

"Put me down. I'll explain it to you the best I can. You can see my mouth isn't moving, so technically I can't talk, but I am able to convey my thoughts to you, and you are able to hear them. It's somewhat like a form of telepathy that works between an owner and their pet."

"Ah, I see."

My head falls a little, and I can feel sadness trying to creep in. "I sure wish we could have done that when..." I try to say the words, but I cannot bring myself to finish.

"I know. It was a hard time for both of us. Don't be sad. You did your best. You were there for me. I was getting old, and that heart murmur Dr. Pawlowski told you about, well, it was really getting the best of me. I know you feel like you were distant, but you weren't. You spent hours with me each day. You couldn't spend all your waking moments with me. I enjoyed every day we spent together."

"Were you in pain?" I ask. "It is the one thing that has always bothered me the most. I feel like I let you live in pain before you passed on."

"I could tell you I wasn't if that would make you feel better."

"So you were," I say sadly.

He looks at me with his deep, mesmerizing cat eyes. "Was I in pain? Yes, I was. But not how you are thinking. My body was numb, so I couldn't really feel any physical pain. My pain came from knowing what you were going through and the decision you were going to have to make."

Tears stream down my face. "I'm so sorry. I'm so, so sorry. I should have done more."

He walks up to me and rubs his face on mine like he used to. "My body was shutting down. There was nothing more that could have been done. Do you remember the promise you made that day? You said if

I let go, so that you wouldn't have to make that final decision, you promised you would find me again."

"Yeah, what a selfish jerk I was." More tears begin to run down my face.

"You were not selfish at all. I was ready. I was just waiting on you to tell me it was okay."

I start sobbing uncontrollably. "I didn't want you to go."

"But you knew it was time, didn't you?"

"I did."

"And you kept your promise."

"I did?"

"You're here, aren't you?" he says. A cat-like grin on his little face.

"I am," I say. A smile penetrates the sadness. "So, what happens next?"

"We play like we used to!"

"I'd love that!"

For what seems like forever, we run through the open fields, chasing each other like we used to. As I watch him run, his appearance changes from a little kitten to a full-grown cat and every stage in between. I smile when I see the little kitten that once fit in my open hand.

"Hey, there's someone I want you to meet. Follow me," I shout as I run over towards Muffin. She is playing with a little white and brown puppy. "Hey, Muffin. Who's your friend?"

Muffin waves. "Oh, hey! This is Bliss. Isn't she beautiful? She says that she is a new arrival here. She is missing someone terribly, but she said it gets a little easier each day. She said all the animals have been so nice to her, and she feels amazing. I told her that I'm sure her loved one is missing and loving her, and that they will be together soon."

I smile and wave at Bliss. She lets out a little bark, then runs off. "Muffin, this is Titus."

"It's very nice to meet you, Titus. I'm looking forward to hearing all about you. I'll give you two a little more time. Find me when you're done, Blue."

"Okay."

"She is very special. I'm glad you found her," Titus says.

"Thanks. Yeah, she is. She is unlike anyone I've ever met before."

"I can see that."

As we walk through the pasture, I can hear music beginning to play. It is soft and soothing. I can't tell where it was coming from. "This song, it's the song that was playing when I held you...in your last moments."

"I hoped you would remember. It's such a beautiful song."

"It's a sad song. I cry whenever I hear it."

"It doesn't have to be. Now you can remember this moment and know that I'm okay, and that I'm happy here. And now you can be happy too."

"But you aren't with me."

"But I am. I will always be with you."

I shed a tear, but it is a happy tear. "How did you get so wise?"

He laughs. "Well, I am much older than you."

We laugh together. I put my arms out. He walks over to me and hugs me in that cat-like way he always did. His purr was deep and powerful. He rubs his face against my cheek.

"I have to go, don't I?" I ask.
"Yes, I'm afraid it's that time."
"Will I be able to come back?"
"When the time is right, we'll see each other again."
I give him one last hug. The music begins to fade out. "Love you, Titus."
"Love you too, Kaleb."
I watch him run off into the pasture. I smile as tears flow down my face. Muffin walks up behind me and takes my hand. "You okay, Blue?"
"I miss him, but he's in a better place."
"You'll see him again."
"I know."
As we walk back over the bridge, Muffin's steps begin to slow. She lets my hand go and turns to look back. A single tear rolls down her face. "Muffin? What's wrong?"
She grimaced "I don't know. Something just doesn't feel right." She looks closely at me. "Are you okay?"
"I don't know. I feel weird. The way Titus looked at me when he first saw me, he looked worried. And I...I remembered things back there. Things I didn't know I forgot. What about you? Did you remember things too?"
"My dad. I remembered my dad. There was an accident. He didn't make it. And my mum—"
"Muffin, I'm sorry, but we have to go. Now!!"

Chapter 64 - Back to the Path

Dreamscape

~Muffin~

A loud boom of thunder shakes the bridge. The sky quickly fills with dark clouds. The clouds begin swirling in a circle, creating a hole in the sky. Constant lightning strikes illuminate the center of the hole. As the clouds swirl, the center appears to get closer and closer to us.

"Blue, we have to get out of here!" I grab his hand and run as fast as I can. The wind picks up and rain begins to pelt us as we run. I can't really see what is in front of me, I just know there is no turning back. I look up at the sky, the center of the clouds is getting closer. I know I have to go faster, but I'm not sure how fast I can go and still have Blueberry keep up. I tighten my grip on his hand. "Whatever happens, don't let go of my hand!" I shout as loud as I can.

Thunder continues to boom, shaking everything around us. I run faster than I've ever ran. Everything is a blur. The only time I can see what is in front of us is when the lightning strikes. I can still feel Blueberry holding on to me. I refuse to let him go. The wind and rain pick up, almost as if it is purposely blowing against us to slow us down. "Stay with me, Blue!" I yell. There is no way I am letting this wind or rain stop me. A large bolt of lightning illuminates the sky. In the distance, I can make out the large tree from the playground. I head straight for it.

"We're almost there, Blue."

"I...can't run anymore, Muffin. I...can't breathe. Just let me go."

"Just hang on! The tree is just up ahead! We'll take cover underneath it!"

As we near the tree, the lightning stops, and the wind and rain begin to let up. It is pitch black and we can't see in any direction. I slow my pace. I reach out with my free hand, frantically trying to find something I could use to guide me. A violent rumble of thunder shakes the area, knocking us off our feet. We stand up, take a few steps, then stop.

"Blue, I don't know which way is forward. I don't know what to do. I don't know what to do!" I say frantically.

"The fireflies," he says. His voice is labored.

"There are no fireflies. They're all gone."

"The song."

"I don't know what you're talking about. What song?"

He takes a deep breath and begins to hum a tune. It is a soft, quiet tune, but it echoes throughout the area. Nothing happens. "Blue, what are you doing? We should just keep moving and hope for another lightning strike." He continues to hum, getting a little louder with each note. Thunder booms again. "Blue, please! We have to move," I plead. He finishes the tune and lets out an exasperated sigh. "What were you trying to do?" I ask.

"I—"

Before he can utter another word, what looks like millions of fireflies, illuminate the giant tree and everything else around us, with their magnificent light. We hurry and make our way to the tree.

"How did you know to do that, Blue?"

"Long story. I'll explain later. Thanks for pulling me through that. You saved my life."

"I guess that makes us even."

"Oh? How is that?"

I wink at him. "Long story. I'll explain later."

"So, what should we do now? Wait this out?"

"I don't think so. I don't think we belong here anymore, Blue."

"What do you mean?"

"I mean, this place, it's dying all around us." A loud boom shakes the ground beneath us. The fireflies disperse. Everything around us is so dark, it looks like nothing is here anymore. A loud boom shakes the ground again. In the distance we can see flashes of lightning. A dark black smoke in the shape of a large man appears to be advancing towards us. Fear grips me. "Blue, we have to run!" I yell.

"Run where?!"

I point to the one direction we had both been avoiding. "That way! Follow the fireflies!"

"We can't go that way. That's the way to the path!"

Lightning strikes again. I can see the black smoke advancing. I grab his hand. "We don't have much of a choice. Run!"

We run towards the path. The fireflies that returned, provide enough light to guide our way. The thunder and lightning stop. We look back. All we can see is darkness. We take slow, timid steps down the path. Up ahead, in the faint light, I can see the shed and the pavilion. "We just have to get past that," I whisper.

"Muffin, I'm scared."

"I'm scared too. But it's our only chance. We just have to stay together."

We slowly walk towards the shed. The fireflies disperse again. The area emits an eerie light that waves in a weird distorted way. I grip Blueberry's hand a little tighter. "That's the strange distortion from before," he says.

"Should we just run past it?" I ask.

"I don't know. I don't feel so spry anymore."

I shake out my legs. "I don't either. It's happening again." I begin to feel sad and terrified.

Blueberry looks at me. He looks terrified. "What do we do?"

I take a deep breath. My heart sinks with the realization that there is only one way out of this. "I have an idea. It's a bit crazy, but I need you to trust me, okay?"

"Of course, I trust you."

"Okay. We are going to walk towards the shed. You have to keep on moving, no matter what. You got that? Don't stop moving."

"But—"

"Don't stop moving!"

"Okay."

Hand in hand we walk towards the shed. With each

step, I can feel my body aging. The wind picks up and the rain begins to fall again. As we near the shed, the distortion gets greater and greater. The rain seems to fall from every direction. We reach the shed door. "Blue, whatever happens here, I want you to know that these were the greatest moments of my life. You've awakened something in me that I thought was dead. I don't know what will happen next, but I need you to promise me that you will never forget me. Promise me that you will find me again."

"What are you talking about? You said we have to do this together."

"I know, Blue. Just promise me, okay?"

"I promise. But it's going to be okay." He places his finger on my chin and lifts my head. "Look at me, Muffin. It's going to be okay."

"Okay," I say. His eyes were holding back tears. His face was older now. If it wasn't for his eyes, I would barely recognize him.

We lose ourselves in each other's eyes. It is like I am replaying everything that happened from the time we got here until now, reliving all of those moments again, feeling all of those feelings again, falling in love with him again. We lean forward. I rest my forehead on his. "I love you, Blueberry."

"I love you, Muffin," he replies in the sweetest tone. The words hang in the air. We lean in a little more and close our eyes. Our noses touch ever so slightly, and we shake our heads back and forth. I want to stay in this moment forever.

I reach my hand to the side of his face. He slowly lifts his head and looks at me. I smile. He smiles back at me. In the reflection in his eyes, I see something that paralyzes me with fear. He notices my fear and looks over my shoulder. A black shadowy figure is approaching. It doesn't seem like it is moving towards us. It almost seems like the area we are in is being drawn into him. I stare at it. I have seen this thing before. I know what it is, and I know what it wants. A loud, distorted beeping sound pierces our ears. Everything around us starts to bend and contort.

Blue shakes me. "Muffin, we have to go!"

I stand there. Anger grows inside me. "You can't have him!" I yell. I grab the shed door and open it. We take steps backwards as it approaches. "Not this time, you bastard!" I shove Blue far back into the shed. I step out and slam the door. I lean up against the door and hold it closed with all my strength. The dark figure lets out a distorted wail.

"If you want him, you're going to have to go through me!" The dark figure hovers before me. Its black soulless eyes peer at me. As I stand there holding the door, I can feel Blue knocking on the door, pleading for me to open it. I close my eyes. Tears flow down my face.

"Muffin! What are you doing?! Open the door!" he yells.

"I'm sorry, Blue. You can't stay here. You have to wake up! You have to wake up!"

"Muffin! Open the door! Open the door! Open the door!"

Chapter 65 - Rude Awakening
~Penny~

"Open the door! Open the door! Streetlight, open the door!

I opened my eyes. I heard banging on the door. I could barely get to my feet. "What? Who's there?" I said wearily. I was confused and didn't know where I was.

"It's Char, sweetie. Can you open the door?"

"Hold on." I gathered myself, made my way to the door, and opened it.

"Oh jeez, Streetlight. You look like holy hell. Are you on that stuff again?"

"What? No. What are you...how...how did you get in here?"

"Never mind how I got in. You need to get yourself together. It's your mom. She's awake, but she's not doing well. You need to go see her."

"My mum? Awake? But...Blueberry needs—"

"Blueberry? Streetlight, snap out of it!" She grabbed my arm and led me to the bathroom. She filled a cup full of cold water and threw it in my face.

"What the hell, Char?!"

"You need to snap out of it! Get yourself together, get in the shower, and get yourself ready to go. Who knows how much time is left."

She walked out of the bathroom and slammed the door. I stared into the mirror and tried to figure out what I just experienced. I didn't know what day it was or how long I was out. I turned the water on and just stared at it. "There's no way that was just a dream. But if it wasn't, then Blueberry..." I thought to myself.

Char banged on the door. "I set some clothes on your bed. I'll be in the kitchen waiting for you."

I showered and got dressed. I threw my hair in a ponytail and headed down to the kitchen. Char was at the table reading the tome. As I approached, she quickly closed it. "You ready? she asked.

I took a deep breath. "Yeah." The sadness of the moment hit me all at once.

"Then we better get going." She took off my necklace and held it up. "Here you go. I fixed the clamps on it. I figured you might want to wear it. I packed you some stuff in a bag too."

I threw the bag over my shoulder. I took the necklace and put it in my pocket. "Thanks."

We headed out the door and got in her car. There was an awkward silence as we drove to the hospital. I stared out the window, still lost in my thoughts. "So, how ya been, Streetlight? It's been a while."

"I'm fine."

"You know, after that horrible night, I was worried sick about you. You just disappeared. The least you could have done was let me know you were okay."

"Sorry. I just wanted to put it all behind me."

"So, how are you, really? Because if I'm being honest, you don't look fine. You don't look healthy, and your skin tone is almost as pale as mine."

"Really, I'm fine. Can we change the subject?"

"Fine. I'll let it go. Just showing concern for you."

"And I appreciate it."

"So, did you write the stories in that weird looking book on the kitchen table? They're pretty trippy."

"No, I didn't."

"Oh, good. Then I guess I can tease you about those silly names. Whoever wrote it could have definitely come up with better names than those."

I sat up in my seat. "What?"

"Nothing. I'm just yanking your chain. I'm sure those names have special meanings. They just sound like pet names, is all. So anyway, why didn't you ever speak of your mom? We just all assumed she passed away."

I turned my head and stared out the window. A tear rolled down my face. "Because basically, she did. After my dad died, she became a shell of herself. She was barely able to function on her own. It was like she didn't even want to try anymore. That's why I was sent to live with my dad's family. I would visit her occasionally, but I eventually just stopped. I was angry at her. I felt like she abandoned me when I needed her the most. One day, she collapsed and was admitted to the hospital. The doctor said it was a case of takotsubo cardiomyopathy."

"Tae-kwon what?"

"It's basically broken heart syndrome."

"Oh, wow. I'm sorry. I didn't even know that was a real thing."

"A lot of people don't. It caused her to fall into a coma. She's been in it ever since. Until now, I guess."

"And you haven't been to see her because you were still angry at her?"

"At first, yes. After a while, I think it was the guilt that kept me away. It's stupid, I know."

"Hey, we all have our demons. I'm not here to judge. I just want you to be sure you say what you need to say. Not all of us get that second chance."

"Thanks, Char."

We pulled up to the hospital. Char parked the car and turned it off. My heart was racing. I kept taking deep, steadying breaths, trying to calm myself down. Char put her hand on my shoulder. "Do you need me to go with you?"

I took one more deep breath. "No, I have to do this alone." I leaned over and gave her a hug. "Thanks again, Char."

"Anytime, sweetheart. Remember what I told you about second chances."

"I will."

I got out and looked at the hospital entrance. I took controlled, measured steps as I walked towards it. Each step corresponded with a deep breath. I made my way to the coma ward. I slowly walked over to the nursing station. The nurse smiled at me. "Hello, may I help you?" she asked politely.

"I'm here to see my mum," I said sadly.

"Okay. And what is your mom's name?"

"Delilah. Delilah Johnson."

"Oh? And you are?"

"Penny Johnson." She looked quizzically at her computer screen. "Micaleah Penelope Johnson, I said."

"Oh, my. Follow me, dear."

She led me into Mum's room. She opened the door. I walked in. "I'll give you two some privacy." She closed the door as she walked out. My heart began to race again. My palms were a sweaty mess. I didn't know how to start. She laid in the bed. Her eyes were barely open. She looked so much older than I thought she would. I walked over and sat down in the chair next to her. I put my hand on hers. Her eyes opened halfway.

"Penny? Is that you?"

"Yes, Mum. It's me," I said weakly.

"Oh, my goodness. Let me look at you." Her voice was weak. She struggled to turn her head towards me. "Look at you. You are absolutely beautiful. You are all grown up. What a beautiful woman you have become. If only your father could see you now."

"Yeah," I said softly. My eyes welled with tears.

"Penny?"

"Yeah, Mum?"

"How's everything with you?"

I shrugged my shoulders. "Good, I guess. Just chugging along, you know."

"You're still upset with me. You never could hide that from me. I don't blame you. Not being there for you, especially when you needed me more than anything, is something I'll always regret."

"Then why didn't you try. Why didn't you try harder for me?"

"Penny, dear. I hope you never have to experience what I did that night, and I don't expect you to understand. I loved your father more than life itself. Losing him was the hardest thing I ever had to deal with. I tried to move past the grief. It just wouldn't let me go."

"You aren't the only one who lost someone that night."

She moved her hand on top of mine. "I know. I'm sorry, Penny. I've replayed that night over and over again. Each time, I think about what I could have done differently. Sometimes, you just can't fight fate."

"I still miss him."

"I still miss him too, more than you know."

"I just wish...I wish you...never mind."

"It's okay, Penny. Speak your mind."

"I just wish you tried harder, then maybe my life would have turned out a bit different, you know. It wasn't easy growing up, dealing with everything alone."

"Oh, Penny. You were never alone. At times you may have felt that way, but you were never alone. I'm sorry I couldn't be there for you. I love you more than words can say. I just need you to always remember that."

I wiped the tears from my face and rested my head on her chest like I did when I was a child. "I know, Mum. You know, sometimes I have these life-like conversations with you. You would tell me stories or your little sayings. They helped a lot."

She stroked my hair softly. "Did you ever wonder where your name came from?"

"My name? I just assumed Daddy liked it. And my middle name is your middle name."

"Your father knew that you were going to be special. So, he picked Micaleah. It means 'Gift from God.' I gave you my middle name because my great grandmother, my nana, my mother, and now you, share a special gift."

"What special gift is that?"

"The name Penelope means 'weaver.' To be more precise, it means 'dream weaver.'"

I stood up. "I don't understand. Are you saying that while I'm sleeping, I can alter my dreams?"

"Yes, but not all dreams take place in your sleep."

"So, what are you saying? I can weave dreams while I'm awake? That doesn't make sense. And you can weave dreams?

"Yes, Penny, we both can."

I stood there in disbelief at what I was actually hearing. I didn't remember anything from my childhood that would have given any indication of this. "Did you weave any dreams when I was a child?"

"A few here or there, if necessary."

"If necessary? What do you mean?"

"If I needed to relax or comfort you."

I could feel myself getting flustered. I wasn't sure how to feel about this information. Part of me wanted to believe she wouldn't make up something like this, especially now. The other part theorized that maybe this was just the ramblings of an old woman who had just awakened from a horribly long coma. I decided to press the issue to test my theory. I held her hand in both of mine.

"Mum?"

"Yes, sweetie."

"Were you able to weave dreams while you were in a coma?"

She hesitated. "Yes, I was."

"Did you weave any dreams for me?"

"Penny, dear, are you sure you want to know the answer?"

"Why wouldn't I?"

She slowly turned her head the other way. "Just two."

"Two? Which ones?" There was a long pause. Her heart rate began to rise, setting off an alarm on the machine. "Mum?" Nurses rushed into the room. They began checking on her and the machines. They put an oxygen mask over her face.

"Ma'am I need you to step back," one nurse said.

"Mum, which two?" I yelled.

"Can someone please remove her from the room?" another nurse said.

A nurse grabbed me and started pulling me towards the door. "Which two?" I shouted as they tried to pull me out. Mum held up a hand to the nurses pulling on me. They stopped pulling me, but held on to me. She pulled the mask off her face and weakly uttered three words.

"Josie and Alexandria."

"No! No!" I screamed as I fell to my knees. "How could you!?" The nurses grabbed me and pulled me out of the room.

Chapter 66 - Weaver of Dreams
~Penny~

The last thing I remember seeing was Mum passing out. I laid in a hospital bed. A nurse stood beside me holding a clipboard. I tried to sit up. "What happened? Where's my mum?"

The nurse rested her hand on my shoulder. "Please, Ms. Johnson. Try to relax. The doctor will be in shortly." She handed me a glass of water. "Drink some of this and try to relax."

A female doctor knocked on the door, then walked in. "Hello, Ms. Johnson. My name is Dr. Baker. I'm glad to see you're awake. How are you feeling?"

"I feel fine. Where's my mum?"

"Well, that's what I'm here to talk to you about. Your mother is resting. She experienced quite a bit of trauma earlier. That's a lot for someone in her condition to deal with. I'm sure you realize this, but it is a miracle that she's even awake after being in a coma for that long, and even more of a miracle that she is lucid. She has asked to see you. However, before I sign off on that, I wanted to speak with you and make sure you knew that it is imperative that she stay calm. I'm not sure she could survive another episode like the one yesterday."

"Yesterday? How long have I been out?"

"A little over fourteen hours. You were severely dehydrated, and I'm sure you must be starving. I'll have some food brought in if you'd like. Also, I'd like you to consent to a health assessment, just as a precaution."

I rolled my eyes. "Do I have a choice?"

"The choice is yours, but I strongly recommend it."

"Fine. Whatever. I'm not hungry though, but thank you."

"I'll have them bring in a little something just in case. I'd feel much better if you ate something. Now, about what I discussed with you before. I'm not sure what went on between you and your mother, but I need to know that you are able to keep your emotions in check before I allow you back in there."

Just when I thought nothing could make my life any stranger, my mum went and did just that. What was I supposed to do with the knowledge that I could weave dreams? I didn't know whether I should be happy or mortified. I didn't even know what was real anymore. In my head I could hear her voice repeatedly saying "Josie and Alexandria." It cut like a knife each time. What else had she intervened in? What else has she not told me about? My mind immediately went to Blueberry. Was that all just another mind game she set in motion? The cruelty of it all made me sick to my stomach. I thought about what Char said about second chances. The anger in me didn't want to give any more chances. The rational side of me decided that I needed more answers.

"I can keep them in check. When can I see her?"

"Like I said before, she is resting. I'll have someone come and get you as soon as she wakes up."

"Thank you."

"You're welcome. And look, I know it's none of my business, but mother-daughter relationships can be messy. I lost my mother when I was young. I was a stubborn teenager and we argued all the time. I couldn't see that everything she did was because she loved me. Now that I have kids, I can see it clearer than ever. As parents, there's no way we can always be there for our kids, but our love is always there, just something to keep in mind."

I wiped the tears from my eyes. "Thank you."

"You're welcome. It shouldn't be long now. Eat a little bit. You'll need your strength."

She walked out and shut the door. I laid back on the pillow and cried. I knew that she was right. If I was being honest with myself, I didn't know where I'd be without Josie and Alexandria. They got me through my darkest days, Blueberry too. I had been so foolish. Mum didn't deserve my anger. She deserved my thanks.

There was a knock on the door. An orderly rolled in a tray with food on it. He smiled. "Forestview's finest. Enjoy."

"Thank you," I said. I removed the lid and picked at the dry sandwich. I walked over to the window and looked out. It was a bright, sunny day. In the distance, I saw kids playing in the park. I thought about Blueberry and Muffin. Tears welled in my eyes. I thought about all the time they shared. I thought about the playground, the waterfalls, and the beautiful cherry blossom trees with their red leaves. And now their dream just ends. It all felt so real. I wanted so badly for it to be. I knew that if it was, then Blueberry is all alone and in a dire situation.

There was a quiet knock on the door. "Ms. Johnson?" a nurse called out.

I wiped any traces of tears from my eyes. "Yes?"

"Your mother is awake. You can go in whenever you are ready."

"Thank you."

I took a deep breath and steeled myself. I was almost as nervous as I was the day before. I made my way to her room. When I opened the door, she was sitting up, looking out the window. Her eyes were more open than they were before, but they were bloodshot. She had been crying.

"Mum?"

She turned towards me. "Oh, Penny." She put her arms out. I ran over to her. "Oh, my sweet Penny. Please don't be angry with me. I'm so sorry. I never even considered your feelings. I just wanted to keep you safe. I just wanted you to always be safe."

"I know, Mum. I'm not angry. I understand why you did it." I half smiled. "I'm actually glad you did. You know I always wanted a sister."

"I know, sweetie." She sat quietly for a moment. She gently placed her hand on her belly. "It was in the plans." She began to sob.

"Oh, Mum." I pulled her in close and hugged her tightly. "Shh, it's okay, Mum. It's okay."

"I'm sorry, Penny. I shouldn't have burdened you with that. I know you've dealt with enough."

"It's okay, Mum. The only thing that matters now is

that you are awake, and we are together again."

"Thank you, Penny. That means so much to me to hear you say that."

We hugged and sat in silence for a few minutes, just enjoying each other's company. I felt so at ease. There's nothing quite like a mother's embrace.

"Are you tired, Mum? Do you need to rest?"

"No, I'm okay for now. Besides, don't you have questions for me?"

"How did you—"

"A mother always knows."

"Really, Mum, if you are tired, I can wait."

"Nonsense. Ask away. No more secrets."

"Okay, I guess I'll start with dream weaving. I can't believe I'm asking this, but is that really a thing? I mean, I've experienced some crazy things in the last few years, which is probably why I haven't just dismissed it as you having brain fog from your coma."

She smiled. "You are your father's daughter. I wouldn't expect you to just accept that sort of information without questioning it."

"Did he know?"

"I suspected he did. For reasons that you'll understand one day, it's very hard to hide it from the ones you love."

"I see. How exactly does it work?"

"Well, that's a bit difficult to explain. You have your normal dream weaving, where you can manipulate things in a dream as you see fit, just by focusing on them. Then there is weaving other people's dreams. This can only be done if the person's dream you are weaving, is connected to you. Typically, it only works with other weavers. Very few people find that connection. It is said that the eldest amongst the dream weavers used spirit animals to reach the ones they wanted to connect with."

"Like the owl you sent me?"

"Owl? I'm afraid not. I do not possess a spirit animal."

"You said you can weave dreams in a person that is awake. How is that possible?"

"There are parts in the human brain that are dormant. In other words, they are sleeping. That is where the dream takes place. Essentially, the person is awake, and yet, they can also be dreaming at the same time. Only the most skilled weavers can pull off such a feat."

"Like you?"

Her face saddened. "Yes, like me."

"I'm sorry. I didn't mean it like that."

"It's alright. You deserve the truth."

"So, this is how Josie came to be?"

"Yes."

"And Alexandria?"

"Yes."

"How were you able to weave while in a coma?

"I haven't always been in a coma as you know it. One of the dangers of dream weaving is that it drains your life force. You can only do it in intervals, and eventually, once your life force is depleted, you will be unable to do it at all."

"Is that why Josie would always disappear and why Alexandria was gone so long?"

"Exactly. I needed to preserve my life force. Eventually, I had to send Alexandria away. It became too much to manage both."

"I see. Why did you make Josie go away?"

"I'm sorry. I am almost out of my remaining life force, my dear. I'm so sorry it ended the way it did."

"It's okay." I wiped a tear away. "She wasn't real, anyway."

"Oh, sweetie. Come here." I laid my head on her chest. She rested her hand on my head. "Of course, she was. Everyone that means something to you is real."

"I just miss them," I said, trying not to cry. "I never really got a chance to say goodbye," I cried out, unable to control myself.

"Shh, it's okay sweetie. It's okay. Let it all out." She stroked my hair in that way she always did when I was upset. I felt like I was five years old again. "There, there. It's going to be alright. Just rest, sweetie. Let Mummy make it all better."

Chapter 67 - Josie's Return
~Penny~

"Oh, for Frank's sake! Are you going to lay there grizzling all day?"

I wiped my eyes and looked towards the door in astonishment. Josie stood there in heels and a beautiful black and red, floral dress. Her long blond hair was down. It was longer than I remembered. She smiled at me as if she never went anywhere. She turned and modeled the dress. "Don't you just love this tea dress? I'm thinking this is definitely a solid autumn staple. What do you think?"

I jumped up and ran to her. "Josie! I've missed you so much!"

"Hiya, lovely. It's been quite some time." She yawned. "I know one thing; I could go for a swift half." She looked around the room. "And where the bloody hell are we? A hospital? What sort of trouble have you gone and gotten yourself into now?"

"So much has happened since you've been away. I can't wait to tell you all about it."

"And I can't wait to hear all about it, love. But first, please tell me you didn't marry that knob."

"I didn't. I actually ended up knocking him out. It's

a long story. Let's just say he got what he deserved."

"Damn right he did. Good for you, love. You should have knocked his arse out a long time ago."

"I know. I kind of just snapped. He was hurting someone I cared about."

"Oh? Someone you care about? Pray tell."

"It's nothing. He's gone." I hung my head and looked at the floor. "I haven't seen him since that night."

"Well, did you try to find him?"

"No."

"Bugger all, Penny. How do you expect to find him if you don't look for him?"

"It doesn't matter," I said sadly. "So much has happened since then."

"You got your memories back?"

"I did."

"Have you made peace with everything?"

"I'm trying. I'm still processing the bombshell Mum dropped on me."

"Ahh, yeah, that. Well I suppose there was no other way around that. You were bound to find out eventually. I imagine that could be quite the scary thing to find out on your own."

"I guess so. Why didn't you ever tell me?"

"Because, love, that wasn't my place. My place was to keep you safe and get you better." She surveyed the room. "Which, apparently I did a bollocks job of, by the looks of it."

Through my tears, I let out a little bit of laughter. "You did fine. I'm actually in the best place I've been in quite some time."

"Then why do you look so sad?"

"I don't know. There is a part of me that feels incomplete. A part of me that misses someone very special."

"Penelope Johnson! Have you gone and proper fallen for someone?"

"What? No! Well, kind of."

"Hmm, well, you better tell me the story. You may want to skip to the juicy bits, life force and all that jazz. Blimey, that's confusing, even for me."

I told Josie everything that happened the day after she left. I told her about the guy from the park. I told her about what happened at the nightclub. She laughed and gave me a high five. She couldn't believe her ears when I told her that I had been sleeping. She looked at me very peculiarly when I told her about the adventures of Muffin and Blueberry.

"What's that look for?" I asked.

"Do you remember me telling you the story about the little boy that you had a crush on in primary school?"

"Now that you bring it up, I do."

"Do you remember his name?"

"I don't."

"Do you remember where he sat in your class?"

"No, I don't. What are you getting at? You think I made him up?"

"No, love. I don't think you made him up at all. I just don't think he actually went to your school. I think you dreamed him. You would always have stories of all the adventures you went on. You had quite the imagination, or so Mum and Dad thought."

I sat there and pondered the meaning of what Josie told me. "So, what do you think it means?"

"I don't know, love. Maybe he's your soulmate."

"My soulmate? My soulmate is a dream? That makes no sense."

"You're talking to me and you're questioning what makes sense? That's a bloody good one."

"Yeah, I suppose you're right." I thought about it for a minute, then an epiphany came to me. One I wasn't eager to address. My face turned to a scowl.

"Oh, bugger all. I know that look. Well, come on. Out with it."

"Mum said that she could weave within other people's dreams. What if he is like you?"

"Does he feel like me?"

"It feels different. I feel young and free when I'm with him. I feel alive."

"Gee, thanks. What am I, Scotch mist?"

"Stop it. You know what I mean. Everything feels natural with him. It feels right. You know that feeling you get when you hear a song so powerful and moving, it makes you cry? I feel like that when he holds me."

"You want my opinion? I think he is your soulmate and you two are reaching out to each other. Maybe the dreams when you were younger were the first time you connected. Maybe this is the second. Sounds too magical to be a coincidence. Penny, just as birds call out to each other on a warm spring morning, so too, do our souls call out to the one we are meant to spend our lifetime with."

"That's beautiful, Josie."

"It's beautiful because it's true."

"So, what do I do?"

"Talk to Mum about it. She may have a little more insight into this than she let on."

"Great. More secrets."

"Not secrets, knowledge. Everything she has ever done was to protect you. You are not like everyone else. These gifts you have, these things you can do, it's pretty powerful stuff."

"Gifts? Plural?"

"Yes, Penny. Like I told you before, your inner light shines very brightly. When you smile and shine that light, the whole world will smile with you. As a child, it was oh so evident."

"In my dreams, I'm a child. I'm happy, and he can feel my happiness."

Josie smiled. "That's your inner child. That is where all faith, happiness, love, hope, and imagination live. For so long, you suppressed your inner child. When you do that, you lose all those things. I'm so happy you found yours again."

"Yeah, me too," I said. Worry covered my face.

"Penny?"

I began to cry. "If he's not a dream of Mum's, then I think he may be in terrible danger. Things weren't good when I last left him."

"There, there, love. I'm sure it will be okay. You just need to get back and save his arse. Easy peasy."

I continued to cry. "Yeah, easy peasy lemon squeezy."

"Come on, now. Get yourself together. You don't want to find the bloke and he sees you looking like a miserable old toad."

I laughed through all my tears. "You troll!"

"Duff!"

"Mouth-breather!"

"Barmpot!"

"You...you butt-face!"

Josie smirked. "Someone is losing their edge. I'll take mooncalf for the win, please."

We laughed hysterically. "I let you win," I said. I was still laughing uncontrollably.

"My arse, you did. Now that's a proper way to ride off into the sunset."

My heart sank immediately. My laughter was replaced with silence. "That's not funny, Josie."

"I'm sorry, love. You know I always did have foot-in-mouth disease." She opened her arms to me. "Come here, love." She gave me the biggest warmest hug I could ever remember her giving me. "Don't think of it as goodbye. Think of it more as a 'to be continued.'"

"I'm really going to miss you."

"Chin up, buttercup. You have a soulmate to save."

"I do." I held her for a minute. I didn't want to let go. "I love you, Josie."

"I love you too, Penelope Johnson. Cheers, love."

As we stood and held our embrace, I could feel another pair of arms wrap around my waist. I looked down. "Oh, Alexandria!" I kneeled down and gave her the biggest hug. "I'm going to miss you too! Be a good girl, okay?"

"I will. I love you, Aunt Penny."

"I love you too, sweetheart."

Josie kneeled down and we all embraced. I held on to them, not planning to ever let them go, until I heard a voice call out to me. "Ms. Johnson. Ms. Johnson. I'm sorry. Visiting hours are over. I need to take you back to your room."

I blinked my eyes open to find myself wrapped in Mum's warm embrace. She looked half awake. "But I need to talk to my mum."

"I'm sorry. It'll have to wait until tomorrow."

"But it's urgent. I need to talk to her!" I said urgently. The nurse was alarmed by my tone. "But Ms. Joh—"

"It's okay, Michelle. Please just give us a few minutes," Mum said. Her voice was weak and raspy.

The nurse nodded. "Yes, Mrs. Johnson."

"Mum! You're awake."

"I am."

"Thank you for that. It meant the world to me."

"You're welcome, Penny. I'm glad I was able to do that for you."

"Your life force?"

She shook her head slowly.

"I'm sorry, Mum.

"It's okay. I've done all the weaving I need to do for a lifetime. All I ever wanted to do was keep you safe."

"Mum, I have a question about Blueberry. Is he like Josie and Alexandria?"

"Who?"

"Blueberry. The one I see in my dreams. Did you weave him to make me happy?"

"Oh, sweetie." She smiled and touched my face. "I did not, but that is how I met your father."

"What? I thought you met at a book writers conference."

"That's where we met in person for the first time."

"So, does that mean that Dad was your soulmate?"

"Yes, and he still is. It's much deeper than you can imagine." She coughed. Her voice was getting weaker.

"How did you find him outside of the dream world?"

"There's always a place...special place...same..." She

began coughing again, only much harder.

I spoke frantically. "Something happened in the dream. The world we created is turning dark. The smoke, Mum. I saw the black smoke. I slept last night, but I couldn't get back." My voice quivered.

Mum's coughing got worse. Blood trickled down her nostril. Her breathing became labored as she tried to speak. She squeezed my hand. "Sorry...help...find him...book...necklace...cr..."

Her heart rate monitor began to beep faster and faster. "Mum? Mum? What's happening?! We need help in here now!" I yelled.

The nurses rushed in. "She's coding! Get me a crash cart! Get Ms. Johnson out of here."

I screamed as someone pulled me away. I could still hear the nurses in the room.

"We're losing her. I need those paddles!"

"Paddles ready. Charged."

"Clear!" There was a loud shocking sound. I could feel it throughout my entire body.

"Clear!" Another shock.

"Clear!"

Part Four

Chapter 68 - Reemergence Dreamscape -Blueberry-

I don't know how long it has been since muffin locked me in the shed. I don't know how long it has been since I've seen her face, heard her voice, or felt her presence. I can feel myself reaching that desperation point. I muster what little courage I have and contemplate opening the door. I figure if I can just get back to the playground, everything will be okay.

I slowly open the door and peek out. It is dark. Northern lights consume the sky. The dim, eerie, amber light is the only thing making it possible to see. I step out and look around. The entire area is ravaged. I barely recognize where I am. I call out to Muffin. There is no answer. I look around the area for signs of her. I can't find anything.

I head in the direction of the playground, hoping she is there waiting for me. As I walk, each step is heavy and labored. I feel like I am being tied down with weights made of sorrow. Everything around me is still. It is so quiet, it is deafening. The bridge that was once here, the only way back to the playground, is now gone. My heart sinks. I fear that I will never get back to her. I have no choice but to head the other way.

With the distortion now gone, the path beyond the shed is now accessible. I am hesitant to venture into this unknown area alone, but with the bridge gone, I don't have much of a choice. I take a deep breath and begin walking. My steps are slow and heavy. My knee is killing me, and the rest of my body feels tired and weary.

I eventually come to a clearing at the bottom of a hill. Tall grass, as tall as me, stands before me. It is dry and withered. It gently sways back and forth. I walk through it, pushing it out of my way. Eventually I come to a clearing where an old withered tree stands. An old, broken swing hangs from it. The area is vastly different than I remember, but I have been here before. Several pieces of the sky are black, like puzzle pieces have been removed from it. At the top of the hill sits what remains of the church.

I slowly make my way to the old church. I look out over a countryside that was once filled with so much color and beauty. Now all that remains is a field of sadness. I open the door to the church. I remember the wedding that I couldn't stop. I remember the old lady. I remember Micaleah. It all seems like a lifetime ago.

"Definitely not the way it was supposed to happen," a voice says. It sounds distant, as if it is from a far-off place. "Sit down and take a load off. You'll need your rest for what's to come."

I take a seat in the pew. "Mother? Is that you?" I ask.

"Yes, dearie. It is."

"Where are you? Why can't I see you?"

"Look a little closer, dearie. Use more than your eyes."

Oddly, what she said made sense. I focus on the area next to me. A thin outline of an elderly woman sits right beside me. She looks like the translucent people that surrounded her the last time I was here, but a bit more faded. "What happened to you?" I ask.

"Oh, don't you worry about little old me. What happened to me is not as important as what's happening to you."

"What's happening to me?"

"You seem to have lost your guide, and now you're lost, wandering aimlessly with no real destination. Am I close?"

"How do you know this?"

"Oh, dearie. I know lots of things."

"Do you know where Muffin is? Is she okay?"

She chuckled. "Muffin. Such a charming nickname."

"Is she okay?" I ask sternly."

"Yes, dearie, she is okay, but she is cut off from you, and only you can restore the connection."

"What do you mean? How do I restore the connection?"

"Follow your heart, dearie. Love is always the answer. You must see this journey to its end. You mustn't stop, no matter what. Or it all ends."

My head sinks low. "My heart was back the other way. How do I get there now?"

"You've come this far. You'll figure it out."

"Yeah, I will. I need to get back to her."

"And she needs you, dearie."

I stare at the front of the church. "Micaleah isn't here, is she?"

"No, dear, she isn't."

"I don't know how, but when Micaleah took my hand, she showed me glimpses of the future. I saw this moment. I didn't understand it then. I understand it now. I saw a lot of things that still don't make sense to me, but I'm guessing at some point they will."

"In time."

"You look like the ladies at the table. What's happening to you?"

"My time here is coming to an end."

"Are you dying?"

"No, dearie. Just beginning anew."

"I see. That was Muffin getting married, wasn't it?"

"It was."

"And I couldn't stop it."

"You weren't supposed to. It hadn't happened yet."

"I guess I'll understand that in time, as well."

"Now you're getting the hang of it."

"Micaleah is Muffin, isn't she?"

She nods "I was wondering how long it was going to take you to figure that out."

"You said you saw the wedding at the church many times before. How?"

"Listen to me. Our time is short, so I'll leave you with this. When our soul has completed its journey in this world, it is reborn anew. Sometimes it follows the same path as before. Sometimes it charts a new course. Sometimes we are the same person. Sometimes we are not. There are those of us who possess a special gift called Soul Remembrance. This is where, despite the creator's intentions, we remember things from our past lives, in our current lives. Initially, it may appear in the form of something as simple as dreams, déjà vu, seeing someone who looks strangely familiar even though you have never seen that person before, or remembrance of a lost love. The more you are reborn, the greater the remembrance. The one thing that remains a constant in each new rebirth is the one you share a soul with. No matter the paths, you and your soulmate are always destined to cross paths, fall in love, and live out the rest of your days together. This is the cycle."

"And what if their paths don't cross?"

"Then the cycle ends, and their cycle comes to an end."

"Forever?"

"I'm afraid so. This is why you must complete your path, my dear."

I sit and contemplate everything she told me. The enormousness of everything begins to weigh on me. The church bell begins to toll. It is a slow, deep toll. "Where do I go from here?" I ask solemnly."

"Follow me, dearie." She walks to the church doors. They open by themselves. The northern lights in the sky still bear an amber hue, but dimmer than before. She walks me to the bottom of the hill. We stand at the beginning of a forest. "Sometimes, the only way out...is in. Take this path to find out who you truly are. Let her light guide you."

"Thank you, Mother, for everything. Will I ever see you again?"

"I hope so, dearie. I hope so."

I take a step into the forest. I turn around to wave to Mother, but she is gone. The entire countryside begins to come apart until there was nothing left but darkness.

Chapter 69 - Visions of Hope Dreamscape -Blueberry-

As I walk through the forest, I can faintly hear the sound of crows in the distance. I notice that this is the forest that I ran through before. All of the colors of the forest have been stripped away and now bear a dull, grey look. Everything is frozen in a sort of suspended animation. Raindrops are frozen in mid-air. A large bolt of lightning is frozen mid-strike. The fireflies that once freely flew about, are now stuck in mid-flight.

I've lost all concept of time. I walk cautiously along the path, careful not to disturb anything. Small uprooted trees sit in mid-air, frozen, as if they have been sucked out of the ground. I keep moving as fast as I can. My body is no longer young and spry. Sometimes it feels as though I am aging with each step. I come to the old abandoned city. All of the houses are now completely destroyed. Some of the crumbled buildings appear to have frozen in time as they were beginning to topple over. I stop and looked around. There is something so familiar about the place, but I can't put my finger on it. I start walking again. My body feels weary, but I don't want to stop. I know I need to keep moving. I need to get to Muffin.

Up ahead at the clearing, I see a pier. A boat tied to the pier rocks back and forth in the water. The sky starts to pulsate. The northern lights change to a brownish hue. My recollection of my previous ride on this boat gives me pause. My eagerness to get back to Muffin is what helps me put my fear aside and get into the boat. I untie the boat and begin to row. Each row only moves the boat a foot or two. The water is thick and heavy, and doesn't reflect the lights in the sky. I continue to row. I can see unfocused visions in the water. I can't make out what they are. I am scared to look closely at them. I remember what happened the last time I looked deeply into this water. I try to row faster, but the water seems to be getting thicker, slowing me down.

Visions appear throughout the water. Some disappear as fast as they appear. A large vision appears in the water on the side of the boat. A young boy sits on a woman's lap as she reads him a story. He smiles at her lovingly. The water ripples and the vision slowly fades away. On the other side, that same young boy sits on a porch with a man, wearing a baseball glove. An old transistor radio sits beside them as they cheer in excitement. The ripples from the oar fade the vision away. A vision appears in the water ahead. I hasten my rowing to get the boat closer to it. A young boy turns back and appears to look right at me. He smiles and waves. Another young boy runs over to him, pats him on the back, and whispers something in his ear. They both run away. The water ripples again, and the vision fades. The water turns black again.

A feeling of immense melancholy overwhelms me. I can't row any further. Tears run down my face. I feel confused. I feel happy. I feel sad. I feel nostalgic for something I know I miss, but can't quite grab hold of. Suddenly I realize that these aren't visions at all. They are memories.

I pick up the oars and begin rowing again. My arms hurt. I can barely move the boat. In the water, a vision appears of the two young boys sitting on top of a garage with their feet dangling off the back. They are eating mulberries while they laugh with each other, before suddenly hopping down. They run away laughing. I smile as the vision fades. On the other side of the boat, the two young boys ride their bikes in a wooded area, frantically trying to get away from something. One of them falls and appears to cut his hand. The other one hops off his bike and helps him up. He picks up an object, cuts his own hand, and reaches it out. They shake hands. The image slowly fades.

My eyes fill with tears. I take a deep breath. "Kaje," I whisper aloud.

The sky begins to pulsate. The northern light's hue slowly changes to a purplish hue. Up ahead a vision appears. I begin to row. Suddenly the water seems more manageable. The vision shows Kaje and I smoking cigars in our cap and gown. Everyone around us celebrates as we all pose for pictures. The vision fades and immediately shows a vision of me, Kaje and a young lady sitting in a diner eating and enjoying each other's company. The young lady throws a fry at me, then picks it back up and eats it. The image slowly fades.

"Monica." I laugh a little bit.

The warmth of the memories give me the strength to press on. In the distance I can see a pier. I continue to row. A large vision illuminates the entire body of water. In the vision, Kaje, Monica, and I are in a club. There is complete chaos. People are screaming. I see Kaje fighting a huge guy. I see him fall to the ground. The huge guy walks over to me. All I can see is the bottom of his boot. As he lifts it, I see someone standing there with something red. It's her. It's the lady from the park. It's Muffin.

The vision fades to black. Sorrow overcomes me. I sit back in the boat and try to come to grips with what I just saw. I know I need to check on Kaje. I know I need to get to Muffin. I lie in the boat staring at the sky. The northern lights pulse with an amber hue again. I take a deep breath and prepare myself for what lies ahead. I feel a bang, and the boat rocks back and forth violently. My heartbeat quickens. I quickly sit up and look ahead. The boat hit the pier. I have arrived.

Chapter 70 - The Six Crystals
~Penny~

I laid in my bed crying. There was a soft knock on the door. The nurse opened the door and walked in. I quickly sat up, fearing the worst.

"Your mother is resting comfortably. It's important that she gets some rest."

"Thank goodness. When can I see her?"

"You can go in soon, but she is sedated."

"That's fine. Thank you for letting me know."

"You're welcome. Maybe you should get some rest as well. I brought you your bag from your mother's room."

She walked out and closed the door. My mind immediately went back to what Mum said about helping Blueberry. I remembered her saying something about the book and a necklace. I got up, grabbed the bag out of the chair. Thankfully, Char put the tome in it.

I opened the tome and flipped through the pages, not exactly sure what I was looking for. Everything was the same as the last time I looked inside it. I was frustrated. I flipped through again, this time skimming each page for anything that may have changed. There was nothing. I slammed it on the bed in frustration and began to cry. "Something horrible is happening to him, and I can't do anything!" I yelled out.

I paged the nurse. She knocked on the door and came in. "Can I see my mother now?" I asked. Tears streamed down my face.

"Oh, my. Come on, dear. Let's get you in there."

I wiped my face. "Thank you."

We walked into Mum's room. She was sleeping peacefully. "I'll give you two some privacy. Page me if you need anything."

I nodded. "Thank you," I mouthed silently.

I pulled the chair over to Mum's bedside. I took her hand in mine. She felt so cold. What remaining tears I had left, ran down my face.

"Mum, I can't get to him. I can't help him. I don't know what to do. I looked in the tome. I don't know what I'm looking for. I need your help, Mum."

I laid my head on her chest and sobbed. I felt a soft hand caress my face. "Penny?"

I quickly lifted my head. "Mum?" I looked around. We were home in Mum's bedroom.

Mum smiled and stroked my hair. "Your skills are beyond anything I could imagine."

"I did this?"

"You did. It's not the first time." She winked. "It is a feat only a truly gifted weaver can accomplish. I take it things aren't going so well out there."

I lowered my head. "Not exactly, but you are resting."

"I see. Why are you crying, Penny?"

"I can't reach him, Mum. I slept, but I didn't dream."
"And the tome?"
"I opened it. Nothing happened. Nothing in it changed. I don't know what to do. What exactly am I looking for?"
"Calm down, Penelope. If you cannot reach him, he may be beyond your reach. Do you have the necklace Josie gave you?"
"Yes."
"There are seven crystals in the necklace. On the cover of the tome is a spot for six crystals. Insert the six crystals. The black one, Tourmaline, must be left in the necklace. You will need its protection."
"Then what?"
"If he is your soulmate, a record of your journey will be kept in the tome. Certain things you will be able to intervene in, others you will only be able to observe. This is how you will guide him back into your reach."
"Intervene how?"
"By writing, of course."
My face took on a worried look. "Oh."
She smiled and looked me in my eyes. "Don't worry, my love. We've been preparing you for this moment your entire life. Now is the time to be brave."
I smiled back at her. "Thank you, Mum." I leaned over and gave her a hug. I'm so sorry for being angry with you all this time. It was foolish. I wish I could stay here with you like this, and make up for all that lost time."
"Oh, Penny. I do too. But we belong where our heart is. Yours is out there, and he needs you."
"I know, Mum. I know. Just a few more minutes. Just

a few more minutes."

"Just a few more minutes, then I'll have to take you back to your room, Ms. Johnson."

I slowly let go of my mother. I opened my eyes and turned around. The nurse was standing there. "I'm sorry. You only have a couple minutes, then visiting hours are over," she said.

I cleared my throat. "That's fine. I'll head back now." I kissed Mum on the forehead. "Goodnight, Mum."

I headed back to my room. The hospital was quiet. I felt like everyone was watching me as I walked back. I walked in my room and quietly shut the door behind me. I grabbed the tome and sat on the bed. I pulled the necklace out of my pocket and held it up to the light. The crystals glistened in the moonlight that shone through the window. I took slow, deep breaths to steady myself. I was a bit nervous about what I was about to do.

I sat the tome beside me. I carefully removed each crystal from the necklace, leaving only the large black one in the center. I placed each crystal in their slot on the cover. Nothing happened. I sighed in disappointment. I opened the book and flipped through the pages. Everything was still the same.

"I don't know what you want me to do!" I yelled out impatiently.

The light in the room appeared to flicker for just a split second. Instinctively, I reached for my necklace and fastened it around my neck. The tome began to vibrate, and each crystal began to light up one by one, until they all glowed, giving off an amazingly beautiful light. The tree on the cover of the tome began to glow so radiantly, it almost looked like a real live tree.

The tome began hovering in the air. It flung itself open to the first blank page. A bright, blue light shone on each word as they began inscribing themselves in the book. Page after page filled with words that brought life to each story they told. I leaned forward and watched the amazing spectacle play out. The pages stopped turning, and the words began to glow. The pages were complete. The chapters were written. The rest was up to me.

I turned back to the first page where the writing began. The words, still illuminated, didn't tell a story of Muffin and Blueberry. It didn't tell a story of him and I. It told a story of us. Of two souls intertwined into one.

I breathed deeply and continued to read. I wanted to read through each page as fast as possible, but that was not the way the pages were intended to be read. Each page felt like something to embrace, each chapter, like something to cherish, each story, like something to experience.

As I read, each page seemed to spring to life. Suddenly, I felt like I was no longer in control of my body. I felt as though I was sharing a body with someone else. I could see through the eyes of the body I shared, but I couldn't see myself. We ran around a playground with a young boy. It was Blueberry. My heart warmed at the sight of him.

We walked down a dimly lit path, holding his hand. We watched as the horrible events unfolded and everything faded to black. We called out to him, but he could no longer see or hear us. We cried out in anguish as we watched him fade away to nothing. We sat in darkness, crying, afraid that we had lost him forever. Behind us, silent lightning strikes illuminated the clouds. A vision of something dark paralyzed us with fear. Another strike of lightning lit up the entire sky.

In the area up ahead, we saw Blueberry sitting on the ground. Behind us, we saw the dark vision moving at a rapid pace. It appeared to be heading straight towards him.

Through our terror, we tried to make our way to him. We suddenly felt a tremendous source of power from within. It felt like the strength of ten people. Somehow, I could feel everything they felt for him. The emotions were almost too much for me to handle.

We needed him to be strong. We wouldn't be able to stand the anguish of losing him again. We walked over to him and grabbed his hand.

"Whatever happens, whatever you see, don't let go of my hand," we whisper.

We ran through the forest as thunder rocked the entire area. An enormous boom knocked us off our feet. He was still holding our hand. He was confused. He didn't seem to have the same sense of urgency we did, so we knew it was up to us. We didn't know exactly where we were heading, we just had to get out of the forest. We knew we couldn't let whatever that thing was, catch us.

Up ahead we saw fireflies. We knew we could use them as a source of light. We started humming the ancient song. Each one of us joined in one after another. The fireflies danced and shared their wondrous light throughout the entire city.

He looked at us strangely. I wasn't sure what exactly he saw, but he looked like he wanted to run away in horror. I focused and tried to look deeply into his eyes. I wanted him to just see me. I'm not sure if it had any effect. We grabbed his hand and followed the fireflies into the park.

Cold rain started to fall, and the lightning and thunder returned. The fireflies dispersed. The lightning was brighter, and the thunder was louder. It was coming again. We pulled him and ran towards the tree as fast as we could. He was having trouble keeping up. We squeezed his hand tighter. We picked up our pace, desperate to get away from it. A loud crack and a blinding light knocked us off our feet. Our hands come apart. "No!" we yelled.

Darkness covered everything. We heard his voice, but he was beyond our reach now. Sorrow and despair gripped us. We lost him. We let him go. We all cried in unison.

We hummed the ancient song, so that the fireflies would light his future journeys and let him know our love would always guide him. There was a giant boom. We called out to him.

Everything was calm. I was alone now. The night sky was lit by the stars. I heard the sounds of waves crashing. I looked around. An owl sat on the tree branch in the distance. It seemed to call to me. Behind me, I saw Blueberry walking. I called out to him, but he could neither see me, nor hear me. The owl hooted again. I took a step toward the pier. The ground underneath me illuminated. I moved to the next section, and it illuminated as well. I slowly moved section to section, imploring him to follow my lead.

We came to a boat at a pier. The lights in the water shimmered with a beautiful blue color. I sat in the boat and waited for him to get in. He hesitated.

    "It's okay. You are safe here" I whispered, trying to urge him on.

    He took a deep breath and got in. I began rowing the boat across the water. I watched him as he carefully examined the water. I tried to speak to him again, but he couldn't hear me. I closed my eyes and tried to open myself up to him. I wanted him to feel what I was feeling. Suddenly, I felt despair and darkness. A loud knocking sound on the boat startled me and brought me crashing back to reality.

Chapter 71 - Convergence
~Penny~

"Knock, knock," the nurse said just before she entered the room.

The tome closed itself and dropped to the floor.

"Oh, honey. I'm so sorry. Did I startle you?" she asked.

"No, it's fine. I just got caught up in what I was reading."

"That must be some story."

I shook my head. "You have no idea."

She smiled. "Well, maybe you'll have to share it with me when you're finished."

I sat in silence. Not sure of what to say. It wasn't exactly the type of story I could tell someone without them thinking I've gone crazy.

"Or not." She laughed. "That's fine too."

"It's not that—"

"I'm just messing with ya. I'm going to be heading out soon. Do you need anything?

"I think I'm good."

"Okay. Well, I'll see you later."

I smiled anxiously. "Goodnight, Michelle."

She left and closed the door behind her. I waited a

couple of minutes to make sure there were no other interruptions. I reopened the tome. It hovered in the air, began to glow, and the words sprang back to life.

I was back in the boat, but Blueberry was not. The sky was starless and the water was dark and murky. I stood and looked around for him, but I didn't see him anywhere. I called out to him. There was no answer. My heart sank. I lost him again.

I got out of the boat and walked along the pier. Each step was heavy with sorrow. I didn't know what to do. I didn't know where to go. My steps became too heavy. The sorrow became too much to bear. I sat down, covered my face, and cried.

"I do, a hundred and one times."

Anger immediately gripped me. I knew that voice anywhere. It was Joey's voice. I was now sitting in a church pew. I was at a wedding. My own wedding. I looked around in confusion at what was going on. There was no way I was going to marry him. I stood up to get a better look. Blueberry sat in the pew in front of me, next to an elderly lady, who, for a second, I would have sworn was Mum. I felt a momentary sense of relief.

"If anyone here can show just cause why this couple should not be joined in matrimony, let them speak now or forever hold their peace."

I looked around, stunned that nobody said anything. "Say something," I whispered.

"Then by the power vested in me—"

"Say something!" I yelled.

Blueberry jumped to his feet and yelled. "I object! I object a thousand times!" She can't be with him. She's not in love with him. She's in love with me. And...and

I'm in love with her."

Everything stood still. I felt warmth throughout my entire body, and all I could do was smile. "He's in love with me," I whispered. "He is in love with me!"

Everyone in the church began to fade away like they were never there. Before long, the church was completely empty. I made my way to the doors and went outside. I watched as Blueberry and the elderly lady walked through the tall grass. There was something about her that I couldn't quite put my finger on.

As I stood at the top of the hill, a little girl ran up to me. It was Muffin. She smiled and waved at me. "Hi!" she said.

"Hi," I replied.

"You're pretty!"

"Thank you. You're pretty too."

"I'm glad you made it. I gotta go now. Bye!"

"Bye."

I heard the church doors open behind me. A bright light shone from inside the church. I took one last look down the hill. I knew it was time to move on. "I'm in love with you too, Blueberry," I whispered as I slowly turned and headed into the church.

I was engulfed by a warm light. I saw a vision of myself sitting on a bench talking to Blueberry. I remembered that moment. My heart warmed. "Hold on to him! Don't ever let him go!" I yelled to myself.

I watched myself grab my things and walk towards the entrance. "Don't leave him!!" I yelled with everything in me. It felt like my voice echoed throughout time and space, but went unheard. The sunlight faded to black.

I heard the faint sound of music playing behind

me. I turned and opened the church doors. I saw myself walk into Tankers with Joey. Just the sight of him brought me anxiety. A few minutes later I saw Blueberry walk in with someone. I wondered who she was.

The sadness of the events to come began to wash over me. "You're too late," I whispered. I shook my head and followed him in. I watched the events of the night unfold. I watched Blueberry as he smiled and laughed with his friends. I blushed when I saw how he looked at me from across the club. I adored him. Just seeing him made my heart happy.

"Hello! Earth to Kaleb," his friend said.

I smiled. "Kaleb. I like that," I thought to myself.

I looked on as the night took a horrible turn. I felt so helpless. Why was I so stupid? Why didn't I just tell Joey? Why didn't I just leave? Anger welled up inside of me every time I looked at him.

I knew what was coming next, but I was powerless to stop it. I stood and watched as Joey threw punch after punch at Blueberry and his friend. Rage built up inside of me with every punch. The lights began to flicker. Joey walked over to Blueberry and raised his foot. I saw myself walking towards him with the fire extinguisher. Enraged, I ran over and somehow merged into my past self. Together, we screamed, and with all the power in us, swung the fire extinguisher at his head.

As we stood there, something strange happened. I was not sharing the body of my past self from that night, rather, my past self from that night was now sharing a body with me. Not realizing exactly what I had done, I slowly took steps backwards. My body felt as if it was extracting itself from hers. I stood back and watched the past version of myself fall to the ground. I stood over her and wept as she held onto Blueberry. He was out cold. I watched as her body gave out under the weight of everything she just experienced.

I heard sirens approaching. Panicked, I knew I had to get her out of there. I picked up the pieces of her necklace. I wrapped myself around my unconscious past self and merged with her again. I slipped back into a dark corner as the EMS workers rushed into the club. I watched in agony as they took Blueberry away.

I stared into the red ambulance lights. My body trembled with sorrow. They were a cruel reminder of what I once lost, but I was determined not to lose Blueberry. I could hear my father's voice telling me to be brave.

I closed my eyes and took deep, steadying breaths. When I opened them, I was back in my hospital room. The tome flipped its pages forward to the next blank page. The tome slowly lowered itself onto my lap. I sat up and took a deep, confident breath, I was ready. It was time for me to complete my story.

I paged the nurse. Nurse Michelle walked in and smiled warmly at me. "Good morning, Micaleah. You need something?" she asked excitedly, almost as if she was expecting me to ask.

"Good morning, Michelle. I need your help with a few things."

"Sure, what's up?"

"The first thing I need is a pen.'

"Sure, that's no problem."

I smiled mischievously. "The second thing,

well...you're going to want to sit down for this."

Chapter 72 - Streetlights Dreamscape
-Kaleb-

I struggle to get off the boat. My entire body aches, and each step is a chore. I follow a long, dark path that leads me to a familiar street. It's the street I grew up on. It is darker than I have ever seen it. The northern lights have all but faded, and I can barely make out anything. All of the streetlights are off. There are no lights on in any house, except for the house at the corner, and they are not inviting lights. They are deep reddish lights that slowly pulsate. It looks as if they are shining through red, stained glass windows.

I begin to walk. I am scared and want to walk anywhere but the direction of that house. However, something draws my footsteps directly towards it. As I pass each house, I try to recall the warm childhood memories that used to envelope each home. I think of Mr. Bergis' mulberry tree, and how we all used to sneak into his backyard and eat mulberries. I think about Ms. Amanda and her daughter Cortnee, and all the hours we spent in their swimming pool. I walk past the Flower's residence. I remember you couldn't walk past there without seeing a volleyball flying, a soccer ball being kicked, or hearing the soft sound of a violin.

I hope that all of these memories of those good times, and just being back on my old street will bring some sort of warmth. But alas, there is no warmth to be found. Sadness is all over this place. Houses, trees, memories, and hopes, all seem to be frozen in time.

My steps keep taking me forward. As I near a streetlight, it flickers on, then turns off. A fear washes over me. I don't want to be in this place. I don't want to go to that house. There is nothing there for me. I turn around and start to walk the other way, hoping to flee from this horrific nightmare of a scene. As my eyes adjust to the darkness, I realize that I am going the exact same way I just turned from. Panicked, I turn again. I see the exact same thing. There is no escaping this. I am trapped in this nightmare.

The worst thing about nightmares is their sinister way of making you doubt what's real and what's not. I entertain thoughts of just sitting down under the streetlight and waiting to see what happens, but time doesn't seem to move here, and I get the feeling that if I try to wait it out, I will be sitting here forever. I know that I am here for a purpose, but my fear has me questioning that purpose.

It grows darker. Everything in my body hurts. I don't know how much further I can go. I want to disappear. I want to yell for help. I want to cry out. I am overcome with fear and sadness. I want Muffin to be by my side.

"Where are you!?" I cry out. Why did you leave me here alone!?" Tears stream down my face as I drop to my knees. "I just want to wake up. I just want to wake up," I say as if I'm a child again, alone in my bed.

At that moment, all of the streetlights illuminate. I struggle to my feet. "Hello?" I call out. There is no answer. I take a step forward and look around. "Hello!?" I call out again. Much louder this time. There is still no response. The streetlight that I am directly under, dims and fades to black. I cautiously walk towards the next one. As I get close to it, it dims and fades. The next one flickers.

"Muffin!" I say with excitement. She is leading me to the house on the corner. With all my remaining strength, I walk towards the house, not remembering that moments ago I wanted nothing to do with it. I don't even notice the streetlights go out above me, until the last one goes out right in front of the house. As I approach it, it flickers intensely, but does not dim. It appears to be brightening, as if to better show me what stands before me.

A warm feeling washes over me. For the first time since that night, I can feel her presence. Although I cannot feel it as strong as I once could, it is definitely there. Emboldened by the fact that she is somehow with me, I muster the courage to do what I know I have to do.

I make my way up the stairs to the front door. The porch light flickers, then turns off. I steel myself, reach for the doorknob, and slowly turn it. The knob fully turns, and I hear a click. Heart racing, I slowly push the door open and look inside. The house is empty and eerily quiet. I cautiously walk around. The inside of the house is huge, but there is only one door. There is no back or side door, and there seems to be no other way out.

    I walk over to the door. It has a butterfly symbol on it. I take a deep breath and hesitantly open it. A surge of light and energy consumes me. This energy is unlike anything I have ever felt. It is so heavy, it brings me to my knees. It is so intense, I can't keep my eyes open. I fall forward onto the ground. I am weary. I can't move. I have no more fight left in me.

Chapter 73 - False Hope
Dreamscape
-Kaleb-

I open my eyes. I am in a hospital. I look around in confusion. I try to say something, but I can't talk.

"Oh, thank goodness you're awake!" We were so worried about you."

"Mom?" I say. The word barely comes out.

"Oh, Kaleb. I'm going to call the nurse in. We've been waiting forever for you to wake up."

"Where am I?"

"Honey, just relax. You're still in the hospital. They're going to get you all better so we can take you home. I have to call your father. He's been so worried."

"Dad?"

"Oh, honey. You're still pretty out of it. I paged the nurse. She should be in any second."

"Where's Kaje?"

"Kaje? Your little buddy? I would think he is at school. I'm sure he will be happy when you are better."

The nurse walks in. She looks very familiar. "Hello, little guy. I'm Nicole." She smiles warmly. "Glad to see you decided to come back to us. How ya feeling?"

I look closely at her. "Confused. Something's not right," I say.

"That's to be expected. It will pass. We just have to get you back in the right direction and you'll be out of here in no time. I'm just going to check a few things, then I'll be out of your hair. The doctor will be in shortly to check on you."

"I'm so confused. I can't remember how I got here."

"Oh, I can help you with that. You came in through the door." She laughs. "Just try to relax. It'll all come back to you soon enough." She writes down a few things on a chart, then walks out of the room.

"Mom?"

"Yeah, sweetie?"

"Why isn't Kaje here?"

"I'm not sure." She looked at her watch. "I suppose he's still in school."

"School?"

"Knock, knock. Hello. How are we doing? The doctor walks in the room. "I'm Dr. Ajal. How are you feeling, young man?"

"Better, I guess."

"That's good news. You gave your parents quite the scare. I'm just going to check a few things, then hopefully we can get you on your way. Can you sit up for me?"

I sit up. My body feels achy all over. The doctor puts the cold stethoscope on my chest and asks me to take some deep breaths. My breathing is hard and labored.

"Well, I don't see any reason you can't go home. Unless, you want to stay. But between you and me, kiddo, I don't know why anyone would want to stay here. You want to get back to your friends, right?"

I nod. "Yeah."

"Okay. Well then, let's get you checked out. Let me just look at one more thing." He pulls out a light. "Say 'ahhh' for me, Kaleb."

"Ahhhh."

"Good, good." He put the light back in his pocket. He places his finger on my eyelid, lifts it up, and looks into my eye. "Know where you're headed when you leave here?"

"Home, I guess."

He lifts my other eyelid up and grabs the light out of his pocket. "Let's hope so," he whispered. "All done. Now, let's get you back on the road home. Good luck to you."

He shines the light into my eye. It is so bright that I can no longer see anything. I reach my hand up to block the light, but I can still see it, and it is just as bright. I close my eyes as tight as I can, but the light is still too bright. I squirm in my bed, trying to get away. "Turn it off! Turn it off!" Enraged, I let out a thunderous yell. All of a sudden there is silence, and the light begins to fade. When the light finally subsides, and I am able to see again, in front of me stands a door with a symbol of an ankh. I am back in the house, sitting on the floor. Panicked, I look around the house. Nothing has changed. I sit on the floor and sob. I am discouraged and don't know how much more I can take. I don't know how much more I want to take.

I manage to get to my feet. I grab the doorknob and take a breath, debating on whether or not I even want to open it. I take several more deep breaths, turn the knob, and open the door. I enter into a misty tunnel. I can see faint light towards the end. "The light at the end of the tunnel. How cliché," I mumble in an exasperated tone. I walk towards the light. Each step weighs me down. I stop and take more deep breaths. The light does not seem to be any closer. I begin walking towards it again. I am barely able to stand. The light is no closer, and the mist is getting heavier. I take a few more steps, then fall forward. The last thing I remember seeing is the faint light fade in the mist.

Chapter 74 - Witching Hour -Kaleb-

I awoke in a car. My head was pounding. I felt groggy and confused, like I had taken a nap that lasted longer than I intended. I turned towards the window. Bright blinding lights shone in my face. A man and a woman with flashlights were standing outside my car door. The woman was banging her knuckles against the window.

"Sir? Are you alright?"

I sat up and rubbed my eyes. I rolled the window down. "I think so. I—. Where am I? What's going on?"

"We were heading in to clean the building and saw your car running. There aren't typically any cars here this late. We heard something in the car, so we came over to check things out," the man said.

"This late? What time is it?

The woman held up her phone and showed me the time. It showed "3:00 AM"

"3:00 AM?"

"Are you okay to drive, sir?

"What? Yeah, I'll be fine."

"Are you sure you're okay?"

"Yeah," I said. I'm sure my tone was unconvincing. "I

just...fell...asleep." My head began to swirl. I was having a serious case of déjà vu. "Have we—"

"We have to get going. Please be careful. It's a bit foggy."

"Thanks, I will."

I put my seatbelt on and took a deep breath. My head was pounding. I picked up my phone. I needed to see what time it really was. My phone showed 3:00 AM. I shook my head and started the car. The car radio showed 3:00. I checked my messages. I had no messages. It was late, but I took a chance and sent Kaje a message asking him if he was okay. I started the car and carefully drove through the fog to my apartment. The streets were quiet. There wasn't another soul in sight. I couldn't believe I fell asleep in the work parking lot.

Nothing about the night felt right. I opened the door to my apartment. My head was still pounding. I made my way to the couch and looked around the apartment. Everything was neatly placed where it was supposed to be. The clocks on the stove and microwave blinked 3:00. I just let myself fall down onto the couch. "I'm not dealing with this tonight," I said. I closed my eyes and tried to sleep.

Something startled me. I woke up and quickly jumped up off the couch. I grabbed my phone. It was dead. I threw it on the table angrily. My head was still pounding. I went to the bathroom and threw water on my face. I got some aspirin out of the medicine cabinet and slammed it shut. I looked at myself in the mirror. I barely recognized my own reflection. I took the aspirin and headed outside to get some fresh air. As I entered the hallway, Monica was standing by her door.

"Hey you," I called out.

She turned to look at me. "Oh, wow. You look terrible. You hungover or something?"

"No, I feel like crap though."

"You look like crap."

"Thanks, Monica."

"I'm just sayin. You want me to lie to you?"

"Shh, just stop talking so much. My head is pounding."

"Whatever. It's not my fault you drank too much."

I shook my head in exasperation. "Hey, have you heard from Kaje?"

"No. Why would I have heard from Kaje?"

"I don't know. I just thought maybe...I don't know. I just feel like something is wrong, and I can't seem to get a hold of him."

"When was the last time you saw him?"

The question caught me off guard. "I, um, I'm not sure, feels like forever."

"Well, that's what happens with success. It goes to your head and you forget where you came from?"

"What success?"

"Are you okay, Kaleb? You're weirding me out a little bit. You haven't heard from him at all?"

"I don't...I can't remember the last time."

Monica laughed. "I have never seen you this messed up." She grabbed my hand. "Come on. I have some errands to run. You can tag along. The fresh air will do you some good. I don't want you acting all weird at Tankers tonight."

"I'm sorry. My head is still foggy. What are we celebrating again?"

"Very funny. Just make sure you are on time."

We walked out of the apartment. The sky was bright, and the air had a briskness to it. There was a quiet calm in the air. I looked around as if I was taking everything in for the first time, or the last time.

"You coming or what?" Monica yelled.

"Yeah." I walked to the car.

As she drove, I sat quietly and stared out the window, trying to make sense of everything. Nothing about it felt right. I felt lost, like I was missing periods of time.

Monica let out an audible sigh. "You're awfully quiet over there. If you aren't going to talk, I'm going to turn on the radio."

I gave her a thumbs up. She sighed again and turned on the radio. Music blasted out the speaker.

See, right about now you have to use precision. Making your car smell fresh, it is a simple decision. When you—

Monica quickly changed the station.

Soar by. Soar by. As I release the pain, I straight drink the rain—

"Are you kidding me?" Monica groaned again and changed the station.

Hot to the touch. Hot to the taste. Hot like a piece of hot steel. Not to be—

"Seriously?!" Monica groaned again, this time even louder, and changed the station.

A song began to play and Monica reached to turn the station. I grabbed her arm. "Wait! I want to hear this."

If your life-long dash is in vain or its worthless, search your soul and you will find your purpose.

From the date you're born until the date you die, don't

let that be the only thing people see of your life. Think about the times we laughed, the times we cried, don't be a John Doe at the end of the ride.

"That's Kaje!" I said excitedly.

"Yeah, and? And that was him on the last three stations. You can't turn to any station without hearing his songs, stupid air freshener, or energy drink commercials."

"What? That's great! Why are you so upset about it?"

Monica turned and gave me a confused look. "Really, Kaleb? Why are you all of a sudden not upset? Look, I don't know what the hell is wrong with you, but I'll indulge in your little fantasy. Do you know why you don't know the last time you talked to Kaje? It's because after that night where we went out and celebrated him making it big, he went ghost on us and disappeared. He got too high and mighty and forgot all about his friends. Now do you remember? Is any of that ringing any bells?"

"I don't understand. He hasn't made it big yet. He just got signed. He wouldn't ghost us like that even if he did."

"Look, I don't know what you drank last night or what kind of drugs you did, but I'm not playing games with you anymore. The hospital is right over there. I should just drop you off. You have obviously lost your damn mind. You either need to go back to sleep or wake the hell up."

I stared out the window in confusion. I frantically tried to make sense of what Monica was saying. My head began to pound again. Across the road, I could see the entrance to the park. That déjà vu feeling washed over me with such an intense rush, I had a hard time breathing.

"Monica, stop the car!" I yelled.

"What? Stop it for what?"

"Just stop the car, please. There's something I have to do."

Monica slammed on the brakes. "Kaleb, I don't know what's going on with you, but I have things I need to take care of. I can't wait here for you."

"It's okay. I'll be fine. I'll get a ride home."

"What? How are you going to get a ride home? You know what? Fine. Whatever. I guess I'll see you later." She sped off.

I looked to the entrance of the park. An odd feeling began to settle in. I couldn't quite identify it. A calling, maybe. All I knew was that I was supposed to be there. I walked slowly through the park, looking around, searching for something. I didn't know what I was looking for. I just knew that I would know it when I found it.

The park was quiet. The only sound I heard was the crunching of leaves as I walked. I made my way to the huge tree in the middle of the park. There was an empty bench by the tree. I made my way over to the bench and sat down. I felt weary. I closed my eyes, took a deep inhale, and tried to gather my thoughts. Everything about the day felt wrong. I tried to remember the days before I woke up in the car, but I couldn't recall them. I reached for my phone, then I remembered I left it at home. Frustration began to set in. I closed my eyes and rocked back and forth.

I'm not sure how much time had passed, but the sun had begun to set. I stood up and began to make my way towards the exit. I looked to the bench across the way. An orange butterfly landed on the bench and slowly flapped its wings. A feeling of warm energy took over my body. I walked towards the butterfly and put my hand out. The butterfly took flight from the bench and landed on my hand. It gently flapped its wings before taking flight again.

"Wait!" I yelled as the butterfly began to fly away. It fluttered down the path as I ran after it, flying further away the closer I got. I was out of breath and barely able to stay on my feet, when it landed on the gate just outside the park. It was dark now and only the glow of the moon made it possible to see the butterfly. I limped my way over to the gate. The butterfly again gently flapped its wings, almost as if it were beckoning me towards it. As I reached the gate and reached out for it, it took off again. It flew a few feet and landed on the ground in front of me. Exasperated, I fell to my knees.

I wanted to give up, but there was something about the butterfly that drew me to it. I crawled towards the butterfly with what little energy I had left. Each inch drained me more than the last. When I finally reached the butterfly, I reached out my hand. It took flight straight up in the air, flapping its wings vigorously before lowering itself back down towards my outstretched hand. Its wings illuminated with an amazing bright light. I heard a loud beeping sound. When I turned my head, I saw two large, bright headlights headed straight towards me at an impossibly fast speed. I tried to yell, but nothing came out. I tried to move...but it was too late.

Chapter 75 - Falsus in Omnibus Dreamscape -Kaleb-

I awake in a fright, face down. My heart is racing. I quickly roll over and pat myself down, fearing that I have been run over by a vehicle of some sort. When I am satisfied with my inspection, I lie on the ground with my eyes closed, taking deep breaths in and out. I know that I haven't been hit by a truck, but my body sure feels like I was. I open my eyes. In front of me is another door. This one bears the symbol of a Celtic love knot. I shake my head in exasperation. I don't want to move. I'm not sure if I have the strength or the courage for another one of whatever those experiences were.

"I must be dead. That's what's going on here. I'm dead and this is purgatory. I guess I'm just supposed to keep going through these doors over and over again. Well, no thank you!" I yell out.

I lie there with every intention of not moving. I think about everything that I've gone through to get to this point. I convince myself that all of it couldn't have been for nothing. I turn over and crawl towards the door. I use the doorknob to help me get to my feet. I stand there with my hand grasping the doorknob, contemplating my decision. I can hear Mother's voice in my head telling me that I mustn't lose hope. That seems so long ago.

    I gather all my strength and courage. I open the door slowly. There is nothing but a dimly lit, empty room on the other side. It is a large room. It is much larger than I would expect a room in this house to be. I walk around the room, examining every nook and cranny. The floorboards creak with each step I take. "Hello?" I call out. My voice echoes as if I called out into a deep, dark cavern.

    I hear faint sounds of music fade in and out. It is distorted, and I cannot make out where it's coming from. I walk to the other side of the room. I see flashes of images of people. They disappear as quickly as they appear. The light in the room buzzes, then comes on before flickering and going out. Suddenly, I hear distorted yelling and screaming from everywhere in the room. It is so loud, it is deafening. I hold my hands over my ears and lean back against the wall, trying to drown it all out.

    The room begins to shake violently, and I am thrown off my feet. My head bangs hard on the floor. I grab my head and try to blink my eyes back into focus. I see a figure cloaked in a brilliant bright light float across the room, and for a moment there is silence. The shaking stops, and the room is calm. The bright figure fades away. It is now dark again. Across the room, a red exit sign flickers and sparks over the door.

    I manage to stand up and walk to the middle of the

room. Suddenly, I hear noises. It sounds like items are being thrown around, followed by yelling and loud screams. I feel bodies whisk past me on my left and right, but I can't see anyone. Something bumps me, and I stumble backwards. Fear overtakes me, and I head towards the door. The exit sign sparks and turns off. The door is now gone. I turn around and look behind me. Out of nowhere I feel a hard punch to my jaw, followed by another one. I fall to the ground. The screams get louder. I try to inch backwards, but I can't move. Suddenly, a large black object appears in front of my face, blocking whatever light I can see. It is as if the darkness itself is attacking me. I try to move out of the way, but I still can't move. Before I can take another breath, I feel immense pain in my face, like I have been hit with an anvil. I fall backwards onto my back. My head slams violently into the floor. The room is spinning, and I can feel myself blacking out. The screams begin to fade, and all I see is darkness. I feel a heavy thump on my body and then everything goes black.

Chapter 76 - Reality Bites
-Kaleb-

I could faintly hear sirens and the sound of voices. My head throbbed. I tried to move, but I couldn't.

"Just lie still, sir," a voice said. He turned to someone and yelled. "We got a big one. Can I get some help over here?"

I tried to open my eyes, but only one would open. The other one was swollen shut, and my jaw ached something fierce. I saw two men grab someone from on top of me and put him on a stretcher as he moaned and groaned in agony.

"Oh, man! That's Joey the Shark," the paramedic said to his partner."

"Who?" the other paramedic replied.

"Joey "The Shark" Bruckner. He was a famous amateur boxer back in the day, until he jacked his hand up fighting some dude in a parking lot."

"Yeah, well it seems he still hasn't learned anything from that experience. Help me get him onto the stretcher."

They lifted him off me and onto the stretcher. I tried to get up. "Sir, please don't try to move until we have a chance to check you out. Sir, do you know where you are?" the paramedic asked.

"Tankers. There was a fight. My friend..." I tried to sit up.

"Sir, I need you to lie still. Can you tell me who the president is?"

"Um, Abraham Lincoln. My friend? Where's my friend!? What happened to Kaje?"

"Can you tell me what day it is, sir?"

"The day after yesterday," I said. I was clearly annoyed with all the questions. "Where is my friend?"

"Your friend is fine. Lucky for him, he has a hard head. Apparently, he isn't the only one."

I laid there feeling relieved as the paramedics did their thing. They put one of those collars on me, lifted me up to the stretcher, and put an oxygen mask over my mouth. I moved the oxygen mask from my mouth. "There was a lady...light skin, long brown hair, very pretty..."

The paramedic put the oxygen mask back over my mouth. "If she was here, she's not now, and she's not one of ours. Just try to lay back and relax." He wheeled me out to the ambulance.

I moved the oxygen mask again. "Can't I just go home? I'm good now."

"Sir, you suffered a concussion and some pretty severe facial lacerations. We're just going to take you to the hospital for observation. If everything checks out, you'll be good to go."

"But I need to find her," I said groggily.

They loaded me in the back of the ambulance. "Yeah, good luck with that, buddy."

When we arrived at the hospital, they wheeled me into a room and put me right beside Kaje. He reached over to me with a closed fist. I returned the gesture and we bumped fists.

"Just another adventure in the life and times of Kaje and Kaleb," I said.

"Yep," Kaje responded.

"In all seriousness, thanks for having my back, back there."

"Always, man. I hope it was worth it. Did you find her?"

"I didn't. The paramedics hadn't seen her either. I would have thought she would have stayed to check on me."

"Don't overthink it, man. Who knows what happened before the ambulance arrived."

"Yeah, you're probably right. I'll find her. If anything, just to tell her thank you. From the way that dude was lying on me, out like a light, I'm pretty sure she saved my life."

A doctor pulled the curtain back and walked in. A police officer stood by her side. "This officer would like to ask you gentlemen some questions," she said in a terse tone. "I told him he has three. You both need to rest."

The officer questioned both of us about what happened that night. We told him our side of the story. I told him about the lady who was in danger and needed my help. He asked me if I knew how the big guy ended up on top of me. I wasn't entirely truthful with him. I told him that I had no clue.

"Well, the bigger they are, the harder they fall, I guess."

Kaje and I looked at each other. I snickered. He tried not to, but despite our best efforts, we laughed through our pain. "Warning. Warning. Cliché alert," we said in unison.

"I'm glad you two think this is a joke. I bet you wouldn't find it too funny if I—"

The doctor loudly cleared her throat. "If that's all, officer. These gentlemen need to get some rest."

The officer shot us an angry look. "We're done for now. I'll be in touch, gentlemen." He said the word gentlemen in a mocking tone.

The doctor shot us a stern look, then whipped the curtain closed.

"Dude! You are going to get us thrown in jail," Kaje said.

"What? You laughed too."

"Yeah, but only because you snickered."

I laughed. "I couldn't help it. Did you hear the way he said it?"

Kaje laughed so hard, he started coughing. "Dude, stop making me laugh. My head is killing me."

"Okay, I'm done. My head is killing me too. I haven't taken an L like that since I was a freshman in high school."

"I've never taken an L like that before."

I laughed. "That's because you're a lover, not a fighter."

"Yeah, right. It's because I don't normally fight guys the size of tanks."

"Yeah, my bad. I kind of wish that all went down a little differently. I just saw him put his hands on her, and I flipped."

"Oh, don't get it twisted, I get it. I would have done the same thing, and I know you would have had my back."

"No doubt."

"Now you just need to find her so all of that wasn't for nothing."

I turned my head and stared at the wall. "I'll find her. I know exactly where to look."

"The park?"

"Yep."

Kaje sat up. "And what are you going to do if she isn't there? It's not like you can look her up. You don't even know her name."

I turned and looked at him. "It's Micaleah."

"How do you know that?"

"I'm not exactly sure. It's weird, I feel like I know her better now than I did before the fight."

"Dude, that concussion is messing with your head. There's no way you could know more about her now than you did a couple of hours ago. And if it turns out her name is really Micaleah, then I'll be officially weirded out."

"I'm a bit weirded out already, because I don't know how to explain how I know her name, or how I'm feeling the way I feel about her."

"And how is that?"

"I think I—"

There was a commotion, and the curtain was suddenly pulled open. "You two get on my nerves!" Monica said loudly. "We can't go out one time without you two causing trouble. Do you know how worried I was?"

"We're glad you're okay too, Monica," I said.

"That's not the point. I didn't know what was going on with either of you. My phone turned off and wouldn't turn back on. I was escorted out of the building and had to give a statement to the police. It was just crazy, and here you two are back here chopping it up like it's a slumber party."

I laughed. "Did you tell them that Kaje started it?"

"It's all a big joke to you, isn't it? Well, it's not to me. I was really worried about you guys."

"No, I'm sorry. Just trying to lighten the mood. It has been a crazy night, but we are all going to be okay."

"Yeah, well, both of you look like crap. You both look like you went twelve rounds with Tyson."

"It feels like it," Kaje said. "He was twice the size of Tyson."

"I know, right! I would have come in and helped y'all, but I just got my nails done, and I was not trying to break a nail on that fool. I figured y'all had it."

"Oh, boy. Here you go again."

She waved me off. "I'm just saying."

"Whatever. How'd you get in here anyway? I'm pretty sure you aren't supposed to be back here."

"Please! You think they were going to stop me from coming back here? I got skills."

"Stalker skills," I mumbled.

"What?"

"Nothing. We're supposed to be resting. You better get out of here before you get us all in trouble."

"You're probably right, for once. I'm gonna let you guys rest. I'll be back tomorrow. Any word on when they'll let you both go home?"

"Not yet."

"Okay. I'll check back tomorrow. Y'all might want to check your phones. Everyone in the parking lot was complaining about their phones not working."

"Okay," we said in unison.

"Goodnight." She stepped out and closed the curtain.

Kaje turned over on his side. "I'd love to hear your weird explanation of how you know that woman's name, but I can barely keep my eyes open. I'll talk to you in the morning."

"Okay. I can't sleep. I'm going to stay up and try to sort through all this stuff in my head."

"Good luck with that."

I laid back in my bed for hours and tried to make sense of everything. That concussion must have really done a number on me. There were pockets of time that I couldn't seem to account for, no matter how hard I tried. I remembered the current day, but the days before that were kind of foggy. I remembered things in pieces. For some reason, I remembered waterfalls and cherry blossoms. I hadn't seen waterfalls in forever and didn't remember seeing cherry blossom trees anywhere. I was giving myself more of a headache, so I decided to just close my eyes and try to sleep.

Chapter 77 - Reaching Out
-Kaleb-

The next day Kaje and I were discharged. If I slept even a little bit, it didn't feel like it. Monica picked us up and took us to our cars. Neither of our phones worked, so I knew the first thing I was going to do once I got to my car. The ride was quiet. Everyone was still exhausted from the night before. We were probably more mentally exhausted than physically. And even though the night was crazy and didn't go as planned, it didn't change the fact that we were all going our separate ways soon.

We arrived at Tankers. Monica pulled up next to my car. Kaje's was several spaces over. She turned off the car and sat back in her seat. "So, I guess this is it, huh? This is where we part ways. It sure doesn't seem like a proper send-off."

"Yeah, I know that's right," Kaje said.

"Yeah, it kind of sucks, to be honest," I replied. A tear formed in my fully open eye. "But you guys have to do what's best for you. I'm sure it will all work out. I have to take care of something. I'll catch up with you guys later."

I quickly opened the door and got out. I could hear

them calling my name, but I kept walking to my car. The moment hit me harder than I wanted to admit, and I didn't want them to see me upset. I fooled myself into thinking I'd be okay because of Micaleah. And even though I never really got to know her, it felt like she had left me too. For some reason, the pain was all too real.

I jumped in my car and began to drive. I felt lost. My head was still a bit foggy. I couldn't seem to keep my thoughts straight. One minute I was thinking about being home on my couch, the next minute I was thinking about the church on the hillside from my dream earlier in the week.

It was a windy day. As I drove, a tempest of leaves swirled around my car. Melancholia washed over me. "Why do I miss her so much?" I asked myself as I banged on the steering wheel. As I continued to drive, leaves continued to fall. Each leaf stirred things inside of me, things that made me think of her.

I decided to drive to the park. I had to see if she was there waiting for me. It was the only place I knew to look for her. I arrived at the entrance of the park. I got out of my car and made my way to the bench by the giant tree where we first met. Déjà vu took hold of me. Something about every step I took felt so familiar. I looked towards the sky. The sun glistened through the remaining leaves. It was a little chilly out, but still warm for the time of year it was.

I reached the giant tree in the middle of the park and looked around. She was not there. I sat down on the bench that I said I would wait for her on. I waited for hours, hoping that she would somehow know that I was there waiting for her and magically show up.

Hour after hour passed with no sign of her. I was determined not to give up. I sat back on the park bench and continued to wait.

I felt something warm around my shoulders. I blinked my eyes open. Dusk had fallen, and I could barely see the other bench. I turned and looked behind me. Kaje and Monica stood there looking at me with concern on their faces.

"No luck, huh?" Kaje said sadly.

I shook my head. "No, not yet."

They both took a seat on either side of me. "We waited for you at your apartment. When you didn't show up, I kinda figured we would find you here," Kaje said.

"So, we did some talking, and we've decided that we were going to stick around for a while. At least until everything settles down and gets back to normal," Monica said.

I sat up and rested my head in my hands. "Oh, did you? You made these decisions without me?"

"Well, yeah. We thought it would be best," she said.

"Well, I don't think it would be. I think everyone should just stick to the plan. I don't want you guys to alter your lives because of me. Things are a little tough right now, but I'll soldier on. I'll be fine."

"Why are you acting like this, man? We are just trying to look out for you, and you just seem angry and upset about it," Kaje said.

I sprang up. "Because I am angry and upset. You both had reasons for doing what you planned on doing and they were damn good reasons. Monica, you need to get out of here, so you can get out of that toxic situation you are in and heal. It's a chance to work on you, so no one can ever do to you what Nate did to you. I want you to learn to never rely on a man for your happiness, because when you aren't relying on a man for your happiness, you won't settle for any old loser that shows you attention."

Monica put her head to the ground. I turned to look at Kaje. "Man, look. You have an opportunity to do something people only dream of. Something you've dreamed of since we were kids rapping at block parties and school talent shows. And you want to throw that away because I'll be sad without you guys? Please! I won't let you do that. Me being sad, but seeing both of you happy, would bring me much more joy than knowing you didn't fulfill your dreams because of me. It'll be tough at first, but I'll manage. Plus, we'll all be in touch. It's not like you'll forget where you came from."

"Never that," Kaje said.

"I'm not sure we'll ever be welcome in Tankers again, but I'm not sure I ever want to go back there anyway."

We all laughed a bit. "I know that's right," Monica said.

"I love you guys. Go out there and make me proud," I said.

"Aww man," Monica said. "Group hug. Come on. Bring it in. Bring it in."

We each walked into each other's open arms. I could feel the warmth and love emanating from them. It made me happy and sad at the same time. I was happy that I was able to experience it, but sad that it would be the last time for a while.

We stepped back from each other's embrace. Each

of our faces were wet from crying. Kaje wiped his face. "So, what are you going to do about Micaleah?" he asked.

"Wait! You know her name?" Monica asked.

"Yeah, it's a long story," I replied. "I'll tell it to you another time. I know how much you love my stories."

Monica rolled her eyes. "Mmmhmm."

"Honestly, I was just going to wait here. I know that sounds crazy, but that's what I told her I would do. Plus, I have some things I need to sort out in my head. If I'm being completely honest, something about all this just feels wrong. I can't really explain it, it just feels like this isn't the way this is supposed to happen. I can't really put it into words, it's just a feeling I have."

"Wait! You are going to stay here all night and wait for a woman you met one time?" Monica said. She looked at me as if I was crazy.

"Yeah, I am."

"Boy, you better get yo—"

Kaje grabbed Monica's arm and started to pull her away. "Come on. Just let him do his thing. I don't always understand the things he does, but when he has a feeling about something, he is rarely ever wrong. It'll work itself out." Kaje looked at me and gave me an approving nod. Monica just shook her head in disbelief.

I sat on the bench and took a deep breath. I closed my eyes and tried to make sense of everything I was feeling. I saw visions of things I couldn't quite explain. I remembered things that I couldn't have possibly done. I remembered her.

I opened my eyes and looked over towards her bench. There was a small pulse of light coming from the top of the bench. Curious, I walked over to get a closer look. "A firefly? In autumn?" I mumbled. Its light was brighter than I'd ever seen on a firefly. Underneath it, there was something engraved in the wood on the bench. It was a tree with three symbols around it. A butterfly, an ankh, and a Celtic love knot. My mind began to race with images of Micaleah and I. Some as children, some as older adults. Calling it déjà vu didn't seem quite right. They felt more like recent memories.

The firefly took flight. It flew high in the air, pulsing its light slowly. As it did, other fireflies joined in. I followed as they led the way through the park, their light lighting the way forward. They led me to a path in the park that I didn't remember seeing as a child. The farther along the path we traveled, the more fireflies joined in, creating a spectacular display of lights.

They led me out of the park and into my old neighborhood. They picked up their pace. Their lights began to flash so brightly, I could only make out a few feet in front of me. I shielded my eyes and kept moving forward. Eventually, they began to slow down and their lights slowly began to fade. We came to a stop. I moved my hands from above my eyes. I stood at the doorstep of the house on the corner of my old street.

All the fireflies dispersed, pulsing their light as they flew into the night. The one firefly that remained, landed on the doorknob of the house and pulsed it light quickly. I walked up the stairs and peeked into the window. Everything in the house looked completely dark, save for an occasional flicker of light. I steeled myself. For some reason, I wasn't as afraid as I thought I would be. As I reached for the doorknob, the firefly took flight. I slowly turned the doorknob and entered the house.

I felt a shock so strong it knocked me off my feet. It was followed by another one that slammed me into the wall. All I could see was darkness all around me. My body ached and I could not get to my feet. In the corner of the house stood a black figure. It was the black figure I had seen before. In front of me was a long, dark stairwell. The shadowy figure looked at me and appeared to vibrate as it moved towards me. I crawled towards the stairs. Each inch it passed, it seemed to swallow it in darkness. I looked up the stairway, a faint light flickered behind a door. Each step I crawled up felt like I was climbing a mountain. I was halfway up. I began to cough. My legs began to give out. I scratched and clawed at the stairs to keep myself moving. I could see the door. It had a symbol on it. It was the same one as the park bench. I kept pulling myself towards the door. The light started flickering more frantically. I took a quick look behind me. Everything was gone except for the black figure, and it was closing in on me. I was three feet from the door, and the black figure was three inches away from me. I closed my eyes and kept clawing the floor, desperately pulling myself up the stairs. I saw a vision of Kaje and Monica waving me on, encouraging me not to stop. I saw Tammy, Liza, Catherine, Ron, and Rob cheering me on, as if it was the end of a hard-fought race. I saw Micaleah's outstretched hand, surrounded by light, beckoning me to take hold of it.

I opened my eyes. The doorknob was a foot from me. I mustered everything I had left and lunged towards the doorknob. I grabbed it and tried to turn it. My hand slipped off the doorknob and I crashed to the floor. The door cracked open. In an instant, I was enveloped by a light that was softer and warmer than anything I had ever felt in my life. I closed my eyes and drowned in its warmth.

Chapter 78 - She is Light Dreamscape
-Blueberry-

I open my eyes. Muffin is standing over me, smiling. She is giving off the same radiant glow she had when we first met. "Hi, Blue."

"Who are you?" I ask wearily. Her face takes on a worried look. I smile. "Hi, Muffin."

"Oh, you are such a butt!" She laughs "How do you feel?"

I wiggle my arms and legs, and give myself a once over. "I actually feel better than I have in a long time. Where are we?"

"We are back where we started. Where we first met."

"How did I get here?"

She smiles. "That is actually a very long story, and I would love to share it with you one day. But now is not the time. We have to get you back. You have people who need you."

"What about you? Will you be there?"

She smiles. "We made a promise, right?"

I smile back at her. "We did."

She reaches out her hand. "You ready for one last cliché?" She winks.

I laugh. "Sure, why not!"

I take her hand. We fly straight up into the air and look down on all the darkness that covers everything.

"Wait here," she says.

I release my grip from her hand and hover in the air. I watch in awe as she flies eloquently through the air. She is beautiful in the way she moves through the air. She is poetry in motion. Her entire body spins as she flies higher and higher. When she reaches the apex of her ascent, she stops and looks over all of the darkness below. She opens her arms and releases the most spectacular light I have ever seen. The light follows her as she flies over everything, spreading her light like a tidal wave, illuminating everything she flies over.

She flies back to me and takes my hand. "What do you think?"

"It's amazing! You're amazing!"

"Shall we?"

"We shall."

We propel forward. The wind against my face feels phenomenal. We fly over all the areas we visited, and even a few places we didn't. The leaves on the trees are a spectacular deep red, accompanied by dazzling cherry blossoms. The warm sands on the beach glitter like white gold, and the water once again sparkles like diamonds. We laugh as we fly through waterfalls. We soar up and through the clouds, then back down again. Birds and butterflies join us in flight as we soar over everything.

The day wears on, and together we manage to

spread our light over the entire world. We fly over to each other and hover above everything. As we embrace, we watch the sun begin to set over the water.

"I'll miss this place." I say.

"Me too," she replies.

"Maybe we can come back and visit someday."

She looks around and smiles. "I'm starting to believe that anything is possible."

We lower ourselves down to the flowery field near the giant tree. We lie in the grass and watch the sky, our hands still locked together.

"While I was trying to make my way back to you, I met this old lady. She said to call her 'Mother.' It was not my first time meeting her. She told me that life was cyclical. She said that we are supposed to meet each other and spend this life together, then find each other in the next life and do it all again."

"Do you believe what she told you?"

"I'm not sure. I guess I never really thought about it. It makes sense. But I guess it's too much to process right now. I just know that I feel like I've been waiting for you my entire life. The thing is, I'm not sure how many times we live this life, but I know if it is only this one time, I want to live it with you, wherever we are."

She looks at me and smiles. A tear rolls down her cheek. "I am speechless. That's the most amazing thing anyone has ever said to me. You sure know how to make a girl feel special. How did I get so lucky to find you?"

I winked at her. "I think we may have had a little help."

The sun is now completely set. Thousands of stars

illuminate the nighttime sky. Fireflies put on a dazzling light show as they fly about. The air is cool, but we lie close and keep each other warm.

"Hey, Muffin."

"Yeah, Blue."

"Should I call you Micaleah or Muffin?"

"It's your choice. I like how you say both."

"I'm Kaleb, by the way. But you can call me whatever you like."

"I know." She winks. "Nice to meet you, Kaleb."

I smile. "Nice to meet you, Micaleah."

"Hey, Kaleb."

"Yeah, Micaleah."

"I'm really sleepy."

"Me too."

She turns and looks at me. "Are you afraid to fall asleep?"

"A little," I say nervously.

"Everything is going to be okay."

I reach my pinky out. "Pinky promise?"

She locks her pinky around mine. "Pinky promise."

I lie there, trying to fight the inevitable for just a little longer, but sleepiness was winning the battle.

"Hey, Muffin."

"Yeah, Blue."

"Did you know that sea otters hold hands while they're sleeping so they don't float away from each other?"

She locks her hand in mine. "Oh?"

"Yep. So, we should make sure we..."

Chapter 79 - Deliverance
-Kaleb-

I blinked my eyes open. Everything was a bit blurry, and it took a minute to get used to the light. I looked over at Kaje. He was sleeping so soundly that I could barely see him breathing. I blinked my eyes again, trying to adjust them to the light. I felt stiff and groggy. I had no idea how long I had been out. I called out to him, but my throat was dry and raspy. I coughed loudly. Kaje blinked his eyes open and looked strangely at me. He jumped out of his chair. "Dude! No way! No freakin way! I knew it! I told them you were waking up! Oh, my goodness! Dude! Dude!"

I looked at him strangely. Everything seemed so fuzzy. I felt like I'd gone to sleep and overslept by a few hours. "Where am I?" I tried to ask him, but my words barely came out.

"Dude! Dude!" He hopped around joyfully. "Uh, don't move. And, uh, don't fall asleep. I'll be right back."

He ran out of the room, calling for someone. I laid there confused, not really grasping what was going on. I turned my head and looked around the room. On the wall was a picture of skinny trees with white trunks and no leaves. I turned and looked out the window. What remained of the leaves on the trees were still a deep red color. I was happy to see it was still autumn.

Kaje came back into the room with several nurses. One nurse leaned over me and looked at me. "Mr. Barnes, I'm your nurse, Michelle. I've been taking care of you. Can you hear me?"

I slowly nodded my head. She looked really familiar, but I couldn't place her face.

"You've been through quite an ordeal. Try not to move too much. How are you feeling?" she asked. She seemed excited to talk to me.

I still struggled to speak, so I gave her a thumbs-up, although I had the worst headache I could ever remember having.

"I'm sure you have a lot of questions. We'll make sure you get all the answers you need, soon enough. Are you thirsty?"

I nodded my head. "Yeah." The words barely escaped. A nurse put a small sponge near my mouth and told me not to suck on the sponge. She dripped water into my mouth.

"Okay. Sit tight. The doctor is on her way."

I gave her a thumbs-up again. Everything around me appeared to be moving in what seemed like a pattern of slow motion, followed by things quickly sped up to fast forward, then back to slow motion again. I saw Kaje standing behind a group of nurses and doctors, talking to someone on the phone. He was very animated and looked overjoyed. I could hear one nurse tell another how amazing it was that this was the second one. One nurse whispered something about a miracle.

A doctor walked in the room. She was very tall, and I could have sworn I had seen her before. She chatted with the other nurses for a minute, then walked over to me. She squeezed my hand, then squeezed my toes.

She smiled. "Hello there. I'm Dr. Baker. Do you know who you are?"

"Yes," I said. My voice was a lot less raspy than before.

"Can you tell me your name?"

"Kaleb."

"Very Good." She motioned for Kaje to come over. "And can you tell me who this is?"

"Kaje."

"Awesome. Do you know what day it is?"

"Friday?"

She gave me a look, then looked at Michelle, who typed something into a small laptop.

"Do you know what season it is?"

"Autumn."

"Very good."

I turned my head to the window, then turned back and smiled at her.

She smiled. "Ah. Well, that's cheating. I can't give you a point for that one, now can I? Let's see...well, obviously you know you are in a hospital. Let's get to the tough questions. Can you tell me the last thing you remember?"

I looked at Kaje. He had an anxious look on his face. A whole slew of memories flooded my mind. I tried to put them in some sort of logical order. I tried to speak. I coughed and cleared my throat. Michelle held the sponge over my mouth and let a few drops fall.

"I remember driving home from work. It was really foggy. Was I in an accident?"

"In a sense, yes. Do you remember anything after that?"

The nurses and doctors that were in the room were mumbling things to each other that I couldn't understand. Kaje gave a peculiar look. "Not really. Just bits and pieces. A church. A boat. Cherry blossom trees."

"I see. Well, I'm sure things will gradually start to come back to you. I'm sure you have a lot of questions. I'm going to check a few things. If you are tired, I'll clear everyone out of the room so you can get some rest. If you are up for it, Kaje and I will be happy to answer any questions you may have."

She turned to Michelle and Kaje and started speaking quietly. I heard Kaje ask the doctor why I was speaking with an English accent. I struggled to keep up with what they were saying. They seemed to be speaking so fast. Kaje was obviously agitated. Dr. Baker did her best to calm him down. The tension in the room was making my head pound. I reached for my head. The machine next to me started to beep rapidly. Dr. Baker ordered everyone out of the room except Michelle.

"How are we doing, Mr. Barnes?" Dr. Baker asked.

"My head is pounding."

"I'm going to give you something to help you relax, okay? Then I want you to get some rest."

She injected something in my IV. Before I knew it, I couldn't feel much of anything. I heard Dr. Baker say that she would come back and check on me in a little bit. It sounded like she was speaking really slowly. I laid my head to the side and stared at the picture of the white trees. My eyelids began to feel really heavy, then I dozed off.

Chapter 80 - Five Years -Kaleb-

I heard a soft knock on the door, and Dr. Baker walked in. "How are we feeling? Better?"

"Much better. Thank you."

"Good to hear. You're doing remarkably well." She checked a few things and typed a few notes on her laptop. "I'll be back later on to check on you, at which time we can talk about your rehab and the plan going forward. Kaje should be in any minute. Feel free to ask him any questions. If you need assistance from a nurse, just push the button and a nurse will be in to assist you, okay?"

"Thanks, doc."

She smiled. "You're welcome. Welcome back."

Kaje walked in as she was walking out. "Please keep in mind what we discussed, Mr. Waters," she said to Kaje.

"I will," Kaje responded.

Kaje walked over and sat by the bed. "How you feeling, man?"

"Honestly, like I've been hit by a bloody truck. But I'm starting to feel a little better."

Kaje winced a little bit. "Good. Good. I was a little

nervous when they said you were resting."

"Thought I wasn't going to wake back up, eh?"

"Something like that."

"So, what are you not telling me? I can see you're hiding something. And where's Monica?"

"She'll be here. She's flying in this evening. I filled her in on the details."

"Flying in? From where? Oh, wait. She was going to stay with her mom for a while. She left already?"

He looked to the floor. "Yeah."

I sat up. "Kaje, it's still autumn. How long have I been out?"

He took a deep breath. "It's been five years, dude."

"Bollocks! Don't joke with me like that." I could feel myself getting angry.

"I'm serious. Five years. Facts, dude."

I looked out the window. Shock and sadness started to creep in. "But it's still autumn."

"Yeah, but it's not the same autumn you remember."

I sat there in silence for a while. I couldn't wrap my brain around what Kaje told me. I didn't want to accept the fact that five years of my life were gone.

"Kaje, tell me what happened, please."

He told me the entire story of me meeting a lady in the park and the incident at the Tankers. He said the lady in the park probably saved my life by hitting a big guy we were fighting. He said she clocked him with a fire extinguisher just as he stomped on my head. He said he wasn't sure exactly what happened to her after that because all of the lights went out, and by the time they got them back on, she was gone.

"So, I lost five bloody years and didn't get the girl.

Splendid," I said. I was still trying to take in what Kaje just told me. Kaje kind of winced again and had an uneasy look on his face. "What's that look for?" I asked.

"Dude, you have this weird English accent now. The doctor said that weird things like that can happen to people who have been in a coma, but it's taking me a minute to get used to it. She said there were cases where people have come out of a coma speaking an entirely different language, so I guess you are lucky."

I stared out the window. My head started to hurt again as I tried to process everything. "What happened with your record deal? It didn't get derailed because of me, did it?"

He paused for a minute. "No. Monica and I stayed by your side awhile. We discussed it, and we knew you wouldn't have wanted us to completely put our lives on hold. We actually joked that you would be really angry at us if we did. So, she eventually moved back home and I traveled back and forth to Cali."

"Did you make an album?"

"I did. Two, actually."

"Man, that's bloody fantastic! I knew you were going to make it. I can't wait to hear them."

"Even had an air freshener commercial." He smiled.

I laughed out loud. "The prophecy has been fulfilled." We both started laughing. It felt like old times. "So, are you working on a new one? What are you driving now? An Escalade? A Land Rover?"

"Nah, I gave it up. It's not all it appears to be. I once told you that it can be a dirty business. It was even dirtier than I thought. People were always trying to get in my pockets. I couldn't deal with it anymore. Plus, I had other things going on, and someone had to keep you company while you were living in your dream world. I can only imagine the dreams you had, especially considering how crazy they were anyway."

"Yeah, I'm having trouble recalling any of my dreams. I keep getting bits and pieces here and there. So, wait a minute, you gave up the rap game for good?"

"Not entirely. I do local stuff, some producing, and I mentor young artists. I'm working with this kid named Coby on a new single. The kid has some pipes. It's weird. He woke up one morning and realized he could sing."

"That's wicked, mate. I still can't believe you gave it up. So, no fancy cars? I remember you always wanted a few."

"I have a couple. I mainly drive the minivan these days." His voice trailed off.

"What was that? Did you say you drive a bloody minivan?" I asked in amazement.

He pulled out his phone and showed me a picture of him next to a pregnant woman and two kids. "That's Nandini. Your nephew, Kaje Jr, and your niece, Chandini. We were thinking of naming the one in the oven Kaleb, but that's a stupid name, so we are still debating."

Tears of joy flowed down my face. "You wanker! That is so amazing, mate! I took a nap for a couple of hours and you went out and made a family. That is phenomenal! Congratulations!"

"Thank you. Thank you. The kids are with her parents. She is traveling for business. They can't wait to meet you though."

"Almost halfway to eight, Octodad." I winked.

Kaje laughed. "Whatever, man! We are done after

this."

I smiled and shot him a skeptical look. "I can't wait to meet them and tell them all the crazy stories I have about you."

"Yeah, I bet."

"Hey, did the Browns win a Super Bowl while I was out?"

Kaje laughed. "Yeah, right. They'd have a better chance of winning it in that dream world you were in."

We laughed. I grabbed the phone and continued to look at the picture. There was a knock at the door. "Knock, knock." Michelle walked in. "How are we doing? I see you two are catching up. I just need to check a few things and then I'll be out of your hair."

That weird déjà vu feeling washed over me again. "Uh oh. I know that look," Kaje said.

"Nicole?" I asked.

Kaje looked confused. "Nicole?"

"Was there ever a nurse that took care of me named Nicole?"

Kaje and Michelle looked at each other and shook their heads. "Nope. Just me," Michelle said. "My middle name is Nicole, but nobody knows that."

Kaje looked at her and shook his head. "See, I told you. Weird things have always happened to him."

"You remember a nurse named Nicole taking care of you?" she asked.

"Kind of."

"Hmm, that's interesting. Well, it's good you are starting to remember things. Hopefully you'll keep remembering things as you and Kaje continue to catch up."

"I'll make sure he remembers everything," Kaje said as Michelle walked towards the door.

"I'm sure you will. Play that music you always played for him. Maybe that'll help."

"What did you play for me? Was it your new music?" I asked.

"I started out playing it, then I switched it up. I put together a playlist of that new age, yogascape music you always listened to when you were trying to relax."

I laughed. "Oh, I bet you loved listening to that. I know how much you love it," I said sarcastically.

"Let's just say I've developed a new appreciation for it."

"So, let's hear it. Let's see what you put together."

Kaje pulled his speaker out of his bag and placed it on the table. He began playing music. I closed my eyes, relaxed, and let the music take me away. I saw myself walking through a field of tall grass. A large church sat atop a hill behind me. The warm setting sun shone down on me as I walked through the grass. Butterflies fluttered all around me. A gentle breeze began to blow. It whispered things to me as it passed through the grass.

A loud obnoxious knock on the door snapped me back to reality. Kaje looked at me and shook his head. I rolled my eyes and smirked at the all too familiar knock.

Chapter 81 - Back Together Again
-Kaleb-

"Kaleb!" Monica barged in the room and danced around ecstatically, before she ran over and hugged me. "You finally realized how much you missed me, huh?"

"Yep, that's it. If only I realized it sooner."

"I know, right!" She did a double take. "Wait a minute. What's up with that accent?"

I shrugged. "I don't know. Apparently, it's a bloody side effect from the coma."

"Mmm-mmm. I like it. It's kinda sexy. Too bad you're like a brother to me."

I rolled my eyes. "I've sure missed that phrase, feels like a whole two days since I heard it."

"Whatever! You know you love me." She walked over to Kaje and gave him a hug. "It's good to see you, Mr. Big-Time. Haven't heard from you since you made it to the charts. Did he tell you about his number one hit, Kaleb?"

"We were catching up on other things. We haven't covered that yet."

"Monica, don't even front like that," Kaje said. "You know I sent you updates every week."

"I'm just saying. It used to be every day," she replied.

Kaje shot her a look. "Seriously?"

"I'm just messing with you." She walked over and grabbed the Lorna Doone cookies off of my tray. "You aren't going to eat these, are you, old chap?"

"You still got jokes. And I see you still act obnoxious to try to hide your emotions. It's okay to just be happy to see me."

"Ooh, say that again. You sounded like Idris."

"I'm going to have the nurse remove you from the room," I said jokingly.

"Whatever! You wouldn't dare." She looked at me and waited for confirmation. "I'm sorry. I'm just so excited. I can't believe you are awake. It was really hard for me to leave knowing the condition you were in." She started to get choked up. "We all figured you'd wake up in a couple of days, and when you didn't, and days turned to weeks, I had to try to make peace with the fact that I might not ever get to talk to you again."

"It's okay. Don't go getting all mushy on me. I'm awake now and we have plenty of time to catch up. You can start by telling me about that huge rock on your finger."

She smiled. "Oh, this little thing. I actually just got engaged."

"Oh, wow! Congratulations!"

"Thank you. He's a good man. To be honest, he's a lot like you. I can't wait for you to meet him."

"Oh, then he must be the second coolest person in the world."

"Who's the first?" Monica asked, then she busted

out laughing. "I've missed you so much."

"I've missed you too, kiddo."

"So, when are you getting out of here? We need to go celebrate!"

"I'm not sure. The doctor is supposed to come back later. She said we'd discuss my rehab and next steps."

"Oh, you have a female doctor? Is she cute? Is she married?"

Kaje and I looked at each other, laughed, and shook our heads. "Are you finished?" I asked. "You have not changed one bit. She is my doctor. I don't fancy my doctor."

"You don't fancy her? This accent is going to take me a minute to get used to. Anyway, I'm just saying, now that you're awake you can get back in the game. Whatever happened to that woman from Tankers? Your future wife. Did she ever come visit? It was the least she could do. You were fighting for her honor."

Kaje shot Monica a look, as if to say "shut up." Monica put her hand over her mouth. "I'm sorry. I keep forgetting it's only been a couple of days for you."

"It's all good. I don't really remember her anyway."

Monica's face took on a sad expression. "That's too bad. You were kind of head over heels for her. She was rather stunning. A bit out of your league though." She winked.

"Yeah, I bet she was." I turned and looked out the window. "Hey, guys, I'm getting tired. I'm going to rest for a while. We'll catch up more in a little bit?"

"No problem, dude. We'll check back in later," Kaje said.

"Sorry, Kaleb. I didn't mean to make you sad and blue," Monica said.

I sat up. "What did you say?"

"I didn't mean to make you sad and blue. I'm sure you'll find someone."

"Yeah," I said softly. Something seemed to stir inside of me when Monica said the word "blue." I couldn't quite explain it, but it sounded familiar, just different than I remembered hearing it.

They headed towards the door. "Kaje," I called out. Is there any way you can play that playlist for me again without leaving your phone?"

"Yeah, no doubt. I'll stream it from my tablet. Did it stir something?"

"Yeah, I think it did."

Chapter 82 - Unlikely Guide
~Kaleb~

"Knock, knock." Michelle walked in. "Are you ready to head over?"

I sat up. "Yep, just let me turn this music off and finish jotting something down in my journal."

"How are the memories coming?"

"Still scattered. Each time I see something different, it's like another puzzle piece added to the collection."

"Well, that's good. Hopefully you'll be able to put them all together soon."

"Yeah, hopefully."

Michelle moved the wheelchair over to the bed. "Do you mind if I ask you something? I'll understand if you don't want to answer."

"Are you kidding me? As long as you have had to put up with me, you can ask me anything."

She laughed. "I didn't have to put up with you. You were great. You were always a great listener, and always agreed with everything I said. Those are rare qualities in a man."

"Oh, bother. Don't start man bashing." I laughed.

She winked. "You never gave me grief when I did it

before."

I smiled. "Maybe I did and you just didn't know." I closed my journal and set it on the table. "Hey, back the wheelchair up a little bit. Watch this."

She backed the wheelchair up a few feet. I swung my feet around and placed them on the floor. I took small unassisted steps all the way to the chair. "Tada!" I said as I sat down in the wheelchair.

"Oh, my God. That is amazing! The physical therapist said that you were making unbelievable progress. He said he has never seen this much progress in just a few short weeks. I didn't know he meant this much progress."

She opened the door and wheeled me down the hall. "So, Kaleb. You said you were remembering bits and pieces of memories, right?"

"Yeah."

"You said the last day you remembered was Friday afternoon. So technically, you are only trying to account for Saturday. People who suffer from concussions typically lose a day or so, and they move on. Why does it seem like you are trying to recall more than just Saturday?"

"Well, I guess the answer is a bit complicated. I have this feeling that I can't quite explain. A yearning of sorts. I'm sure Kaje told you a lot of the stories of how weird things always seemed to happen to me. It always felt like I had a sixth sense or something. I feel like while I was in the coma, I experienced things. I'm sure they were just dreams, but they felt way more bloody powerful than regular dreams. In the week leading up to the day I lost, these weird things were happening to me. I had these dreams that felt more like out-of-body experiences than dreams. Some of the fragments I see when I rest and listen to that music feel the same way. They bring about these powerful sensations that I can't really explain. Sometimes it's an overwhelming joy, other times it's an incredible sadness, like I lost something very special.

"And I'm sure you've heard about the lady in the park. Kaje and Monica told me that I met the girl of my dreams that Saturday morning in the park. Which was the same lady that was at Tankers that night. They both said that I felt some sort of way about her. Kaje said when I ran over to help her, we exchanged looks. He said he had never seen two people look at each other the way we looked at each other, let alone two people who had just met."

"That's so beautiful."

"Yeah, except I can't remember her face. You know what's weird though? I can remember her essence. But only in the fragments of the dreams from the coma. It's like, somehow, she was there, and now I'm here chasing time. The weird thing is, each day that has gone by, I've found myself missing her more and more."

"Maybe she actually is the girl of your dreams."

"That's a bit cliché, don't you think?"

"Yeah, maybe. Most, if not all love stories are cliché. What's not cliché is our personal journey to love. Everyone has their own."

"You're right. I never thought about it like that."

Michelle wheeled me off to the side. She kneeled down in front of me. "These fragments that you remember, what can you tell me about them?"

"I'm always in a field of tall grass. There is a church

that sits atop a hillside. Someone is always there with me, holding my hand, but I can't see them. We follow the butterflies along a path, but never make it to a destination."

"Butterflies?"

"Yeah, they were everywhere. They seem to be guides or something."

"I see," she said, as if she just had a sudden realization. She stood up and wheeled me to the physical therapy room. "Call for me after your session. I may be able to help you with your memories."

"Really? How?"

"We'll talk later."

Chapter 83 - Preserving Memories
-Kaleb-

I struggled through my therapy session. I was completely distracted by what Michelle told me. I immediately used the nurse call button when I got back to my room. Michelle walked in looking at her phone. She had a disgruntled look on her face.

"What's wrong?" I asked.

"Oh, it's nothing. I was just looking at the weather forecast. It looks like snow is coming in the next couple days. I guess autumn is finally coming to an end." She sighed. "I hate winter."

"That stinks. Autumn is my favorite season. I haven't even had a chance to enjoy it this year."

"Well, maybe we can get you outside, tomorrow."

"That would be awesome."

She pulled up a chair and sat close to me. "What I want to discuss with you, it is very important that it stays between us. You can't even tell Kaje or Monica. I could lose my job for doing this."

I was a little concerned, but I nodded my head in agreement. "I won't tell anyone."

She reached in her pocket and pulled out two large pills. "These pills are part of an experimental drug trial. They are used to treat patients with memory loss due to conditions such as amnesia or dementia."

I examined the pills in her outstretched hand. They each had a different imprint on them. One read ME, and the other read FH. "So, I take these pills and my memories come back?"

"It's not quite that simple, and there is no guarantee they will work. You'll need to take the pills before you go to sleep. I would suggest listening to the same music you have been, since it already helps you recover some of your memories. There is one potential side effect. While you may recover your long-term memory, you will lose most, if not all of your short-term memory."

"So, I won't remember anything that happened since I woke up?"

"I'm sorry. No, you won't. But you'll remember her."

I took a deep breath and tried to process everything Michelle said. In my head, I weighed the options, trying to think of all of the possible downsides. "I have to admit, this all sounds a little crazy."

"Believe me, it is crazy. It's very risky, but it might be your best shot."

"You said you could lose your job, right? Why would you risk your job to help me?"

She rolled up the sleeve on her shirt to reveal several butterfly tattoos that covered her entire arm. "You're not the only one that has weird things happen to them."

"Whoa!" That déjà vu feeling grabbed hold of me.

"Imagine how I felt when I heard about your

dreams."

"Okay, so, how do we do this?"

"I need you to listen carefully and do exactly as I say. So, the first thing you need to do is write down every little detail of everything you remember happening since you woke up from the coma. Make sure you include everything I told you and everything Dr. Baker said to you. Make a note of everything you talked to Kaje and Monica about. You'll also need to write a note to yourself about what we're going to do, so you can start to make sense of things more quickly. Try not to mention the pills."

"Can't we just pretend that I had a setback and it's affecting my memory?"

"No, because they'll want to run tests, and if they find any traces of those pills in your bloodstream, I am screwed."

"Right. I didn't think of that."

She smiled sheepishly. "Make sure you write something nice about me in that journal, since you may not remember me at all."

The realization of what she said made me sad. "I didn't think about that."

"Just think, you'll get to meet me all over again."

"That'll be fun."

"Okay, I'm going to get out your hair, so you can get to writing. Remember, spare no details. Also, set an early alarm and a reminder so you know to read your journal as soon as you wake up. I imagine things will be kind of weird at first, but once you start reading, it will start to make a little more sense." She handed me both pills. "Put them somewhere that's out of sight. Oh, and I almost forgot, take the ME pill before the FH pill. That's important."

"Okay," I said nervously. "Anything else we're forgetting?"

"No, I don't think so." She leaned over and gave me a hug. "Good luck. I'll see you in the morning."

"Cheers." I smiled nervously. "I can't wait to meet you again for the first time."

She smiled and walked out of the room. I grabbed my journal and nervously began writing. I wrote things, erased them, and wrote them again, all in an attempt to make everything sound clear and rational as possible. The truth was, I knew it was all going to seem like the ramblings of a crazy person once I read it. I just had to make it sound as convincing as possible.

After a while, I took a break from writing. I rolled myself over to the window. The daylight was fleeting. I had almost forgotten how quickly the sun sets in late autumn. I watched the wind whirl the leaves all around the parking lot. Beyond the parking lot, I could see the park. Déjà vu set in again. I let my mind go and tried to follow where it led me. The feeling ended almost as abruptly as it began. Frustration set in, and I quickly closed the blinds. I stared at the ceiling, contemplating why I was even putting myself through the trouble of remembering.

There was a knock on the door. Kaje walked in. "Yo! What's good, brother man?"

"Just relaxing. It's been quite the day."

"How so?"

I almost started telling him about the plan, but I remembered what Michelle said. "Just mentally exhausted."

"Remember anything new?"

"Nope. To be honest, sometimes I ask myself why I'm so bloody obsessed with trying to get a day and a half back. From what the doctors told me, I'm lucky to be alive. Despite getting my clock cleaned, I scored a three on the Glasgow scale. My blood pressure was through the roof, and probably has been for quite some time. They found traces of carbon monoxide in my blood. Not to mention, hardly anyone wakes up from a five-year coma and recovers like I have."

"Yeah, and not to mention we thought we were going to lose you a few times."

I sighed. "Even more reasons why I'm questioning myself."

Kaje shot me a look. "You know why. Just hang in there, man. It'll all come back. You know crazy Monica was actually trying to track her down, right?"

"Seriously?"

"Yep."

"Any luck?"

"Not yet. But it's not like Monica is some super-duper sleuth." Kaje laughed.

I let out a small laugh through my frustration. "Let her tell it, she is."

"Right! Something will turn up though. It's just been such a long time since that night. I just—" He cut himself off mid-sentence.

"I know what you were going to say. I hope she hasn't either. But if she has moved on to someone else, at least I'll still get the chance to thank her for saving my life."

"True that."

"I just can't believe there is no security cam footage

or anything. If we were fighting in the middle of the club, you would think at least one person was recording it on their phone."

"Dude, there were so many weird things about that night I haven't told you. For one, when the lights went out, everybody's phone went out too. I mean everybody's. We all had to get new phones. It was crazy. Then, right before the ambulances came, there was this light—"

"Hold up. Don't tell me anymore right now."

"Why? What's up?"

"Uh, nothing. I'm just getting a headache, and I want to be able to keep my memories straight and not overload them, so when I do remember something, I know it's my original memory."

"Yeah, I feel it." He walked over to the table where I kept my journal. "Is this your memory journal? Do you need me to confirm any memories you wrote in here?"

"No!" I shouted nervously. "Don't open that. That's something else. I'll tell you about that later."

Kaje set the journal down. "Okay, dude. Relax. You're acting a little weird today. You sure you're okay?"

"Sorry. Yeah, I probably just need to get some rest."

"Alright, I'm gonna head out. Get some rest so you aren't acting weird tomorrow."

"No promises," I mumbled.

"What was that?"

"I said 'See you in the afternoon.'"

Kaje walked out the door. "Later days."

I wheeled myself over to the table and continued to write in the journal until I put in everything I could think of. I then wheeled myself over to the bed and got in. I placed the journal right beside me. I put the speaker on top of it. I grabbed the pills and held them in my hand. I took a deep breath. The thought of knowingly replacing memories with journal entries brought me angst, but the thought of seeing her again brought warmth to my heart.

I grabbed my phone and nervously set an alarm. I tore a page out of the journal and wrote a reminder. The reminder read "Trust thy heart." I folded the paper and put it on the journal. I started the playlist, then set my phone on the journal beside the speaker. I sat back, took a huge breath, then let all of the air out. I grabbed a bottle of water. I took the first pill, then the second. I laid my head back on the pillow. A childlike anticipation washed over me. I smiled, closed my eyes, and let the music take me away.

Chapter 84 - Saudade Dreamscape
-Kaleb-

I awake in the old church, lying on my back in one of the pews. I sit up and look around me. I am alone. Rays of sunshine shine through the windows. I stand up and walk to the doors. I push them, but they don't budge. I feel a soft tap on my shoulder. I look behind me, but there is no one there. I try the doors again. This time they open easily.

The sun is bright overhead. I look down over the tall grass field. A majestic blue bird circles the sky. I suddenly feel a soft, warm hand in mine as I begin to walk. I turn and look beside me, but there is no one there. There is something about the feel of the hand. I hold on to it and search it for answers as we move through the field. Butterflies flutter in the air above us. As we walk, they flutter to an area ahead of us. We follow them to a dimly lit path. As we walk the path, I can hear soft music and the laughter of children.

In the rays of sunlight that shine down through the trees, I can somewhat make out a vision of children running along the path. As they exit the rays of sunlight, the images change to more of a translucent look. I move us closer to get a better look, but they are running at a dizzying speed and never stay in the light long enough for me to make them out.

"Hey!" I yell, but they don't stop. They continue along the path, laughing and chasing each other. We follow along the path. I take in everything as we pass it. A feeling of nostalgia begins to set in. It is as if I am looking at pictures in an old photo album. We approach a bridge. The hand tugs on me gently. It leads me down to a muddy area under the bridge. In the wet mud there is a drawing. It has little hearts with one large heart around them. Next to the hearts are two stick figures.

"I heart you with me," I whisper. I feel a sudden surge of warm energy and a vision quickly appears in my head. It disappears as quickly as it appeared. The soft hand holding mine is now a woman outlined in a mesmerizing, sparkling light. I cannot see her face, but I know her by the way she makes me feel. She leads us back to the path.

We come to an opening. The area is dark and completely void of anything. She gently tugs on my hand, and I follow her into the void. The light behind us fades into darkness, closing us off from the area we entered from. The only light that shines is from her.

She lets go of my hand and stands in front of me. Her face is close to mine. Behind the light, I can see a pair of beautiful, brown eyes. I know these eyes. I almost drown in an overwhelming feeling of pure elation. She reaches out to my shoulders and steadies me. She rests her hands on my face. I lean forward. Our foreheads touch. Without her saying words, I can hear her call out to me. The feeling is so powerful, it takes everything in me to hold on. I reach my hands out and rest them on her face.

"Micaleah," I whisper softly. "I'm ready. Show me." I lean my face forward, our noses touch, and there is light. We are light.

When the light fades, we find ourselves floating above the void, in a place outside of time and space. As we look down at the void, everything we experienced is being shown to us. Only, it isn't like watching a movie, it feels like we are reliving it and feeling everything all over again. The void fades to black and Micaleah begins to float away, but for some reason it doesn't feel like a sad parting, it just feels like it is supposed to happen this way.

The light inside the void begins to illuminate. I see myself walking towards the park on a beautiful autumn day. I can feel the breeze. The smell of burning wood fills the air around me. I arrive at the park and sit on the bench. I see Micaleah on the bench and walk over to her.

"I remember this," I whisper.

I see Micaleah's face. I see those eyes. She is beautiful. She smiles at me. A surge of memories begin to rush in. I remember all of it. She gets up and rushes off.

Time quickly advances. I'm in a car driving with Monica. Time quickly advances again. We are in Tanker's parking lot. Time advances again. I see Kaje, Monica, and me, laughing and having a good time. Time advances again. I see the big guy grab Micaleah. I hear her scream out in pain.

I remember everything.

"I remember now! Make it stop!" I yell.

Time advances. The lights start to flicker. Kaje jumps in and starts hitting the big guy.

"Make it stop! I don't need to see anymore!"

Time advances again. Kaje takes punch after punch! His face is covered in blood.

I begin to sob. I ball my fist up and put them to my head. "Please make it stop. Just make it stop." I fall to the ground.

Time advances again. The big guy stands over top of me, his foot is raised. In the next instant, there is only darkness.

Time advances again. There is only silence and darkness. I feel a warm touch lift my head. It's Micaleah's touch. She rests my head in her lap and holds my face. Without words, I can hear her speak to me. "I'll wait for you. Find me there."

Time advances again...

Micaleah rejoins me and holds my hand. We watch Muffin and Blueberry meet. We feel what they feel. We become what they are. We watch as they begin to create their own beautiful world. We hold each other. We hold on to each other and watch it all.

Chapter 85 - What was Meant to be
~Penny~

I closed the tome, set the pen down, and took a satisfying breath. I walked over to the window. It was a beautiful autumn day. I closed my eyes and smiled warmly with thoughts of what the day would bring.

There was a knock on the door. "Morning, sunshine. I have something for you. I'll set it on the bed. I'll stop back in a little bit to see if you're ready."

"Thank you," I said.

The door closed. I walked over to the box. There was a card on top of the box. I quickly opened the envelope.

Didn't I tell you they were the cutest?
Cheers, love.

I opened the box to find a pair of boots and the dress I wore the day I first met Kaleb, all those years ago. I held it up and smiled. I ran into the bathroom and put it on. I looked at myself in the mirror. I smiled and twirled the same way I did the first time I tried it on. For the first time in a long time, I loved what was looking back at me in the mirror.

As I was putting my boots on, Michelle walked in. "Knock, knock. Wow! You look amazing, girl!"

"I blushed. "You really think so?"

"Hell yeah. They don't make 'em much prettier than you."

I blushed again. "Stop it."

"I'm serious, and don't you ever believe otherwise."

"Thank you, Michelle."

"Are you ready to head out?"

"If it's okay with you, I want to stop and see Mum for a minute."

"No problem. Take your time. Buzz me from her room when you are ready."

"Okay."

I headed into Mum's room. She laid in bed resting. I stared at her. She looked so much older than she did just a couple of weeks ago. I pulled up a chair. I caressed her hair. "I did it, Mum. I found him. I can't wait for you to meet him. You're going to love him. I have to go now. I'll be back soon, and we can talk. I love you, Mum." I stood up and kissed her on her forehead. "Thanks for the boots, by the way. I love them."

I called for Michelle, and she came in smiling. "Ready?" she asked.

"I think so. I'm a little nervous," I said.

"Why? You already did the hard part."

"I know. I just want to make sure I say the right thing. I mean, what do I even call him?"

Michelle laughed. "Would you just relax? Just do what comes naturally. I'm sure everything will be fine."

"I know. You're right. I just don't want to mess this up again."

"Look at me. There's never been a surer thing in the world. Now, take a breath, relax your mind, and go finish your story."

I hugged her. "Thank you, Michelle. I couldn't have done this without you."

"You are very welcome. Now, get out of here before he gets away again"

I smiled. "Yes ma'am. Thank you again."

I got in the elevator and nervously pushed the button. In my head I recited what I planned on saying. The elevator doors opened. I stepped out and stared at the main doors. I took slow steps towards the door.

"Micaleah!" a voice called from behind me.

I turned around. Michelle was running towards me with the tome. She winked. "Just in case."

"Right. Thank you."

"You're welcome. Now go. I can't believe you are still in the building. What are you waiting for? This story isn't going to finish itself."

She was right. It wasn't. I took a deep breath and walked outside into the warm sunlight.

Chapter 86 - Just in Time
-Kaleb-

I heard a loud beeping sound. I blinked my eyes open and looked around. My heart was racing. I was in a hospital. I was confused as to how I got there. On the table next to the bed was a folded note on top of a journal with the words "Trust thy heart." I knew that phrase. It was a phrase my father would always say to me. I unfolded the note.

Stay calm. Before you do anything or talk to anyone, read this entire journal very carefully. No skimming! None of this will make sense at first, but eventually it will all make sense. No matter how crazy what you read may seem, you have to stay calm and trust that it will all make sense. Michelle, the nurse, will help guide you. She knows everything. You can trust her. Good luck. Oh, and P.S. No, you aren't dreaming.

I shook my head. I figured someone must be playing some sort of joke on me, but the note was in my handwriting. I grabbed the journal off of the table and read through it.

I put the journal down and took deep breaths to keep myself calm. I figured there was no way that anything in that journal was true. There was no way five years had passed. I had to learn to walk again? Kaje is married with kids? Monica engaged? That was probably the most far-fetched of everything in the journal.

I grabbed my phone and looked at the date. "Holy Mother of Pearl!" I said loudly. "I've officially lost it." I put the phone down and kept taking deep breaths. I picked up the journal and started reading again. At the top of every page, "MEMORIZE THIS!" was written in large bold letters. I put my palm to my forehead and muttered to myself. "Why would I think I, of all people, could memorize this? I guess I forgot how bad I did on tests in school."

I kept flipping through the pages, re-reading every word I wrote. Each time I read them, the shock was just as great as the first time I read them. I studied it as much as I could. My head was starting to hurt, so I closed the journal. I figured if there was something I forgot, I would just have to wing it.

I sat back in the bed and looked outside. The sun was beginning to rise. A few leaves hung on the trees, refusing to let go. I couldn't believe I had been in a coma for five years, then awake for almost four weeks. It seemed like just yesterday we were at Tankers.

Suddenly, a moment of clarity washed over me. I sat up quickly in my bed. A feeling of immense euphoria flowed through me. "Micaleah!" I smiled. "I found you!"

There was a knock on the door. A nurse walked in. It was Michelle. She looked exactly how I described her in the journal. "Hi, Michelle," I said.

"Good morning, Kaleb. You're up early. How do you feel today?"

"Wonderful!"

"Well, that's good news. What's got you feeling so wonderful today?"

"It worked," I whispered excitedly. "Thank you so much!"

"What worked?"

"You know, the pills."

"She smiled and looked at me strangely. "I give you pills every day, silly. Are you sure you're feeling okay?"

"Oh, I get it." I shot her an exaggerated wink and made a zipping motion across my lips.

She laughed. "You crack me up, Kaleb. I'll be back to check on you in a little while. Don't forget your little field trip outside today. It's your last chance to enjoy autumn before it ends."

I laughed. "I'm looking forward to it. I know just where I want to go."

I got out of my bed and into the wheelchair. I wheeled myself over to the window. The sun had almost fully risen. Its golden rays shone on the two remaining leaves on the tree outside. I sat there and reflected on the journey that I went on to get to this point. What apparently took five years, felt like one magical night to me.

I smiled as I thought about Muffin and the walks along the path, the unbridled joy of playing on the playground, the wind in my face as we flew through waterfalls, and the cool nights when we laid in the grass as we watched the stars.

I reflected on what the lady from the church told me about soulmates. I laughed at myself and thought about all the times that I dismissed any notion of that. And there I sat, giddy as a child, beaming with anticipation of meeting my soulmate.

As the day went on, I had a hard time containing my excitement. I wheeled my chair back and forth. I went over what I was going to say. I went back and forth with myself over whether I should call her Micaleah or Muffin. I must have paged Michelle twenty times or more, asking her stupid things like, "How do I look?" or "Was it time to go yet?"

Early in the afternoon, there was a knock on the door. Kaje and Monica walked in. Kaje had a bag in his hand. "What's up, mate? Kaje said playfully.

I looked at his wedding band. My heart warmed, and I smiled at him. I stood up and gave him a hug. A tear rolled down my cheek. "Good to see you, mate."

He looked at me and shook his head. "Dude, I literally just left a few hours ago. I see you are still acting weird."

"Oh, my goodness. He's got that glow. I remember that glow, "Monica said. She walked over and gave me a hug. "I'm going to be nice to you since he's being a jerk."

Kaje laughed. "Whatever!" She just wants those cookies on your tray."

"Shut up, Kaje. I do not." There was silence for a few seconds. "Okay, I do, but that's not why I'm being nice."

I laughed at both of them. "It's fine. You can have them."

"Thank you," she said. She turned to Kaje and stuck her tongue out.

As she reached for the cookie, I noticed her ring. "Blimey, that's a big rock on your finger."

"No bigger than the last time you saw it," she replied.

"See, I told you he's been acting weird. Maybe we should get Dr. Baker in here."

"Stop it. I'm fine. I was just saying how big it looks with the sun shining on it."

Monica held it up and examined it in the sunlight. "Yeah, it does look bigger, doesn't it?"

Kaje sighed. "Weirdos." He threw the bag in my lap. Put that on."

I reached in the bag and pulled out a jacket. "What's this for?"

"We're going outside. It's nice out there, but I know you'd still want a jacket."

"You guys are taking me?"

"Yep! Michelle had something come up. She said she pulled some strings and it's okay if we take you," Monica replied. "We just have to be sure to bring you back."

"Well, let's go already."

I put the jacket on. Kaje pushed the wheelchair out the door and down the hallway to the elevators. Monica pushed the button and we all got in.

"Kaleb," Monica said sadly. "I'm not sure if Kaje told you, but I had been trying to find the mystery lady from Tankers. I couldn't find her. I'm sorry. It's like she's a ghost."

"It's okay, Monica. I appreciate you looking."

The doors of the elevator opened. We exited the elevator and walked out the front doors. It took my eyes a minute to adjust to the sunlight. It was a perfect autumn day. The sun was warm. The air was crisp and inviting, and the gentle breeze created an almost surreal feeling. I breathed in the fresh air. Each breath filled me with excitement, joy, and hope.

"So, where are we going? You just want to go around the parking lot?" Kaje asked.

"There." I pointed to the large tree in the park across the way. "There's something I need to do."

"Something you need to do, huh? Well, technically, we're not supposed to leave the premises, but whatever. Let's do it!"

Monica laughed and shook her head. "Y'all are crazy, always causing trouble."

"You know it!" We said in unison.

We arrived at the entrance of the park. An intense feeling washed over me. I could feel her presence everywhere. It felt like the day we first met, only magnified. I smiled nervously. Kaje kept pushing me towards the tree. I began to get butterflies in my stomach. As we got closer, I noticed her sitting on the bench, holding a large book. She was wearing that same beautiful dress she wore on the day we met.

"Kaje. Kaje. Slow down!" I whispered excitedly.

He stopped pushing. "What's up?"

I pointed to Micaleah sitting on the bench.

"Oh, my God! Is that her!?" Monica asked."

"No way!" Kaje exclaimed. "How did you know?"

"She told me to find her there." I was so nervous. I just sat there and stared at her.

"Dude! You ready? I'm about to push you over there."

"Wait. Push me halfway. I'll walk the rest."

"You sure, man?"

"Yeah, I got it."

"Okay. Here goes nothing."

Kaje wheeled me over to the bench that I sat on

the day I first met Micaleah. I got up and took careful steps towards her. With each step, my mind recalled each feeling, each memory, each lifetime that brought us to that very moment. I approached her. She turned and looked at me with those beautiful, brown eyes. She was the most beautiful thing I had ever seen. She smiled. It melted me. I smiled back. She stood up. We locked in an embrace and lost ourselves in each other. We slowly pulled back and rested our foreheads against each other. Our noses touched ever so gently.
　"Hey, Muffin."
　"Hey, Blue. You're late."

Epilogue

"You ready to get a wiggle on?" I asked.

"I am." Muffin turned around and smiled at me. "How do I look?"

"Beautiful as ever."

She blushed. "Thank you." She continued to look at me. I would often catch her staring at me, lost in her thoughts.

I looked at the clock. "Hey you. You ok?" I asked, snapping her back to reality.

"Sorry. Yes, I'm fine. Sometimes I still can't believe you are really here and all of this is really real."

I walked over to her and gave her a reassuring hug. "I thought I was the only one who thought like that. But, yes, I'm real. And yes, this is all real. And we are going to be really late if we don't leave soon, and I'll never hear the end of it if I'm late."

She laughed. "We won't be. If we are, you can tell them it was my fault."

I laughed. "There's no way they would believe that." We put our coats on and headed towards the car.

"Get a wiggle on? Still hanging on to that English accent, huh?"

I smiled at her. "Nah. It's pretty much gone. I just

use it every now and then to make you smile."

"Aww, how sweet of you."

The car ride was surprisingly quiet. I could tell she was a bit nervous about meeting everyone. I reached over and gently touched her hair. "It'll be fine, you know. Everyone is going to love you. I'll stay close to you."

"I'm not worried about that, silly. We've gotten through a lot worse."

We both laughed. I put the blinker on and slowly pulled into the driveway of the house address listed on the invitation. "You ready?" I asked.

"Mhm." She smiled and stared at me.

I winked at her. "You're doing that staring thing again."

"I was not."

I laughed. "If you say so. Let's head in."

We got out of the car and headed towards the door. Out of nowhere, a cold breeze blew against my face, sending chills throughout my body. I zipped up my coat and picked up my pace. "Have I mentioned that I don't do well in the cold?"

"I may remember you mentioning it once or twice."

My teeth chattered as I rang the doorbell. Rob opened the door. He had a big cheesy grin on his face. I suspect he was doing his best to hide his pure elation.

"Who is it honey?" a female voice asked. Her accent sounded French.

Rob escorted us into the house. He hugged me so hard, I think he may have cracked a rib or two. "It's good to see you, man!"

A very tall, beautiful woman entered. "Oh, are they here?" she asked excitedly.

Rob released me from his clutches. "Yeah, they made it. Guys, this is Faith, my girlfriend."

"Very nice to meet you, Faith." I smiled. "You'll have both of your hands full with this one."

Faith shot back a playful grin. "Oh, I already know."

I turned to Muffin. "This is Mu...Micaleah. My soulma...my girlfr...my everything. I'll just go with that."

"Aww, that's so sweet. It is a pleasure to meet you," Faith said.

"Yeah, dude, that's pretty awesome. It's nice to meet you, Micaleah," Rob said.

Micaleah smiled. "It's a pleasure to meet both of you."

"Well, come on in, Rob will take your coats. Micaleah, you can come with me. I'll give you the tour while they catch up a bit." Faith took Micaleah's hand and led her towards the kitchen. I smiled at her and shrugged my shoulders. So much for staying close to her.

Rob nudged me with his forearm. "She is a looker, man. Where did you find her?"

"That is actually a long and crazy story. Let's just say she found me in the park."

"Cool. I can't wait to hear the story."

"What about you, man? You look like you hit the jackpot yourself. She is stunning."

"Dude, I got super lucky, for real." He pulled me into an office and shut the door. He reached into a drawer and pulled out a little box with a ring in it. "It's love, man. She is definitely the one. I'm going to ask her to marry me."

"What!? That's great, man! But what are you going to do with the ring when she says no?"

We both laughed really loudly. We had to quickly cover our mouths so no one else would hear. There was a knock on the door, then the door slowly started to open. Rob nervously tried to put the ring in his pocket but it dropped to the ground. As he knelt down to pick it up, the door swung open and Tammy walked in.

"I guess this means we're officially broken up, huh?" she asked. Her face was bright red from holding in her laughter.

We all started laughing. Tammy opened her arms. "Come here, trouble! I've missed you so much!"

I walked over and hugged her. I held her close for a long time. Tears of joy began to fill my eyes. "I missed you so much. I'm so glad you're okay. I thought I was going to lose you."

"Five and a half minutes."

"Huh?"

"I was dead for five and a half minutes before they bought me back."

"Seriously?"

"Yep. I almost kicked the proverbial bucket. I saw the pearly gates and all sorts of crazy things."

"Did you see the big sign on them that said 'Do No Enter?'"

Tammy laughed. "Still an ass. Actually, I turned away from the gates because I knew you couldn't survive without me. Besides, they aren't ready for this jelly."

I laughed. "No, not many people are."

We both laughed and hugged again. "I really missed you, sweetie. I'm really glad you are doing well. And I see you brought my replacement with you. There's no way I'm competing with that."

I shrugged. "Yeah, it kind of just happened. You know how that is. Besides, you were never going to tell your parents about me anyway."

"Oh, whatever! You were never going to tell yours. It's okay. I'm happy for you. She seems like she's really special."

"Thank you. She is very special."

"Well, we better get out there. I'm sure everyone is waiting to see you."

"You're right. I better go get this over with."

"Where's Kaje? I expected him to be here."

"His wife is due any day now. They didn't want to take the chance."

"Oh, how exciting! I still can't believe both of you went over to the dark side. You'll never catch me there."

I laughed. "You never know."

We walked into the dining room. Everyone smiled and cheered as they saw me approach. Shockingly, Brenda was the first person to come up and hug me. Liza, Catherine, and Ron followed suit. There were a few other people from work that I barely knew, but I was happy to see them nonetheless. Everyone had aged a bit. It was an odd feeling. I was expecting everyone to look exactly how I remembered them. Sometimes I had to remind myself that five years had passed.

We all laughed and joked about the good old days. They filled me in on all the things that had changed at work, and how they kept my cubicle exactly the same as it was. It was weird reminiscing when it had only felt like a couple months.

After a while, everyone began to file out. We stayed and talked with Rob and Faith for a bit before heading out.

"Are you happy with how everything went?" Muffin asked.

"I am. It was good to see everyone again."

"They all seem to care for you very much."

I laughed. "Or they did a good job of faking it."

"Shut up. You know they do. Especially Tammy. She's got the hots for you."

I smiled. "Tammy was my work wife. We helped each other get through the day."

Muffin smirked. "Yeah, I bet you did."

"Uh oh. Are you jealous, Muffin?"

She laughed. "No way. I know you are all mine."

"Never doubt that for a second."

Muffin stopped suddenly and looked off in the distance. "Do you mind if we stop somewhere on the way back?"

"No, not at all. Everything okay?"

"Yeah. I just want you to meet someone. I'll drive."

"Okay," I said suspiciously.

It was late in the afternoon, but the sun was still bright. It was a bit warmer than it was earlier, but still cold. She didn't say much as she drove, she just focused on the road. I sat back and closed my eyes. I was exhausted. I still hadn't regained all of my energy back yet.

She parked the car and took a deep breath. She turned to me. I opened my eyes and looked at her. Her eyes were holding back tears, but she smiled lovingly at me. "I want you to meet my father," she said, still holding back tears.

"Ok. Sure. Right now?"

"Yes. Right now. Come on."

We got out of the car. She took my hand and led me to a large tombstone near a large tree. Her steps were slow and hesitant. I could feel everything she was feeling.

She let my hand go and knelt by the grave. "Hi, Daddy. It's me, Micaleah. I...um...I'm sorry it took me so long to come visit. Things were just kind of bad, you know. I know that's not a really good excuse, but I'm here now, and...um, I miss you, Daddy. There isn't a day that goes by that I don't think of you. I really wish you were here. I'm in a really good place now. I met someone. Well, we kind of met each other. His name is Kaleb. I want you to meet him."

She turned and looked back at me. I nervously took a couple steps towards the tombstone. I had never talked to a grave before. I wasn't sure exactly what to say. I cleared my throat. "Hello, Mr. Johnson. I wish I could have met you in person. Your daughter is very special to me. I wouldn't be here without her. She saved my life. So, um, I guess I should thank you too, because she wouldn't be here if it wasn't for you. I love her, and I promise to take good care of her."

I felt like I was just rambling so I didn't say anything else. Muffin took my hand. Her hand was warm and comforting. We closed our eyes and stood in silence over the grave site. The air suddenly had a cold chill to it. I opened my eyes to see large flakes of snow began to slowly fall. The warmth from Muffin's hand faded. I turned to her, but she was not there. I called out to her, but I could hear no sound.

As I looked around, the large snowflakes suddenly

froze in midair. I turned to head back to the car. The entire parking lot was gone. I found myself in the middle of a forest. I called out again. The silence was deafening. I was paralyzed by the fear that I was still trapped inside of a coma, and Muffin was not there with me.

The sun began to set behind the trees. As I began to take steps in the direction the car was parked, I thought I could make out the sound of faint laughter.

"Muffin?!" I called out. There was only silence.

The large snowflake in front of me had crystallized. Inside of it, I could see a blurry vision of Muffin and her father laughing at a park. I reached out to touch it. It shattered and formed several smaller snowflakes that gently fell to the ground. I moved to the next snowflake. I saw another vision of Muffin and her father dancing. I saw another one of them writing in a book. Each snowflake showed me a different vision of them. In each one, they looked so happy together.

The sun had set. The bright light from the moon made the remaining snowflakes glisten. They led me to a cityscape. I looked around in awe. Everything was pristine. I had seen that cityscape in my dreams, but in my dreams, everything was crumbling and falling apart.

In the sky above, a giant blue bird continually flew in the aura that surrounded the moon. It flew in what appeared to be a figure-8 pattern. The large snowflakes in front of me began to sparkle and give off an intense light as they converged into each other. When the light subsided, a giant glistening snowflake floated just in front of me. Inside it, a blurry vision showed me a man dangling from a car, struggling to hold on. I could feel an intense sadness and anguish pulsing through me. I watched as he spoke, and his fingers started to loosen. He was letting go. In my anguish, I reached out to him with both hands. I could feel his wrists in my hands. I pulled as hard as I could. I could feel him moving towards me. With everything in me, I leaned back and pulled again. He was through. I fell backwards and onto the ground. When I got back to my feet, Muffin's dad stood before me. He looked around. He looked happy, but confused. His expression quickly changed to a nervous one as he looked up at the moon. I looked to see what he was looking at. The bird that had been circling the moon was gone. Muffin's dad examined himself. He looked at me and began to speak. There were no words, only silence. He palmed his head in exasperation.

Darkness began to slowly eclipse the moon. He looked at the moon again. His face saddened. He desperately began signing something repeatedly. The moon was half eclipsed. He frantically began pointing and gesturing for me to go. Panicked, I took several steps backward.

In the next instance, he was wailing his arms and legs as if he was falling. Only, he wasn't falling down, he began falling upwards towards the moon. Instinctively, I reached out my hand to try to grab him, but he was just out of my reach.

"Noooo!" I yelled. The last of the moon's light was eclipsed from view, and Muffin's father was no longer in sight.

"No what? Are you okay? What just happened!?"

I could feel Muffin's warm hand in mine. The rest of my body trembled. I opened my eyes and looked at her. Tears flowed down my face.

"Blue? What's wrong? What happened?"

I looked at her. My mind contemplated all of the repercussions of what I was about to utter. "I..."

"It's okay, Blue. You can tell me. We'll get through it."

"I...I think your father needs our help."

Acknowledgement

Writing a book was so much harder than I ever thought it would be. Every aspect of it consumes your daily thoughts. However, the sense of accomplishment is so much greater than I could have ever imagined, and I wouldnt trade it for anything.

First, I want to thank my wife, Jennifer. I am so grateful for her encouragement and belief that I can do anything I put my heart and mind to.

I would also like to thank all the people who helped along the way with their encouragement and support.

Heartfelt thank you to Nicole Brunner, who awakened my creative writing side and started me on the path of writing a book.

To Jo-Ann Garnsey, who I argued with endlessly over the "correct" way to say things. Thank you for never getting tired of me bugging you with questions about how the British say things. Its "aluminum." xx
Thanks to Katherine, Amanda, Jake, and Bob for your

knowledge and encouragement.

Big thanks to Jai Perrin for the awesome book cover.

Special thanks to Hailey for reading my crazy dreams and helping me believe that I could actually make this work.

A heartfelt thank you to all my readers. To whom I will forever be grateful for reading the ramblings of my crazy mind.

About The Author

Jared A. Perrin Sr.

Jared A. Perrin Sr. is a first-time author whose deep love of music, movies, video games, books, and fascination with dreams, inspire his writing.

He is a husband, father, and grandfather. He was born and raised in Cleveland Heights, Ohio and currently lives in Northeast Ohio where he enjoys being out in nature as he reads, writes, explores new music, daydreams, and continues his love-hate relationship with commas.

www.jaredaperrin.com

Made in the USA
Middletown, DE
04 August 2024